T0363179

HISTORICAL

Your romantic escape to the past.

One Waltz With The Viscount
Laura Martin

When Cinderella Met The Duke
Sophia Williams

MILLS & BOON

ONE WALTZ WITH THE VISCOUNT
© 2024 by Laura Martin
Philippine Copyright 2024
Australian Copyright 2024
New Zealand Copyright 2024

First Published 2024
First Australian Paperback Edition 2024
ISBN 978 1 038 93562 5

WHEN CINERELLA MET THE DUKE
© 2024 by Jo Lovett-Turner
Philippine Copyright 2024
Australian Copyright 2024
New Zealand Copyright 2024

First Published 2024
First Australian Paperback Edition 2024
ISBN 978 1 038 93562 5

MIX
Paper | Supporting
responsible forestry
FSC® C001695

Published by
Harlequin Mills & Boon
An imprint of Harlequin Enterprises (Australia) Pty Limited
(ABN 47 001 180 918), a subsidiary of HarperCollins
Publishers Australia Pty Limited
(ABN 36 009 913 517)
Level 19, 201 Elizabeth Street
SYDNEY NSW 2000 AUSTRALIA

Cover art used by arrangement with Harlequin Books S.A.. All rights reserved.

Printed and bound in Australia by McPherson's Printing Group

One Waltz With The Viscount
Laura Martin

MILLS & BOON

Laura Martin writes historical romances with an adventurous undercurrent. When not writing, she spends her time working as a doctor in Cambridgeshire, where she lives with her husband. In her spare moments, Laura loves to lose herself in a book and has been known to read from cover to cover in a single day when the story is particularly gripping. She also loves to travel—especially to visit historical sites and far-flung shores.

Books by Laura Martin

Harlequin Historical

The Brooding Earl's Proposition
Her Best Friend, the Duke
One Snowy Night with Lord Hauxton
The Captain's Impossible Match
The Housekeeper's Forbidden Earl
Her Secret Past with the Viscount
A Housemaid to Redeem Him
The Kiss That Made Her Countess

Matchmade Marriages

The Marquess Meets His Match
A Pretend Match for the Viscount
A Match to Fool Society

The Ashburton Reunion

Flirting with His Forbidden Lady
Falling for His Practical Wife

Scandalous Australian Bachelors

Courting the Forbidden Debutante
Reunited with His Long-Lost Cinderella
Her Rags-to-Riches Christmas

Visit the Author Profile page
at millsandboon.com.au for more titles.

Author Note

Always when I come to the end of writing one book, the ideas for another start to blossom and take hold. I will find myself lost in thought at the most inopportune moments. When writing *One Waltz with the Viscount*, I was walking through the streets of Cambridge as the first scene took form, and I knew I couldn't risk losing a single word of it. I had to abandon my Christmas shopping and quickly dive into a coffee shop to jot down the chapter unfolding in my mind.

I've often wondered what the writing process is like for others. Mine I find hard to articulate when asked. The ideas come in surges, often too many and too complex for one project, but over a few days, that initial rush will get whittled down until there's something I feel excited about. That was certainly the process with this book. After the first barrage of ideas, I couldn't think of much else until I began writing in earnest a few days later. I hope you enjoy *One Waltz with the Viscount*. If anyone would like to connect and talk about writing or historical romance, then please reach out on social media.

To Mum.

I don't say it enough, but I know
how lucky I am to have you.

Chapter One

At the grand old age of twenty-three, Miss Sarah Shepherd had never seen anything quite like this. It was a beautiful midsummer's evening, with the doors to the ballroom thrown open. The rise and fall of the music, played perfectly by a string quartet, floated on the air. Women in magnificent dresses twirled in the arms of dashing gentlemen. Even the servants looked fancy, and every few feet a footman stood, holding a tray of drinks or delicacies, offering them to whoever walked past.

From her position in the foliage outside the ballroom window, Sarah yearned to be part of it. The desire took her by surprise. Normally she prided herself on being a wholly practical person, never succumbing to the daydreaming or fantasizing that so often plagued her twin sister, Selina.

Reluctantly she pulled herself away. This was a world she would never be part of. She reminded herself, not for the first time, to be thankful for what she did have. Her future might not contain the beautiful ballgowns of the *ton*, but—as long as her trip to London to find her sister did not last too long—she had a secure job as a music teacher to three children from a lovely family in Kent. It was a position that would give her security and stability alongside her weekly wage. These past few months Sarah had learned to treasure her independence—this job would allow her to make her own way in the world, and not have to rely on anyone else.

She tried to block out the scene in the ballroom and focussed on the rest of the house. It was large, especially by London standards, a sprawling mansion, detached from other residences with a good-sized garden. Most of the house was in darkness, but light flickered in a few windows at the very top, no doubt those of the servants not needed for the night's festivities. Her eyes flitted across the façade until she paused on a first-floor balcony. All the other windows were closed, but these doors had been left slightly ajar—every so often a wisp of curtain would billow out, caught in the evening breeze. The room beyond wasn't completely dark either, but Sarah watched for a good minute and saw no movement within.

'That's the one,' she murmured to herself. Her eyes trailed from the stone balcony to the wall below. It was shielded from sight—anyone stepping out of the ballroom onto the terrace would be blocked by a line of trees—although there would be a few seconds when she was vulnerable just before she pulled herself up onto the balcony.

Silently she cursed her decision to wear a ballgown. She had hoped to slip inside, concealed amongst the other guests. But when she'd arrived she'd spotted a footman carefully checking invitations, before escorting guests into the ballroom and announcing them to the room. Now that she had resigned herself to finding a different way in, she wished she had worn something a little less cumbersome.

Sarah waited until the swell of music signalled a new dance. With the dance floor filling up it was less likely anyone would step onto the terrace. After the first few notes she made her move, darting through the darkness. In the moonlight her dress shimmered. It was a beautiful gown, made of royal blue satin with a white sash around the waist. From a distance it looked almost regal, although close up, in good light, the frayed and mended hem was apparent. She wore tiny sapphire earrings in each of her earlobes. They matched perfectly with the dress, although that was more coincidence than anything else. Sarah did not have much jewellery of her own, but these earrings had been a gift from her mother, and she rarely took them out.

Not allowing herself to hesitate, Sarah grabbed hold of the wisteria that snaked up the wall of the house and began to pull herself up. A childhood spent in the country meant she'd climbed many trees in her life, although none quite like this. This was far from a relaxed outing with her sister, where they would spend their day playing in the stream and climbing trees before having a picnic in the sunshine. In many ways it had been an idyllic childhood, filled with fresh sea air and all the family she thought she ever needed in her mother and her sister. Of course there were hardships—money worries that worsened with each year, as well as the odd looks her mother received from a few of their neighbours—but all in all it had been happy.

Quietly she muttered encouragement to herself under her breath, hoping the branches of the wisteria tree would not buckle or break under her weight. When she was halfway up her dress snagged on a twig—for a moment, she felt off balance. Her heart thumped in her chest as she gripped the branch tighter, but thankfully she regained her control and was able to reach down and unhook herself without too much damage.

The hardest part of the climb was near the balcony. The wisteria curved away from the stone balustrade, leaving a three-foot gap for her to navigate. It was just a little too far for her to reach out and grip the edge.

Sarah made the mistake of looking down, wondering if she would break a bone if she fell from this height. It was a sickening thought, and quickly she pushed it away.

Without another moment of hesitation, she twisted her body and launched herself through the air, feeling a rush of elation as her fingers gripped hold of the stone of the balcony. The muscles in her arms screamed as she pulled herself up and, after a few more seconds, she was over the balustrade. She sank down, her chest heaving from the exertion, and sucked in great breaths of air, only straightening when she had recovered enough for the next part of her plan.

* * *

Silently Lord Henry Routledge blew out the candle as the shadowy figure climbed onto the balcony. He stayed completely still, not moving a muscle, watching as the person outside paused for a moment to catch their breath. There was no way he would allow a thief to creep into his host's house without challenge.

Lord and Lady Shrewsbury were good friends. They'd helped him recover from the death of his first wife—through the mourning period and the months after, when he'd tried to build himself back up again. They had supported him in his ongoing feud with his father, encouraged him to reach out to the old man and try to rebuild the relationship for the sake of his sister, before it was too late. They had even given him a place to stay as he searched for a new set of rooms, after his old house had burned down in the fire that had killed his wife.

He half suspected this ball had been arranged with the sole purpose of encouraging him back into society, and to push him into meeting some of this year's debutantes.

Henry, in his angst, almost forgot the person on the balcony, about to break into the house.

It was a bold move, climbing up the wisteria that grew outside the library whilst guests danced and socialised only a few feet away. Only a certain type of thief would attempt such a feat. No doubt they hoped to find the rest of the house deserted, with the guests and servants all gathered in the downstairs rooms or running between the basement kitchen and ballroom.

Stealthily he used the lull in movement to creep over to the open balcony door. He stayed in the shadows, invisible to anyone outside.

After what seemed like an eternity, the balcony door began to inch open and the thief slipped inside. Henry moved immediately, striking before the intruder was aware there was anyone else in the room. He lunged, grabbing hold of the thief's arms, pushing back forcefully so they ended up pressed against the wall.

Henry froze as he looked down at the intruder, his mind not

able to make sense of what he was seeing. Even in the darkness it was painfully obvious the intruder was a woman. He could feel the curves of her body through her clothes, and the softness of her skin under his hands. This woman was not dressed as a thief either. Rather than an outfit of dark breeches, or clothing that was easy to manoeuvre in, she was wearing a ballgown. It *was* dark in colour, perhaps blue or purple—it was difficult to see without proper light—but the white sash around her middle shone like a frozen river in the moonlight.

For ten seconds they just looked at each other, both as shocked as the other.

'Please unhand me,' the young woman said, her voice cultivated with the sharp clip of authority. She was no street urchin in stolen clothes.

Henry did not move. They were in a compromising position, his body much closer to hers than was appropriate, but that was hardly the most pressing matter.

'No,' he said, his eyes raking over her. She was pretty, despite her slightly dishevelled appearance. Brown hair was pinned back in the current fashion, but some had been pulled free and curled around her neck. Even in the darkness he could see her eyes were green, sparkling with life and vitality.

'No?'

'No.'

She spluttered, trying to find the words to convey her disbelief, but he silenced her with a look.

'I find you breaking into Lord and Lady Shrewsbury's house, sneaking in through a first-floor window, and I would be a fool if I released you without finding out who you are and what you want.'

Her eyes narrowed a fraction and he felt her body tense. Anticipating her next move, Henry shifted to the right just in time. The young woman's knee came up but connected only with empty air rather than his groin.

'That isn't very friendly.'

'You're hurting my wrists.'

'Tell me who you are and I will consider letting you go.'

There was silence for a moment whilst she considered his offer.

'Sarah,' she said eventually.

'Sarah. A pretty name, but not enough to win your freedom I am afraid.' He saw the darting of her eyes to the left and quickly continued. 'No lies please. I have a peculiar flair for being able to tell if someone is lying to me.'

'Shepherd.'

'Miss Sarah Shepherd?'

A single nod of her head as she strained again against him, despite them both knowing there was no way she could physically overpower him. She wasn't short, but even so, the top of her head only came up to his chin, and her body was lithe and slender. Good for climbing up to first-floor balconies, but not so much for a contest of physical strength.

'A pleasure to meet you Miss Shepherd,' Henry said, wondering what was wrong with him that he was actually enjoying himself more now than he had been fifteen minutes ago, dancing with the debutantes in the ballroom. 'I am going to let go of your hands, but if you make any sudden movements, you will find I am not as gentle the second time around. Do you understand?'

'Yes.'

Slowly he released her hands, taking a step back so their bodies were not pressed together. He saw her exhale in relief.

'Are you a thief, Miss Shepherd?'

She tensed again.

'No,' she answered quickly, a hint of outrage in her tone.

'I am struggling to see what other reason there could be for you to climb all the way up here into Lord and Lady Shrewsbury's house.'

Her eyes trailed over him, inspecting him. 'I need to talk to someone in this house.'

'Did you try knocking at the front door?'

'I did that just this morning. I was turned away.'

'So your response was to break in through an open window?'

'This may be merely a matter of jest to you,' Miss Shepherd tossed the loose strands of hair back over her shoulder, 'but it is vitally important I speak to Agnes Pepper who works here as a maid.'

'Could you not have sent her a note? Or waited for her to have her afternoon off?'

'There is no time,' Miss Shepherd said, the words bursting forth with such feeling that they made Henry pause.

'I should alert Lord Shrewsbury of your presence,' he murmured after a moment. 'And perhaps the local constable.'

He watched as some of the fight left her, and he suddenly realised how young she was. Miss Shepherd could only be twenty-two or twenty-three. Her skin was smooth, her face unlined and her hair was thick and deep in colour. She spoke as if born into the middle or gentry classes. If she was telling the truth about needing to speak to one of the servants in the household, whatever motivated her must be of great importance. You did not often find gently born young ladies climbing trees and breaking into houses.

Miss Shepherd pressed her lips together before speaking again. 'I implore you not to call the constable. Let me be on my way. No harm has come to anyone.'

Her tone was stiff and formal, and he got the impression it was hard for her to ask for his assistance.

'I will make you a deal, Miss Shepherd. You have five minutes. Five minutes to tell me your story and convince me not to call the authorities. If I deem you are telling the truth, I will escort you from the house and let you go on your way. If not, I will ensure the full force of our justice system is used against you.'

Miss Shepherd regarded him for a full minute before answering, inspecting his face so thoroughly he felt like a racehorse being put up for auction.

'Very well,' she said, her shoulders sagging. 'I came to London in search of my missing sister and, with every passing day, I become more and more convinced she is dead.'

Chapter Two

❦

Sarah watched the expression on the man's face change from mild interest to intrigue. It was a fascinating story she had to tell, at least it would be if she wasn't so closely involved.

'May I sit, Mr...' She motioned to the comfortable chairs positioned in front of the fireplace.

'Routledge,' he said. 'Lord Henry Routledge.'

She nodded, trying not to feel intimidated. There were not many titled gentlemen strolling around the streets of St Leonards where she and her sister had grown up. Her mother had raised them as well as she could within her limited means. She had given Sarah and Selina the education they would need to provide for themselves once they reached adulthood, teaching them to speak French and read Latin as well as play the piano and sew. Yet she could not prepare them for an interaction such as this.

'Shall I start at the beginning?'

'Please,' he said, reclining back in his chair as if he had all the time in the world. She wondered about this man who seemed to prefer hiding away from the festivities downstairs, talking to her rather than returning to the dancing and the debutantes. He would be popular, there was no doubt about that. He had a title and probably the fortune that came with it, and he was charming. It was the easy charm of a man who had grown up confident in himself, knowing he would one day be one of the privileged few. When he smiled it was half indulgent, half knowing and even Sarah, who thought herself immune to most men's charm, found herself leaning in, wanting to be that little bit closer to him, to bask in the warm glow that surrounded him.

She realised she'd been staring. He was smiling at her and she wondered if he thought her just another of the simpering girls that batted their eyelashes and tried to get his attention.

Quickly she sat a little straighter, forcing a serious expression onto her face, crossing her hands one over the other in her lap.

'My sister Selina and I were raised by our mother. For most of our lives we were told that our father had been an officer in the army and he had died in a skirmish when we were young. Neither my sister nor I remember our father.'

'He didn't die?'

Sarah bit her lip. It went against everything she'd learned to reveal such a family secret to a stranger, but she had no choice. The truth was mortifying and would result in scandal if it were widely known, but she would have to tell Lord Routledge—or risk being hauled in front of a judge, accused of breaking into the Shrewsburys' home.

'My mother, God rest her soul, passed away six months ago. As we sorted through her personal papers we found letters sent to her from her lover. We were able to work out our father had not been in the army, and he had not died in a skirmish. From the scant details we gathered he was a gentleman.'

She risked a glanced at Lord Routledge and saw his expression had turned serious. He nodded slowly. 'Unfortunately it is not an unfamiliar story. A gentleman gets a young woman pregnant and then refuses to marry her, because of family expectations or the need to marry someone from his own class.'

'My mother was the daughter of a vicar. Her family was respectable, but from the letters in my mother's possession it was clear they wanted nothing more to do with her after she met our father.'

'You were born out of wedlock?'

Sarah closed her eyes for a moment, hating the question. For twenty-two long years her mother had kept this secret, in the hope that Sarah and Selina might be able to avoid scandal and make good matches with decent young men. It felt like a betrayal of her memory to openly admit the truth.

'We are not sure. There was some suggestion of a small wedding ceremony in one of the letters, but it is hard to tell. It is deliberately vague I think.'

'What's this got to do with your sister going missing?' Lord Routledge asked.

Sarah sighed. 'As I mentioned, six months ago my mother died and we found out our father might still be alive. However, I decided to focus on the future, to find a position as a music teacher and to try to forget the circumstance of my birth.'

'You were not even a little curious as to who your father might be?'

Sarah shrugged. 'Curiosity is all very well if you have nothing to lose, but I was not about to waste my time chasing a man who may or may not exist, and may or may not acknowledge us.'

'I sense you are a highly practical person, Miss Shepherd.' It should have been a compliment, but Sarah felt the sting of the barb as he said it. Her sister always called her practical, as if it were a character fault.

'There is nothing wrong with being realistic,' she said primly.

'Am I to take it your sister held a different view?'

'She was determined to find our father. Each day she came up with more and more fantastical stories to explain why he had abandoned us, and she convinced herself he must be waiting, tortured, in purgatory, not knowing how to find his daughters.'

Sarah sighed. Selina had always been a dreamer. She was impulsive and fun and the sister everyone wanted to spend time with. In anyone else it would be an annoying trait, but Selina was generous and loving, and Sarah couldn't bring herself to feel any jealousy towards her. Most of the time.

'Unlikely, but possible I suppose.'

Sarah gave a short, sharp laugh, without any hint of humour. 'I would say the likelihood that our father wishes for his two long-abandoned daughters to turn up on his doorstep is close to nought.'

Lord Routledge could not argue. No man wanted his past indiscretions showing up to embarrass him in his current life.

'Selina became so obsessed with finding our father that she gathered up my mother's diary, and all the letters we'd found in her possession, and made her way to London. She thought she could piece together the little information we had, follow the clues and identify our father.'

Sarah sighed and closed her eyes. She should never have let her sister go. They'd argued about it and, one day, she had been at the end of her tether and told her sister to do as she pleased. It had been a careless comment, one she had regretted immediately, and the next day she had woken to find Selina's bed empty and a note saying she had used her small savings on a ticket for the stagecoach to London.

'She followed his trail to London?'

'Yes. Each week she would write me a letter, detailing her progress, or lack of as it normally was, but in her last letter she wrote of her excitement. She thought she had really found something. She told me she was coming here to speak to Agnes Pepper, a maid in the Shrewsbury household, who she thought might have had a connection to our father. Her name was mentioned in an anecdote in one of the letters.'

Lord Routledge was sitting forward in his seat now. Sarah felt a surge of hope, and with relief realised it had been the right decision to tell him the whole truth. His interest in her tale might save her from being handed over to the authorities.

'Which is why you are here.'

'I waited patiently for a letter from Selina, but week after week nothing arrived. I grew so worried I wrote to my new employer, asking if they might allow me to search for Selina before I took up my position. They said I could have four weeks, but if I was not back after that they would find a new music teacher.'

'So you have four weeks to find your sister.'

'Two and a half. That is why I am so desperate to speak to

Agnes Pepper. I would never have done something so risky as breaking into a house otherwise.'

'Do you know, Miss Shepherd, I believe you.'

Slumping back in her chair, Sarah closed her eyes. She felt exhausted and overwhelmed. All she wanted to do was return home, to go back to the small house with a view of the sea, to hear the gulls calling overhead as she walked to the shops, to taste the salt in the air on her lips. All of that was gone now. She had packed up their belongings before she had left for London. They could no longer afford the rent and it was silly to waste money they didn't have on a house they were not using.

'What is your decision, my lord?' Sarah asked, her voice weary. 'Am I to be hauled off to gaol to await a date for a trial, or will you let me slip away?'

He tapped his fingers on the arm of the chair, as if still deciding.

'I have an alternative proposition for you,' he said, his voice low.

Sarah felt a stirring of something deep inside her, and quickly pushed it away. Now was not the time to be thinking about how Lord Routledge's body had felt as he pinned her up against the wall.

'Let me help you,' he said.

'Help me?'

'Yes. I have heard your story, I am intrigued. I would like to help.'

'Why?'

He shrugged. 'I find myself at a loose end at present. Parliament has a recess for the summer months, and I have no wish to retreat to the country. This matter piques my interest.'

'I could not ask you to help me,' Sarah said, feeling a surge of panic. She had confessed all the sordid details of her origins in the hope he might believe her story, but she had never thought he would want to get involved.

'You do not have to ask. I am offering. Consider it for a moment before you answer. Not only do I help you escape from the Shrewsburys' house without anyone else knowing you were ever here, I also have the contacts to arrange for you to meet with Agnes Pepper, without having to resort to nefarious methods. My name alone opens doors in this city.'

Sarah still hesitated.

Lord Routledge leaned forward, tapping her on the knee as if she were a faithful hunting dog. 'Do not fear, I am not an imbecile. I will be very discreet when we are making our enquiries. There will be no mention of your possible illegitimacy, and no question of anyone impugning your honour.'

'Then I accept,' Sarah said. She was already filled with misgivings, but she had no other choice. If she refused his offer he may still send for the constable. There was no chance of finding Selina if she was incarcerated, and even a few days' delay might be the difference between picking up her sister's trail and losing it for ever.

'Good. Let us get you out of here.'

'What about speaking to Agnes Pepper?'

'Tomorrow. Tonight we work on keeping those delicate little wrists of yours free from manacles.' He stood and strode over to the door, opening it a crack. A weak light shone through, suggesting a candle still burned somewhere in the hall.

'Wait here,' he said, slipping out and disappearing from view.

He returned a few minutes later, holding a candlestick, with a grim expression on his face.

'We have a problem,' he said without preamble.

'What?' She hated any suspense, always wanting to know the worst possible outcome for any situation.

'The guests have spilled out of the ballroom into the hall. If we start descending the stairs we will have to pass a half dozen guests, including our esteemed hostess.'

'What about the servants' stairs?'

'Not an option either I'm afraid. They lead directly down to the kitchen, I just checked. There's a lot of people down there.'

Sarah felt the panic begin to rise inside her. It must have shown on her face, for Lord Routledge stepped closer.

'Do not fret, I have a plan. You wait in here until the guests move away from the hall or they start to leave. I will return for you, then and we can spirit you away.'

She glanced at the little clock on the mantelpiece. It was just after ten. She had never been to a ball like this before, but she suspected they went on until the early hours of the morning.

'I could be in here for hours.'

'Can you think of a better plan?'

'Perhaps I could go back out the way I came,' she said, moving towards the balcony doors. She paused on the threshold and looked down, swallowing hard. The descent would involve an initial leap over to the wisteria, whilst praying she caught hold of one of the branches, that it held her weight, then a shimmy down, which somehow seemed harder than going up.

'The ballroom has grown warm and there are couples on the terrace, enjoying the evening air. I doubt you will make it half-way down without someone seeing you.'

She exhaled sharply in frustration.

'Fine. It looks like your plan is the only option. Please do not forget about me whilst you are twirling with some simpering young woman who is angling to become Lady Routledge.'

'I doubt that will be possible, Miss Shepherd. You make quite the impression.'

He moved to the door again, and Sarah had the absurd urge to call out, to ask him to stay with her. Quickly she suppressed it, biting back the words. She would be perfectly fine on her own here in the library. It was comfortable and cool and not altogether dark.

'I shall return when I am able,' Lord Routledge said, moving towards the door. 'I should show my face again downstairs, or someone might wonder where I've got to. The last thing we want is anyone searching up here.'

Without a backwards glance he disappeared into the hall, closing the door swiftly behind him.

Sarah flopped back into the chair and looked around her. She wondered if she should conceal herself. It was unlikely anyone else would come into the library whilst the ball was ongoing, but not impossible. In the end she decided she would take her chance and sat in the comfortable chair. If she was going to spend hours in this room, there was no need to make it even more of an ordeal.

Chapter Three

'You seem distracted, Henry dear,' Lady Shrewsbury said as she cornered him at the edge of the ballroom, placing a hand on his arm, shooing away a young woman who had been nervously approaching. 'Are you enjoying yourself?'

'Of course he isn't,' Lord Shrewsbury boomed as he joined their little group. 'The poor man is at a ball where every single unmarried young woman knows he is in search of a wife. He has been subjected to an endless stream of inane small talk about mutual acquaintances and the weather.'

'Nonsense,' Lady Shrewsbury said, turning on her husband. 'Young women are not all fools with air where their brains should be.'

'Perhaps he would be having a better time if you hadn't let it be known he was out of mourning and looking for a wife,' Lord Shrewsbury countered.

'I am not looking for a wife,' Henry said quickly, although he wasn't sure anyone was listening. 'Though don't tell my father that.'

'Henry, darling, you must dance with Miss Lippet. She is a very accomplished young woman and I think you will like her very much,' Lady Shrewsbury said.

'Leave the poor man alone.' Lord Shrewsbury ushered his wife away, only to catch her arm and plant a kiss on her cheek. 'Leave him to me,' he murmured, quiet enough it was clear Henry wasn't meant to hear.

'I am fine, Shrewsbury,' Henry said quickly as his old friend turned to him.

'You're anything but fine, although no one could blame you. This is the first time you've attended a ball since Anne's death, isn't it?'

'Yes.' His late wife, Anne, had passed away two years earlier. There had been the obligatory mourning period, which had lasted a year, but after that Henry had been surprised at how many people expected him to slip back into normal life. He had struggled, shutting himself away, unsure what he wanted from life and how to navigate all the guilt and sorrow he still felt.

'Ignore my dear wife. She loves you, and she wants to see you happy, but I don't think she quite understands that it's going to take time. You do not need to choose a wife on your first outing in society.'

'I do not *wish* to choose a wife at all.'

'Yes, that might be a problem,' Shrewsbury said with a frown. 'Your dear old father isn't likely to be swayed on the matter, is he?'

'No.' Henry thought of his father, the austere man he had only ever visited in his study, even when he was a young child. He couldn't picture him anywhere else but the oppressive room, surrounded by is ledgers and books, a look of disapproval on his face. 'I have never known him to change his mind on any matter.'

'Then you have a choice to make. Do you satisfy your father and search for a respectable, wealthy wife, or do you honour your own feelings and stay a single man?'

Henry closed his eyes—for a moment it was as if he had been whisked away from the ballroom. The noise faded, the chatter of the guests a mere hum, the music from the string quartet no more than a soft trill on the air. These were decisions he didn't want to make. Once he had been so certain of his own

judgement, so ready to make difficult decisions. Then he had
defied his father with his head held high. After everything had
gone wrong, his confidence in himself had been crushed, and
now he found it difficult to make even the easiest of decisions
about his life.

The choice he was faced with wasn't as straightforward as
Shrewsbury suggested either. He could quite happily spend the
rest of his life without ever speaking to his father again, but his
father controlled access to his sister, and Henry did want to see
her, to ensure the old man was treating her well.

'Have a drink. Have three. I will ensure my darling wife does
not push any more young ladies your way tonight.'

'Thank you,' Henry said.

Lord Shrewsbury clapped him on the shoulder and then
moved away, already smiling at his next guests. Henry surveyed
the room. The ball was a roaring success. Everyone was in high
spirits. Despite the late hour the dancing continued—hardly
anyone made their excuses to slip away. Silently he cursed,
thinking of the young woman waiting for him upstairs.

He had thought of little else in the hour since he'd rejoined
the ball. These last few weeks he had found it difficult to summon interest in anything, but her story was intriguing, and her
practical manner was strangely endearing.

He could admit to himself what he probably liked was the
element of distraction this matter promised. If he was dashing
across London, trying to find Miss Shepherd's missing sister,
he didn't have to think about his own predicament. He didn't
have to make any decisions about his future.

With a glance around the room to check no one was watching, he lifted two glasses of champagne from the table and
slipped from the room.

Upstairs he paused outside the door to the library, not wanting to scare Miss Shepherd by bursting in. He knocked quietly
and then opened the door. Before he entered he transferred the
two glasses to one hand and picked up a candlestick from one
of the tables, taking it into the dark room.

Miss Shepherd sprung to her feet as he entered, her eyes seeking his before she calmed and slid back into her chair.

'You have been gone for ever,' she said, her tone completely serious with no hint of exaggeration.

'The ball continues. There are guests everywhere downstairs.' He held out one of the glasses. 'I brought you champagne.'

She sipped at it gingerly, then gave a surprised little nod before taking a bigger gulp.

'It has been a tedious hour,' she said, motioning to the room around her. 'This could have been designed as a form of torture. Surrounded by books but with no way to see them.'

'You could have got a candle from the hall.'

'You told me to stay in here.'

He inclined his head, motioning to the candle he had placed on a table, far away from the bookshelves. 'Now you can read whilst you wait.'

'That is something at least.' She paused, took another sip of champagne. 'Thank you. For the candle and for the drink.' Her eyes roved over his body—for a moment he wondered what she was going to ask of him next.

'Did you bring any food?'

He laughed. 'No, Miss Shepherd, I did not think to smuggle you a pastry in the pocket of my jacket.'

'Hmm. Shame,' she said, standing and taking the candle to move closer to the bookshelves. 'How is the ball?'

'Tedious.'

'It did not look tedious.'

'From what you saw peeking in from the bushes?'

'Exactly. It looked…magical.'

He paused for a moment, considering what it would be like to look in from the outside, to see the glamour and the splendour when you led a much less extravagant life.

'I sound like a poor little rich boy, don't I?'

She smiled at this, and he felt something stir inside him. She had a lovely smile. It was a little tentative, as if she were

not used to smiling in public, but that made it all the more endearing.

'Have you been to a ball like this before?'

'No, never.'

'Have you been to any ball?'

'No.'

'A dance at the local assembly rooms then?'

'My mother never wanted us to attend. I realise now she
was worried about the gossip. She was terrified of a possible
scandal, I suppose. After everything that had happened to her
it made her a little cautious. Selina sneaked out a few times,
but I never did.'

'So you have never danced a waltz before.'

'I have learned the steps with Selina, but I have never danced
anything with anyone other than my sister.'

Henry knew he should leave Miss Shepherd to her glass of
champagne and her book, but he had no desire whatsoever to
go back downstairs to the ball. Before he could stop himself,
he stood and held out a hand.

'Would you do me the honour of the next dance?'

She stared at him as though he'd grown a second head.

'Here?'

'There is ample space, we can hear the music through the
balcony door and there is no one else watching. I do not like
to boast, but I am an excellent dancer. You are in safe hands.'

She did not look convinced, but he didn't waver, holding his
hand out until she put the candle on the table, alongside her
glass, and placed one delicate hand in his. She exhaled softly
as he pulled her to him, her cheeks flushing.

As if it were a sign from heaven, the first few notes of a waltz
floated up from the ballroom below.

'Try to relax, Miss Shepherd. As I said, you are in safe
hands.' She was stiff, her posture erect and her shoulders tensed
so much they were raised towards her ears. Slowly he coaxed
her into a more natural position, before exerting just the right
amount of pressure on her lower back to guide her in the right
direction.

With the first step he felt his spirits lift a little. He had always enjoyed dancing, the art of anticipating your partner's movements, two people moving as one for at least a short while. His late wife, Anne, had not ever wanted to dance. Much like Miss Shepherd, she had not had the privilege of a dance tutor, or the expectation that she would be able to dance perfectly by the time she attended her first ball. On the two occasions they had danced together she'd hated every minute, and he had been left feeling guilty for even suggesting it.

Miss Shepherd was hesitant at first, but as they spun, their bodies moving in unison, he saw a flicker of a smile on her face. And then, when he executed a rather flamboyant spin, she actually laughed in delight.

'Stop trying to look at your feet,' he said, catching her hand and placing it on his chest. 'Feel the music in here, find your rhythm and stop thinking about it too much.'

'Is that what you do?' She was looking up at him, her green eyes glinting in the candlelight.

'I have not danced for quite some time, but yes, I try not to think of each individual step.'

'I cannot believe the much-esteemed Lord Routledge is not in demand at every ball he attends.'

'You assume too much, Miss Shepherd,' he said as he twirled her again. In the darkness of the library he was daring to hold her a little closer than would be acceptable on the dance floor downstairs, but there was no one there to raise a disapproving eyebrow.

'You wish me to believe that you are not a man held in high esteem by the rest of society?' She had a teasing note to her voice that Henry realised he rather liked. He felt happier than he had in a long time, hiding in the shadows with Miss Shepherd.

'Certainly not by all society.'

'Ah,' she said, looking up at him appraisingly. 'Let me guess. Your father? He is the one who disapproves of you?'

'He does indeed.'

'Am I to understand your antics are too wild for him? You bring the family name into disrepute?'

Henry felt a heaviness descend on him as he thought of everything that had happened in the last few years.

'My wife,' he said. 'He did not approve of my wife.'

'I am sorry.' She looked genuinely appalled at having touched on such a sensitive subject.

He shrugged, not wanting to go into the details. He could barely talk of Anne to the people who had known her, let alone explain the impossibility of their situation to a stranger. With a firm resolve he pushed all thoughts of the past from his mind. He found it easier to thrust them away rather than deal with uncomfortable truths.

Focussing on the woman in front of him, he worked on losing himself in the dance. Miss Shepherd might not have danced in public before, and every so often she stepped in the wrong direction, but she was a natural. Her body was lithe and graceful, and he was reminded how easily she had climbed the wisteria to the first-floor balcony.

Together they swayed and stepped and twirled, Henry thankful of the distraction from darker thoughts that nipped at the edge of his consciousness.

Sarah made the mistake of looking up and for a long moment she was lost in Lord Routledge's eyes. Of course she'd noticed them before—even in the semi-darkness it was impossible to ignore the man's good looks. His eyes were a wonderful deep brown, full of sadness and intrigue.

She swallowed, her pulse racing and heat rising through her body.

She knew she was passably attractive, and there had been offers from a couple of young men of her acquaintance to step out over the last couple of years. Never had she been tempted. But, right now, if Lord Routledge asked her to run away into the night with him, she would find it hard to refuse.

Silently she scoffed at the idea. As if the poised and eligible Lord Routledge would ask her that. No matter what he said, he probably had five or six elegant and well-bred young women waiting for him downstairs.

'You look sad,' he said, an expression of genuine curiosity on his face. 'The waltz isn't meant to be a melancholy experience. At least not if I'm doing it right.'

With a press of his fingers he spun her quickly, and somehow they ended up closer than they had begun, her body brushing against his. She inhaled sharply, and for a moment it felt as though time had stopped. Their eyes met. Ever so slowly, he raised a hand to her face, tucking a stray strand of hair behind her ear.

In that instant Sarah wanted to be kissed. She felt her lips part slightly, her breathing become shallow. She'd never been kissed before, but instinctively her body swayed towards Lord Routledge. Her heart thumped within her chest as he moved a fraction of an inch towards her, and then stopped.

Immediately Sarah felt like a fool. She looked away, hoping Lord Routledge had not noticed the pathetic way she'd been staring at him, like some lovesick puppy. It would be a miracle if he had missed it, but hopefully in the darkness he could convince himself he had been mistaken.

The last few notes of the waltz drifted up to the library. Lord Routledge gently let go of her and bowed, taking a step back.

'Thank you for the dance, Miss Shepherd.'

Sarah turned, not trusting herself to keep a neutral expression on her face.

'I expect you need to get back to the ball.'

'I expect I do. I shall check downstairs and return when I think we can get you out of here without anyone noticing.'

'Thank you.'

She felt strangely bereft as he slipped out of the library, closing the door behind him. Sarah had been the one to push him away, shooing him back to the ball downstairs. It was a protective action, done to stop any further inappropriate thoughts on her part.

Letting out a loud sigh she sat back down in the chair, allowing her head to drop back against the soft fabric. She blamed the uncertainty and worry around Selina's disappearance for her uncharacteristic behaviour. Never would she have ever imagined breaking into someone's house, and her thoughts about kissing Lord Routledge were similarly out of character.

Chapter Four

It was half past two in the morning by the time Lord Routledge reappeared. Despite the long hours, which he must have passed dancing and socialising in a warm ballroom, he still looked impeccably smart, with not a single hair out of place. By contrast Sarah felt a mess, even though she had spent the last few hours doing nothing more vigorous than sitting in a chair reading.

'Are you ready to make your escape?' Lord Routledge asked as he slipped back into the room. His eyes glinted with anticipation—he didn't try to hide the fact he was enjoying this.

'Will we escape unseen?'

'Most of the guests have left, and the few gentlemen that remain are so engrossed in their card game they wouldn't notice a stampede of elephants flattening the house. The only person we have to be wary of is Lady Shrewsbury, our hostess. I do not think she has retired for the evening, and even with a glass or two of champagne inside her she is an observant woman.'

'What is the plan?' This was the moment Sarah had been patiently waiting for these last few hours, but now it had come she felt suddenly nervous.

'I will descend the stairs and, if there is no one in sight, I will motion for you to follow. Move quickly, and I will escort you out.'

'Will you not need to bid your host and hostess goodnight?'

'They will forgive me for slipping away.'

'Very well,' Sarah said, rising to her feet. She smoothed the fabric on her dress, resisting the urge to grip the material of her skirt in her hands and lift it above her ankles, as if getting ready to run.

Lord Routledge led the way out of the library, treading quietly and motioning for her to keep directly behind him. Sarah's focus was on getting out of Shrewsbury House without anyone catching her, but as they crept down the hall she couldn't help but be distracted by the opulence. Even in the darkness she could see it was by far the grandest residence she had ever set foot inside. The carpet on the floor was thick and plush, and beautiful cream wallpaper decorated the walls. There were paintings hung at regular intervals, colourful scenes of foreign shores as well as a few portraits of serious-looking men and women in the fashions of bygone decades.

They reached the stairs and the soft hum of conversation drifted up, although there was no one visible in the hall. Lord Routledge touched her shoulder and then leaned in close, his breath tickling her ear as he spoke, sending involuntary shivers across her skin.

'Come downstairs as soon as I signal to you.'

Sarah nodded, feeling her heart lurch as he set off down the stairs.

He paused at the bottom, looked around and then beckoned her down. Now she did lift up her skirts, not wanting to trip on the material and end up in an inelegant pile for all to see. She hurtled down the stairs, and was halfway down before she looked up to see Lord Routledge's panic-stricken expression and the hand he held up to stop her descent.

Sarah froze, flattening herself against the wall as best she could, but aware that if anyone looked up they would see her acting oddly.

Below an elderly man walked up to Lord Routledge and clapped him on the shoulder.

'Good to see you out in society again, Routledge. A man cannot stay in mourning for his wife for ever.'

Lord Routledge muttered something Sarah could not hear, a scowl crossing his face, before he managed to fix a smile as he addressed the old man.

'Enjoy your trip back to Yorkshire, Lord Humphrey, I hope the journey is not too arduous.'

Lord Humphrey murmured a few further platitudes, clapped Lord Routledge on the shoulder again and disappeared into one of the open doorways.

Immediately Lord Routledge beckoned for her to move. Sarah was paralysed, frozen to the spot, and she had to force her legs to start working again so she could descend the stairs. It felt as if it took for ever to cover the final eight steps, but once she was at the bottom Lord Routledge immediately put a guiding hand in the small of her back and propelled her along the hall. They were outside in a matter of seconds, the door closing behind them with a reassuring click, but Lord Routledge did not stop there.

'Bend your head and look to the ground,' he said quietly. 'There are still a few carriages waiting outside, with inquisitive footmen who have nothing better to do than gossip. If they get a good look at you, the whole of London will be talking of the pretty young woman acting strangely as she left the Shrewsburys' ball.'

'Perhaps we should go our own ways now,' Sarah suggested.

'I may not have been at my most gentlemanly tonight, but please do not think I would be callous enough to send you out into the streets of London unaccompanied at this time in the morning.'

Sarah glanced around her, with a sinking feeling she realised he was right. It was past two o'clock in the morning. No one respectable was out on the streets at that time, and she had to walk a good distance to get back to her lodgings.

At home she wasn't in the habit of taking a stroll in the middle of the night, but if she did she would know which parts of St Leonards to avoid and which would likely be safer. Here, in the city, everywhere seemed like it could be teeming with danger.

'I can't ask you to walk me home. It's miles away.'

'You don't have to ask. I'm not even offering. I am insisting.'

'Thank you,' Sarah said softly. Throughout much of the night she had felt exasperated that her plan had failed, panicking that she might be found out. It hadn't left much time for her to consider what a favour Lord Routledge was doing her. Not only had he helped her escape unseen from Shrewsbury House, he was now planning on walking miles out of his way across London to ensure she got home safely. She glanced up at him, not for the first time wondering what his motivations could be.

Bending her head, they walked briskly down the path, out through the gate and onto the street. They passed the five carriages that were sitting motionless at the edge of the road, waiting for the gentlemen to finish playing cards inside before transporting them home.

'You do not have a carriage?' Sarah asked. She would not normally consider setting foot inside a carriage unchaperoned with a man, no matter how helpful he had been the rest of the evening—if anyone found out her reputation would be in tatters—but given that she had already spent a long time alone with Lord Routledge, adding on a private one-on-one carriage ride could hardly make things worse. What was more, she was exhausted and craved the comfort of a swift journey back to her narrow single bed in the rooms she was renting whilst in London.

'No,' he said with a grimace. 'A decision I am coming to regret right now. I normally relish the walk both before and after a ball. It gives me time to clear my head before I get home.'

'That is a pity.'

'Where are your rooms?' he asked.

'Close to Fleet Street.'

'Then we had better get walking, Miss Shepherd.'

The trek across London was further than he had anticipated, but after ten minutes Henry was beginning to enjoy himself, and after twenty he had all but forgotten it was after half past two in the morning.

The streets were quiet, but not deserted. As they walked and talked he kept alert, knowing a well-dressed man and woman would be likely targets for any thieves roaming the streets at this time.

'Why don't you tell me about the other avenues you've explored to find your sister,' Henry suggested once they had settled into a comfortable pace.

Miss Shepherd sighed and looked at him out of the corner of her eye. 'I am thankful for your assistance tonight, Lord Routledge, but forgive me, I am struggling to understand your interest in my plight. Surely a man of your station in life has many more interesting and important things to occupy his time than helping a stranger look for her foolish sibling.'

'What do you think occupies my time?' he asked, aware he was dodging the implied question by asking his own. It was a mechanism of defence he had developed over the last few years. People were naturally curious when they heard of his tragic situation. He had insisted on a marriage that had shocked and scandalised society, and then had to endure the endless interest of acquaintances as the marriage had spiralled into a disaster, which had ended only with his late wife's death. Even now, two years on, people were morbidly curious about how he was coping, and what he might do next that they could gossip about whilst at the breakfast table.

It was one of the reasons he normally ensured his life stood up to any scrutiny. If he didn't dally with unsuitable young ladies, didn't frequent the wrong sort of clubs, didn't do anything out of the ordinary, one day surely people would stop talking about him.

By helping Miss Shepherd he was breaking his own set of rules, but there was something enchanting about her stubborn insistence on doing whatever was necessary to find her sister. It had made him forget his resolution for a few minutes. He'd felt that spark of excitement that had been missing from his life for so long. Also, he knew it was a way of putting off the inevitable task of searching for a new wife.

She looked at him, head cocked to the side and raised an eyebrow. 'You are good at deflecting questions about yourself, my lord.' She smiled gently before letting him off the hook. 'I can only assume a lord spends some of his time in Parliament, but as you said earlier we are in the middle of the summer recess. I always assumed lords had land to manage, tenants to oversee, property to invest in.'

'Ah,' he said with a smile, feeling grateful that she had allowed the distraction, 'you are thinking of titled gentlemen who have property and money.'

'You are not one of these?'

'No.'

'A pauper lord, just my luck,' she murmured. He was beginning to enjoy her quiet, dry sense of humour. 'Although I am not sure how poor you can be, if you wear clothes like this and have your own carriage to spirit you around.'

'You are of course correct, everything is relative. I do not pretend I am forced to beg on the streets for enough money to buy a morsel of food, but you would be surprised at what lifestyle one can maintain with quite meagre funds and the promise of a fortune to come one distant day in the future.' He lowered his voice as if about to confide something important. 'The secret is to make everyone think that distant day is fast approaching, even when it isn't.'

'This is when your father dies and you inherit?'

'Yes. The old man is sixty and in such good health I expect he will be around to torment everyone for another twenty years at least. I have to make my creditors think differently.'

'Is that possible?'

Henry shrugged. 'Every so often I throw a comment into our conversation about how the doctor's bill for my father get higher every week or some such nonsense, although after years of saying such things I think people become impatient.'

'Wouldn't it just be easier to get a job, Lord Routledge?'

He laughed, although it was a forced sound. 'You would be surprised at how difficult that is for a Viscount who will one day be an Earl. It is assumed a man, even one with such a strained relationship with his father such as mine, is given a small yearly income.'

He made light of the situation, but it was something that hurt more than he could say. In the years before he had married Anne, his relationship with his father had already been difficult, and he had become tired of relying on the old man to fund his lifestyle. Much to his father's disgust he had become a working man, using what little funds he could scrape together to buy a small property in a cheap part of London, turning it into a lodging house. The property had been in a terrible condition and in dire need of repair, and every day he would go and supervise the tradesmen as well as rolling up his sleeves to do some of the manual labour himself. It had been satisfying to see the property transform from a tumbledown dwelling into a smart lodging house, even more so because it was the first time he had felt as though he had properly earned something for himself.

His father had never been loving, always distant and cold, but when he was a child Henry had received what he had needed to thrive. Lord Burwell was cruel in how he withheld affection from his son, but he wanted to mould a man worth taking over the title and all the responsibilities associated with it. It had meant the finest tutors, attending the best school and being ushered along to Cambridge University when the time came. Only when Henry had started to think and speak for himself had the withdrawal of money and support started in earnest.

'I am hardly qualified for anything.'

'No,' Miss Shepherd said, her face suddenly serious, 'I suppose it is difficult for anyone to step outside of what is expected for them. The opportunities are not there, unless you conform to society's expectations. I had the choice of becoming a governess or music teacher, or trying to find a position as paid companion or housekeeper. There are no other choices available for a woman with my background. We are expected to eschew more manual jobs, even something like becoming a seamstress or milliner. We are told to stick to our path, to not deviate.'

'And the consequences if you do can be dire,' Henry said, more to himself than to her. He was thinking of his late wife, of the chance they had taken to be together, of the blind hope he had based their relationship on. He had stepped off his prescribed path when he had married Anne and now, years later, he was still reeling.

They walked on a little further in silence, both a little melancholy as they considered their situations.

'At least no one will bother to rob us whilst we walk home,' Miss Shepherd said after a while.

He looked at her quizzically.

'They would be able to sense the self-pity we emanate half a mile away, and no doubt would not want to become embroiled in our sorrows.'

Henry laughed, enjoying the little smile that bloomed on Miss Shepherd's lips at his response. He wondered if her wit was normally so well received, or if she had to keep it hidden for fear of people's reactions.

They were only a few minutes away from Fleet Street now. But, as they walked, Henry began to have the sense of being watched. The few times he had nonchalantly turned, to see if he could spot anyone behind them, he had detected a flicker of movement in the shadows, but no more.

'You're worried about something,' Miss Shepherd said, making to look over her shoulder.

'Don't look, not yet. It may alert whoever is following us that we are aware of them and force them to make a move.'

'You think they mean to rob us?'

'I cannot see why else they would be following us at three o'clock in the morning.'

She chewed her lip and Henry realised Miss Shepherd didn't like not being in control of a situation. Although he knew little about her, he could tell she had spent much of her life being sensible and making the difficult decisions needed to keep a family afloat. Even the story of how she had come to London— having to postpone starting her new job to chase after a sister whose actions were at best reckless, but also could be viewed as highly selfish.

'It is only a couple of minutes to my lodging house,' she said, motioning with her hand in the general direction of Fleet Street. 'If we run for it, I am sure whoever it is will not be able to catch us before we make it.'

'Do you have a key?'

'Yes. There is a woman who rents out the rooms, Mrs Angel.

She has a bedroom close to the front door, but I expect she will be sleeping. There is a rule that no men are allowed in the lodging house, but I am sure even Mrs Angel will not begrudge you stepping over the threshold to keep you safe, if the thief does decide to follow us.'

'As long as you are delivered home safe,' Henry murmured, risking another glance over his shoulder. For a moment he wondered if he were imagining the muted footsteps matching their speed, and then he saw another dart of movement in the distance.

'Make haste, Miss Shepherd.'

She slipped her hand into his, and he was surprised by the familiarity of the movement, but he gripped hold of it. As one, they ran. Without looking back they darted along the streets, Henry matching his speed to hers, and before long they were outside the door to a respectable lodging house, and Miss Shepherd was fumbling with a key.

Henry stood with his back to the door, his eyes darting in all directions.

'I think somewhere back there they gave up,' Henry said.

'What if they are waiting for you when you return, alone?' There was genuine concern in her eyes and Henry felt touched. Miss Shepherd had her own troubles, but she was not so caught up in them that she ignored everything else going on.

'I will be fine,' he said with a shrug. 'I have nothing they could wish to steal anyway. I did not come out with any money, and I do not carry an expensive pocket watch or similar. I doubt they will risk a fight to take nothing more than the shirt from my back.' He motioned at the earrings that sat in her ears. 'I was more worried about your jewels.'

Her hand flitted to her ears and she touched the little sapphire earrings. They were only small, but probably were the most expensive thing she owned.

'Do you wish to come inside to wait a little longer?'

'No, thank you, Miss Shepherd. I will not risk the wrath of your landlady. I do not want her throwing you out on the street.'

Suddenly he realised quite how close they were standing. Miss Shepherd looked up at him and, for a moment, he was transported back to the moment in the library, as the last notes of the waltz had played, the moment when he'd had an overwhelming urge to kiss her. It was a foolish idea, one he had banished as soon as it had occurred, yet here it was again. His hand even started to move up, ready to cup her face, to pull her towards him.

Quickly he stepped away, clearing his throat. The thought was unforgiveable. Miss Shepherd was nothing like the sort of young lady he needed to focus his attentions on. Once before he had married a woman of a different social class to his own, thinking love would conquer all. Despite his youthful optimism it had been a disaster, and never again would he think he could overcome society's rules and prejudices. If he did decide to find another wife in the next few years, he would force his head to choose, not his heart.

'Goodnight, Miss Shepherd,' he said, somewhat stiffly.

'Thank you again, Lord Routledge.'

'I will send a note with the details once I've set up a meeting with Agnes Pepper.'

Chapter Five

It felt as though his head had only just hit the pillow before the pounding at the front door forced him awake. Somewhere below one of the servants opened the door, and he heard distorted voices drift up through the floorboards. Even without being able to hear the words he knew who it was that had deigned to pay a visit so early in the morning.

With a groan he sat up. For five years his father had refused to speak to him. From the moment he found out about Henry's intended marriage to Anne, a woman of a much lower social class, Lord Burwell had met with his only son once, to warn him off the marriage, and then no more. When it became apparent Henry was going to go through with the union—with or without his father's blessing—Lord Burwell had cut him off. Henry had been married for four years and not once had his father broken his vow to cut Henry out of his life. Even after Anne's death, his father had remained silent, choosing his frosty displeasure over sending any sort of condolences to his heir.

It had only been in the last few months Henry had looked to repair the relationship. His father was a narrow-minded, pompous man who did not have many redeeming features, but Henry had been forced to admit that, in one way at least, his father had been right. A marriage between two people of vastly different classes could not work out.

Right now, having had only three hours of sleep, he couldn't bear to face the man, but he hauled himself up out of bed all the same, quickly pulling on his trousers and a shirt that was draped over the back of a chair. His father would not think twice about bursting into his bedroom uninvited if Henry did not meet him downstairs.

'Good morning, Father,' he said, running a hand through his hair as he descended the stairs. 'Do come up.'

He was currently living in a set of modest rented rooms. His home was upstairs and another young gentleman, recently graduated from Oxford and trying to make his fortune like so many others in London, lived downstairs. They shared one entrance, as well as a maid and a footman, who also fulfilled the role of valet as needed.

'Did you choose a wife?' Lord Burwell asked once they'd ascended, throwing himself down in an armchair in Henry's sitting room without being invited.

'Excuse me?'

'The Shrewsbury ball last night. I hear it was well attended, despite half of London having retired to the countryside for the summer. The Gough girl was there, and the Tattership daughter. Both are very wealthy and have impeccable bloodlines.'

'I spoke to Miss Tattership,' Henry said, recalling the insipid young woman who had struggled to step out of her mother's shadow.

'You spoke to her? God's blood boy, sometimes I despair that you will ever marry. You need to do more than speak to her.'

Henry raised an eyebrow, but did not remind his father he had already been married for four years. Lord Burwell would not acknowledge Henry's union with Anne, and it was too early in the morning to get into such an argument.

'I am in no hurry, Father.'

'You might not be, but my years on this earth are limited. I want to see my bloodline secured before I shuffle off towards the grave.'

Henry knew his father was in excellent health—there was

no concern that he was shuffling off towards the grave any time soon. It was just another method the old man employed to manipulate him.

'I agreed I would start to look for a wife, Father. I have started that process. I attended the Shrewsbury ball last night, and tomorrow I am going to the opera. Ask around, the eligible young women of London are aware of my intentions. I have upheld my end of the bargain, now it is time for you to uphold yours.'

'You want to see her,' Lord Burwell said, his voice dropping low.

'Yes.'

His father curled up his lip and sneered. 'Present to me a *suitable* woman who has agreed to marry you, then you can see her.'

'That wasn't our agreement.' Desperately he tried to keep his temper from rising to the surface. His father did not respond well when he was challenged, and over the years Henry had learned it was foolish to make the man angry. He would never deign to see someone else's point of view, never admit he was wrong. Instead, Henry had learned to find other ways to get what he wanted.

'You say you went to the Shrewsbury ball to look for a wife, but for all I know you could have spent the whole evening at the card tables.'

'I did not.'

Lord Burwell shrugged. 'Bring me a fiancée and you can see your sister. Until then, she will remain shielded from your unsuitable influence.'

Sophia had been nine years old when he had seen her last, a lovely little girl who was inquisitive and kind. Now she was fourteen, and Henry often wondered how much his sister remembered him. During the years his father had refused any contact, it was the loss of a relationship with Sophia that Henry had regretted the most. He'd been all too aware that she was growing up secluded from the world, her only role model their father. As he had slowly emerged from his grief and shock after his late wife's death, it had been Sophia his thoughts had turned to, and it had been the reason he'd reached out to his father all those months ago. The crafty old fox had seen how much Henry

wanted to rekindle a relationship with his sister, using it to ca-
jole and manipulate his son into finally doing what he wanted.

Lord Burwell clapped his hands together and stood, looking around him, taking in the simple dwelling and cheap furnishings.

'You should return home to One Grosvenor Square,' Lord
Burwell said. 'It is not fitting for my son to live in lodgings
such as these.'

Henry shuddered at the idea of being completely under his father's control, as he would be if he returned to the family home.

'People expect the son of an Earl to have his own rooms,'
Henry said, trying to keep the emotion from his voice. He
wouldn't ask for more money, it was hard enough to take the
small stipend his father gave him every month, but without
any other source of income at the moment his hand was forced.

Lord Burwell grunted. Without another word, he stood and
walked to the door.

'Farewell, Father.'

He watched the older man from his window, allowing his
body to sag once the carriage had rolled away, disappearing
around the corner.

After a visit from his father he always felt battered and
bruised. This time had not been terrible, but he had been reminded of how much he had lost, and how much his father still
withheld from him.

Carefully he checked his reflection in the mirror. Later he
would refocus his energies on finding a bride his father would
deem suitable, who he could tolerate well enough for a lifetime
spent together, but right now he had a promise to fulfil.

Sarah had seen the carriage draw up outside and was down
the stairs and out the front door before Lord Routledge could
approach. She did not want her landlady opening the door to
him and appraising him in the suspicious way she looked at
anyone of the opposite sex.

'Good morning, Miss Shepherd, I trust it is not too early for
a trip out?'

'Every second is precious if I am to find Selina before I

have to return to Kent,' she said quickly. 'Thank you for keeping your promise.'

She felt his eyes on her and suddenly she felt self-conscious. Today she wasn't looking her best. It had been a late night and, even once she had slipped into bed, she had found it hard to sleep. Her mind had been racing with thoughts of all that had happened, as well as worries about her sister.

'Shall we be on our way?'

He held out a hand to assist her into the carriage as if she were a grand lady, ensuring she was settled on her seat before hopping up and sitting opposite her. The carriage lurched off almost immediately, rocking slightly as they picked up speed over the cobbles.

Sarah looked around her, trying not to let her mouth fall open. The carriage was unlike anything she had ever been in before. On her trip to London she had taken the stagecoach, but that had been a very different experience, squashed inside with seven other people. This was luxurious by comparison.

'It is a bit tatty, I apologise,' Lord Routledge said, following the direction of her gaze.

'Tatty?'

'Yes. It isn't mine, at least not really. My dear friend Lord Shrewsbury gave me the use of it when his wife insisted on a new one. Even the horses are his.'

'That is generous,' Sarah said, reaching out and touching the velvet that lined the walls.

'He is a generous man. He is one of the wealthiest people in the country, which of course makes it easier to be magnanimous with one's fortune, but I think it is just in his character. I suspect even if he was down to the last two coins he would insist on sharing.' Lord Routledge stared out of the window absently for half a minute, then turned back to her. 'He is kind too, and I am sure will have no objection to you speaking to the maid you wish to question.'

'You will not tell him I broke into his house?'

Lord Routledge grinned. 'Not yet.'

'Not yet?'

'Once you are far away from London, teaching Beethoven

to those little children in Kent, I can't see the harm in sharing the story with him.'

Sarah closed her eyes. Lord Routledge was right, and it wasn't as if she would ever cross paths with someone like Lord Shrewsbury ever again, but just the thought of someone else knowing how she had so recklessly broken the law was mortifying.

The journey that had taken well over an hour on foot was much quicker in the carriage, and in no time at all they were rolling to a stop in front of Shrewsbury House.

It looked even more magnificent in the daylight. It was a large building with a white façade and columns spaced at regular intervals. The whole house was immaculate from the outside, from the paintwork to the flowers and shrubs that grew in the pots that flanked the door.

A flutter of nerves started in her stomach, working its way up until she felt flushed and a little breathless as they stepped from the carriage and approached the house.

'I will explain everything to Lord and Lady Shrewsbury,' Lord Routledge said. 'And in no time at all you will have your answers from Agnes Pepper.'

He knocked on the door. It was opened almost immediately by a footman who bowed deeply.

'Please come into the drawing room, Lord Routledge, I shall let Lord Shrewsbury know you are here. Who shall I say accompanies you?'

'This is Miss Shepherd. Thank you, Jacobs.'

The footman showed them into the drawing room, and Sarah had to remind herself not to gawp. If she had thought the carriage was plush this was even more so. The room was airy and large, with gilded mirrors at either end, giving it the appearance of going on for ever. Two windows looked out onto the street, allowing the late-morning light to flood into the room. A piano stood at one end, and beautifully upholstered chairs were set in a horseshoe configuration at the other.

Sarah's eye was immediately dawn to the piano. It was a magnificent instrument, polished so it shone, reflecting the rays of sunlight from the windows. She longed to trail her fingers across the keys and to hear the depth of sound from such an instrument.

They were not kept waiting long before the door opened and an elegant woman a little older than Sarah entered. Everything about her was perfect, from how the silk of her skirt rippled as she walked, to the intricate way her hair had been pinned. A broad smile broke onto her face when she saw Lord Routledge, which made her look even more radiant.

'Henry darling, I am so pleased you...' she began, the words trailing off as she saw Sarah. She recovered quickly. 'Forgive me, Lord Routledge, I did not know we had company.'

'This is Miss Shepherd. Miss Shepherd, it is my pleasure to introduce simply the best woman in London, Lady Shrewsbury.'

'Are you flirting with my wife again, you reprobate?' Lord Shrewsbury asked as he lumbered into the room.

'We have a guest, my dear,' Lady Shrewsbury said quietly to her husband whilst smiling at Sarah. 'Miss Shepherd.'

'Miss Shepherd, pleasure to meet you,' Lord Shrewsbury said, unabashedly looking her up and down. 'Do I know your people?'

She had to suppress a smile at the question. *Perhaps* wasn't going to be an acceptable answer, not when she didn't want to declare herself illegitimate to the whole world.

'Sometimes I wonder how you survive, Shrewsbury,' Lord Routledge said, shaking his head. 'No, you don't know her people. Miss Shepherd is an orphan.'

'Ah.'

The Shrewsburys regarded her with interest, and for a moment they all just stood looking at one another.

'I have a favour to ask, on behalf of Miss Shepherd.' Lord Routledge flopped down onto one of the chairs as if it were his own home. Lady Shrewsbury motioned for Sarah to take a seat as well, before choosing one herself.

'Miss Shepherd needs to talk to one of your maids. Agnes Pepper.'

The request took Lord and Lady Shrewsbury by surprise.

'May I enquire what this is about?' Lady Shrewsbury asked with a frown.

'Miss Shepherd's sister is missing. She thinks Agnes Pepper might know something of her whereabouts.'

'You came to the house a few days ago,' Lady Shrewsbury said, her eyes narrowing a fraction.

'Yes, my lady,' Sarah said, trying to sit confidently in her seat. 'As Lord Routledge says I am very worried about my sister. She has disappeared and I know she spoke to Agnes Pepper before her disappearance. I am most eager to find out what they discussed, and hopefully this will lead to finding out what happened to my sister.'

'What a worrying time for you,' Lord Shrewsbury murmured.

'If you would excuse us for a moment, Miss Shepherd,' Lady Shrewsbury said, standing. She flashed a look at the two gentlemen who stood and followed her from the room.

Sarah felt her heart sink, wondering if Lady Shrewsbury would refuse to help, or worse, if somehow they knew she had broken into their house the night before and were sending for the authorities. In any other circumstance she would have considered running, but the information Agnes Pepper had might lead her to her sister, and she couldn't jeopardise her chance of finding out where she was.

'Are you unwell, Henry?' Lady Shrewsbury asked, laying a hand on his forehead.

'Leave the man alone,' Lord Shrewsbury commanded, pushing gently past his wife. 'Clearly he's smitten. Who is she?'

Henry closed his eyes. 'I am neither unwell nor smitten. I am merely trying to do a good deed for a young woman who is distraught over the disappearance of her sister.'

'You're too kind, too good,' Lady Shrewsbury said with a sigh. 'People see that and take advantage.'

'No one is taking advantage.' Henry felt a ripple of irritation. Lord and Lady Shrewsbury were his closest friends. Over the last few years they had seen him at his worst, and never faltered in their support or love. However, after the heartbreak he had suffered, sometimes they treated him as though he were fragile, something to be protected.

'She is pretty. Lovely eyes. And a good figure. Not too skinny,' Lord Shrewsbury mused.

'Thomas,' his wife scolded. 'You shouldn't be looking.'

'I'm not passing judgement, but I have eyes in my head. All I'm doing is making an honest observation. The girl is pretty.'

'I hadn't noticed,' Henry lied. Miss Shepherd was attractive, with those sharp, green eyes and her thick brown hair. It was her smile that transformed her face though. When she could be coaxed into smiling or laughing, she looked radiant.

'How do you know her?' Lady Shrewsbury stepped closer, taking on the role of interrogator.

'I met her in the street outside.'

'In the street? Oh, Henry, as I said, you are too good, too naïve.'

He raised an eyebrow. 'I am nothing of the sort.'

'No, the man is not naïve, my dear,' Lord Shrewsbury said quietly. 'A hopeless romantic, yes, but he is aware of the ways of the world.'

'What is the harm in bringing Miss Shepherd here to ask your maid a few questions? You can sit in, ensure nothing inappropriate occurs, and then Miss Shepherd will be on her way.'

'You have no obligation to her beyond bringing her here?'

'None at all. My good deed will be done, and we can all move on.'

Lord and Lady Shrewsbury exchanged a meaningful look, but to Henry's relief they both nodded.

'I shall go and fetch Agnes from her duties.'

'Thank you.'

He watched as Lady Shrewsbury left the room.

'I would apologise, but she is only protective of you because she loves you,' Lord Shrewsbury said.

'There is nothing to apologise for. I have always been thankful for the friendship of you both.'

They were silent for a moment before Lord Shrewsbury spoke again. 'Did you meet anyone last night who you might be interested in courting?'

Henry sighed. 'No, but I confess I did not try very hard. I

know it is what I must do to satisfy my father and try to build the bridge between us, but I hate the idea of marrying again.'

'It would not have to be like last time.'

'I know. I am not a lovesick, optimistic fool any longer. This time I will be more practical in choosing a wife. I suppose any of the coming season's debutantes will do.'

Lord Shrewsbury looked at him sadly. 'I never used to be a romantic. Although you know that changed when I met Louisa. I do not think you need someone you are madly in love with when you marry, love can grow and develop in all sorts of ways, but I do think it important you feel *something* for your future wife. That might be friendship or respect, but choosing a wife based on a list of criteria, as your father would have you do, is not going to make for a happy union.'

Henry shook his head. 'He did give me a list you know, said my judgement wasn't to be trusted after last time. He wrote down which families she could be from, the minimum dowry I would accept and even reminded me that he had final say on whether the woman I chose was suitable.'

'You should cut him off Henry. He can't disinherit you entirely, you will be the next Earl of Burwell. Most of the property is entailed.'

'I don't care about any of that. I care about Sophia.'

Lord Shrewsbury fell silent. There was nothing he could say in argument there.

'I do not wish to marry again, but if it means I get to see my little sister, to ensure that *man* we call our father is not making her life an utter misery, then it is something I need to do. I acted selfishly when I married Anne, and look where that got me.'

'Following one's heart is not acting selfishly.'

'I was self-indulgent. My father was not the only one with misgivings about our relationship, although he was the only one to react quite so terribly.'

Their conversation was cut short by Lady Shrewsbury re-entering the room with a scared young maid following her.

'This is Agnes Pepper. Shall we take her to Miss Shepherd?'

'Thank you.'

Next door Miss Shepherd was standing close to the piano.

He had noticed her interest in it as soon as they had entered the room, and now she was examining the instrument without touching it. She jumped a little as everyone entered, quickly returning to her seat.

'This is Agnes. Agnes, Miss Shepherd has some questions she would like to ask you about her sister. You are not in any sort of trouble, so answer truthfully.'

'Yes, my lady.'

The maid was in her mid-twenties, with coppery hair that twisted in tight curls as it sprung from her head. Despite the numerous pins used to try to hold it in place, Agnes's hair looked as though it could not be tamed. She was tall and hunched her shoulders, likely thinking the action made her seem smaller.

'Go ahead, Miss Shepherd, ask your questions.'

'Good morning, Agnes,' Miss Shepherd said, smiling softly at the maid. 'Thank you for talking to me this morning. I have come to London to look for my sister, Miss Selina Shepherd.'

Agnes nodded.

'From her letters I understand she was planning on coming to see you.'

'She did. She caught me when I went out on my afternoon off. I was going home to visit my ma, and she asked if she could walk with me.'

'What did she ask you?'

'She wanted to know about her father. She said she was trying to find him and she had come across my name in an old letter. I think she was a bit disappointed when she saw me, she kept saying I was too young, that she must have got the wrong Agnes Pepper.'

'Were you able to tell her anything?'

'No, Miss. I said I was very sorry, but I didn't know anything about her father. She asked me where I had worked before I came here to work for Lord and Lady Shrewsbury and I told her that I'd only had one previous position, as a maid in Mr and Mrs Warner's household.'

'Did she say anything else? Or ask you anything else?'

'She asked me if I was named after anyone, but I told her I

was the first Agnes in my family. She thanked me for talking to her and then she left.'

'She didn't say where she was going next?'

'No. I'm sorry Miss. She seemed like a nice girl.'

'She is a nice girl,' Miss Shepherd murmured. 'Thank you, Agnes. Perhaps I could write my address down, and if you remember anything else, anything at all, you will know where to contact me.'

Agnes looked quickly at Lady Shrewsbury, who nodded, and directed Miss Shepherd to the small writing desk in the corner of the room. Once the piece of paper was handed over, Agnes bobbed a curtsey and left.

'I am sorry this visit was not of more use,' Lady Shrewsbury said. 'I wish you the best of luck in finding your sister.'

'Thank you.' Miss Shepherd looked as though she was about to burst into tears. She gave hurried thanks and bid Lord and Lady Shrewsbury good day. As she rushed outside, Henry had to take the steps two at a time to keep up.

Chapter Six

Sarah walked briskly down the road, the tears stinging her eyes as she tried to gain control of her emotions.

'Miss Shepherd,' Lord Routledge called after her. She walked faster, not wanting him to see her like this.

His stride was much longer than hers and, despite her best efforts, he caught her just as she rounded the corner.

'Wait, Miss Shepherd,' he said, his voice laced with concern.

'Thank you for your assistance,' she said. Her voice was muffled by emotion, and the tears were starting to flow in earnest down her cheeks. 'I doubt I would have been able to persuade Lord and Lady Shrewsbury to let me speak to their maid without your help.' She spun and walked away.

After a minute she was aware Lord Routledge was following her. He kept pace easily, walking alongside her quietly, his head bent as if they were two old friends going for a companionable stroll.

'You've done what you promised.' The words came out sharper than she had intended, but she didn't apologise. She was too upset at losing the trail of her sister to consider if she was being unforgivably rude.

'I am not going to abandon you in the middle of London when you are so visibly distressed.'

She spun to face him, halting abruptly. 'Why are you insisting on helping me? You do not know me. You do not know my sister. Don't you have your own problems to solve? Or do you just like being surrounded by the misery of others so you don't have to think about your own?'

Never before had she been so rude, but Sarah wanted to lash out, to hurt someone as she was hurting, and Lord Routledge was conveniently there. Immediately she felt ashamed of her outburst, but Lord Routledge looked unshaken.

'Might I suggest we make a detour through the park? Some people swear by being surrounded by nature if they become overwhelmed.'

Seeing she wasn't going to evade him that easily, Sarah shrugged and allowed Lord Routledge to lead her through a set of gates into Hyde Park. It was a warm day, the sun shining, and dozens of couples strolled arm in arm along the paths. Lord Routledge chose their route and, after ten minutes of walking, they reached a relatively secluded spot that overlooked a pretty fountain. There was an unoccupied bench and Sarah nodded in agreement when he suggested they sit.

For a long time neither of them spoke. The trickling sound of the water in the fountain was hypnotic. Sarah felt some of the overwhelming tension begin to ebb and then flow away.

'I have a sister,' Lord Routledge said quietly. 'You asked me why I wanted to help you.' He shrugged. 'There are many complex reasons, but I think the most understandable is that I have a sister, and I hope that if she was ever in trouble someone would help her.'

Sarah cleared her throat, suddenly feeling ashamed of her outburst. Lord Routledge had been nothing but kind since she had met him, and she had been unforgivably rude.

'I doubt your sister would get into this sort of mess,' she said, her eyes fixed on the fountain.

'I wouldn't know.'

She looked up sharply and saw the sadness in his eyes. He'd looked that way when he had spoken about his late wife, and Sarah got the impression his life had been marred by tragedy.

'My sister is fourteen years old, but my father has not let me see her since she was nine.'

'That's terrible.'

'Yes. It is. He keeps her cloistered away on one of the family estates in Yorkshire. The only news I hear about her is what he deigns to impart. He says she has a governess and everything she needs, but he has lied to me before.'

'Why will he not let you see her?'

Lord Routledge didn't answer for a second, and she saw pain flashing across his face. 'My father is a cruel and complex man, who derives pleasure from other people's pain, but more than that he loves to be in control of everyone. He likes to have people dangling on a string like a puppet, and then he makes you dance to his tune.' He shook his head. 'Once I was old enough to strike out on my own, I rebelled, refused to conform. It culminated in my marriage to my late wife, whom he did not approve of one little bit. When I announced the wedding, he told me to call it off or I would never see Sophia, my sister, again.'

Sarah thought of all of the good times she had shared with Selina—the secret conversations in bed at night, the laughter they'd shared as they jumped over waves on the seashore. She couldn't imagine someone telling her she could never see or speak to her sister again. Selina had only been gone for a few weeks, and already Sarah felt as though a piece of her heart had been ripped out.

'I thought he was bluffing, that once he saw I would not be controlled by him he would relent, but I should have known better.'

'He's kept you from seeing your sister for all that time?'

'Yes. So you see, Miss Shepherd, I cannot be there to protect her, from him or from anything else. It is always my hope that other people would show her kindness if she was in need of some.'

'I am sorry. I shouldn't have snapped at you. I lashed out, and you were closest and easiest to hurt,' Sarah said, looking up and holding his gaze.

'I understand why you are so upset. The talk with Agnes Pepper was not at all helpful.'

'It was the last thing Selina mentioned in the letter. She was really excited about going to see Agnes Pepper. I've followed every other lead, chased down every other name she talked about. There's nothing, no clue of where she would have looked next.' She wrung her hands together, worrying at the skin at the side of her thumb with her nail. 'It feels as though she has just disappeared into thin air. I do not know what to do.'

'I will not force my help upon you, and I cannot promise to uncover anything that you have not, but sometimes a new perspective is all that is needed. If you want my assistance to go over everything, then I would be happy to offer it.'

She considered the man sitting next to her. Sarah normally liked to do things alone, without the help of anyone else, but here she would have to admit defeat. The stakes were too high for her to indulge her pride.

'That would be very kind, thank you.'

'Good,' Lord Routledge said, clapping his hands together. 'Where do we start?'

Three hours later they were back in Hyde Park, this time seated on a blanket on a patch of grass close to the Serpentine. It was a glorious day, although the clouds had just started to bubble up as they did when it was hot and humid, and there were plenty of families seated in a similar way dotted over the grass. A group of children giggled as they tried, without much luck, to set a paper boat floating on the water. Their nannies sat and gossiped, stretched out and enjoying the sunshine and freedom from the nursery.

Sarah had returned to her lodgings to collect the letters she had received from Selina, arranging to meet Lord Routledge back in the park a few hours later. It was a very public place for them to be discussing Selina's disappearance, but they could hardly retire to either of their lodgings.

Carefully Sarah set out the letters in date order.

'Unfortunately, Selina took all of the original letters, the ones sent by our father to our mother when they were courting. I did read them when we first discovered the truth after our mother's death, but I cannot remember much. I was in shock, unable to take much in.'

'So we have to rely on what your sister said in her letters, and from them try to work out where she might have looked for clues next.'

Sarah felt a sudden surge of anger towards her sister. It was typical of Selina to disappear without a thought for anyone else. She had always been flighty and carefree, never thinking about the consequences of her actions. Not that anything bad ever seemed to happen to Selina. Her natural charm and positive outlook always meant that, somehow, she landed on her feet, even when doing the most reckless of things.

'That's right.'

'You must have discussed the situation with your sister, either when you found the letters or since. Did you talk about who you thought your father could be?'

Sarah thought back to the moment she had stumbled across the letters. It had been soon after their mother had passed away, and she had been clearing out the few personal effects their mother had kept private. There was a large wooden chest she kept locked, the key around her neck. Sarah had only seen inside a few times. She had always thought it contained her mother's most valuable items of clothing, and perhaps the few pieces of jewellery she had that she didn't wear day to day.

Under the layers of material, right at the very bottom of the trunk, she'd found the neatly tied bundle of letters. Immediately her instincts had told her these letters were important. Even without reading them, she had realised this was the reason her mother had kept the chest locked, not out of fear of thieves breaking in and stealing her valuables.

She'd handled the papers carefully, at first thinking they were letters from the father they had been told about, perhaps whilst he was posted away in the army, but once she had started reading the truth dawned quickly.

'There was nothing specific in any of the letters, they were all very vague. He wrote of the tedious, never-ending round of balls and dinner parties in London, and how he wished he was in the countryside with our mother. That was why we suspected he may have been wealthy. Very few people attend the London balls.'

'It does narrow it down quite considerably.'

'He talked of his parents pushing him towards a certain young woman, but he only referenced her as Lady P. I know from her letters that Selina was trying to work out who Lady P could be, but she did not have any luck—or, at least, not that she told me.' She screwed up her eyes, desperately trying to remember the details of her father's letters. It was many months ago and, after reading all the letters through once, she had refused to read them again. It had been quite clear to her that their father, although likely wealthy and titled, had been a scoundrel. She was under no illusion that he had probably promised their mother marriage and a life as his wife, but instead had used her until he'd grown bored, then moved on to marry a woman of his own class.

'Did the letters have a date on them?'

Sarah thought back, trying to recall all the details.

'Seventeen ninety-two. Does that help?'

'It may help with identifying Lady P. I do not know who was out in society that year, but if Lady P was an eligible young woman who had her debut that year, or possibly the year before, she should be easy to identify. Perhaps she went on to marry your father, perhaps she didn't, but there will be someone who can remember the gossip of the season from twenty-three years ago.'

'It's that simple?'

He shrugged. 'If you know the right people it is. Although I'm not sure it helps us find your sister. She would not have known anyone to ask about Lady P, so she couldn't have had much luck following that trail. Shall we have a look at Selina's letters?'

Sarah handed him the first one. She had most of the contents memorised—she had poured over them so many times.

'In this one she details her journey to London and her hopes for finding our father,' Sarah said as Lord Routledge's eyes skimmed over it. 'I do not think there is much of use in there.' She handed him the second, and then the third. 'She puts where she is staying, but that is the first place I went when I came to

London. They hadn't seen her for weeks and were grumbling about an unpaid bill. Thankfully the man who rented her a room finally took pity on me and gave me her bundle of things.'

'Was there anything useful in there?'

'No, just her clothes, and a few mementos from home.'

She waited for him to read the two letters, then handed him another. 'This one she sent after her first week in London. She started by visiting some of the places mentioned by our father in his letters. There was a gentleman's club and the opera house in Covent Garden.'

'You have been there as well?'

'Yes. Both turned me away pretty quickly, and from what she wrote I think they did the same to Selina.'

'I cannot see either establishment entertaining enquiries from an unknown young woman who has no clear ties to the aristocracy.'

'Then, in her letter the next week, she wrote she had tracked down a few of the people mentioned, although she had not been able to get close to them. In one letter our father writes of a Mr Peterson, apparently a friend from school, who was one of the few people who knew about the relationship. Selina expresses her excitement about possibly finding the man in this letter, although she had not worked out a way to get close to him.' Sarah handed over the next two letters. 'Although in the next one she talks of paying one of the serving staff at the gentleman's club to point out Mr Peterson to her, and then approaching him when he left the club one evening. It sounds like he refused to speak to her, dismissed her without even listening to what she had to say.'

'Mr Peterson,' Lord Routledge mused, nodding his head. 'He would be about the right age to have gone to school with a man who could be your father. I would guess that he is about fifty.'

'You know him?'

'London society is very small. I expect I am at least acquainted with your father.'

Sarah blinked, finding it difficult to believe.

'Selina also talks of a woman mentioned in the letters, Mrs Otterly.'

'She's dead,' Lord Routledge said, taking the last of the letters from Sarah.

'Yes, apparently she died last year.'

'She was old and I think a particularly bad winter fever carried her off.'

'You really do know everyone, don't you?'

He shrugged. 'Most men of the aristocracy went to one of three or four schools, and then to Oxford or Cambridge to continue their education. We frequent the same gentlemen's clubs, play cards at the same tables, attend the same balls and dinner parties. I would be most surprised if I didn't at least know *of* your father, if he is as wealthy and well connected as you suspect.'

Sarah swallowed. She hadn't come to London to find her father, all she wanted was her sister. Yet there was a real possibility that, with a little digging and help from Lord Routledge, she would succeed where Selina had failed. She might uncover the identity of the man who had abandoned them when they were just babies.

'Do you...' she began, then trailed off.

'Do I have a suspicion of who he might be?'

Sarah nodded, not able to bring herself to put the question into words.

'Not as yet, but I expect I could have a viable list for you in a few days. Do you want that?'

She shook her head, her instincts answering for her, and then sighed. 'I suppose it would be helpful to know. There is the chance that Selina discovered his identity and went to see him, even though there is no indication of her being close to finding the truth in her letters. It would be foolish to spend all this time looking for her only to fail because I am too much of a coward to confront my father.'

'I do not think you are a coward, Miss Shepherd,' Lord Routledge said, his voice low and soft.

She looked up sharply and met his eye. For a moment it felt like everything else faded into the background. She forgot they were sitting in the middle of Hyde Park, and she felt an overwhelming urge to throw herself into his arms.

Quickly she rallied. She was feeling this way only because he was being kind. These past few months, ever since Selina had left, Sarah had felt so very alone. She had no one to confide in—she'd kept her friends at a distance, not wanting to tell them about her illegitimacy. Now Lord Routledge was here, offering help and asking nothing in return. It was as though he had been sent by a guardian angel, who had seen her struggling and delivered Lord Routledge to her with all his calmness and connections to the *ton*.

He reached out to take the last letter from her, his fingers brushing hers. She wasn't sure if she imagined it, but she thought he lingered for a moment longer than was necessary, his little finger gently sweeping over her hand before he pulled away, breaking the contact.

Sarah quickly turned away, trying to regain her composure. She felt the skin on her chest and cheeks begin to flush, and she hoped if Lord Routledge noticed he would think it was from the sun and nothing more.

'Is something amiss?' he asked, looking at her with genuine concern.

Sarah shook her head, not trusting herself to speak. 'I just need a minute.' She gestured vaguely at the letters, hoping he would assume thinking about her sister had resulted in her feeling overwhelmed. She stood, taking a few steps away, looking out over the Serpentine but not really seeing anything.

To her surprise Lord Routledge stood too, moving behind her. He was careful to keep an appropriate distance away, there could be no hint of impropriety, watched as they were by the ladies and gentlemen strolling through the park, yet still she felt the heat of him. Sarah wanted to lean her head back, to rest against his shoulder and draw strength from him.

'You're being ridiculous,' she muttered to herself. She barely knew the man. Their acquaintance had been intense over the last twenty-four hours, but there was no getting away from the fact that she had known him for less than a day.

'We will find your sister, Miss Shepherd,' Lord Routledge said, his words tickling her ear. More than anything right then she wanted to lean in, to bury herself in his chest and to feel his arms pull her close. She felt the heat rising in her body at the thought of their bodies being pressed so closely together and she tried to take a step away, but her feet refused to move.

Never had she felt such an intense attraction to a man, although over the last few years she had avoided most situations where she might meet someone she wanted to be with. Her mother had always advocated for a quiet, private life, forbidding Sarah and Selina from attending the local dances at the assembly rooms, discouraging them from stepping out with any young gentlemen who were keen to get to know them better. Sarah had been a dutiful daughter, going along with her mother's wishes, even when she had not understood the motivation for them.

In the last six months since her mother's death, Sarah had eschewed any chance of developing a relationship. She had been shaken by the discovery that all her life their mother had lived a lie. She had given her heart away when she was young, been promised the world, then left with two young children and no support from the man she thought had loved her. Sarah had seen the melancholy that had tainted her mother's life. She'd resolved that she would focus on building her happiness in ways that were not reliant on other people. It had been one of the reasons she'd been so keen on taking the position as a music teacher to the family in Kent. It was a well-paid position for someone of her background, and the family seemed pleasant enough. She would have her own room and meals with the other servants. Sarah wasn't naïve enough to think that life would satisfy her for the next thirty or forty years, but it would be enough for now.

Slowly she regained her composure and turned to face Lord Routledge. He looked concerned, which somehow made him even more attractive.

With great resolve she told herself that a physical attraction was nothing that couldn't be overcome. Lord Routledge was an attractive man, it would be a lie for anyone to say otherwise. And he was being kind to her. No doubt any young woman in her situation would feel a flutter of desire.

The key was not to act on anything—to accept Lord Routledge's help and not scare him away by allowing her imagination to build something up that was not really there.

Sarah shivered suddenly and looked up at the sky. The day so far had been gloriously warm and, as they had entered Hyde Park for a second time, she had worried that her skin might turn pink from the intensity of the sun. Yet as they had been sitting, discussing the letters, great grey clouds had bubbled up and now covered the sky. There was a chill to the air that hadn't been there minutes before. As Sarah looked up, a fat raindrop fell from the sky and landed on her upturned face.

'The letters,' she and Lord Routledge said in unison and they both dashed back to the blanket, gathering up Selina's precious letters.

Lord Routledge tucked them inside his jacket and picked up the blanket, but by the time he had roughly folded it the rain had started in earnest. All around them nursemaids and governesses were gripping the hands of their young charges, pulling them away from the Serpentine and towards the paths that led out of the park.

Overhead the clouds grew even darker. Somewhere in the distance there was a rumble of thunder.

'We need to shelter,' Lord Routledge said, casting his eyes around for possibilities.

'A tree?'

'Over there,' he said, pointing to a massive oak that stood some distance away. Its branches were heavy with leaves and there was ample room to stand underneath it. It was some distance away from the other trees, and as yet no one else had sheltered there.

With every second that passed the rain grew heavier, falling in great droplets that soon saturated the grass. Sarah eyed the tree, still fifty feet away, and then made the decision to run, picking up her skirts and taking off through the park. She was thankful for her sensible boots, glad she had not chosen anything more elegant. Though, an hour earlier, her feet had felt hot and she'd worried about her choice of clothing amongst the elegant young ladies, strolling through the park in their dainty shoes and light, almost sheer dresses.

After thirty seconds she made it to the shelter of the tree, Lord Routledge close behind her, and they bent their heads to step under the lower of the branches, heading for the trunk in the middle.

Sarah shivered. The rain had collected in droplets and was now running down her arms and her back. Her dress was sodden.

'I would offer you my jacket,' Lord Routledge said, 'but I do not think it would do much to keep you warm.'

Henry brushed the excess water from his hair and glanced over at Miss Shepherd, then quickly looked away. The material of her dress was not thin, but the downpour had soaked through it and it now clung to her body as if it were moulded to her. He could see every curve, from the outline of her hips and waist to the swell of her breasts.

He tried to be gentlemanly, but after a moment he found himself looking again.

The attraction he felt was unsurprising when he thought of it rationally. He had been a widower for two years. He had never seriously considered taking a mistress—his life was complicated enough already, added to the fact that he barely got by on the little funds he had. There was no way he could support a mistress as well.

Given the length of his celibacy it should be no surprise that he felt attracted to a pretty young woman, yet it was inconvenient. He had promised to help her. The last thing he needed was to be fantasising about Miss Shepherd whilst they searched for her sister.

A flash of lightning forked across the sky, followed soon after by a rumble of thunder.

'Suddenly I am questioning our choice to shelter under the tallest tree,' Miss Shepherd murmured, looking at the sky with concern.

'It is better than being out there in the open.'

'I saw someone struck by lightning once,' she said, biting her lip as the sky lit up again.

'Actually struck by lightning?'

'Yes. I come from a little seaside place, St Leonards. It neighbours Hastings.'

'Of the famed battle?'

'Yes. Hastings has these beautiful cliffs that stretch for miles. The views out to sea are unparalleled, and sometimes you can spot seals swimming offshore. On occasion, Selina and I would walk the few miles into Hastings and then climb the windy path up the cliffs, but once we were caught in a storm. It came about quickly, much like today, one minute glorious weather and then the next the sky clouded over.' She shuddered, although whether from the memory or the dampness of her clothes, it was impossible to tell. 'We had to walk slowly, the cliffs were sandstone and covered in grass on the top, but they became slippery. We were about to descend when there was a flash of lightning, and it struck a man walking on the path a few feet ahead of us.'

'What happened to him?'

'He died. Instantly I think. He just dropped to the ground. Selina and I rushed forward, thinking we might be able to help, but there was nothing to be done for him. One moment he was there and then suddenly he wasn't.'

'That must have been terrible to see.'

'I couldn't sleep for weeks after.'

'You are remarkably calm today, being caught in a storm.'

'My heart is pounding,' she said, with a nervous little smile. He had the inexplicable urge to place his hand on her chest, to feel the thud of her heart within, and his hand was halfway there before he caught himself.

'It happened about six years ago, and every time there was a storm I was so scared I would hide beneath a blanket. Selina would sit with me the whole time, telling me the storm would pass. She would do that even though she must have been petrified herself.' Sarah bit her lip. 'People don't always see that side of her. She's fun and charming and everyone loves her on first meeting, but they don't always get to see the kind young woman underneath. Sometimes she can be selfish, but often it is only because she is impulsive, and when it matters she is the most generous person you could ever meet.'

'We will find her.'

Miss Shepherd nodded as she looked up at him. Somehow her eyes appeared even greener today, and he found he couldn't look away. She swayed towards him, and this time he couldn't stop himself. He placed his hand around waist and drew her to him. She dipped her head, resting her forehead on his shoulder, and for a long moment they stood there, unmoving.

After a minute she looked up, a question in her eyes that he didn't dare to answer. It would be so easy to dip his chin, to catch her lips with his own, to kiss her whilst the rain fell around them.

Eventually the rational part of him won and he cleared his throat, breaking the contact between them and stepping away. He turned, pretending to look out at the storm, thankful when another bolt of lightning forked across the sky.

'I think the storm is getting further away.' His voice was so gruff it was unrecognisable.

Miss Shepherd had turned so her back was to him, but he could see the tension in her shoulders. She was an impressionable young woman, away from home for the first time, in a situation that was highly stressful. No wonder she had sought comfort in him—there was nothing more to it than that. He had been kind to her and she had reached out in her moment of vulnerability.

For the next few minutes they watched the storm in silence. Miss Shepherd relaxed a little as the thunder and lightning moved away, and after five more minutes the rain eased as well.

'I should return to my rooms. I am soaked to the skin,' she said, turning to him with an overly bright smile.

'Shall I escort you?'

'There is no need. It is not too far, and now the storm has passed I will be perfectly fine.'

'May I keep the letters and have a look over them? I will draw up a list of the people your sister mentions, and how best to approach them, as well as noting down some ideas of who could be your father.'

'Thank you,' Miss Shepherd said.

'I am due to attend the opera tomorrow night, perhaps you

might like to accompany me? I have a spare seat. We can talk in the interval.'

Her eyes widened. 'The opera? Are you sure?'

It was a terrible idea. Half of the *ton* would be in attendance, and everyone would be curious to know who his companion was, especially as word would have got around that he was searching for a new wife. Yet, as he saw the excitement on her face, he realised he couldn't withdraw the invitation.

'Yes. We can say you are a distant relative, visiting London from the country.' As long as they didn't engage anyone he knew too well in conversation, then there was a chance the lie would be believed. 'I will call for you at seven.'

'Thank you.'

Chapter Seven

There was a crowd outside the opera house as they approached, and quickly Henry checked for any familiar faces. He couldn't regret inviting Miss Shepherd, she had talked of nothing else but her love for music all the way to Covent Garden, asking him about all the operas he had seen. She looked radiant this evening, wearing the same dress she had when he'd first met her sneaking into the Shrewsburys' library. It was a midnight blue with a white sash around the middle. There was no adornments or embroidery, but the dress was well cut and the material fell in soft lines, giving her a lovely silhouette.

'I am glad to see you are taking this seriously.' Henry jumped at the voice that came from over his shoulder. With a sinking heart, he turned to see his father approaching. The crowd of people parted before him as if the old man had a leper bell around his neck.

'Good evening, Father,' Henry said, cursing his bad luck. His father was not all that keen on the opera and only attended a couple of times a year. It was unfortunate one of those times was tonight, although perhaps not entirely unforeseeable. Many of the wealthy residents of London had left for their country estates weeks earlier, and society events were few and far between in the summer months. His father was the opposite of a social butterfly, but he did enjoy having something new to moan about, and that couldn't happen if he sat at home counting his money.

'Is this her? The woman you were spotted with yesterday?' He peered at Miss Shepherd with undisguised judgement.

Henry swallowed. He did not want to subject Miss Shepherd to his father's rudeness, and equally he would prefer it if his father thought he was doing his utmost to search for a wife.

'This is Miss Shepherd.'

'Miss Shepherd? Never heard of her. Who is her father?'

Henry glanced at Miss Shepherd and saw her expression turn quickly from horror to faux warmth.

'It is a pleasure to meet you, my lord,' she said, dipping into a pretty little curtsey.

Lord Burwell grunted, although his expression wasn't quite as hostile as she rose.

Henry thought quickly, trying to come up with some story to mollify his father.

'Miss Shepherd is a distant relative of Lady Shrewsbury. She is newly arrived in London from Sussex, and Lady Shrewsbury asked if I would bring her to the opera tonight.'

'A relative of Lady Shrewsbury?' Lord Burwell asked, looking her over again. Miss Shepherd's dress was of decent quality, but Henry was suddenly very aware that it did not compare to some of the beautiful gowns of the *ton* that surrounded them. No, it was more akin to the best frock of a vicar's wife, worn to a country dinner party.

'Yes, my lord,' Miss Shepherd said to Henry's relief. 'A distant cousin on my mother's side of the family.'

Lord Burwell gripped hold of Henry's arm and drew him to one side.

'You're wasting time. I can see even from a perfunctory look that Miss Shepherd is not of the right calibre to be a candidate for your new bride. All the time you are ferrying her around the city you are not focussed on finding someone suitable.'

'This is a favour for Lady Shrewsbury, that is all.'

Lord Burwell grunted but Henry saw him soften ever so slightly. There were many things his father disapproved of in his life, but his friendship with Lord and Lady Shrewsbury was not one of them. Lord Shrewsbury was one of the richest and most influential men in the country, which was all that mattered, it seemed. Of course his father didn't bother to look past that fact to the man beneath, not caring that Shrewsbury was also one of the kindest, most generous men, and Henry considered himself lucky to count him as a friend.

Just as it looked as though his father might move on, a heavy hand clapped onto Henry's shoulder.

'Routledge, I didn't know you were attending tonight.'

With a sinking heart Henry turned to see Lord and Lady Shrewsbury. He managed to suppress a groan, but he could not stop his eyes flicking to where Miss Shepherd was standing.

'Surely you knew he was bringing Miss Shepherd here tonight,' Lord Burwell said. For all his faults, no one could accuse the Earl of being slow-witted. A hint of suspicion was back in his eyes as everyone turned to look at Miss Shepherd.

Henry felt his chest constricting. At any second everything was going to come crashing down, and his chance of ever seeing his sister would become slimmer.

'Cousin, dearest,' Miss Shepherd stepped forward, taking hold of Lady Shrewsbury's arm, 'I am so glad you could make it this evening. I am very much looking forward to the opera. Lord Routledge has been kind enough to explain what to expect.'

Lady Shrewsbury looked startled—Henry thought she might protest at being led away by Miss Shepherd. He did not see what looks passed between them, but after five excruciating seconds she stopped resisting and turned away.

Now he only had Lord Shrewsbury to stop from revealing his secret.

'I don't know...' Shrewsbury began. Over the top of his father's head, Henry shot him a pleading look. Shrewsbury clamped his lips together.

'I think everyone is heading inside,' Henry said, hoping it would prompt his father to go and find his seat.

'Don't let yourself get distracted, boy,' Lord Burwell said, with one final, meaningful look at Miss Shepherd.

Henry nodded seriously, holding his breath until his father had disappeared into the crowd.

'That was bizarre,' Lord Shrewsbury said, raising an eyebrow at Henry. 'Miss Shepherd is here I see. And apparently she is my wife's distant cousin?'

'Your wife is a rare gem.'

'I know,' Lord Shrewsbury murmured. 'You're lucky she likes you so much. She would not have gone along with that for anyone else.'

At that moment Lady Shrewsbury and Miss Shepherd reappeared, no longer arm in arm.

'I know,' Henry said, raising his hands in defence. 'I have a lot of explaining to do.'

'I suggest you start immediately,' said Lady Shrewsbury.

'As you know, my father has been increasingly insistent that I focus all my energies on finding a suitable wife to be the second Lady Routledge. He was not impressed to find me here with Miss Shepherd.'

'From how I dress he could apparently see I was not worthy of being the sort of woman a Viscount would court,' Miss Shepherd said. She did not look upset or perturbed, and even gave Henry a little half-smile. He reminded himself to thank her later—only her quick thinking had saved him from his father's wrath.

'He thinks my every waking hour should be dedicated to finding a wife, and with his threats to keep Sophia from me I thought it best he did not know Miss Shepherd's true identity. I didn't want him to think I was courting her.'

'Are you courting her?' Lady Shrewsbury asked, her eyes widening.

'No,' Miss Shepherd said, so quickly that in any other circumstance he might be offended. 'Lord Routledge has been very kind to me, that is all.'

'Wait a moment,' Lord Shrewsbury said, 'I can't see how we got from Miss Shepherd being someone you met in the street and persuaded you to help her access an audience with our housemaid, to you two attending the opera together.'

'Ah,' Henry said. 'Yes, I can see how that looks to be a bit of a leap.'

'Was any of it true? The story about your missing sister? The need to talk to Agnes Pepper?' Lady Shrewsbury fixed her gaze on Miss Shepherd, and Henry marvelled at how well she handled the scrutiny.

'Yes. I came to London to try to find my missing sister, and in her letters she mentioned Agnes Pepper, which was why I wanted to talk to her.'

'I have offered to help Miss Shepherd find her sister, if I can provide any assistance.'

Both Lord and Lady Shrewsbury turned to Henry, looks of incredulity on their faces.

'Would you excuse us a moment, Miss Shepherd,' Lady Shrewsbury said, stepping to close the gap between her and Henry, moving them a few steps away from Miss Shepherd.

'Have you gone mad? Do you have a fever? Is there some sort of parasite eating away at your brain?' Lady Shrewsbury whispered, her hands flying as she spoke.

'Now, my dear, I am sure—' Lord Shrewsbury began, but he was cut off by his wife.

'You know nothing about the girl. It is obvious you are a wealthy man, have you not considered that she may be luring you in, hoping you will compromise her and then need to compensate her to satisfy your honour?'

Henry opened his mouth, but Lady Shrewsbury was not finished.

'You cannot take in waifs and strays without knowing anything about them. She could be anyone, you know nothing of her family, her background. It is beyond reckless, Henry. You need to get rid of her.'

Henry had always prided himself on his even temper, but right now he was struggling to maintain his composure.

'I have the utmost respect for you, Louisa,' he said quietly, his voice low but dangerous, 'but I cannot allow you to speak of Miss Shepherd like that.'

'Henry—'

'She may not be born into the wealthiest of families, or have had the privileges and opportunities we have enjoyed through-out our lives, but she is so much more than you are suggesting.'

'You barely know her.'

'But you know me. I would hope you trust my judgement at least a little, given how long we have known one another. *I* have given my word to help Miss Shepherd in her search for her sister, not because she has coerced me, or enchanted me, but because it is the right thing to do. She is a young lady, alone in this city, petrified that she may never see the sister that she loves again.'

He saw Miss Shepherd move a little closer, aware she was listening to his every word.

'I do not think she is out to bewitch me, or to trick me into compromising her. I think she is merely a woman who is in need of help and kindness. If I refused, what sort of a man would that make me?'

Lord and Lady Shrewsbury looked suitably chastised. He knew they both only wanted what was best for him. He soft-ened a little.

'One day it may be Sophia who is in need of a friend.' He said this quietly, and saw the tears form in Lady Shrewsbury's eyes.

'Forgive me,' she murmured, holding his eye, then she turned to Miss Shepherd. 'I owe you an apology too. I was rude, I am sorry.'

Miss Shepherd smiled and nodded, accepting the apology gracefully.

'Shall we go inside? The opera is about to start, and Miss Shepherd has never been before,' Henry said, eager to leave the conversation behind them.

Henry offered his arm and led Miss Shepherd into the opera house, followed closely by Lord and Lady Shrewsbury.

Sarah stepped carefully, aware of her heart pounding in her chest. Never before had anyone defended her honour in such a way, and she felt a little giddy from Lord Routledge's words.

As they joined the crowds in the foyer, Lord Routledge placed his hand over hers and squeezed her fingers gently. Sarah looked up and felt her pulse quicken.

Carefully she examined the rush of emotions she was feeling, trying to tell herself it was from the excitement of the last ten minutes, yet not quite believing it.

It was difficult to ignore the gratitude she felt for Lord Routledge, but she couldn't deny there might be something a bit more.

'That would be inconvenient,' she murmured to herself. With his speech he had made it quite clear that he viewed her as a charity case, someone he could assist as his good deed of the week. She didn't mind that, it was an apt description of their relationship, but she wondered if she might be developing an affection for the Viscount.

It was absurd, and Sarah was well aware nothing could ever happen between them. The difference in their social status was a big hurdle, but she had begun to piece together the fraught relationship Lord Routledge had with his father from the little he had told her, and watching how he reacted to the older man a few minutes earlier. It was clear she would never be of the right social status to satisfy the people around Lord Routledge.

She scoffed that she was even considering it. All she needed Lord Routledge for was his assistance in finding Selina. After that she would return to Kent and take up her position as music teacher. She had chosen a life that was likely to be chaste, and without the likelihood of marriage, and she couldn't start second-guessing her decisions just because of one man's kindness.

'Sit with us,' Lady Shrewsbury said. 'We have empty seats in our box.'

'Yes, sit with us,' Lord Shrewsbury said.

Lord Routledge glanced at her and she was absurdly pleased that he sought her opinion in this matter. Many young women would have been offended by Lady Shrewsbury's assumptions about her character, but Sarah had not been. She *was* using Lord Routledge, but not in the way his friends had feared. She would do anything to find her sister, and she knew she would get further in London with someone who could gain access to the places she could not.

'That sounds lovely,' she said, and Lord Routledge smiled at her.

He leaned in close, his lips almost brushing her ear as he whispered, 'Thank you.'

They climbed the stairs up to the boxes and made their way inside. Sarah had to fight to keep her mouth from falling open. There was a throng of people taking their seats below them, all talking loudly, the ladies wafting fans to help with the stifling heat. But the real spectacle was on their level, with the other well-dressed ladies and gentlemen taking their seats in their own boxes.

'Sit here,' Lord Routledge said, directing her to a seat at the edge before positioning himself next to her. It made for an intimate little corner and, as he leaned in, she felt the heat of his body. 'This first part of the evening is about being seen.'

She touched her face self-consciously.

'Everyone watches everyone else, so much so that sometimes the performers on the stage become frustrated by the lack of attention from the audience.'

'Surely people come to see the performance?'

'Some do, I'm sure, but for many it is an opportunity to show off their newest set of emeralds or finest silk gloves.'

'And we mustn't forget you are here to search for a wife,' she said, immediately regretting the words—she worried they sounded bitter.

Lord Routledge did not seem to notice and grimaced. 'Yes, or so my father thinks.' He shuddered as he let his eyes trail over the people in the other boxes.

'Surely the idea of marriage cannot be that terrible, my lord?'

'I did not think so once.'

She longed to ask him about his first wife. She did not think it was purely grief that stopped him from wanting to marry again. His expression hinted at a deeper tragedy.

'Then perhaps you can learn to like the idea again. Is there a young woman you favour?'

She wondered what she was doing, torturing them both. She supposed her subconscious thought was that, if she helped him choose a candidate to court, no one would think she was interested in him romantically.

Looking at the frown crinkling between his eyebrows, she

had the urge to reach out and smooth it, to take away some of his angst—but she stopped herself, instead folding her hands demurely in her lap.

'Miss Gough is here,' he said, not sounding overly excited. 'She is sitting with my father, poor girl.'

Sarah followed his gaze to a pretty young woman with blonde hair, and a set of diamonds around her neck that looked as though they weighed her down.

'Do you like Miss Gough?'

'I barely know the girl. She is seventeen years old, barely more than a child.' He closed his eyes and then leaned in as if to confide in her. 'I see what Lord and Lady Shrewsbury have, and then I look at Miss Gough or the other young debutantes, and I wonder what I will have to talk about with a wife that young.'

'Then choose someone older.'

'I can't.'

'Don't be ridiculous. Of course you can, it is your choice.'

'No, it is not, not really. The only way I satisfy my father is if I marry a wealthy, well-connected woman from a good family. The problem is each year the young women are introduced into society, and the cream of the crop are quickly snapped up by anyone looking for a wife.'

'Ah, so you're saying that the best ones from each year have already married,' Sarah said, understanding now.

'Yes. Only by looking to the debutantes of the next season can I satisfy all of my father's demands.'

'Do you have to satisfy your father?'

He gave a mirthless laugh, but Sarah was prevented from asking any more by movement on stage. The opera had begun.

Chapter Eight

Miss Shepherd sat leaning forward, resting her arms on the balustrade of the balcony, enraptured by the opera. It was refreshing to come with someone who enjoyed the music, someone who was so intent on the stage her eyes did not waver.

Henry allowed himself to sit back and relax, letting the music wash over him. It had been a stressful evening so far, with his father turning up unexpectedly and then having to explain Miss Shepherd's continued presence in his life to the Shrewsburys. He enjoyed the few moments of peace he had available to him, aware that, in the interval, things would only become more difficult.

As the curtain fell on the second act Miss Shepherd turned to him with tears in her eyes. 'Thank you for bringing me tonight. This is the most wonderful thing I have ever seen.'

'I'm glad you are enjoying it. Shall we step out for some air?'

Miss Shepherd inclined her head and he offered his arm. After informing Lord Shrewsbury they were going to take a little stroll in the interval, Henry escorted Miss Shepherd from the box.

They had only taken a few steps when he spotted his father, with young Miss Gough in tow, making his way through the crowds of people in their direction.

Quickly he grabbed Miss Shepherd's hand and pulled her the other way, darting through the groups of people in a bid to get away from Lord Burwell. He spotted a door and, without thinking, pulled it open, guiding Miss Shepherd through it before closing it quietly behind him.

It was completely dark and it took Henry a moment to realise that he had pressed Miss Shepherd up against a wall. It had not been by design—in his haste to escape his father and Miss Gough he had lost all sense of reason. Yet even now, as he realised what position they were in, he didn't immediately step away.

In the darkness he felt the soft rise and fall of her chest, and was reminded of the first time they had met, when he had held her against the wall in the library. Before he could stop himself he reached out, his fingers finding her face, and trailing a soft caress across the skin of her cheek.

'Lord Routledge,' she said, her voice barely audible above the crowd beyond the door.

'Henry. My name is Henry.' He longed to hear his name on her lips. Hardly anyone ever used his given name, and he craved the intimacy that came with such familiarity.

She hesitated, then whispered his name. 'Henry.'

The sound of it lit something inside him and he moved forward, increasing the contact between them. He could feel her soft body underneath his, and felt her rise up to meet him. Before he could stop himself he bent down and brushed a kiss against her lips, testing her response. When she let out a little moan of satisfaction—opening her lips ever so slightly to meet him—he surged forward, one arm around her waist, pulling her to him and deepening the kiss.

For a moment it was frenzied, uncontrolled, and Henry's free hand tangled in Miss Shepherd's hair, then slid down her back, cupping her buttocks. She kissed him harder and he wished there was a little light so he could see the desire he knew would be reflected in her eyes.

He wanted to abandon himself to this moment, to do exactly

what he wanted and not think about the consequences, and Miss Shepherd was warm and willing in his arms.

There was a sudden swell of noise from outside the door and they both froze, jolted back to a reality neither of them wanted to face. Henry stood—one hand on Miss Shepherd's lower back, one behind her head, holding his breath—wondering if the door was going to open and expose them to the world. The was a click and a sliver of light shone through, illuminating a small slice of them, and then inexplicably the door closed again without anyone coming in.

With great effort Henry disentangled himself from Miss Shepherd and took a step back, feeling for the wall behind him. His pulse was still racing, the desire still flooding through him, and he knew if he touched Miss Shepherd again, he would be lost.

Neither of them spoke for a minute. Outside they heard the sound of people moving around, going back to their seats as the interval came to an end.

'I apologise—' he began, once it was quiet beyond the door.

'No.' Miss Shepherd cut him off, her tone curt. She took a shuddering breath in. 'I cannot go back to the box like this. My hair is a mess and I cannot fix it in the dark.'

'We can leave. Once everyone is seated no one will notice us slipping out of the opera house.'

'Your friends will notice you are gone, and your father.'

It was not ideal, but unavoidable.

'It does not matter,' he said, hating the note of panic in Miss Shepherd's voice. He had taken advantage of her and he hated that he'd allowed himself to be ruled by his baser instincts. Miss Shepherd had not been unwilling, she had kissed him back fervently, but that did not excuse him pinning her to the wall in the first place.

'You stay. I can make my way to my lodgings on my own. I am sure you can think of an excuse to tell your friends.'

'I am not letting you leave by yourself.'

'Do not be a fool, Lord Routledge. One moment of weakness does not need to ruin both our lives.'

He paused before speaking, conscious that they needed to make a decision—they could be discovered at any moment.

'It will not. I will escort you to your lodgings and tomorrow I will make my apologies to the Shrewsburys. They already think I am acting strangely, one more instance will not matter.'

She started to speak again but he reached out, feeling for her hand in the darkness.

'Either you accept my escort home, or I follow you five paces behind. I know which option will look more conspicuous.'

Miss Shepherd hesitated and then exhaled loudly. 'Fine. You may walk me to my lodgings.'

Sarah was shaking as they peered out through a crack between the door and the frame, checking to see if any of the opera patrons were still in the corridor. Once they could be sure it was deserted, Lord Routledge opened the door and slipped out, offering her his arm as she followed.

It was petty, but Sarah pretended she had not seen the offer. She could not touch him right now. The kiss had taken her by surprise, but as soon as his lips had touched hers it had felt as though she was finally complete after a lifetime of missing something essential. She would have given herself to him entirely in that dark and dirty corridor if they had not been interrupted, and the realisation had shaken her. She'd always thought of herself as someone with good morals and a high standard of virtue. It was disconcerting to know a little attention from an attractive man had her abandoning all her values.

This is what happened to Mama.

It was an unwelcome thought, but once it had popped into her head she found she could not get rid of it. She refused to let history repeat itself. Her mother had most likely been fooled by a rich man's sweet words—promises that he would look after her—only to be abandoned when he grew bored. Sarah would not make the same mistake. Her future lay elsewhere, with independence and freedom, not tied to a man who would discard her once it was time to get married.

She caught sight of her reflection in one of the gilded mirrors that lined the staircase as she hurried down, and had to stifle a gasp of surprise. She looked dishevelled with her hair falling around her shoulders, her cheeks flushed with colour. If anyone saw her they would be able to tell immediately she had been doing something she shouldn't.

Thankfully, apart from a few stares from the staff at the front of the opera house, they escaped without anyone else taking any notice.

Once outside she took in some deep breaths of air. All she wanted to do was gather her skirts in her bunched fists and run. She wanted to get far away from Lord Routledge and his seductive eyes and all the rest of the ladies and gentlemen of high society, who could ruin her if they found out what she had been doing. No doubt the Huntleys in Kent would not employ a music teacher if they were aware she had loose morals. Scandalous gossip travelled far and wide, so there was no hope of keeping something like this a secret if anyone spotted them.

She walked as fast as she could, head bent and her gaze fixed on the ground. Lord Routledge kept up easily, but he didn't try to touch her or talk to her, sensing perhaps she might either snap at him or burst into tears.

The walk to her lodgings did not take much time, given her speed, and she was soon ascending the steps to the front door, key in hand.

'Miss Shepherd,' Lord Routledge called out.

She paused, but did not turn, not trusting herself to look at him.

'Forgive me. I took advantage of you in the worst way imaginable. I am sorry.'

Her mind flashed back to the way his lips had felt on hers, the wonderful warmth that had flooded through her body as he had pulled her into his arms. She didn't want to admit how good it had felt to have that intimacy. It went against everything she had promised herself, to keep her from suffering the same fate as her mother, yet she knew if she were to relive the moment again she would not push Lord Routledge away.

'Thank you for taking me to the opera, I think it best we end our acquaintance now, Lord Routledge.'

'There is no need for that, Miss Shepherd. This was a moment of madness, nothing else. No one saw us.'

Sarah pressed her lips together, digging her fingernails into the palm of her hand. She shouldn't be surprised that Lord Routledge was unshaken by their kiss, no doubt he had women clamouring for his attention all the time. He'd probably shared a dozen such kisses with different women over the last few years.

Closing her eyes to ward off momentary vertigo, she turned to face Lord Routledge. She couldn't tell him that, for him, it may have been a moment of madness, but for her it was her first kiss. Perhaps her only kiss. Her focus at least over the next few years needed to be on building a life where she could support herself. There would be no time for courtship, and any dalliance no doubt would be frowned upon by her employers. She was determined to be independent, not to rely on a man for her security. Her mother had struggled their entire lives to provide for them, eking out the little money she'd received from their father and supplementing it with whatever job she could find. Sarah wanted a different life for herself, a better life.

Despite all of this, despite the sensible part of her telling her to walk away, as she looked at Lord Routledge she felt the invisible pull, the attraction that had plagued her ever since he'd first pressed her up against the wall in the library.

She glanced at his lips and then quickly looked away.

'It is late,' she said curtly. 'I cannot think properly. I will consider things tomorrow after a night's sleep.'

Forcing herself to turn and climb the last few steps she found she was disappointed when Lord Routledge did not call out. Somewhere deep inside, she could admit that a small part of her wanted him to run up the stairs and pull her into his arms, declaring he could not live without her before kissing her senseless.

Of course it didn't happen. Sarah slipped into the dark hall of the lodging house and closed the door behind her, resting her head on the cool wood. She let out a little self-indulgent whimper and then rallied. Tonight had been a terrible mistake, but Lord Routledge was right, there should be no long-lasting consequences. At least...none beyond her bruised heart.

Chapter Nine

Henry had not slept and had risen at the crack of dawn, frustrated with the hours he had spent in bed without any rest. He felt like a cad. Miss Shepherd was a vulnerable young woman, someone with no family or friends to look out for her welfare, and he had taken advantage of her. He'd allowed himself to act on the desire he felt for her when he should have suppressed it.

He thought of the kiss, the sweet taste of her lips and the way her body had felt pressed against his, and for a moment he was back in the dark corridor in the opera house. It had been a dangerous situation and, what was worse, he knew if they had not been interrupted by the door opening he would have gone further. They had both been so caught up in the moment and their attraction for one another, who knew where it would have stopped.

He needed to make things right, on two fronts. Firstly, he would focus his efforts on narrowing down the selection for a suitable wife. She needed to be wealthy and from a good family, someone who would satisfy his father as well as be tolerable to live with. He didn't trust his own judgement after his awful marriage to Anne, but he was willing to put aside his reservations for the sake of mending the rift that had separated him from his sister.

The second thing he needed to do was make things right with Miss Shepherd. He was thankful she was a highly practical young woman, who had not even hinted that his impropriety should lead to a proposal. In truth he *should* offer to marry her. He had compromised her, kissed her in public, and it was only through sheer luck that no one had seen.

He shuddered at the thought. Miss Shepherd was a pleasant young woman who he felt an undeniable attraction to, but his previous marriage had taught him there could not be happiness when two people of vastly different social classes married. The gulf between them was too big, the obstacles impossible to overcome.

What he could do was apologise again and then help her find her sister. He knew all would be forgiven and forgotten if he could reunite Miss Shepherd with her errant sibling.

That was why he was standing outside Miss Shepherd's lodging house at three o'clock in the afternoon, steeling himself to approach.

He knocked on the front door and waited, hearing shuffling footsteps inside. An elderly woman opened the door and inspected him from head to toe, softening only slightly as she took in his well-tailored jacket and smart appearance.

'No gentleman visitors allowed inside,' she said, starting to close the door on him.

'I am calling for Miss Shepherd, I am due to meet her this afternoon.'

'Not in here.'

'I am happy to step out with her, but please could you let her know I am here.'

The old woman muttered something under her breath and closed the door. Henry listened carefully but couldn't hear anything through the thick wood. He had no way of knowing if she was going to alert Miss Shepherd to his presence at all.

He waited five minutes, then ten, arms crossed and foot tapping on the stone of the steps. He was just about to contemplate if there was another way to get a message to Miss Shepherd when the door opened and she slipped out, closing it firmly behind her.

'Mrs Angel is not happy. Her one rule is no gentleman visitors.'

'I hardly barged into the lodging house.'

'She thinks by darkening her doorstep you bring her house into disrepute.'

Henry saw that Miss Shepherd looked tired and drawn. He wondered if it was from a night tossing and turning, thinking about their kiss the evening before, or if it was from worry about her sister.

'What do you want, Lord Routledge?'

'I know where Mr Peterson is going to be this afternoon.'

Miss Shepherd stilled, every part of her frozen, as if she were a perfectly carved statue in a museum.

'Do you think he will talk to me?'

'There is only one way to find out.'

Miss Shepherd bit her lip, no doubt weighing up her desire to talk to Mr Peterson about her sister—and also perhaps about the identity of her father—against her better judgement not to spend time with him.

'Where will he be?'

'Mr Peterson is a gambler. He plays cards, but his vice of choice is betting on boxing matches, and I have it on good authority that he will be attending a boxing match south of the river later this afternoon.'

She chewed her lip more, her eyes downcast but darting around. He watched, mesmerised as her tongue darted out, and for a second all he could think about was kissing her again.

'I could go alone,' she said, but sounded unconvinced.

'It would not be safe for a young lady to attend alone.'

'Perhaps you know where Mr Peterson may be this evening, or tomorrow?'

'No. I had to work hard just to find his location this afternoon. He may even be leaving London soon for his house in the country.'

Miss Shepherd groaned and then gave a little nod. 'Very well. It is of the utmost importance I speak to Mr Peterson.

'Do you have everything you need?'

She shook her head and disappeared inside for a few minutes.

It was another warm afternoon, but the sky was overcast and grey, and the sun had been struggling to break through all day. It meant the air felt humid and sticky, as if another storm were needed to cool things down.

Perhaps due to the heat they walked slowly. It was a fair distance through the streets of London to the river, and then they had to cross to the other side. Henry had visited Southwark on a few occasions, but he did not regularly frequent the less salubrious neighbourhoods. He had felt a prickle of anxiety about taking Miss Shepherd there, but he had meant what he said earlier when he'd explained it might be their only chance of seeing Mr Peterson. With the warm weather looking set to continue, many of those who had stayed in London these last few weeks were finally quitting the capital for their cooler country estates.

They walked in silence for a while but, as they did, Henry sensed some of the tension Miss Shepherd had been holding ebbing away. As they approached the river he spoke softly. 'I am sorry about last night. My behaviour was unforgiveable.'

'We do not need to talk about it.'

'Will you let me say what I need to say, and then we can agree never to mention it again?'

She hesitated for a moment, glancing up at him with a hint of sadness in her eyes, and then nodded.

'I am sorry I kissed you. I know what a horrible position it puts you in, and also the possibility of a scandal would hurt you immeasurably. I would like to tell you I am not normally that reckless, which is the truth, but losing control is unforgiveable.' He took a deep breath, needing to acknowledge more. He did not want her thinking she didn't deserve his full consideration. 'I compromised you, Miss Shepherd, and I am well aware I should be making arrangements for our union, of taking your hand and proposing.'

She looked at him sharply and he hurried on.

'I like you and I respect you, but I cannot marry you.'

'I have not asked you to,' she said, an edge of anger in her voice.

'I know. You are too unassuming and kind to think of it, but if I were a true gentleman I would be proposing to you.'

'I understand you do not want someone like me as a wife.'

He paused, wondering what to say. In many ways she was right. He had resigned himself to marrying again, but only to mend the rift that had come about from his choice of first wife. It would do nothing to mollify his father, or secure him a position back in his sister's life, if he rushed into marriage with someone not from the aristocracy. What was more, he didn't actually want a wife. He had thought himself in love once, and had been willing to give up everything he is for his wife, but it had been a total disaster of a marriage.

'I do not want a wife,' he said, deciding honesty was the only way he would have a chance of making Miss Shepherd understand.

'Yet you are scouring London for one.' She sighed and waved a hand. 'I do not want a proposal, my lord.' He thought of the night before, when she had called him by his given name, and for one mad moment he almost asked her to do so again. Quickly he caught himself.

'Will you sit with me a moment?' he asked, indicating one of the benches that lined the north bank of the river.

'Should we not make haste?'

'Mr Peterson will linger the whole afternoon if the rumours are to be believed.'

She perched on the edge of the bench, looking out over the river. Her face was pale, but she had two spots of colour on her cheeks.

'Would you indulge me whilst I told you about my wife, my first wife?'

'You do not need to…'

'I would like to.'

She inclined her head, waiting for him to speak. Henry tried to summon the words, his throat instantly dry, his tongue thick and heavy.

'I met Anne one cold winter's evening when I was walking home from a dinner party. It had been filled with beautiful, wealthy people, talking loudly and eating to excess.'

'I sense that irritated you,' Miss Shepherd said quietly, with a hint of a smile.

'It did. It didn't help that my father was also present, and pressing me to propose to one of the eligible young ladies.'

'Much like he is now.'

'Indeed. I was walking home and I saw a young woman slip on some ice. She fell into the road and a carriage came trundling round the corner. I do not think the coachman saw her and she was winded from the fall, unable to move.' He closed his eyes for a moment, that night still so vivid in his mind. 'I ran forward and pulled her from the road just in time, and we collapsed onto the pavement together.'

'The woman who became your wife?'

'Yes, it was Anne. She was in shock, so I walked her home and ensured she was safe before leaving, then the next day I returned to check she had recovered.' He paused, finding it hard to explain quite how he had fallen in love. 'We went for a walk together, in the park, and talked. It was refreshing to speak to someone about the real world, and their hopes and dreams, instead of discussing the price of silk and who was the best artist to commission for a new portrait. We talked for hours, and when I walked her home I asked if I could see her again.'

'She must have been a very special young woman,' Miss Shepherd said, and Henry thought he heard a hint of sadness in her voice, but when he looked up she was smiling at him softly.

'I became infatuated. I was only young, but already disillusioned with the world I had been born into, frustrated by the path my life had to follow. I wanted to make my own way in the world, but at every turn there was my father, trying to dictate how I should live my life.' He shook his head. 'I realise I sound like a spoilt child, and in many ways I was. I didn't appreciate the privileged upbringing I had. All I could think of was rebelling against it.'

'Wealth is not the only thing that makes for a happy childhood.'

'Indeed. I was infatuated with Anne and I thought she felt the same. I proposed to her within a few weeks of meeting her and she accepted. My father was furious, of course. He told me he would cut me off entirely if I went through with the wedding. I had a little income from the property I'd renovated, and over time I invested it and bought another, but we had to live a modest life. Even my friends were wary—they tried to warn me how difficult our union would be, that we would be shunned by society, and I would not be able to lead the same life as all my peers.'

'And yet, you went ahead anyway.'

'I thought all that wasn't important, not when the alternative was losing my true love.'

Miss Shepherd was looking at him with interest now, invested in his story. It wasn't one he told often. Of course, his close friends knew most of what had occurred, but there were some parts he still felt too ashamed to discuss.

'We were married in a small ceremony with just a couple of witnesses.' He shook his head at the memory, unable to believe he had been so naïve. 'I thought it was the start of the rest of our lives together.'

'It wasn't?'

He grimaced. 'I had explained to Anne that my father would cut us off, that we would have to live on a small income, in a modest fashion, but I don't think she really believed me. She did not know my father, and thought once he had got over his initial anger and disappointment he would come round.'

'She knew she was marrying a Viscount, so she did not believe you truly could be poor?' Miss Shepherd ventured.

'I think she had visions of grand balls and spending her days shopping for fine silks. The reality was vastly different. As I had been warned, everyone except a few close friends from my world shunned her, and she was too ashamed to go back to the people she had grown up with, the people she had told she was escaping for a better life.' He'd hated how sad she had always looked, how miserable, after being told there were no invitations for her, no social events she would get to go to. 'I was prepared to leave my old life behind, but I think she did not realise it would be as difficult as it was. She was miserable.'

He sighed and slumped back against the bench. It was improper posture for a gentleman out and about, but right now he could not bring himself to care.

'I found out a few years later, during a terrible argument, that Anne had been engaged to another man, before we met. A butcher's assistant. I never knew about him, never knew they were due to be married, never knew she had chosen a life with me over marrying the man she loved.'

'She didn't love you?'

'No,' Henry said, still feeling the pain of the realisation cut through him. He had thought they were united in their love, a single entity bound together to face the challenges of whatever life had thrown at them. In reality, Anne had seen his infatuation with her and thought she had the opportunity for a better life as a Viscountess. When she had realised he was telling the truth, and had very little by way of income, she had turned bitter. Things may have been better if they had been accepted by society, able to attend events together and get out of the house, which had slowly felt as though it had turned into a prison. 'She never loved me. And as the months and years went by, she increasingly resented me.'

'I'm sorry,' Miss Shepherd said, the warmth back in her eyes. He hadn't told her this story to gain her sympathy, but he wanted her to understand why he could not marry her, not under any circumstance.

'There is more. Anne fell pregnant a few years into the marriage but lost the baby a few of months before she was due. We were both devastated, but I think it was the final insult to Anne's poor mind.'

Miss Shepherd grew still, as if sensing the tragedy he was about to tell her.

'At the time we lived in a set of rooms in the lodging house I owned. I had painstakingly renovated it and we'd moved in a year or so earlier. It was comfortable, with our own entrance. Three other families lived in the rest of the building.' He swallowed, thinking of how he had been out just walking around, not wanting to return to the oppressive atmosphere of his own home. 'I had been out and I was walking home when I heard shouts of fire. I think I knew immediately what had happened.'

'It was your house?'

'Yes. The blaze had taken hold and the neighbours had started a water chain to try to stop it from spreading to nearby buildings. There was no hope for our house though. The fire burned for two hours before it could be put out completely. Thankfully the families who lived upstairs were all either out or had managed to escape, but Anne...'

'She died in the fire?'

'Yes. The inquest recorded a verdict of accidental death, but I have my doubts that it was an accident. Anne was in extremely bad spirits, and no matter what I tried she pushed me away. That day I actually thought she was a little better. She had talked of maybe taking a trip somewhere together. Now I see it was because her mind was made up and she had a plan to resolve her situation. She was at peace.'

Miss Shepherd reached out and took his hand, gently laying her fingers over the top of his. It was a small movement, one that no one passing by would notice, but he was grateful for it. In the months after Anne's death he had sunk into a deep melancholy, alternatively blaming himself for the tragedy and hating the anger he felt towards his late wife.

'You lost your wife and your home all in one moment.'

He inclined his head. In the aftermath of the fire he had been scooped up by Lord Shrewsbury, taken first to his London home, and then, when all the formalities requiring Henry's presence in London were completed, to one of his country estates. Shrewsbury was a true friend, and he and his wife were still so invested in Henry's happiness.

'I told myself I would never marry again. It was an unmitigated disaster. I married a woman who I thought loved me, who only wished for the trappings she thought came with the title. We made each other miserable for four years and then she became so overwhelmingly sad she took her own life.'

'Yet you are searching for a wife again.'

'For the sake of my sister. When I married Anne my father stopped me from having any contact with Sophia. He said I was a bad influence. I have not seen her for years.'

'And she has been left in the care of your father,' Miss Shepherd said, nodding in understanding. He was thankful she was so level-headed. Many young women would not have taken his treatment, his refusal to even contemplate marriage after risking her reputation, without a great fuss. Thankfully, Miss Shepherd was much too practical to hold a grudge.

'Through friends and mutual acquaintances I have been able to keep an eye on her from a distance, but I have had a lot of time to think these last couple of years. I feel guilty for having abandoned my sister for so long, and wish to find a way to see her again.'

'Even if it means marrying someone you do not love?'

He gave a short, mirthless laugh. 'I tried marrying for love, for ignoring the social norms, and look where that got me.'

'Is there not…'

He shook his head. 'I know what you are going to suggest, that I look for another way to satisfy my father and gain access to my sister, but I have had *years* to consider this. There is no other way. If you knew my father, you would see what I mean. He is cruel and unreasonable and does not mind doing anything to maintain the upper hand and get what he wants.'

Miss Shepherd was silent for a moment, studying his face in that serious way of hers. Eventually she nodded. 'I know our acquaintance has not been a long one, but thank you for telling me.'

He was surprised himself at this need to be unburdened of his story. His closest friends knew the sordid details of his marriage, but no one else was aware of what an awful disaster it had truly been. All the outside world had seen was him marrying a young woman of a lower class, retreating from public social life and then tragically losing his wife in a fire four years later.

'You are welcome. Now, shall we see if we can find Mr Peterson?'

Chapter Ten

Sarah had remained quiet on the walk across the river and into Southwark. Lord Routledge's story had been heavy with emotion and heartbreak, and she felt genuine empathy for him. She understood why he had told her about his disastrous first marriage—he didn't know her all that well and wanted to ensure she knew there was no possibility that he would propose to her.

She had never expected a proposal and felt a little mortified that he had felt the need to tell her some of his most personal secrets. Closing her eyes for a moment, she pushed the embarrassment aside. It had been his choice to tell her, she hadn't forced him.

Now she needed to forget about Lord Routledge—and how her stomach flipped when she looked at him—and focus on getting whatever information she could out of Mr Peterson.

'We're here,' Lord Routledge said, gesturing to a nondescript door set, on a street that made up the maze of Southwark. From the way people spoke of the area south of the river, she had expected something much worse, but most of the people hurrying through the streets looked merely a little less wealthy than their counterparts north of the river.

As they approached, two men pushed through the door

they were heading to, talking loudly and staggering a little on their feet.

'You do not have to come inside if you do not wish to,' Lord Routledge said, the hint of a frown on his face. 'I can see if I can persuade Mr Peterson to step outside.'

'No, I want to come in.' She had no real interest in the boxing—the idea of two men punching each other for the satisfaction of the crowd didn't promise to give her any sort of pleasure or enjoyment—but she wanted to have the best chance of speaking to Mr Peterson.

The door opened onto a dark corridor. To one side a man sat at a small table, looking up expectantly as they entered. He raised an eyebrow as Lord Routledge purchased two tickets, but said nothing, and once the money was paid the man motioned for them to continue further down the corridor.

Sarah would never have reached out for Lord Routledge's arm on her own, priding herself on her independence and spirit, but she was thankful when he paused to ensure her hand was tucked into the crook of his arm.

'Stay close, Miss Shepherd.'

At the end of the corridor there was another door to the left, which opened out onto a huge space. In the middle was a roped off area, around the edges of which there were some benches for people to sit on. But for now most were standing, crowded around the ring.

The atmosphere was jovial, the crowd loud. It was mainly men, although there were a few women dotted throughout, their dresses cut low enough for Sarah to wonder if they were here touting for customers.

'Do you see him?' Sarah asked, her eyes darting round the room, even though she had no idea what Mr Peterson looked like.

'There,' Lord Routledge said, eventually, pointing to the far corner where a group of men were gathered. 'He looks like he may be in his cups.'

'Do you think he will speak to us?'

'I think the odds are better for us than we might have expected, as he is likely to be much more agreeable drunk than sober.'

They began to work their way through the crowd. On her own Sarah would have found it almost impossible to navigate the darkened room, but Lord Routledge's size and air of importance meant people stepped aside.

After a couple of minutes they were almost there, but then there was a moment when the chatter in the room quietened a little followed by a deafening roar.

Sarah turned to the roped off area. By standing on tiptoe, she could see two men emerging into the ring. They were both tall and muscular, their torsos bare and glistening, and their expressions grim. The air grew thick with anticipation as the two men took to their corners, bending to listen to final pieces of advice from the men that accompanied them.

After a minute a fully clothed man stepped into the ring and announced the boxers. He hurried out again before there was a ding of a bell, and the two fighters started to circle one another.

As the first bout commenced Sarah found herself torn between fascination and repulsion. The sounds of fists meeting flesh echoed through the room, mingling with the cheers and jeers of the crowd. She winced every time a blow was landed, wanting to turn away but unable to stop looking, mesmerised. At first she thought the men were just lashing out, hitting as fast and hard as they could, but the longer she watched the more she could see the technique and training the two boxers must have had. They were light on their feet, darting backwards and forwards, taunting one another, trying to trick their opponent into making a misstep.

After a short time it became clear that one of the boxers was just slightly more talented than the other. He was fast, jabbing with his fists, landing heavy blows, but would then quickly pull back out of reach, so the other man only managed to land glancing blows.

There was a roar through the crowd as the first bout came to an end. Lord Routledge leaned down, speaking into her ear. 'Now is our chance.'

He took hold of her hand and, for a moment, Sarah felt her

heart beat faster in her chest, before she told herself he was only doing so to prevent her being swept away by the crowd. She hated the flare of desire she felt towards the man who had only half an hour earlier taken great pains to explain why he could never marry a woman like her.

Lord Routledge shouldered a path through the excited on-lookers, and after a minute they were standing next to the group he had pointed out earlier. Close up it was clear these were gentlemen. Their clothes were of a higher quality than the other men that jostled around the boxing ring, and they would not have looked out of place in a ballroom or fancy dinner party, if they deigned to smarten themselves up a little. They were all terribly drunk, at present acting jovially, slapping each other on the back and making jokes, but it would not take much more alcohol to make them dangerous.

'I will see if I can persuade Mr Peterson to step outside with us,' Lord Routledge said, glancing at the ring. It would only be a few more seconds until the boxers started fighting again.

'Maybe we should wait until this fight ends. He might be more likely to agree to come outside once the winner has been declared,' she suggested.

'You are right,' Lord Routledge said, pausing. 'Do you mind watching another bout?'

At that moment the second round began—a raucous cheer went through the crowd. Sarah glanced at the man she now knew to be Mr Peterson. There was a good chance he had once been friends with her father, that he probably knew his identity and his awful secret. Perhaps they had laughed together over a glass of whiskey at how her father had deceived an innocent vicar's daughter into losing her virtue, and how he had abandoned her once he had taken his pleasure. She felt a wave of revulsion and quickly looked away.

Initially, the second boxing match followed in much the same vein as the first, but after a particularly daring feint and punch from the more quick-footed of the fighters, his opponent reeled for a moment. The crowd reacted, shouting loudly for their favourite, calling encouragement or cursing depending on who they were supporting.

The younger man followed up his attack with a blow that snapped his opponent's head back. As if the world had slowed, the man took a staggering few steps back, reeled around and then collapsed to the floor.

An almighty roar erupted in the room and the crowd surged forwards, sensing the boxing match was over.

'Will he recover?' Sarah asked, peering in horror at the blood seeping from the head of the man laying prostrate on the ground.

'I hope so, although it is not guaranteed,' Lord Routledge said, watching as the victor stepped over his unconscious foe, raising his arms like a conquering king. 'Come, let us see whether Mr Peterson backed the winner. If he is in a good mood it may make our job easier.'

They turned back to the group of gentlemen and Lord Routledge stepped amongst them, greeting them by name. There were lots of hearty slaps on the back and slurred jokes before Lord Routledge singled Mr Peterson out.

He was a short, rotund man, with thinning hair and a sweaty face. His cheeks were rosy from the warmth of the room and his eyes had a glazed, unfocussed look about them.

'Might I have a word outside, Peterson?' Lord Routledge said.

'Not before he pays his debts,' another of the men said, shouldering his way in between the two men.

'You'll get your money, Greenacre,' Mr Peterson slurred, but made no move to reach for his coin purse.

'You see I do. Everyone knows you're the tightest man in England.'

'Steady on,' a third man said, although he looked as though he was enjoying the exchange immensely.

'Our business will only take a couple of minutes. You will be back inside ready for the next match,' Lord Routledge said, taking Mr Peterson firmly by the arm.

'Business? What business?' Mr Peterson said, trying to focus on Lord Routledge but failing, his eyes crossing before he blinked and settled on looking over his shoulder instead. Mr Peterson's gaze settled on Sarah and she thought there was a flicker of recognition in his eyes. She wondered if he was remembering Selina. She and her sister shared certain features.

Although Selina was considered the fairer of the two, in a dim light it would be easy to mistake one for the other.

'Private business,' Lord Routledge said, a little more firmly.

To her relief Mr Peterson murmured his agreement and Greenacre stepped aside, allowing his friend to walk away. Sarah followed quickly down the corridor, glad when they slipped out of the door into the fresh air of the street. She took a few deep breaths and then gagged. There wasn't the strong scent of sweat and unwashed bodies out here, but the streets of Southwark weren't exactly fragrant.

'You're a pretty little thing,' Mr Peterson said, turning to Sarah. 'I feel like we've met before. Is she your mistress, Routledge?'

She shuddered as the inebriated man's eyes swept over her body, taking an involuntary step back.

'This is Miss Shepherd, a friend of mine.'

'If that's what you young people call it these days. I'd like Miss Shepherd to be my friend.'

Sarah saw a muscle twitch next to Lord Routledge's eye, but he managed to keep control of himself.

'A couple of weeks ago a young woman approached you, asking what you knew about her father.'

'Ah yes, *that* is where I know you from,' Mr Peterson said, a hint of disappointment in his tone.

'It was my sister.'

'I remember,' Mr Peterson said, although his words were a little slurred. 'Pretty girl like you. Brazenly approached me in the street, then got offended when I assumed she was a whore.'

'What did she ask you?' Sarah pressed, fighting to ignore his offensive suggestion about her beloved sister. It was crucial that they got the answers they needed from this man.

Mr Peterson considered for a moment, then he stilled, seeming to regain control of himself a little. 'She was going on about her father and how I was mentioned in some letter. I didn't pay much attention.'

'Did you tell her anything? Did you tell her who her father was?'

'Good lord, no. She was just some chit off the street.'

Sarah felt a swell of anger but pushed it down. Shouting at the man would not achieve anything—it would only give him cause to mock her and walk away.

'Have you seen her since?'

'No. I can't say I have.'

'I think you know who Miss Shepherd was talking about,' Lord Routledge said quietly. 'You knew who her father was.'

'I'll tell you exactly what I told the other one, I have no clue what you are blathering on about.'

Lord Routledge stepped closer, drawing himself up so the older man was aware of the size difference between them.

'Twenty-three years ago a friend of yours entered into an affair with the daughter of a vicar,' Sarah said, trying to keep calm. She felt a sinking disappointment. He might know who her father was, but she wasn't overly interested in that detail. All she wanted to know was what had happened to Selina. 'He made her certain promises about the life they would lead together. They were involved with one another for some time, but he left her when he knew she was pregnant.'

She watched Mr Peterson carefully, and thought she saw a flicker of recognition in his eyes before he stumbled sideways.

'I have no idea what you are talking about.' He went to move away but Lord Routledge put a hand out to stop him.

Sarah shook her head. 'I do not think he knows where Selina is. It does not sound as though he saw her after he dismissed her in the street.'

'Which school did you attend?' Lord Routledge asked, surprising them both with the question.

'Eton, of course.'

'Which year did you start?'

'Seventeen eighty-two.'

'University?'

'Oxford.'

'Year?'

'Seventeen eighty-eight.'

The questions were barked out, but it had the desired effect. Mr Peterson answered before his brain could even think about stopping him.

'Thank you.'

He released Mr Peterson's arm and the older man staggered to one side, almost losing his footing.

'I think that is all we are going to get from him right now,' Lord Routledge said, shaking his head in disgust as Mr Peterson retched and then vomited in the gutter.

Feeling disappointed, Sarah nodded, and with one last look back at Mr Peterson they walked away.

Chapter Eleven

The disappointment and frustration were evident on Miss Shepherd's face as they made their way back through Southwark. Henry had never been overly hopeful that Mr Peterson would be the key to unlocking what had happened to Miss Shepherd's sister, but it would have been foolish to pass up the opportunity of speaking to him. Perhaps when he had sobered up he might be convinced to give up the identity of Miss Shepherd's father, but Henry thought he could probably work that out on his own.

By asking when Mr Peterson had been at school and university, he would be able to compile a list of his peers, and no doubt within that list Miss Shepherd's father would sit.

He glanced at the young woman walking beside him and felt a flush of guilt. For the last half an hour he had not thought of his own predicament once. It was refreshing to have something to distract him, and he wondered whether subconsciously one of his motives for helping Miss Shepherd was as a distraction from his own complicated personal life.

'Thank you for taking me to see Mr Peterson,' Miss Shepherd said. She sounded dejected. He knew she saw the chances of her finding her sister shrinking before her eyes.

'I am sorry it was not more useful.'

'You could not have foreseen that. It was important we spoke to him in case Selina had approached him again.'

'I will go to the gentleman's club your sister mentioned later this afternoon, once I have escorted you home.'

'Thank you.'

'Then perhaps tomorrow evening you would like to accompany me to the Vauxhall Pleasure Gardens.'

She turned a cautious face towards him.

'After last night do you not think it would be best if we were not seen out together socially?'

'Probably,' he said. She was completely right of course, he should stick to helping her find her sister and nothing more. Yet she looked so sad he couldn't bear to think of her sitting in the impersonal lodging house all alone night after night. 'But I do not think it would be too much of a risk. They are having a special event, a masquerade. No one would know who you are.'

She hesitated, and he found himself willing her silently to say yes. He knew he shouldn't have invited her, shouldn't have risked the scandal that being linked with a woman of a much lower social class could cause, but he couldn't help himself. He wanted to see her smile, to wipe the melancholy expression from her face, and for one night at least enjoy the company of a woman he liked to be around before he started in earnest to look for a wife.

'I suppose you could tell me what you had discovered from the gentleman's club.'

'Does that mean you will come?'

She bit her lip, an endearing habit that drew his eyes to her mouth. For a moment he could only think about kissing her. Quickly he looked away. He wouldn't make that mistake twice. He couldn't deny the attraction he felt towards Miss Shepherd, but more than that he *liked* her. He respected her single-mindedness, her devotion and her loyalty to her sister. She was kind and understanding and he felt comfortable with her. She was the first person he had ever told the story of his first marriage. Other people knew about it because they had lived through it with him, but never had he felt comfortable enough to actually tell them the story.

He shook himself. He was beginning to sound like a lovesick fool, and only a buffoon made the same mistake twice. Once before he had allowed his sentiments to rule his head and it had caused nothing but heartache. Now all his decisions had to be made in a logical fashion.

Grimacing, he realised his last offer to Miss Shepherd had not been logical. The logical thing to do would be to offer to visit the gentleman's club and then deliver her a note with the outcome. It had not been sensible to invite her for an evening, where their only protection from the curious eyes of society would be flimsy masks.

'If you are sure?'

'Yes.' The word was out before he could stop it, despite his misgivings. He didn't want to examine what had pushed him to extend the offer, or why he was feeling quite so elated that she had accepted.

Duty. That was what he needed to focus on. The time for self-indulgence and making decisions based on what he wanted was long past. He was still paying for all the mistakes he had made. Now he should be putting all his effort into fulfilling his duty.

Pressing his lips together in displeasure at the word, he told himself it was a means to an end, nothing more. He had no other choice but to tolerate his father's demands, not if he wished to see his sister, and perhaps find a way to rescue her from their father's malign influence. He didn't know what Lord Burwell had planned for his only daughter when she reached an age to be launched into society, but he doubted it would be a happy marriage to a man she loved. If he could be part of her life he might be able to influence his father's choices in the matter.

'You look serious,' Miss Shepherd said, 'and a little sad.'

'I was thinking of my sister.'

She gave a rueful smile. 'We are quite a pair, are we not? I have a troublesome sister who has disappeared without a trace, and you have a sister who is in need of rescuing.'

'It is certainly something we have in common, Miss Shepherd. We are both changing the course of our lives for the sake of our sisters.'

'I hope my change will only be temporary.'

'I am positive it will. In two weeks you will be sitting in the music room of your new home in Kent, teaching your charges the basics of piano.'

She closed her eyes and inhaled, a look of serenity on her face, and for a moment he envied her. He had been prepared to live a simple life with Anne. He'd wanted to make enough money from his properties to support them and any children they may have, but to eschew the trappings of the very wealthy. It had all seemed a little pointless to him, to always need the latest fashion or the fanciest house. Miss Shepherd would not have an easy life, he didn't wish to belittle her need to work for her living, but she would have the satisfaction of waking up each day knowing she was in control of her own destiny.

Sarah watched through the gap in her curtains as Lord Routledge disappeared around the corner. He had once again walked her back to her lodgings, leaving her with a promise that he would visit the gentleman's club later that afternoon.

She thought of the invitation he had extended, asking her to accompany him to the pleasure gardens, and tried to suppress the bubble of excitement that rose inside her.

For him it would be nothing more than a way to impart what he had uncovered without changing his plans. He had made it perfectly clear that he did not wish anything romantic to happen between them. She reddened a little at the memory of how painstakingly he had ensured she knew that, telling her of his disastrous first marriage.

'He could never want someone like you,' Sarah murmured to herself. She needed to hear it—despite her resolution not to think of Lord Routledge in that way, she had found herself on edge the entire afternoon. Although his reasons were valid, she also had plans that did not involve any liaison between them. She was not going to repeat the mistakes of her mother.

She sighed. It was not the same. She may have only known Lord Routledge for a couple of days, but she could tell he was a man who took his responsibilities seriously. It was endearing how much he was willing to endure to help his sister, and she knew he was the epitome of a good man.

He would not leave a young woman ruined, as her father had done to her mother, but she would not put him in that position. He had made it quite clear the only thing he truly cared about was seeing his sister, and entangling himself with Sarah would only complicate matters.

'Stop it,' she told herself. She needed to stop thinking about the attractive Viscount. She'd only known him a couple of days, and now he was dominating her every thought.

She was about to look away from the window when a fine carriage pulled up outside, pulled by four huge white horses. Her interest was immediately piqued. This was not a bad part of London, but it was a long way from Grosvenor Square, where this sort of carriage would look at home.

A liveried servant hopped down from the front of the carriage and opened the door, holding out his hand to assist the lady inside to step down onto the street. Sarah inhaled sharply as she recognised the willowy, elegant figure of Lady Shrewsbury. The Countess looked up at the lodging house, and Sarah quickly stepped away from the window, hoping she hadn't been seen.

A minute later Mrs Angel was knocking at her door.

'All these comings and goings, I don't know what to think, Miss Shepherd. This is a quiet lodging house.'

'Do I have a visitor, Mrs Angel?'

'Outside. She opted to wait in her carriage.'

'Thank you.'

Sarah contemplated closing the door and pretending she was not there, but Lady Shrewsbury struck her as a tenacious woman who would stop at nothing to get what she wanted. With a sigh she picked up her bonnet and left the bedroom, wondering what Lord Routledge's friend could want with her.

'Thank you for coming out to meet me,' Lady Shrewsbury said, beaming out at her. 'Would you come and join me? I thought we could go for a ride. The weather is becoming unbearable again, but with the curtains drawn back it is quite pleasant in the carriage.'

Inside the space was small but the upholstery luxurious. Sarah sank back into the seat of the carriage, opposite Lady Shrewsbury, taking a moment to arrange her skirts. She was conscious of the much inferior cut and material of her dress compared to that of the Countess, which was a beautiful garment made out of green satin.

'Is there something you wished to discuss, my lady?' Sarah asked, looking at the other woman directly, refusing to be cowed by their difference in social status.

'Miss Shepherd, you must understand my position,' Lady Shrewsbury began, softening the words with a diplomatic smile. 'Lord Routledge is a dear friend, in many ways like the brother I never had, and I worry about his welfare.'

Sarah bristled, but tried not to show it.

'Lord Routledge is a Viscount, whereas I am a mere miss from Sussex.'

'Yet in just a few days you have managed to bewitch him,' Lady Shrewsbury murmured.

Sarah's head shot up—she had not expected the Countess to be so blunt.

Lady Shrewsbury held up a placating hand. 'Perhaps my turn of phrase is too strong, too accusatory, but the fact remains that ever since deciding he was going to dedicate his life to regaining contact with his sister, Lord Routledge has not once acted rashly. Then you come along and suddenly he is bringing you to the opera and sheltering under trees with you during thunderstorms.'

She was glad Lady Shrewsbury did not know of their latest foray out into the world together, to the seedier parts of London.

'Lord Routledge has been kind enough to help me find my sister.'

'He *is* very kind. He would hate it if I insinuated that he was sometimes too kind, but I have my opinions.'

Sarah blinked a few times, taken aback again by Lady Shrewsbury's directness.

'What would it take for you to go away? To disappear from his life and never come back?'

'There is nothing you could offer me,' Sarah said, feeling the first stirrings of anger deep inside her. For now she kept her voice calm and neutral, although tension gathered in her shoulders.

'Nothing? I am a very wealthy woman.'

'There is nothing you could offer me because, in a couple of weeks—sooner, if I find my sister—I will be leaving London anyway, and I don't expect to have any further contact with Lord Routledge.'

Lady Shrewsbury frowned, studying her.

'I do not want to seduce Lord Routledge, I do not wish to divert him from his plans to marry some young debutante his father approves of, I do not wish to prevent him from reuniting with his sister. All I want is to find out what happened to my own sister, and if Lord Routledge is kind enough to offer help with that then I am hardly going to refuse, am I, Lady Shrewsbury?'

There was silence in the carriage for a full minute as Lady Shrewsbury contemplated Sarah's speech.

'You are telling me if Lord Routledge came to you tomorrow and asked for your hand in marriage, you would refuse?'

Sarah laughed. 'The question is preposterous. We have known each other but two days. Surely you have more faith in Lord Routledge's judgement than that?' She knew she should not speak in such a disrespectful tone, but Lady Shrewsbury had plucked her from her lodging house and was now accusing her of scheming to entrap Lord Routledge into marriage.

'Sometimes a good and kind man can be taken in by an ambitious minx.'

'Please Lady Shrewsbury, choose your words carefully. I may not be a Countess, but I think you owe me the courtesy of not insulting me so directly when you do not know me.'

Lady Shrewsbury sighed and looked out the window, irritation mixed with angst on her face. Sarah wondered if she was just a very good friend concerned for a man who had been hurt before, or if she harboured her own feelings for Lord Routledge.

'If you had seen him after his wife's death,' she said, shaking her head. 'And even the months before her death. His vitality drained away, sucked out by that scheming woman. She married him for the life she thought she would have with him, not for the wonderful person he was.'

'I am sorry for what happened in his first marriage, but I am not Anne. I have no desire to marry a man of a vastly different social class. I have my own life to live, and once I find my sister I will be leaving London.'

'Immediately?'

'Yes, as soon as I have found my sister.'

Lady Shrewsbury looked thoughtful, and then leaned forward, placing her delicate hand over Sarah's.

'You must forgive me, my dear. If you had seen what a mess Lord Routledge was in a few years ago you would understand my concern. He is a good man, who sees the best in everyone. You may not be planning on using that to your advantage, but there are many who would.'

Sarah pressed her lips together, cautioning herself not to say more than was needed, but after a moment the words flowed anyway.

'I think you do not give him credit. He is an astute man alongside his kindness and generosity. Yes, he was naïve in matters of the heart once, but he was younger then and had less experience of the world. I do not think one mistake made years ago should be how he is judged today.'

'You are forthright, Miss Shepherd,' Lady Shrewsbury said sharply, and then relaxed again. 'But I expect my husband would agree with your words. He is always telling me that Lord Routledge is a different man than the one who fell for Anne, that we should not expect him to make the same mistakes.'

'Your concern for him is admirable,' Sarah said, hoping if she said the right thing this interview would come to an end. 'You must have been friends with him for a long time.'

'Yes, from before my marriage to Lord Shrewsbury. Though my husband's friendship with Lord Routledge goes back even further of course.'

Sarah fell silent, glancing out the window. She did not know London well enough to be able to recognise where they were, but already they must be a fair distance from her lodging house.

After a moment Lady Shrewsbury smiled brightly, the smile Sarah suspected she kept for when she had company.

'Look at me, plucking you from your home and interrogating you. I am sorry, Miss Shepherd, my behaviour leaves a lot to be desired. Let me make it up to you. Come to Shrewsbury House for tea and cake.' She held up a hand to quiet any protest. 'I insist. It is the least I can do.'

'That is very kind, my lady, but I have to focus my efforts in searching for my sister.'

'One hour cannot hurt. And perhaps there is something that Lord Shrewsbury and I can do to assist your search. We have many contacts between us.'

Sarah was not quite sure why Lady Shrewsbury suddenly wanted her company, and she doubted there was much the Countess could do to assist in her search for Selina, but she knew she could not turn her down if there was even a miniscule chance she could help.

'Thank you, that is very kind.'

'Wonderful. Then we can get to know one another properly. This is going to be so fun.'

Lady Shrewsbury wasted no time in thumping on the roof of the carriage so it rolled to a stop. A moment later the liveried servant appeared at the window.

'Tell Samuels to take us home.'

'Yes, my lady.'

Throughout the journey Lady Shrewsbury kept up a continuous flow of polite conversation, about nothing much at all, and within ten minutes they were rolling to a stop outside Shrewsbury House.

It was no less grand than she remembered, and Sarah had to tell herself not to be intimidate by the huge size of the house and the impressive façade. A footman opened the door as they stepped down from the carriage, and within a few seconds she had been swept inside.

They went straight to the drawing room where she had been seated on her previous visit to the house. Lady Shrewsbury stopped to ask a footman to arrange tea and cake.

'Do sit down,' the Countess said, positioning herself on one of the delicate chairs, perching on the edge and smoothing her skirts around her.

Sarah felt out of place in the beautiful room. She wore her practical dark blue work dress, which had been carefully mended over the years but still looked a little worn. She had another dress, in grey, which was much smarter, but she was keeping that for when she took up her position as music teacher. The Huntley family expected her to be presentable from the first day of her employment, even though she would not get her first wages for a week. Sarah planned to save up with the money she earned so she could buy a second respectable dress, before she started to put money aside for savings.

Everything in the Shrewsbury drawing room was shiny and gilded, and Sarah felt frumpy and plain. It wasn't something that normally bothered her. She had made peace with her place in the world a long time ago, thankful that she had been fortunate enough not to need work as a kitchen maid from a young age. She might not have a fortune and a big house like Lady Shrewsbury, but she was much more fortunate than many young women in the world.

Self-consciously she touched her hair. At home Selina would often help her pin her hair, both of them enjoying the ritual of brushing through Sarah's thick locks whilst she sat in front of the small mirror. From childhood they had taken turns to do the other's hair, and it was one of the thousands of things Sarah missed about her sister now she was gone. Sitting for a few minutes, talking of their plans for the day or the latest gossip or even nothing at all, had been a wonderful way for them to stay close.

A minute later the door opened—a tray with a teapot and cups, as well as two slices of cake, was brought into the room.

'I confess I often indulge in a piece of mid-afternoon cake. I find the gap between breakfast and dinner so very long if there is not something to sustain me mid-afternoon.'

Lady Shrewsbury motioned for her to take the second slice. Sarah picked it up before taking a bite. The cake was delicious, light and fluffy with a hint of lemon. She'd only tasted lemon once before, but it was a flavour that had stuck with her, luxurious and sharp.

'Tell me about yourself, Miss Shepherd. You are from Sussex I think?'

'Yes, a little town on the coast, St Leonards.'

'I have heard of it. It must have been idyllic growing up by the seaside. I fondly remember trips to Brighton and Lyme Regis from my childhood.'

'I feel very lucky to have spent my childhood there, yes,' Sarah said, feeling on edge. She could not understand why Lady Shrewsbury had invited her to have tea and cake and share in small talk in her huge mansion, not so soon after accusing Sarah of trying to manipulate her friend into marriage. It was bizarre—she would have felt more comfortable if the Countess had dismissed her once she'd been assured there was nothing developing between Lord Routledge and Sarah.

'And you came to London to find your sister.'

'Yes. After I have tracked her down I have a job waiting for me in Kent.'

'Oh?' Lady Shrewsbury tried not to sound too excited, but failed as she leaned forward, placing the plate with the cake down on the table.

'I have a position with a family to teach music. I am eager to start.'

'That is what you wish to do with your life then, Miss Shepherd?'

Sarah considered the question. She loved music, loved the way she felt when her fingers touched the piano, gliding over the keys. She could get lost in music, taken away from the present for minutes at a time.

It was her passion in life, although becoming a music teacher was less so. She liked children, but instructing them day after day on how to play the piano was not how she would choose to spend her time if she had limitless opportunities. The fact of the matter was she did not. Her options were limited, and she was lucky enough that she could become a music teacher instead of searching for a position as nursemaid or general household servant.

'Yes, my lady,' she answered simply.

'A noble profession, teaching young minds. I never was a quick study with music. I can play the piano of course, and sing, as all young ladies can, but it was not something that came naturally to me.' She paused. 'Perhaps you could play for me.' She indicated the beautiful piano sitting at the other end of the room.

'I don't...'

'It would make me very happy. I do love to listen to music.'

Sarah stood, smoothing down her skirt and moving towards the piano. She took her time, adjusting the position of the piano stool, wondering at the strange set of circumstances that had led to her being pressed to play the piano for a Countess, in a house she had broken into only a few days earlier.

She needed no music, selecting one of the pieces she knew from memory, and positioned her fingers on the keys. After a moment she began to play. As the clear notes rang out through the room, she felt some of the tension leave her. This was one of the reasons she loved to play the piano. Music was freeing—it allowed you to escape for a while, to float away on the musical notes. It brought people together. You did not need to be a certain class or creed to enjoy a perfectly composed symphony. For her it was a little more personal too. Her mother had been a talented pianist, her fingers gliding over the keys of their old piano.

When Sarah and Selina had been very young the piano had belonged to their next-door neighbour, who had invited their mother to play whenever she wanted. Although Mrs Shepherd was a very private person, she had not been able to resist this offer. Twice a week she would take her two young children to the kindly neighbour's house and spend an hour playing. When Sarah was six their neighbour passed away, and much to the chagrin of the neighbour's daughter, left the piano to Mrs Shepherd in her will. Every day, once the piano was moved to their modest cottage, Sarah and her mother would sit side by side as Mrs Shepherd taught her daughter everything she knew. Selina never had the patience to perfect the art of making music, although could play passably well, so it was a passion Sarah alone had shared with her mother.

Now she was playing one of her mother's favourite pieces. As her fingers danced over the keys she felt a pang of sadness. With all the discoveries that had followed their mother's death there had not been time to mourn her properly. Sarah had been caught up in a whirlwind—trying to stretch the little money they had to cover their expenses and pay for their mother's burial, as well as tempering Selina's excitement at the discovery of the letters from their father.

But she would not cry here, not in this house with Lady Shrewsbury looking on. This was not the place to mourn her mother.

After a couple of minutes of playing the door to the drawing room opened. Sarah glanced up and saw the portly figure of Lord Shrewsbury standing there. He was frowning, but when his wife gestured for him to come and sit with her he did so without comment. Sarah continued with the piece until the end. Once she had played the last note, she looked up at her audience of two.

'That was exquisite, Miss Shepherd,' Lady Shrewsbury said.

'Yes, you are very talented. I beg your indulgence whilst I speak to my wife for a moment. Do take some more tea whilst we step out,' Lord Shrewsbury added, taking his wife firmly by the arm and guiding her through the door.

It didn't fully close behind them, and Sarah's curiosity got the better of her. She took a few steps over to the door and listened carefully.

'What on earth do you think you're doing?'

'Henry has been running around London with her. Someone even saw them sheltering under a tree during a storm in the park.'

'It is none of our business.'

'Of course it is. Henry is our friend.'

'Louisa,' Lord Shrewsbury said, his voice firm, 'you need to let the man live his own life. If he wants to gallivant around London with Miss Shepherd, then that is his choice. He is thirty-two and perfectly capable of looking after himself.'

'Past endeavours suggest that is not entirely true.'

'You cannot blame the man for falling in love. We were all young and naïve once. He is hardly going to make the same mistake again, and if he does we have to let him. It is his life to live.'

'I thought you were meant to be his closest friend.'

'Friendship does not mean control, Louisa. It means supporting him whatever decision he makes.' Lord Shrewsbury scoffed. 'And tell me you haven't noticed the spark in his eyes these last few days. The man has looked half-dead for two years, finally there is a bit of life about him.'

'You cannot think *she* could be good for him. Maybe for a few days, a throwaway girl for fooling around with, but he has been through this before. What he needs is a wife from his own social class, someone he can introduce into society and who will become his Countess one day when he inherits the earldom.'

'Someone who will make him miserable you mean?'

'Oh, pish-posh. You do not know that. And even if he only finds his wife mildly tolerable, he will have other things that give him pleasure. His friendships, *not* being ostracised from society…'

'Louisa…'

'I'm not meddling.'

'Then why is that young woman sitting in our drawing room looking petrified, no doubt wondering what to do when a Countess kidnaps her.'

'I have not kidnapped her.'

'I doubt you gave her much choice in coming here.' Lord Shrewsbury sighed loudly. 'I know you have a particular regard for Henry. I have made my peace with it, but you cannot keep interfering in his life. He is very patient with you, I know he holds you in high esteem, but he will push you away if he thinks you have overstepped the mark.'

The couple fell quiet outside the door and Sarah hastily made her way back to her chair, managing to refill her teacup and sit down before Lady Shrewsbury re-entered, followed closely by her husband.

'Thank you for coming to take tea with me,' Lady Shrewsbury said with a beaming smile that didn't quite reach her eyes. 'And for playing that lovely piece on the piano. Once we have finished, I will arrange for a carriage to take you back to your lodgings.'

Sarah smiled cautiously. 'Thank you, my lady.'

'And we wish you luck in your quest to find your sister. If there is anything we can do to help, then please just ask.'

'You have been generous enough already,' Sarah said. She did not want to owe Lady Shrewsbury anything, although if she thought any intervention from them would help her to find Selina quicker, then she would do whatever it took. But there wasn't much the Countess could do at this time.

Quickly she drank her tea, eager to be out of the house and back in her own lodgings. Just as she was about to declare herself ready to leave, there was a murmur of voices in the hall outside.

'Lord Routledge,' the footman announced as Henry walked through the door.

He looked so surprised to see Sarah sitting there, drinking tea with Lady Shrewsbury, it was almost comical.

Chapter Twelve

'Miss Shepherd?' Henry said, reeling. He had left her at home only an hour earlier, and now she was sitting with his friends, sipping tea, looking right at home in their drawing room.

No, he thought, that wasn't quite right. Miss Shepherd looked decidedly uncomfortable.

'Good afternoon, Lord Routledge.'

'I do not wish to be rude, but what is Miss Shepherd doing here, Louisa?' he said, turning his attention to his friend's wife.

Lady Shrewsbury had been born to be a Countess, raised with the sole intention that she marry some wealthy gentleman, provide him with children and be a dutiful wife. Every lesson of her childhood had been focussed on that one goal, but it had also prepared her well for moments like this. She sat looking as serene as a summer's morning, her hands folded demurely in her lap, her face set into an expression of gentle curiosity.

'I asked her to come for tea and cake. We've had a lovely afternoon. Miss Shepherd even played a piece on the piano for me. Have you heard her play?'

He regarded her suspiciously. 'How did you know where Miss Shepherd is staying?'

Lady Shrewsbury gave a dismissive wave of her hand. 'I must have heard it somewhere. You know what gossip is like.'

'Gossip does not concern itself with the living arrangements of penniless young women from Sussex.' He turned to Miss Shepherd. Despite his surprise at finding her at Shrewsbury House, he could not deny the surge of pleasure he felt at seeing her again. It was concerning just how quickly his feelings for Miss Shepherd were developing. Only once before had he ever felt like this, and that mistake had ended up ruining two lives for many years.

He cleared his throat. 'Are you well, Miss Shepherd?'

'Very well, thank you,' she said, but the tone of her voice was flat.

Lord Shrewsbury stepped forward, looking uncomfortable. His old friend had never been able to hide his emotions, which was helpful in this sort of situation.

'I think my wife was about to arrange for a carriage to take Miss Shepherd home.'

They all looked at one another in awkward silence for twenty seconds, and then Lady Shrewsbury stood.

'Yes, let me do that. You boys can discuss whatever business you need to, and I shall ensure Miss Shepherd is delivered home safely.'

'I am quite happy to walk,' Miss Shepherd said, looking as though she would be quite happy to swim through a crocodile-infested river if it meant getting out of this house.

'Nonsense. I brought you here, I shall have my carriage take you home. It is no trouble.'

Lady Shrewsbury waited for Miss Shepherd to rise and then slipped her arm through the younger woman's. Together they left the room, with Miss Shepherd sparing a quick backwards glance in his direction.

'What was that about?' Henry asked.

Lord Shrewsbury waved a hand, trying to dismiss his curiosity. 'You know what Louisa is like, she worries about you.'

Henry groaned, imagining the scene. Lady Shrewsbury turning up unannounced, insisting Miss Shepherd accompany her to an interrogation, poorly disguised by delicate crockery and cake.

'Excuse me, Shrewsbury. I think I need to check on Miss Shepherd.'

Quickly he left the neat drawing room, rushing past the footman and throwing open the front door himself. The carriage outside was just starting to move away as Lady Shrewsbury watched from the pavement.

Without a word he dashed past her, leaping forward to grab hold of the handle of the carriage door, pulling it open and throwing himself inside as the horses picked up speed.

He landed with a jolt on the upholstered seat—thankfully the empty one, or he would have crushed Miss Shepherd entirely. Taking a moment to straighten himself out, he ensured the carriage door was not still open before turning to his travelling companion.

'Lord Routledge, that was quite the entrance,' she said, amusement clear in her tone.

'Please forgive me for leaping into the carriage, I wished to check you were well.'

'Most people would send a note.' She raised an eyebrow. With relief, he saw a hint of a smile on her face. In the Shrewsbury's drawing room she had looked uneasy and out of place, as if she would grasp any excuse to escape. Out here in the carriage she was beginning to look like her normal self again. It struck him that he should not know what normal was for a woman he met merely a few days earlier, but he did, and he found he quite liked the idea.

'I like the more personal touch.'

'Is it something I am wearing? Or perhaps the way I am acting? There is something that means my company is irresistible to the aristocracy this afternoon.'

'It was a shock to come into Shrewsbury House and find you sitting and having tea with Lady Shrewsbury.'

'It was a shock for me as well,' Miss Shepherd murmured.

'She turned up with no warning and invited you to go with her?'

'You make it sound as though I had a choice. When you are someone like me you do not argue with a Countess, certainly not in public.'

'I am sorry.'

'It was not your fault. Not directly at least.'

'Not directly? So you do blame me a little?'

Miss Shepherd regarded him in a manner that reminded him of one of his governesses when he was a young boy. Each morning she would rouse him from bed and immediately ask him to recite the kings and queens of England from the past five hundred years. As he spoke she would regard him over the top of her glasses, pushing them up her nose with a tut of disappointment every time he got one wrong.

'I would not know Lady Shrewsbury if it were not for you.'

'That is not true. You climbed into her library well before we became acquainted.'

'A few seconds before we became acquainted, although I concede that you are correct. Except I probably would never have actually met the Countess. I would have found Agnes Pepper, asked her my questions and been on my way.'

'Or you might have been caught and escorted to gaol where you would still be rotting, awaiting trial.' He shook his head. 'I digress. I am sorry you were pressed into coming here.'

Miss Shepherd was quiet, regarding him thoughtfully.

'I suppose you know Lady Shrewsbury is in love with you.'

Henry appreciated the directness of her words, even if he wished she had not uttered them. There would be no delicate skirting around the subject until they finally found the words to speak in metaphors and suppositions.

'I have known Lord Shrewsbury for a long time,' he said quietly. 'We were friends from the first day at school, two scared young boys forced to grow up quickly in a hostile environment. He inherited his title and all the land and properties that went with it when he was twenty-one. He told me, one day soon after, sitting in the huge chair that had once been his father's, that he would always be there for me. Of course, he knew of my problems with my father and he wanted me to know that, however I chose to deal with them, I would have a powerful ally.'

Miss Shepherd sat with a straight back, her hands folded in her lap, listening to him with her full attention.

'Over the years he has done more for me than anyone else,

and although his family life is a little more straightforward, I have been there through every bereavement, every period of mourning.'

'He's like the brother you never had.'

'Yes. About seven years ago we both decided it was time to stop our youthful fooling around and think about settling down. We swapped the late-night card games for more respectable balls and dinner parties. That was when we met Lady Shrewsbury, Louisa.' He cleared his throat, feeling embarrassed about the story, but needing to explain the history, so she would understand a little better the relationship between all of them. 'Shrewsbury fell head over heels in love with her. She was pretty and accomplished and the perfect woman to become a Countess.'

'But she set her sights on you.'

He nodded, remembering back to the awkward moment he had realised the woman his closest friend loved wanted *him* to propose instead.

'I liked her, but there was no way I could ever allow any romantic feelings to develop, not knowing how Shrewsbury felt about her.'

'That is very noble.'

'It didn't feel noble at the time. After a few weeks of this awful awkwardness, I told her I could never consider anything more than a friendship between us.'

'How did she take it?'

He thought back, remembering her serious expression, the tears in her eyes.

'She was upset, but she said she understood. She disappeared for the rest of the season, and I assumed she had set her sights elsewhere. The next year I was a little distracted, as that was when I met Anne. I barely paid any attention to what was going on outside of my own infatuation, but suddenly Shrewsbury and Louisa announced they were engaged. I was ecstatic for my friend, although at first wary of Louisa.'

'You thought she might still harbour feelings for you?'

With a rueful smile he shrugged. 'That sounds rather conceited, does it not?'

'It would be a legitimate concern to have.'

'One evening Louisa took me to one side and told me how happy she was. She apologised for her behaviour the previous season, for acting like a lovesick pup, and assured me of her affection for Lord Shrewsbury. She said she knew how much our friendship meant to him, and she hoped one day we would have a similar relationship.'

'So they married.'

'And they have been very happy.'

'But...'

He sighed. He wasn't entirely sure when he had realised his friend's wife was in love with him. It certainly hadn't been whilst he was married—he had been too distracted by his own troubles. Or when Lord and Lady Shrewsbury had collected him after the fire that had killed Anne and destroyed his main source of income. It had been later than that, when the fog of grief and shock had finally started to clear, that he had sometimes caught her looking at him with a wistfulness in her eyes.

It was an impossible situation, and he had not known what to do about it. But, as always, his old friend had been much more aware of what was going on in his house than Henry had given him credit for.

'I came to realise Louisa still harboured certain feelings towards me.'

Lord Shrewsbury had sat him down one evening and poured out two glasses of whiskey. He had done the hard part of putting into words what he had seen and sensed, never once blaming Henry or asking him to leave.

'Lord Shrewsbury knows,' Miss Shepherd guessed.

'Yes. Louisa loves him too, in her own way. I don't think she would ever act on her feelings towards me, she is aware I value my friendship with her husband too highly, and that I love her as a friend, nothing more. Shrewsbury accepts what he cannot change, and has never once placed the blame at my door.' He motioned vaguely at the carriage they were sitting in. 'Most of the time it manifests in a concern for my happiness, which is not in any way scandalous, but sometimes she does get a little overprotective.'

'I am hardly a threat.'

Henry regarded the young woman sitting opposite him and realised there was no guile behind her words, no desire for him to react, to compliment her. She truly believed she was insignificant, not worthy of notice.

He swallowed, his eyes raking over her, feeling that pull of attraction, that desire to reach out for her.

'Lady Shrewsbury is an astute woman,' he said, his voice low.

Miss Shepherd stiffened a little, her eyes searching his.

'You are beautiful, Miss Shepherd.'

She let out a bark of laughter. 'I know you jest, my lord. I do not think I am ugly, all my features are in vaguely the right proportions and in the right places, but no one has ever called me beautiful.'

'Then everyone in the world is a fool.' He knew this was a dangerous subject. By talking about it, he was giving himself permission to study the woman in front of him, to see the way her face lit up when she smiled, the stunning emerald green of her eyes, the perfect smattering of freckles across her nose. As his eyes roved over her he had to remind himself why nothing could ever happen between them. Not four hours earlier he had told Miss Shepherd why he could not get involved with her. He had told her things about his life that he had never told anyone before, all in the hope that she would understand why he could not do the gentlemanly thing and propose after the kiss they had shared.

Yet right now in this moment he could feel all his resolve slipping. One more kiss couldn't hurt. Not in the privacy of the carriage. One more kiss to sustain him, and then he would return to his search for a suitable wife.

'You are looking at me strangely,' Miss Shepherd said, her voice catching in her throat.

'Strangely?'

'Like you are a wolf and you want to eat me.'

He laughed. 'You do not know how right you are, Miss Shepherd.'

She shifted in her seat and her knees brushed against his. It was an accident, but it sparked another flare of desire in him. She must have seen it in his eyes, for she let out an involuntary little gasp.

'We cannot,' she said decisively.

'Definitely not,' he agreed.

'It would be worse than foolish.'

'It would be disastrous.'

They sat facing each other, eyes locked on one another as the carriage bumped through the streets. It was as though someone else had taken over his body for, despite his words, he reached out and drew the curtains on both sides, shutting out the world outside.

'No one would know,' he murmured.

'We would know.'

'We can keep a secret.'

Despite the throbbing desire that pulsed through him, Henry knew Miss Shepherd had to move first. He held all the power in their relationship, and it meant she had to be the one to decide.

She was breathing fast now, her chest rising and falling rhythmically.

'This is a terrible idea...' she said, and then suddenly she leaned forward.

Their lips met and he kissed her deeply, feeling the pent-up passion of the last few days come flooding out. She tasted sweet and her mouth was soft and inviting underneath his. For a moment he forgot all the reasons they were supposed to be keeping apart, forgot his resolve to disregard his own wants and desires, forgot he had promised himself again and again that he would think rationally about all matters of the heart. For a moment he allowed himself to pretend the world consisted just of him and Miss Shepherd. There were no sisters to think about, no families to consider, no meddlesome friends.

She let out a little moan and he was lost completely. He moved closer, narrowing the gap between them until their bodies were pressed together, held by the tiny confines of the carriage. As she arched her back, he trailed kisses down her neck, pausing at the little notch at the bottom of her throat. He'd never considered anyone's collarbones before, but right now Miss Shepherd's seemed exquisite.

She gasped as he dipped his head lower, kissing the tops of her breasts, pushing at the material to reveal more of her velvety soft skin.

'Do you want me to stop?' he asked, desperately hoping she would not say yes.

'Don't stop.' Her voice came out as a gasp, and he felt such desire as he never had before.

A little voice somewhere deep inside screamed at him to stop, but it was easy to ignore. All he wanted, all he could think about, was the woman in front of him. He gripped at the material of her sensible dress, pulling it until he exposed her chemise underneath. The top was held together by a delicate bow that he untied within seconds.

'You're so beautiful,' he murmured as he lowered his head again, his lips meeting her skin. The carriage jolted a little as it swung round a corner, and Henry took the opportunity to sit back on his seat, pulling Miss Shepherd with him so she landed in his lap. He was about to kiss her again when she stiffened.

'We're slowing down,' she said, her voice laced with panic.

'No,' he murmured, peppering kisses down her neck.

'We are. We're slowing down.'

He paused for a second, realising she was right. He tweaked the curtain that covered the window to look outside.

'Damn,' he muttered. He recognised the street they were on—they were very close to Miss Shepherd's lodgings. The carriage would be rolling to a stop in less than a minute.

Miss Shepherd scrambled off his lap and fell onto her seat, leaving him feeling bereft. She looked beautifully dishevelled and he contemplated thumping the roof and calling out for the coachman to do another lap of London, but already Miss Shepherd was lacing her chemise together and trying to adjust her dress. She was looking down, refusing to meet his eye.

The weight of what they had done hit him, and he could not

believe he had lost control again. For the past few years he had worked and worked on his self-control, on making sacrifices so that he could achieve his long-term goals. Now every promise he had made to himself he'd broken, after just a few minutes in a carriage with Miss Shepherd.

'I expect you are sorry,' she said, eyeing him warily.

'I am. Of course I am. Miss Shepherd...'

She held up a finger and silenced him with an icy glare. It was chilling how quickly she had changed from moaning in pleasure underneath him to looking as though she never wished to see him again.

'Please spare me the lecture on how much you like and re-spect me, but couldn't possibly think about marrying me,' she said, quickly removing a few pins from her hair and jabbing them back in. He winced as she pushed them in with force, feeling every scrape of her scalp. 'Thankfully no one saw our indiscretion...' She grimaced and then corrected herself. 'Our mistake.'

'Miss Shepherd...'

She held up the finger again and he fell silent, not wanting to enrage her further.

'I have no desire to become the next burden to your con-science, so I suggest we meet one further time to discuss what progress you have made in tracking Selina down, and then we bid each other farewell. For good.' She looked as though even spending five more minutes in his company would be too much, but she would tolerate it for the sake of her sister.

The carriage slowed and Miss Shepherd flung open the door before it had even come to a complete stop, jumping down into the street. He watched her stride up the steps to her lodging house, not once looking back, her shoulders tense. Just before the carriage began moving again he saw her fumble with the key, jabbing it three times into the lock before she managed to open the door.

Henry slumped back against the seat. He should go after her, even if there was no way he would be admitted to her rooms, and he doubted Miss Shepherd would deign to step outside to speak to him now.

'Damn, damn, damn,' he said, thumping his fist against the seat. He had handled this poorly, very poorly indeed.

Sarah rushed up the stairs, unlocked her door and dashed into her room, only allowing the tears to spill from her eyes when the door was firmly closed and locked behind her. She threw herself on her bed, buried her face in the pillow and let out a deep sob.

For a minute she allowed herself to cry, letting out all the disappointment and heartache. She used the pillow to muffle the sound of her weeping, not wanting her neighbours to know she was so upset.

Once she had let the tears flow for long enough she sat up, wiping her cheeks and breathing deeply, gritting her teeth to stop more droplets escaping her eyes. Lord Routledge was a distraction, nothing more. There was no point in getting so upset over him.

Her rebellious mind flashed back to the moment he had looked at her as if she were the most irresistible woman on earth. How his lips had claimed her, how expertly he had touched her, bewitching her, so in that moment she would have agreed to anything.

'He does not want you,' she told herself, annoyed when the thought made her sad. She should not want him either, but she did. The whole point of her being in London was to find Selina—anything else was a distraction. Twice now she had allowed herself to succumb to his charms, to give in to her desire and kiss him, even though she knew nothing good could come of it. She needed to focus on finding her sister and then leaving London for the job she had worked so hard to find. *That* was her future, not obsessing over a Viscount who had very clearly told her there could never—not a chance, not even if they both wanted it—be anything between them.

She did not think Lord Routledge was playing games. He was a kind and genuine man, and he had so far been true to his word, offering assistance in tracking down Selina. The kisses they had shared had been the result of an overwhelming attraction between them. She had felt it, and from the possessive look in his eyes he had felt the same too. They desired one another so much it had been impossible to keep their hands to themselves.

Even so, she felt a surge of anger towards Lord Routledge. He had been the one who had sat her down and explained why he could not do the honourable thing and marry her after their first kiss. She didn't expect marriage, she didn't really know what she expected or wanted, but she wished she didn't feel quite so rejected.

Crossing her arms over her body, Sarah went to the window and peeked out, wondering if he had alighted from the carriage and tried to follow her into the lodging house. But the street was empty, the carriage gone, and with it Lord Routledge.

That told her exactly what she needed to know. He might desire her—and feel genuine regret that he had allowed his baser instincts to take him over—but not enough to keep him from his real life, not even for a few minutes.

'Enough,' she declared to herself. She would meet Lord Routledge one final time to find out what he had discovered from the gentleman's club Selina had tried to gain access to. Then she would thank him for his help and release him from any further obligation. Lord Routledge could return to his balls and his debutantes and his search for a suitable wife to placate his father, and she would continue looking for Selina alone.

'Always alone,' she murmured and then shook her head. It was her choice to be alone. She could have spent the last six months dancing at the assembly rooms and hunting for a husband, but instead she had diligently applied herself to finding work that would give her a good life. It was her choice to be alone—a positive decision, not a negative one—and she would learn to embrace it.

With a sigh she turned away from the window and sat down on her bed. She had to hope Lord Routledge would uncover something at the gentleman's club, for she was struggling to find any other trace of Selina. She did not want to leave London without her, but in a few weeks she would have to make the choice of whether she should continue looking and forfeit her job, or leave without knowing what had happened to her sister.

Chapter Thirteen

Henry glanced around him, feeling on edge. Everywhere he looked couples strolled arm in arm, their faces obscured by the masks they wore and the darkness of the gardens. Now he was regretting his decision to meet Miss Shepherd here, rather than pick her up in the carriage.

He'd thought it would be the safer option, given how they had lost control in the carriage the day before, but now he was doubting whether Miss Shepherd was going to turn up and, if she did, whether he would see her.

Earlier in the day he had sent a note to her lodging house suggesting they meet at Vauxhall Pleasure Gardens at eight o'clock. He had included a ticket for the gardens, given it was a special evening event with the masquerade, and packaged up a pretty mask for Miss Shepherd to wear.

Now he was standing a little inside the entrance, watching the guests coming in. Everyone was merry and in high spirits, as often happened with a masquerade. There was an air of mischief, as if the flimsy demi-masks could completely conceal people's identities, and they may engage in more scandalous behaviour than normal.

It was about a quarter past the hour when he saw her. She was the only person coming through on her own, but she did not hesitate. It must have been the first time she had been anywhere like the pleasure gardens, yet she stepped forth with confidence. That was one of the things he admired about Miss Shepherd the most. Whatever the situation, she did not turn away or hang back. She dived in head first, whether that was visiting South-wark for a boxing match or sneaking into Shrewsbury House via a first-floor balcony door.

She looked around her, taking in the glowing lanterns that lit the paths, the women dressed in fine silk and satin dresses. Tonight she was in the same dress she had worn that first night he had met her. It was simple and elegant, and although it prob-ably cost a fraction of what most of the dresses on display here tonight did, he found his eyes were drawn to it.

He shook his head as he corrected himself. His eyes were drawn to *her*.

The attraction fizzed and surged inside him as he fought to restrain it. Even from this distance he was mesmerised and, de-spite the disaster in the carriage yesterday, he knew he would have to tread carefully so he did not lose control tonight.

'Good evening, Miss Shepherd, I trust you are well?'

'Yes, thank you,' she said, her tone clipped and cool.

'You look exquisite tonight.'

Even from under the mask he could see the admonishing look she gave him.

'I do not think you should speak to me like that.'

'My apologies. I never meant to cause offence.'

'It is not offensive. Merely unnecessary.'

He understood why she was being so formal towards him, why she was trying to keep him at a distance. Twice now they had been overcome with desire for one another. Twice he had risked ruining her, and done nothing about it. He was thank-ful she was such a reasonable young woman. She'd demanded nothing from him, but tonight she was keen to show him she would not allow herself to slip a third time.

He squashed the surge of disappointment he felt at the thought of never kissing Miss Shepherd again. Her lips were soft and inviting and tasted ever so sweet. His eyes drifted down to where they were set in a firm line, and quickly he remembered himself.

'Shall we take a stroll through the gardens? It would be a shame not to make the most of the entertainment on offer tonight. I understand it is to be quite the spectacle.'

He offered her his arm—she slipped her hand into the crook of his elbow after a moment's hesitation.

'What did you find out?'

He had to bend in close to hear her over the sound of the music and the people talking, and he didn't answer for a second. After everything that had happened between them, he understood her desire to discuss the matter at hand immediately. Once he had imparted everything he had found out it would mean she could make her excuses and leave.

Inside his chest he felt a sharp pain at the thought. After tonight there would be no reason to see Miss Shepherd again, not if she got her way. Even if she agreed to let him help her for another couple of days, it was not long before she would leave London for ever and be for ever out of reach.

The rational part of him knew it was for the best. Whilst Miss Shepherd was here in London she would dominate his thoughts. Once she left he hoped the desire he felt—this urge he had to seek her out—would fade, and he could return to his normal self. These last few days he had hardly thought of his plan to find a respectable woman to marry. He felt guilty about it. For the past two years he had vowed to put aside his own wants and focus instead on helping Sophia, yet he had allowed himself to be distracted.

They strolled down a narrow path that opened out after a few hundred yards in a clearing. Trees surrounded the central space, heavy with blossom, illuminated by lanterns so it glowed and looked as if it were something from a magical realm. A string quartet played softly at one end, and couples danced in the middle under the light of the moon.

Miss Shepherd paused as they stepped into the clearing, looking around her in wonder, clearly forgetting for a moment her resolve to be as direct as possible.

'It is quite the spectacle, is it not?'

'It is beautiful,' she conceded as she took her time looking around. Her eyes lingered on the dancing couples, and he thought he caught a hint of wistfulness there.

He wanted to ask her to dance, but he did not wish to scare her off. Instead he led her to an empty set of chairs laid out close to the dance floor. The hour was still early—the pleasure gardens were not too busy. There were only a few couples on the dance floor and a half dozen more dotted around the edge. As the night went on it would no doubt get much more crowded, as guests ambled through the rest of the pleasure gardens and made their way back here.

'I have some news,' he said quietly. 'I do not wish to get your hopes up, but I spoke to some of the staff at the gentleman's club. One remembered your sister.'

Miss Shepherd's whole body tensed as she waited for him to continue.

'He was the one Selina spoke to?'

'Yes. He was reluctant to talk to me at first. I think he was worried he would get in trouble for discussing the members. I assured him all I wanted was information.' He had paid handsomely for those scraps of information, but it was worth it if it led to Miss Shepherd finally finding her sister.

'What did he say?'

'As we thought, your sister tried to gain entry to the club a few weeks ago and was quickly thrown out. She was told that admittance was for members only and their guests, but certainly no women. He said she went away that day without too much fuss, but returned a few days later.'

Miss Shepherd reached out and gripped his arm, her fingers surprisingly strong.

'When she returned she wanted to know who Mr Peterson was. She approached the waiter discreetly, waiting outside until he finished for the day. She told him she would pay if he would just point out Mr Peterson to her.'

'She paid him?'

'Yes. He smuggled her in through the back door when it was quiet and pointed Mr Peterson out to her. I gather your sister then waited for Mr Peterson to leave and confronted him in the street.'

'That fits with what Selina said in her letters.'

'Yes, it does, doesn't it.'

'There's more?'

'Apparently your sister came back a third time, a couple of days after she confronted Mr Peterson. She waited for the waiter to finish work again, and this time she asked about Mr Peterson and who he spent his time with at the club.'

'She was thinking she might identify our father that way, I suppose many people keep the same set of friends throughout their life.'

'Yes, especially people of aristocratic origins. Our world is very small, and there are only about fifty families that socialise together here in London.'

'Did the waiter tell her?'

'From what I gather he was reluctant and refused any more of her money, but then your sister threatened to reveal to his employer that he had accepted money in exchange for information about the clientele. Sharing information about the gentlemen is strictly prohibited.'

'What did the waiter say?'

'You are sure you wish to know?'

'You think this man that was named could be my father?'

'I think there is a very good chance. He is the right age and has a reputation for being a hard man. I can see he would have been attractive to an impressionable young woman in his youth, but he does have a ruthless streak.' He grimaced. 'He is friends with my father, as far as two deadly snakes can be friends.'

Miss Shepherd sat looking into the distance for a moment, her eyes glazed, then she nodded decisively.

'Yes, I wish to know.'

'Sir William Kingsley. He was granted a knighthood a few years ago. He's very wealthy.'

'Sir William Kingsley,' Miss Shepherd repeated. Her face was pale, and he realised she had never expected to find out the truth of her parentage. Of course there was still a chance they had the wrong man, but Henry did not think so.

'He went to school with my father and Mr Peterson, and in his youth was briefly entangled with Miss Otterly before she married and became Mrs Hiltshire. Which could explain the mention of her mother, Mrs Otterly, in your father's letters. He was also briefly entangled with Lady Pryce, a widow who had a bit of a scandalous reputation back then, although I am not sure why he would mention her in his letters to your mother.' He paused, resisting the urge to reach out and take her hand. 'I really think this could be your father. I do not know if it brings us any closer to finding your sister, but I suppose there is a chance she discovered his identity too and decided to confront him.'

'We need to see him. Immediately.' Miss Shepherd rose from her seat as if planning on storming his residence straight away.

All thoughts of abandoning his help seemed to be forgotten, and he found he was inordinately pleased. Deep inside he knew his reaction was two-fold. Firstly, he wished to spend more time with Miss Shepherd, even though it would make it harder when she did finally leave his life. Secondly, it meant he had a few more days before he had to start his search for a wife in earnest. He could not send Miss Shepherd out alone now, not when they were so close.

'I hardly think banging on Sir William's door this late in the evening is going to produce the best result.' He caught hold of her hand and her eyes met his. 'I will take you there first thing tomorrow morning, but you will not achieve anything tonight, except upsetting the people you want to ask for help.'

For a moment she stood, contemplating his words, and then she sighed.

'Very well,' she said, 'I expect you are right. You promise to take me first thing tomorrow?'

'Yes.'

She sank back down into her seat and smoothed out her dress. 'Thank you,' she said quietly.

'I am glad I could help.'

It said a lot about her character that she could be gracious in her thanks when she was clearly annoyed at him.

'Perhaps in the spirit of putting aside your worries until the morning you would like to dance?'

Miss Shepherd looked at the dance floor, uncertainty blooming on her face. He could tell she was remembering their first dance, the waltz in the semi-darkness of the library, whilst music floated up through the open window.

'Lord Routledge, I am not sure that is a good idea.'

'It is a dance, nothing more. I will be on my best behaviour.'

Still, she did not look convinced. 'Why do you wish to dance with me?'

He was about to give some glib response when he saw her expression. This answer mattered.

Suddenly he felt as though his cravat was tightening around his neck, and the air had increased in temperature by a few degrees.

'Why do you wish to dance with me, my lord?' she repeated.

He leaned in and lowered his voice, even though there was no one else close by. 'I know that after tomorrow our paths have to diverge. I understand that it needs to happen, yet I find the idea of never seeing you again painful.'

'It is your choice never to see me again.'

'That is not true.'

'It is. I might have put into words the need for our relationship to be limited, but that was necessary to protect my heart. I cannot be around you much longer without acknowledging the feelings I have.' She sighed. 'But I am not the one who is still in mourning and is unable to open his heart or mind to anything other than a convenient, loveless marriage.'

He could not believe they were speaking of these things so openly. They had only known one another a few days, but those few days had been some of the fullest and richest of his life.

'I am not still in mourning.'

'Perhaps not for your wife, although I do not wish to minimise the pain you felt at losing her, but I do think you are mourning the loss of your former self.'

'I am not sure one can mourn losing a part of oneself.' He tried to keep his voice light, but he felt something heavy pulling deep inside, threatening to drag him into an abyss.

Miss Shepherd looked at him intensely. 'This conviction you have that you have to sacrifice any possible future happiness, that you are not worthy of wanting things for yourself—it is very noble to want to rescue your sister, and I think it is a wonderful thing to do, but I wonder if, as well as wanting to build a relationship with her, you have found a way that you never have to risk your heart again.'

'You think I am scared to love?' The idea was preposterous. He wasn't scared, but his experience of giving his heart to a woman had ended in pain and heartache for both him and her.

'I think you were hurt terribly by your first wife. You loved her, and you dared to go against convention and marry her, even though you knew it would mean losing many things in your life. You took that risk, and then you found out everything you had believed was a lie. Then you were forced to live with your mistake and all the terrible consequences for four years, trying to make the best of it. I do not know how I would feel in that situation, but I suspect sometimes you hated your wife and hated your own life.'

He swallowed. It was impossible to ever say that you hated someone who had died tragically, but Miss Shepherd was right. When Anne had told him that she had never loved him, that she had only married him because of the life she thought he would give her, it was the closest he had ever come to hating a person who wasn't his father. What made it worse was that he still loved her at the same time.

'Then there was the fire, and I suspect ever since you've been wracked with guilt, because you wished for a way out of your unhappy marriage and the fire made that wish come true.'

'I never wanted Anne to be hurt. All I wanted was my freedom.'

'You have suffered more than one man should have to suffer in a lifetime,' she said softly, 'but it has made you wary. That is not a bad thing in small doses, but you have constructed a scenario where you cannot get hurt.'

'That is unfair. This battle with my father is not of my making.'

'I know, but you have chosen to engage with him. For years

you refused to toe the line. It meant estrangement, surviving on very little money, having to find your own way in the world. I understand you feel there is no other way to build a relationship with your sister, and you may be right, but choosing this path means you will not have to risk your own heart again. You will be married to a woman you do not care about, who therefore will not be able to hurt you as your first wife did.'

If he had not been sitting, Henry would have staggered back at this point. He had told her all the details of his past so she might understand his position better, but here she was analysing his every action and accusing him of choosing an easy path.

He felt his emotions rise, his voice thick with suppressed anger. 'None of this is easy.'

Her face crumpled. She reached out and touched his hand ever so lightly with her fingertips, not caring for a moment who saw the overly familiar gesture.

'No, none of it is easy,' she said, her voice warmer now. 'You've had the worst few years, your heart has been battered and bruised again and again.' She took a deep breath, her lips moving without making any sound—she was trying to find the right words. 'I do not mean to accuse you of taking the easy path. I do not think any decision you've had to make in recent years has been easy.'

He felt some of the anger simmer and then recede, but his body was still stiff, as if his tense muscles could protect him from the words that were yet to come.

'Will you look at me, Henry?' She spoke softly, his given name like honey on her lips. Slowly he raised his eyes to meet hers. 'I think you are the best man I have ever met. You are kind and generous, despite everything you have been through. I would hate to see you condemn yourself to a life without love because of what happened with your first wife.' She bit her lip, searching his eyes. He could see she was desperate for him to understand that she wasn't saying this out of malice. 'You deserve love and happiness, not marriage to a woman you do not like to satisfy someone else's demands.'

It was too much to take in and Henry slumped back in his chair. If anyone looked over and focussed their attention on them right now, they would not see the composed Viscount and his companion who had entered the pleasure gardens. Henry was glad of the little protection the mask gave him.

'Please say something,' Miss Shepherd whispered.

'What do you wish me to say? That the idea of ever trusting someone again with my heart seems completely and utterly impossible. Why would I do that to myself again? Or that it seems a little hypocritical that you have put your own future at risk to come to London to find your sister, but you counsel against me risking mine for the sake of Sophia.'

'That's not what I meant.'

'Miss Shepherd…'

'Sarah,' she interrupted him. 'Please call me Sarah.'

He only wished it was that easy to throw propriety aside. To throw expectation aside—that of his father and of society.

'Miss Shepherd, I have tried marrying for love. It did not work. Marrying for duty may produce a more favourable result.' It was petty to continue to be so formal with her, a horrible way to lash out and hurt her. He regretted it almost immediately when he saw the tears forming in her eyes.

'You will be unhappy,' she said, gripping his fingers tighter. 'You are already unhappy.'

'Who is to say I will be unhappy. Hundreds of marriages are arranged every year between couples who barely know one another. Some are unhappy, but most are tolerable.'

'You deserve more than tolerable.'

'Perhaps tolerable is all I want.'

She looked at him then, and it was as if her eyes were burning into his soul, teasing out every little secret, every hope and desire.

'Is it?'

He searched for an answer, forcing himself to consider the question instead of just lashing out, but before he could form a cohesive thought they were interrupted.

'Good evening, miss. I wonder if you would care to dance? I think the musicians are about to play a quadrille.'

Henry had never snarled at anyone in his life before, but his expression must have been terrifying—the young man recoiled as Henry looked up at him.

'She is otherwise engaged,' he growled.

The other man was much younger than him, likely no more than twenty-two or twenty-three, but he stood his ground despite his discomfort, leaning in so he was a little closer to Miss Shepherd.

'In truth, I couldn't help but notice how tightly this gentleman was holding your hand, and I wished to ensure you did not need any help.'

Henry glanced down in surprise—his hands had moved, from underneath Miss Shepherd's delicate touch, to him gripping her so hard the tips of her fingers had turned white. With great effort he relaxed his grip.

'Thank you for your concern, but I am perfectly fine,' Miss Shepherd said, managing a small smile to reassure the young gentleman.

He looked between them uncertainly.

'She said she was fine,' Henry said firmly, standing up. 'In fact, she has promised me this dance.'

The young man took one final look at Miss Shepherd and then backed away, holding up his hands as if in surrender. Miss Shepherd looked stunned as Henry took her hand and led her to the dance floor, where half a dozen couples now congregated.

He held her stiffly at first, ensuring there was the proper distance between them, but as the first few notes sounded he found himself pulling her just a fraction closer.

Henry did not look at her as they danced, even though he could feel her eyes searching for his. Instead he fixed his gaze over the top of her head, his expression serious. He felt every brush of her hand, every swish of her skirt as she danced the lively steps of the quadrille. It was torture, but perhaps all he deserved was torture right now.

For four minutes they twisted and twirled, until the music started to quieten then fade. At the end he glanced down at Miss Shepherd to see her looking completely devastated, her hand resting on top of his but she pulled it away as soon as was acceptable. He said nothing, still trying to work through everything she'd told him a few minutes earlier, as her face crumpled.

As the other couples began to move away from the dance floor Miss Shepherd spun, wrenching herself out of his grip, and fled, darting into the darkness beyond the clearing.

For a moment Henry was so surprised he could not move. Then he cursed loudly, drawing curious glances in his direction. He didn't care, instead thinking of Miss Shepherd running, upset and unthinking, to a deserted part of the gardens, where dangers might lurk in the shadows.

Quickly he followed her, hoping to see a swish of fabric or a glimpse of her retreating form, terrified he might lose her in the maze of paths.

Chapter Fourteen

Sarah ran, the tears streaming down her face, head bent against the crowds of people making their way through the gardens. When the path forked she took the left side, the quieter side, which curved away into the darkness. There were no lanterns lighting the way down here, and a couple of times she slipped and stumbled, the grip on her delicate shoes not ideal for the outdoor terrain.

As she ran she kept replaying the conversation with Lord Routledge—Henry—in her mind, and the awful, stiff way he had held her for the dance after. She hadn't wanted to hurt him, but perhaps her blunt delivery had left a lot to be desired. She wanted him to see how wonderful he was, how any young woman would be lucky to have him. She wanted him to realise that he deserved to be loved. Of course she understood he had been through so much, that wasn't something to be dismissed. She just wished he wouldn't resign himself for a life without love.

Letting out a sob, she felt the tears flood onto her cheeks. It had gone so badly. He'd looked at her as if she had just coldly and deliberately ripped out his heart, thrown it to the floor and stamped on it. She'd felt the anger underneath the disbelief too—although as ever Lord Routledge had managed to keep a relatively calm façade. Then, when he had escorted her to the dance floor, he had spent the entire time not looking at her. It had been the most cold and impersonal quadrille ever danced.

Sarah slowed, looking around her. The only light in this part of the gardens was from the moon and the stars around it. Her eyes had started to adjust to the darkness, but she was suddenly aware of how vulnerable she was out here, away from the other revellers. She checked over her shoulder and listened for a moment, relief flooding through her when she did not hear anyone approaching.

She screamed when she felt a hand on her shoulder, whipping round and lashing out. She would have caught the man in the abdomen but her assailant jumped back, light on his feet. She was about to kick out with her own feet when Lord Routledge's familiar voice cut through the air.

'I would thank you not to kick me.' His hand pressed against her half-raised leg, stopping her from acting on instinct.

It took a minute for her heart to stop thumping in her chest and return to a normal rhythm. For that time they stood facing one another in the darkness of the gardens.

'You shouldn't have run off,' Lord Routledge said, his voice gruff.

'I needed to be alone.'

'However upset you are, it is not worth risking your safety.'

Even after everything she had said, he still cared for her wellbeing. She took a deep, shuddering breath, trying to gather her thoughts.

'I am sorry, I did not think of my safety.' They stood in silence for a long moment before Sarah spoke again. 'I am sorry for speaking so bluntly before.'

'You spoke your mind. I cannot criticise you for your honesty.'

'I was insensitive in how and where I told you what I thought.'

'Why do you care what happens to me, Miss Shepherd? After tomorrow we shall go our separate ways, never to see one another again.'

His words nipped at her, stinging and biting, and she flinched.

'I wish I did not care,' she murmured. 'It would make it all that much easier.'

'But you do?'

'I may have only known you for a few days, my lord, but I meant it when I said I think you are the kindest, most generous man I have ever met. You saved me from a run of foolish mistakes at the Shrewsbury ball, listened to my story and promised to help, even though you did not know me. These last few days you have been attentive and true to your word, despite everything you have occurring in your own life.' She glanced up and met his eye, knowing she should leave her speech there, but unable to stop. 'I wish I felt nothing for you, I wish tomorrow I could say goodbye and move on with my life, but I will not be able to, not easily.'

He remained silent, his face impassive, and she wished she could tell what he was feeling.

'Ever since I found out what my father did to my mother all those years ago, how a few weeks of happy recklessness led to a lifetime of being alone, I promised myself I would never get into the same situation. I would either devote myself to my work and grow old a spinster, or I would ensure I was wed before allowing anything intimate to happen. Yet a few days in your company and I find myself yearning for…' She trailed off, still too much of an innocent to put into words what she wanted from him.

'Yearning for what?'

'You,' she said quietly.

A fire blazed in his eyes, and she saw the warring emotions in him. Finally, desire won out—he stepped forward, without saying a word, and pulled her into his arms. He kissed her hard, not like the gentle, passionate kisses of the day before, and Sarah responded to his touch immediately. She knew she should push him away, break off this contact and do the sensible thing, but she wanted more than anything to sink into his arms.

His hands roamed over her body, pulling at her dress, and she gasped as his fingers grazed her skin.

All her life she had been good, she had done what she was told and followed the rules. For once she wanted to break every rule, to do what she wished and damn the consequences. She wanted to feel the heat of his body on hers, to writhe in passion underneath him. She wanted to give every part of herself to him and revel in his attention.

But not like this. She'd felt his passion before, but this evening there was a hard edge to it, as if he could not forgive her for her words earlier. As much as she wanted him, she could not give herself to him when he was angry with her.

It was one of the hardest things she had ever done, pulling away from him, and she saw the surprise in his eyes as she stepped back.

'I can't do this,' she said quietly. 'Not like this.'

'What do you mean?'

'You're angry with me. I can feel it.'

She wanted him to deny it, to approach her with a gentle sensitivity, to reassure her it was only desire he felt, not anger. Instead he sighed, deflating a little.

'You're right. We shouldn't do this.'

He didn't move, but she could see him shutting her off, putting up walls to protect himself.

'I'm sorry,' Sarah said, unsure if she was apologising for kissing him or pulling away, or perhaps for the words she had said earlier. She felt a lump form in her throat, taking away her ability to speak clearly. All she wanted was for him to take her in his arms, to tell her she was right, and then kiss her until she lost all sense of doubt. She wanted him to admit he wanted more than a convenient marriage, that he wanted *her*, not just because of a base, physical desire, but because he enjoyed every aspect of her company.

Quietly she scoffed. He was not going to say any of that. The best she could hope for was that he would consider her words over the next few weeks, then decide he could look for a wife that he at least liked and maybe could grow to love. She could expect nothing more from him. It was pure fantasy to think they had a future together. Their acquaintance was short, and she was exactly the sort of woman he had vowed to avoid.

Sarah tried to compose herself, knowing that in a few minutes she would have to walk back through the crowds of people without alerting any of them to the fact her heart was breaking. She didn't want to care so much for Lord Routledge, but she did. He clearly desired her—even after her earlier tirade he hadn't been able to keep his hands off her—but that was not a basis for an ongoing relationship.

'I think I am going to return home now,' she said, taking another step back.

Lord Routledge looked at her, his eyes raking over her body. A small part of her hoped he might say he could not be without her, that he did not want her to go, but eventually he gave a short, sharp nod.

'Very well. I will escort you to the entrance and find you a carriage.'

'Thank you.'

They walked in silence, retracing their steps through the dark until they reached the main path. Sarah kept her head bent and her eyes fixed on the ground, hoping she would not have to interact with anyone. It took for ever to make their way back to the entrance. The gardens were busy now, and most people were wandering in the opposite direction to Sarah and Lord Routledge, having just arrived to enjoy all the pleasure gardens had to offer. Finally they were outside the gates and Lord Routledge spent a few minutes finding a carriage to take her home.

'I have paid the driver to see you to your door,' he said as he helped her up. She felt her heart squeeze at the contact of his fingers on hers, but he dropped her hand quickly once she was inside the carriage.

'Thank you.'

He nodded and stepped back, closing the carriage door without saying anything more.

Sarah forced herself to sit back, refusing to act like an over-eager fool. Lord Routledge had made his position clear—she should follow his lead.

As the carriage started to roll away she closed her eyes, feeling an unmistakable wrench in her chest as her heart broke a little.

'If this were a book he would come running after me, throw himself into the carriage and declare his undying love for me,'

she murmured to herself. But the carriage doors stayed firmly closed and there was no sound of running footsteps. Sarah sighed, hating herself for even entertaining a little bit of hope.

She told herself it had been worth it. She had been unable to sit back and let Lord Routledge sacrifice himself into a loveless marriage when he deserved so much more. He might ignore everything she had said, but at least she could continue her life with a clear conscience.

Chapter Fifteen

Henry was a mess. He hadn't slept at all, choosing instead to spend the night walking home from Vauxhall Pleasure Gardens, and then, once he had reached his rooms, pacing the floor. He felt restless and agitated, so on edge he couldn't even sit down.

Again and again he replayed the events of the evening in his mind. He saw Miss Shepherd's worried face as she had plucked up the courage to tell him what she thought of his future plans. He heard each and every one of her words over and over. He could remember them entirely, as if they were seared into his brain. She had been bold, pulling apart his every decision of the last few years. Then he had pulled her onto the dance floor and they had danced that intense waltz, spinning and twirling until all he could think about was how much he wanted her but how he could never have her.

When she had run he had found it difficult to follow, until he had realised she'd slipped into the darkness of the gardens. Then concern for her safety had become paramount.

He had winced every time he remembered their kiss, ashamed at the passion-filled but insistent way he had kissed her. She was right, he had been angry with her, and he shouldn't have taken her in his arms whilst he was angry.

It was an impossible situation. Miss Shepherd was exactly the sort of woman he had vowed never to get entangled with again. Though if he dared to think about a future between them, he was not worried about her betraying him. Despite his poor experience with Anne, he knew Miss Shepherd was a good and sweet young woman without a malicious bone in her body. What he worried about was having a life set apart from the rest of society, without having anywhere to fit in, and the toll it would take on both of them.

He shook his head, disbelievingly. He shouldn't even be thinking about the pros and cons of a life with Miss Shepherd. He'd only known the woman a few days.

Henry stopped pacing for a moment and looked out the window. It was going to be another glorious day. Already the sky was bright and cloudless, the sun bouncing off the windows of the houses across the street. He wished it was enough to distract him, but thoughts of Miss Shepherd were still there.

He knew he needed to think on the things Miss Shepherd had said. These past two years he'd tried to become more reflective, taking his time to come to decisions and weigh up the evidence and facts. She was right in that she did not have any motive to lie to him. If everything went to plan, she would be out of his life in a few days, never to return. Her comment that he deserved a life filled with love had come from a place of kindness—friendship, perhaps. He did not think she was scheming to get him to propose to her. Despite his indiscretions with Miss Shepherd, he did not think she was angling for marriage.

Groaning, he remembered how they had parted the night before. Miss Shepherd had looked green with regret and anxiety as she had settled herself onto the carriage seat. He should have accompanied her back to her rooms, it would have been the right thing to do. Instead he had sent her off alone, albeit having paid the carriage driver to deliver her to her door.

'*Enough,*' he murmured. He stopped his pacing in front of the window. Today he would do as he had promised, he would take Miss Shepherd to visit the man they believed to be her father. Hopefully the old man would know where Miss Shepherd's errant sister was, and before the day was done the two sisters would be reunited.

He felt a trickle of panic that, after today, there would be no further reason to see Miss Shepherd again. He would have no excuse to postpone searching for a suitable wife any longer, and Miss Shepherd would be making her way to Kent to take up her position as a music teacher.

It was still early when he took to the streets, walking briskly so that no one would think about stopping him. As he walked he allowed himself to consider further Miss Shepherd's words the night before. When she'd said them, all he could think of was the feeling of pain and disbelief, but now, with a little distance, some of her points started to resound within him.

These last two years he had worked so hard to recover from the tragedy of not only Anne's death, but also the unhappiness in the marriage. Before their marriage he had trusted his instincts, valued his own judgement, and then to find out neither was reliable was a heavy blow. Now he analysed everything carefully, weighing it up from every direction, and yet he still didn't trust his feelings. Only cold, hard facts were allowed.

He wondered if she was right, if in a few years' time he would regret putting his own wants and needs aside, choosing a bride who would satisfy his father. Marriages were made for worse reasons amongst the *ton*, and even those that started loveless could develop into a union with mutual respect and affection. Love was not the only positive thing in a marriage.

He supposed it was possible that in a few years he would meet someone and wonder what his life would have been like with them, someone who turned his world upside down, but that was true of everyone. Henry was a loyal person, he would never allow anything to happen to betray his wife, even if he didn't love her.

You've already met her, the little voice in his head told him.

In frustration, he shook his head, trying to rid himself of the thought. He did not love Miss Shepherd, he could not. They had only known one another for a few days, and he was not foolish enough to think you could fall in love in that time, not any more.

He was thankful when he arrived outside her lodging house off Fleet Street, wondering if it was too early to knock, but approaching the front door all the same. She had waited long enough to find her sister—today she would get some answers.

Sarah watched Lord Routledge approach from her window. She was only a little surprised to see him. Despite all that had happened between them the evening before, Lord Routledge was a man of his word. He'd promised to take her to see this Sir William, to ascertain if he really was her father, and if he'd had any contact with Selina in the past few weeks. She felt strangely optimistic about it—not about meeting her father, but hopeful that she might pick up her sister's trail once again.

She hurried downstairs, hoping to get to the door before her landlady. She threw open the door before Lord Routledge could knock. It left him standing on the top step, hand raised, staring at her in surprise.

'Good morning, Miss Shepherd,' he said. He looked terrible, or at least terrible for him. His face was pale and his hair ruffled, and she wondered if he had slept at all.

'Good morning, my lord.'

'Are you ready?'

'Yes,' she said, searching his face, wondering if he was going to say anything about the previous evening. But he remained silent and impassive. She took her time putting on her bonnet, wishing her fingers were not shaking so much as she tied the ribbon under her chin.

She pulled it low so that she shielded the top half of her face, hoping he would not be able to see her expression from his vantage point.

They walked in silence, covering a mile through the London streets without talking. Sarah felt nervous—she did not really want to meet the man who had probably abandoned her mother all those years ago. If it was her choice, she would happily go through life without knowing anything about him. She did not wish to have any sort of relationship with such a man, especially not one under these circumstances.

'When we arrive I will tell his footman or butler my name. It should ensure we at least get a meeting with Sir William. I understand he is not the most amiable character, and if we forewarn him of your identity he may just refuse to see you whatsoever.'

'I will keep quiet until he is in the room,' Sarah said. It was a sensible ploy. As Sir William hadn't made any effort to find her or Selina these past twenty-three years, he wasn't likely to be happy at seeing her now. Especially if she just turned up at his house unannounced. She didn't really care if he was angry, so long as he answered her questions about Selina.

They continued in silence for a while longer, as the houses they walked past grew larger and grander. Lord Routledge came to a stop opposite a huge townhouse, immaculately kept, set on a pretty square with private gardens in the middle.

'This is it?' Sarah asked, feeling a little intimidated.

'Sir William is a very wealthy man. He owns a lot of land around the country, he's always looking for the next area to invest in.'

Sarah swallowed and felt Lord Routledge move closer. 'Remember he is only a man.'

'A wealthy and influential man.'

'Very true, but a man all the same. He cannot harm you, he holds nothing you need except, potentially, information about your sister.'

'Do you think his servants will let us in, with us turning up without an invitation?'

'I expect so. Sir William is a canny man, but he has one weakness I know about. He is a relentless social climber. Until a few years ago he was plain old Mr William Kingsley, but the Prince Regent granted him a knighthood for some service he rendered to the crown. He is known to covet a title and access to the aristocracy, but despite his huge wealth he is excluded from that very inner circle. My name should intrigue him enough to want to meet with me. All we have to do is get him in the room.'

Sarah nodded, knowing she just needed to move, to approach the house, but feeling as though her feet were stuck to the ground.

'Thank you for coming with me,' she said, turning to Lord Routledge. 'Even after...'

He nodded, not meeting her eye. It would seem he did not wish to talk about the way she had ripped apart his character and all his plans for the future.

'Come, let us get this over with,' he said instead, stepping out into the road.

Once they had knocked on the door it took only a few seconds for it to be opened by a smart footman. He looked Sarah and Lord Routledge up and down before opening the door a little wider.

'Lord Routledge,' he said, slipping the footman his card. 'I have come to pay a call on Sir William. Please apologise for the early hour of the visit, but it is a matter I think he might be interested in.'

The footman hesitated. He'd probably been instructed not to accept any calls before noon, but would also be aware that he could incur Sir William's wrath if he turned away someone important.

'Please come in and wait in the drawing room whilst I see if Sir William is available,' he said after a moment, clearly deciding it was better to break with protocol than to be on the receiving end of Sir William's temper.

The drawing room was immaculate, with light green wallpaper and matching upholstery. The room faced the street, and there was a view out across the road to the private gardens beyond.

Sarah felt so nervous she did not know what to do with herself. She felt immense gratitude when Lord Routledge took her hand and led her to a chair. He pressed her into it, sitting down next to her.

'A few minutes and this will all be over,' he murmured.

She tried taking deep breaths, but they caught in her throat, and she returned to her rapid, shallow breathing.

The door opened and Sarah thought she might pass out her

heart was beating so fast, but it was a woman who entered, not Sir William.

Sarah and Lord Routledge stood, waiting for this woman to introduce herself.

'Good morning, my lord. I am Lady Kingsley.'

'A pleasure to make your acquaintance, Lady Kingsley. I apologise for the early hour of our call.'

She smiled indulgently. 'Thank you, although I am sure my dear husband will be happy to make an exception for you.'

'Sir William is at home?'

'Yes, he is just concluding some business in his study. He is aware that you are here and will be down as soon as possible.' He eyes flicked to Sarah, as if realising she had not been introduced. 'I am sorry, I do not think we have met before.' Her eyes narrowed as she took in Sarah's plain dress and sensible shoes.

Sarah hesitated, then drew herself a little taller. 'I am Miss Sarah Shepherd.'

As Sarah uttered her name she thought Lady Kingsley's eyes narrowed just a fraction further, and she felt a flicker of hope. She certainly had never crossed paths with Lady Kingsley before, so there was a good chance she recognised the name from Selina visiting.

'Perhaps I can hurry my husband along. What did you say your business with him was pertaining to?'

'I didn't,' Lord Routledge said, softening his words with a smile. 'But it regards an opportunity I wish to talk to him about.'

Lady Kingsley held his eye for a moment, then returned his smile with one of her own. Sarah felt as though she was trapped in a game where she did not understand the rules.

After a tense few seconds Lady Kingsley excused herself and left the room.

'Did you see that?' Lord Routledge murmured.

'She recognised my name.'

'Either Lord Routledge has been very honest with his wife about his previous indiscretions, or she has met your sister recently.'

Sarah tried not to allow her hopes to rise too much, but finally it felt as though she was a step closer to finding her sister.

There were heavy footsteps on the stairs and the door to the drawing room burst open. Standing on the other side was a man in his mid-fifties, scowling as he looked into the room.

'What is the meaning of this?' he demanded, forgoing any pretence at niceties.

Next to her she felt Lord Routledge take a tiny step forward, so his body was in between her and Sir William's.

'Good morning, Sir William,' Lord Routledge said, his voice totally calm.

'What is the meaning of this?' Sir William demanded again, as Lady Kingsley appeared behind him in the doorway.

'Might I suggest we take a seat and discuss things calmly and rationally.'

Sir William's face turned an even deeper shade of red. 'You're lucky I respect your father so much. Coming into my home and telling me what to do.'

Sarah felt some of the nervous anticipation drain out of her. Standing in front of her was a preposterous middle-aged man. She did not wish for anything from him, so he had no way to hurt her, nothing he could hold over, her except perhaps some knowledge about where Selina was or when he had seen her.

'Hello, Father,' she said calmly. It was meant to inflame the situation and Sarah had judged right. Sir William roared and took a few steps into the room. Lady Kingsley let out a dramatic moan.

Sir William came within touching distance before Lord Routledge put his hands on the older man's chest to restrain him, keeping him out of reach of Sarah.

'There will be no violence,' he said firmly. 'I suggest you calm yourself and we sit and discuss this like rational adults.'

Sir William looked as though he was considered violence as the only way forward, but after a moment some of his anger dissipated and he stepped back. He motioned for them to take a seat.

'I do not appreciate being ambushed like this. In my own home no less.'

'You would rather we did this in public?' Sarah asked, her confidence returning as she remembered she cared nothing for this man or what he thought of her.

'Do not be insolent, young lady.'

She bit back a retort, realising she did not wish to argue. She wanted only to know if he had seen Selina.

'I am here because I think you are my father,' Sarah said, ignoring the second dramatic moan that came from Lady Kingsley's direction. 'After my mother passed away, my sister and I found some letters you had sent to her.'

'Unsigned,' Sir William muttered, but motioned for her to go on.

'I want to be clear, Sir William. I want nothing from you. I do not wish to get to know you, I do not ask for any money or advantage.'

Lady Kingsley snorted and Sir William turned to her, irritation in his eyes. 'Be quiet,' he snapped, evidently not caring about the upset and embarrassment on his wife's face.

He turned back to Sarah. 'If you want nothing, then I would have to question why you are here.'

'I have a sister. Selina. She came to London to find you a few weeks ago. At first she wrote to me every week, detailing her progress, or lack thereof. Then she stopped writing. She has disappeared.'

Sir William looked at her curiously. 'You wish to have nothing to do with me,' he echoed, ignoring her comments about Selina's disappearance.

'Nothing at all.'

'You do not want to know what happened all those years ago?'

She hesitated and then shook her head. 'I do not need to. It doesn't make a difference. It does not change the fact that our mother was a wonderful and brave woman who raised us alone, on the outskirts of reputable society, despite having very little money and no support. It doesn't change that you, for whatever reason, abandoned her. I don't care if your motivation was money or love or power. It will not make a difference to my life one little bit.'

'You just wish to reassure yourself that your sister is well?'

Sarah's eyes widened. 'You know where she is?'

Sir William considered for a moment. 'A few weeks ago, a young lady approached me on the street. At first I dismissed her claims of who she was, but she was persistent. She was starting to make a scene, so I brought her back here.'

Lady Kingsley's expression hardened, but she did not say anything. It would seem she did not approve of her husband's decision.

'You brought Selina back here?'

'Yes. I questioned her closely, trying to work out her motivations. I am exceedingly wealthy, and it is not the first time someone has tried to claim a connection to gain an advantage. Perhaps money or a position in the household or something else entirely.'

'What happened to Selina, after you satisfied yourself she was who she said she was?'

He grimaced. 'It is a delicate matter. A man is not expected to be chaste, to live without some comfort before he is married, but discretion is important. I did not know what to do with my bastard daughter so I told her she must stay here.'

Sarah felt relief flood through her.

'She's here?'

'Yes. She has been here ever since.'

'I need to see her.'

Sir William regarded her for a moment, and then motioned for his wife to go and fetch Selina.

All the worry and fear from the last few weeks, the terrible thoughts she'd had, thinking Selina had been attacked in the street and her body thrown into the Thames, all those distressing thoughts rose together and she felt them lifting away. Selina was alive and well, staying with their father.

She heard a patter of familiar footsteps, then the door was thrown open and Selina rushed into the room, throwing herself into Sarah's arms. The tears started to flow freely down Sarah's cheeks as she felt her sister's familiar form in her arms.

'I thought I had lost you,' she whispered.

'Lost me?' Selina asked, pulling away slightly. 'Did you not receive my letters?'

'Up until a few weeks ago, and then they stopped. I have been so worried.'

'Shouldn't you be in Kent, teaching those little children to play the piano?'

'I thought you were dead, Selina! I couldn't start a new job not knowing what had happened to you.'

'You didn't receive the letters telling you I had found our father?'

'No.' Sarah had a sinking feeling, and slowly she turned to face Sir William and Lady Kingsley.

'It was a condition of Selina's stay that she not tell anyone about her circumstances or whereabouts,' Lady Kingsley said smoothly. 'Naturally we checked her letters to ensure she was not inadvertently breaking her promise.'

'You read my letters?' Selina's eyes widened.

'And they destroyed them,' Sarah said, seething.

'You never knew where I was? That I was safe and well?' Selina asked, turning back to Sarah.

'How could I? The last letter you sent you made no mention of Sir William at all. I have been searching for some clue as to where you disappeared to for weeks.' She couldn't even properly summon the anger she knew she should be feeling towards Lady Kingsley for interfering with Selina's letters, she was just so pleased to have finally found her.

'You must have been so worried. And now you have lost your position in Kent. I'm sorry Sarah, I never meant for things to turn out this way.'

'I am just pleased nothing terrible has happened to you.'

Selina took her hand and looked into her eyes. 'I am fine, Sarah.'

'Perhaps you would like a few minutes together, just the two of you,' Sir William said, motioning to doors at the side of the room, which led out onto a terrace overlooking the garden.

Sarah was momentarily taken aback by the show of kindness from Sir William—their father—but quickly composed herself. She gripped her sister's hand, pulling her outside, wanting to hear everything.

They sat on a little bench surrounded by flowers in a beautifully designed garden. It felt peaceful out here in the shade and Sarah was glad of a few minutes to gather her thoughts.

'Who is that extremely attractive man you arrived with?' Selina asked, glancing over her shoulder. Sarah suddenly felt a pang of protectiveness. She and Selina had been born twelve minutes apart, with her the elder, but Selina had more than made up for being younger in many other ways. She was everyone's favourite, her personality naturally happy and vibrant, so people were drawn towards her. She was prettier too. Sarah had never begrudged her sister her attributes, but she felt a surge of jealousy now. Lord Routledge could not have failed to notice that Selina was the more personable and more beautiful of the Shepherd sisters.

'Lord Routledge. He has assisted me in my quest to find you.' She waved a dismissive hand, not wanting Selina to focus on Henry for too long. 'How has it been, living here? I cannot believe they stopped your letters from getting to me.'

'Father says we must be discreet for all our sakes, but most especially for Catherine. She is his daughter with Lady Kingsley.'

'We have a half-sister?'

Selina pulled a face. 'I would not get too excited. She is absolutely rotten. She *hates* me and she does not mind letting her feelings be known.'

'What about Sir William? Has he been kind to you?'

Selina considered, and Sarah was disappointed to see it wasn't an instant affirmative.

'To a degree. He agreed I could stay here and get to know him a little, if I was very careful about keeping secret who I am. I got the sense he would rather I wasn't here, but he's worried I will go and shout my identity to the world if he does not allow me to stay.'

'Surely that would not be catastrophic for him?'

She shrugged. 'I don't know the details, but there has been a lot of talk about a peerage. I think he does not want anything to jeopardise his chances.'

'I'm sorry they have not been more welcoming.'

'I confess that I had hoped he would have denied knowing that we existed, and been happy for my appearance in his life, but I did not really expect that. He knew our mother was pregnant when he cast her aside, and he knew we were living, scraping by on a small income, in Sussex. I have no illusion that he is keen to be our father, but I think I have a chance here, Sarah.'

'A chance for what?'

'To get to know him, perhaps build a relationship with him.'

'Is that what you want?'

'Yes. Very much.'

'Even when they treat you like this.'

'It is not so bad. Lady Kingsley should not have destroyed my letters to you, but I am treated as a house guest at the moment. It has been dull at times, as I am not invited to go out and socialise, but I do understand why that has to be the case.'

Sarah just felt so relieved that her sister was safe and well she did not argue too much. In her heart she did not think this was going to end well, but she knew her sister, and she knew Selina would not listen to her warning. She had to find out for herself. If someone told her not to do something she would stick at it twice as long, just to make her point.

'Do not let them mistreat you.'

'I will not.' Selina paused. 'Will you stay with me?'

Sarah didn't answer straight away, even though she was clear on her response. She did not want it to seem like she didn't want to spend time with Selina.

'No.' She reached out and gripped Selina's hand. 'This is what you want, not what I want. Now I am satisfied you are not in any danger, I will leave London and continue with my plans.'

It was a painful decision on so many levels. Now that she had found Selina she did not want to leave her again, but it had to be. Spending time getting to know the man who had so cruelly abandoned their mother was not something she wished to do. It would be better for her to take up her post in Kent and get on with her life.

Of course that meant leaving Lord Routledge too. Quickly she dismissed the thought. He had made it clear there could never be anything between them, and she would not go begging for him to reconsider.

Selina nodded, as if it was the answer she had expected.

'I will miss you,' she said softly.

'And I you. But think of the adventures will we have. Then in a few months you can come and visit, and tell me everything that has happened.'

'I would like that.' Selina took Sarah's hand and then rested her head on her sister's shoulder. 'Gosh, I've found it hard these last few weeks without you to talk to.'

'They are not locking you in here are they? Please tell me you are allowed to leave.'

'It is not a prison,' Selina said with a smile. 'I can go out for walks, and Father gives me a small allowance each week so I can go shopping. There is talk of Lady Kingsley taking me to the modiste one day for some more suitable dresses. Of course, they will have to make up some story of me being the daughter of an old friend or distant relative, but I am sure no one will take much notice.'

'That does sound exciting.'

'I am hopeful that perhaps, once they can see I am trustworthy, they might let me attend some of the balls and parties they are invited to. I do so wish to go to a London ball.'

Sarah thought back to the Shrewsbury ball, to the moment she had met Lord Routledge—as he had pressed her against the wall, convinced she was a thief sneaking into steal valuables. She had not made it to the ballroom, but it had still been a magical night.

'Protect yourself against disappointment though, Selina. Perhaps it may happen that they allow you to join them on social outings, perhaps it may not. Do not pin all your hopes on it.'

'I will be realistic,' she said, but Sarah could see already she was weaving dreams from this situation. She didn't like to see her sister disappointed, but Selina had clearly made up her mind. There wasn't any real risk to her, only the possibility of hurt feelings, so Sarah did not push the subject.

They talked for half an hour, discussing Selina's time in London so far and Sarah's search for her. Sarah kept trying to steer the conversation away from Lord Routledge, but Selina was clearly intrigued by the Viscount who had helped her so much these past few days.

'Come back inside now,' Lady Kingsley said, her face set and hard. Sarah could not imagine choosing to live in a house with this woman, who clearly resented Selina's presence, disrupting her life and potentially damaging the family's reputation.

Arm in arm the sisters returned to the drawing room where Sir William stood in front of the fireplace. Lord Routledge was sitting in a chair, his expression wary. Lady Kingsley closed the doors behind them, then took her place beside her husband.

'Have you decided what you are going to do, Miss Shepherd?' Lady Kingsley asked.

'I would like to stay.'

'You are sure you will not return to the south coast with your sister?'

Selina straightened her posture and met Lady Kingsley's eye. 'No. Sarah has decided she will take up her position as a music teacher as planned. I would like to stay here.'

'There are a few conditions,' Sir William said, turning his attention to Sarah. 'I am happy to accommodate Selina, but as part of our agreement I must have your word that you will not breathe a word of this arrangement, or our connection, to anyone.'

'You have my word,' Sarah said quickly. She had no desire to confess her illegitimacy, and certainly not to claim a father who had treated their mother so despicably. Who seemed more interested in protecting his reputation than the wellbeing of his daughters.

Lady Kingsley's eyes narrowed. 'That means no gossiping to your little friends, no boasting of your connection in the servant's hall of your new home.'

'I am fully aware of what it means,' Sarah snapped, wondering if she was making a mistake not trying to persuade her sister to come with her. 'As far as the world is aware I am an orphan, with my father dying before I was born, and my mother more recently. I at least appear respectable, even if the truth is different. I would not jeopardise that respectability to be associated with Sir William.'

'I think she speaks the truth,' Sir William said after studying her for a moment. 'How about you, Lord Routledge? You have been privy to a lot of private, family business here today. Can I rely on your discretion?'

'I will do as Miss Shepherd wishes,' he said simply. 'If she wants me to keep quiet about her parentage than I will, but if you do anything to upset her, remember I know everything that has passed between you, as well as the sordid details of your past. With my contacts the *ton* could be discussing all the dirty little details within a couple of hours.'

'You dare to threaten me? Your father will be hearing about this.'

Lord Routledge held Sir William's eye. 'I mean it,' he said. 'Treat Miss Selina Shepherd well and leave Miss Sarah Shepherd alone. Then I will have no cause to tell anyone what I know.'

Sir William grumbled something incomprehensible, but eventually nodded.

'I think it is time for you to take your leave, Miss Shepherd,' Lady Kingsley said firmly.

'You will allow Selina's letters to reach me,' Sarah demanded.

Lady Kingsley hesitated, glancing at her husband.

'Do you promise to write nothing of our relationship?' Sir William asked.

'I promise.'

'Then your letters can be sent to your sister.'

'Thank you.'

Sarah leaned in, embracing Selina long and hard, hating that she did not know when she would see her again.

'I love you,' she murmured.

'I love you too.'

It was hard to walk away, and she felt a sense of doom as the door closed behind them, leaving just her and Lord Routledge out on the street.

Chapter Sixteen

Miss Shepherd was quiet as they began the walk back to her lodgings, her head bent and a worried expression on her face.

'I shouldn't have left her there, in that den of vipers,' she said suddenly, glancing back over her shoulder.

'They were not the most pleasant people in the world, but your sister has already survived a good few weeks in their company. Perhaps you underestimate her.'

'Perhaps I do.' She sighed and shook her head. 'I am relieved we found her. I cannot believe they stopped her letters from getting to me.'

'I am not altogether surprised. As I said before, I do not know Sir William personally, but I do know his reputation.'

'His wife seemed equally as bad.'

'Yes. Let us hope the daughter is kinder, or your sister is living with three of them who are highly unpleasant.'

Miss Shepherd simply nodded, falling silent. They walked a little further without saying anything. He found it difficult to work out what she was thinking as her bonnet was pulled down low on her head, shielding half her face.

'Thank you for all your help,' she said after a few minutes. 'I do not think I would have found Selina without you. I know they would have had to let her out at some point, or she might have managed to slip a letter past them, but I would have been ever so worried whilst I waited.'

'I am glad to have been of assistance.' He should feel pleased that he had managed to see this through to the end, and that it was a satisfactory ending, even if not an entirely happy one. Yet all he could think about was that Miss Shepherd now had no reason to linger in London. Her employers were waiting for her and she must hurry away to them. Tomorrow, or at the latest the day after, she would leave the capital and begin her journey to Kent.

'You are free now, my lord. You can go about your business without having to worry about me.'

If they hadn't been in a busy street, he would have caught hold of her arm and had it out with her there and then. He wanted to tell her how much he was going to miss her, which sounded ridiculous—they had only known one another for a very short time.

He noticed a tear glistening on her cheek before she surreptitiously brushed it away, her head still bowed.

'Stop,' he said, coming to an immediate halt. He drew irritated looks from the people around them, who had to sidestep suddenly, but he found he did not care.

Miss Shepherd stopped and looked up at him.

'Why is this so hard?' he asked, his voice barely audible above the din of the London streets.

She shook her head, and he got the sense she was unable to speak, the emotions getting the better of her.

'I barely know you, Miss Shepherd. I accept we have spent a lot of time in one another's company these last few days, but it hasn't been enough for me to be feeling *this*.' He gripped hold of her arms, forgetting they were out in public. 'I should be celebrating that we found your sister, yet all I can think about is that I will never see you again. And that hurts. It shouldn't hurt.'

'My lord, we need to do this somewhere private,' Miss Shepherd said, glancing around them.

She was right, he knew she was right, yet he couldn't wait long. He had so much he wanted to say to her, and he felt as though a clock was ticking nearby, telling him he only had a limited time to tell her before she disappeared for ever.

Grabbing hold of her hand he started walking fast, pulling her through the streets. He checked a couple of times she was keeping up, but mainly strode with a sense of purpose like never before.

'You're taking me to your lodgings?' Miss Shepherd said, stopping dead in the street outside his front door.

'We need to talk somewhere private.'

'I thought you meant a quiet spot in the park, or a bench by the river.'

'That's not private.' He was aware of the emotions roiling inside him, and knew when he began talking they could all start to slip out. He did not want to be out in public when that happened.

'It will ruin my reputation.'

'There is no one here, no one to see. Please, Miss Shepherd. Sarah.'

It felt good to call her by her first name, and he saw something soften in her as he did so. She looked up at the house apprehensively, then gave a quick nod.

Before she could change her mind he went to the door and unlocked it, ushering her into the quiet house. They went for the stairs leading up to his set of rooms quickly. Within a minute she was inside his sitting room.

Henry felt some of the tension leave his body. He had a little time now that Sarah had agreed to come into his home. A little time to formulate his thoughts and tell her how he felt.

'Would you like a drink?'

'No,' she said, stepping cautiously into the room.

Now he had her here he didn't know how to start. Sarah must have seen this—she stepped forward, a little tentatively, and took his hand.

'Perhaps we can sit,' she said, indicating the sofa that was bathed in sunlight from the window. It was large enough for the two of them, and would allow them to sit side by side comfortably.

'Is this real?' he asked as they sat and Sarah gave a soft smile.

'I've asked myself that every morning since meeting you.'

'Ever since what happened with Anne, I have struggled to trust my own emotions. I doubt what I am feeling, and try to second guess everything.'

'I know. I can see.'

'Yet I find the idea of you leaving hurts me physically.' He looked away, not wanting her to see how much he was struggling. Sarah reached out and touched his chin ever so gently, waiting for his resistance to ebb, and then she turned him back to face her.

'I cried myself to sleep last night, thinking I would never see you again,' she said, shaking her head. 'I should be happy that I found my sister, that I finally know she is safe and well, and I am, but it is overshadowed by this feeling of loss, knowing that I will never see you again.'

'I do not wish to be cruel, but you are everything I promised myself I would avoid in a woman.'

'Everything?'

He looked at her and shook his head. 'You're right. Of course not everything.' His eyes raked over her, as if seeing her for the first time, and it dawned on him how stupid he'd been. 'Of course not everything,' he murmured again. 'You are sweet and kind and generous and loving. You are brave and headstrong and beautiful.'

He had been so focussed on her social status, so worried that it was history repeating itself, that he had never stopped to consider that Sarah was a different woman to Anne.

'I was so fixated on not wanting to make the same mistakes again, I only saw the similarities to my marriage to Anne, not the many, many differences.'

'What does this mean?'

It was a question he wasn't ready to answer yet. It felt as though a musket ball had exploded in his brain, scrambling his every thought. These last few days he'd felt tortured, trying to deny the overwhelming feelings he had for Sarah, telling himself again and again nothing could happen. So much of their meeting had mirrored how he had met and fallen in love with Anne. Yet the meeting and the difference in their social status was the only thing the two relationships had in common.

'I need to consider my sister,' he said slowly. It was still important to him to help his sister escape their father's clutches, or at least find some way of supporting her until she was able to marry and get away from their father. He would not abandon her just because his own feelings had changed.

'Of course.'

'The question I suppose I need to ask is what do you want, Sarah?'

She looked at him long and hard. 'I promised myself I would never get involved with a gentleman above my social class. I vowed I would not end up like my mother.' She reached out and trailed her fingers across his cheeks. 'But I do not think you would abandon me like that.'

'Never,' he said quietly, but with conviction in his voice. 'Never.'

'You are sure you wish for this? I cannot quite believe it. I have yearned for you these last few days, I've been unable to think of anything else, but never did I think you would consider we might have a future together.'

'The idea of you leaving hurts, Sarah. I wonder if I am going mad. My friends would certainly think I was, but they do not know you like I do.'

She leaned in closer, her eyes alight with happiness, and kissed him gently on the lips.

Sarah felt her heart sing as he kissed her back. She could not quite believe that, in the space of a few short minutes, they had gone from nearly having to say goodbye for ever to considering their future together. She was thankful she had been brave enough to tell him what she thought the night before at the masquerade. It must have helped him to realise that, sometimes in life, you had to take risks.

It was petrifying and exhilarating at the same time. She didn't want to think about the practicalities involved, or ask for details of how everything would work, it was enough to know that he wanted her as much as she wanted him.

With a moan of pent-up desire he reached out and pulled her onto his lap. She wriggled, eliciting another groan, before he stood, lifting her up and carrying her in his arms from the sitting room and into his bedroom.

He set her feet down on the floor, holding her as she staggered slightly. Her head was spinning as he kissed her again and then gently broke away, turning her round.

'You do not know how many times I have imagined this moment,' he murmured, his lips meeting the skin of her neck, making a shiver run down her spine. 'Ever since we first met at the Shrewsbury ball I have thought almost non-stop about ripping your clothes from your body.'

His fingers followed his lips, tracing a pattern across her upper back. Sarah arched her neck, inviting him in, and was rewarded as his lips lingered for longer.

With expert fingers he unlaced her dress, pulling at the ties, stepping away just for a moment to lift it over her head. She was left standing in her chemise and petticoats, and suddenly felt naked in the bright sunlight.

'Don't cover yourself,' Henry murmured. 'You're beautiful.'

With his eyes on her she felt beautiful, and slowly she let her arms fall to her side.

They kissed again, his hands scrunching the material of her thin cotton chemise, caressing the skin underneath.

She reached out and pulled at his cravat, discarding it as it came loose in her hands, and he helped her by shrugging off his jacket. It felt surreal to be undressing the man she had fallen in love with in just a few short days, but completely right. If anyone had told her a week ago that she would be giving herself to someone she hadn't yet met, she would have thought them mad, but with Henry's hands on her everything felt as it should.

Deftly he lifted off her chemise and she wriggled out of her petticoats, and finally she was standing naked in front of him. No one apart from her sister and mother had ever seen her naked before, but she strangely didn't feel self-conscious. His eyes lingered on her body—he shook his head in wonder.

'This doesn't feel real,' he murmured as he closed the gap between them again, lifting his shirt off in the process.

Now they were skin on skin, and she gasped as his chest

rubbed against her sensitive nipples. He grinned and gently lifted her onto the bed, then lowered his body on top of hers.

She was a complete innocent—until a few days ago she had never even kissed a man before—but right now it was as though her body knew exactly what to do. Every time Henry touched her, her back arched to meet him, every time he kissed her, she was there waiting.

'You taste so good,' he said, peppering kisses down her neck and onto her chest. 'I want to kiss every single inch of you.'

'Surely you couldn't kiss every inch of me.'

'That sounds like a challenge,' he said, a wolfish grin on his face.

He started at her lips, then moved slowly down, teasing her until she felt like she wanted to scream and hold him to her. His lips trailed around her nipples as she writhed, silently begging him for more. When he relented she let out a contented sigh, savouring the pulses of pleasure that darted through her body. He toyed with her for a moment, nipping and kissing one breast, then the other, before continuing on his downward trajectory with his lips.

She took in a shuddering breath as he came to her lower abdomen. Her body tensed in anticipation, but he lifted his head and smiled, moving down to the bottom of her leg and starting his journey up towards her thigh.

Sarah felt the heat rising from her body, and she wondered if it would always be like this. She could not imagine ever wanting to leave the bedroom—then she was distracted from every rational thought as Henry kissed her inner thighs, travelling ever closer to her most private place.

He teased for a bit longer, then placed a kiss at her centre, and Sarah let out a long gasp of pleasure.

'You like that?' he murmured, and then lowered his head back down. Sarah lost all rational thought as he kissed her again and again until her whole body tensed, and she was overcome by wave after wave of pleasure.

It seemed to take a long time for her body to float back to earth, but when it did she realised Henry had kicked off his trousers and was naked on top of her. Tentatively she reached out and took him in her hand, revelling at the hardness of him.

'Are you sure you want to do this?'

She nodded, not able to get the words out, and gently he pushed into her. She felt an exquisite fullness and a wonderful warmth as he began moving inside her. Her hips came to meet his, their bodies coming together again and again until she felt something tense and then release inside her, and she was overcome with pleasure once again. She was vaguely aware of Henry thrusting inside her a few more times and then he groaned, holding her tight.

For a long time they lay side by side, not talking. It took Sarah a good few minutes to regain control of herself, to stop her head from spinning.

Once she was certain she could trust her body, she sat up and looked across at Henry.

'I do not have any prior experience to go on, but something tells me you are good at that.'

'That's just what a man wants to hear,' he said with a grin.

'Is it always so…' she searched for a word to do it justice '…spectacular?'

'I hope it will be with you.'

With a feeling of supreme satisfaction and happiness, Sarah collapsed back onto the bed, laying her head on Henry's chest and watching his smooth muscles rise and fall.

Chapter Seventeen

'**D**o you have any regrets?' Sarah asked as they lay naked together on the bed. It was early evening and the last of the sun's rays were filtering through the window. Soon he would have to get up to light a candle, but not yet. They had spent a wonderful afternoon in the bedroom, making love and talking, and he felt satisfied with life.

There were still so many details to work out, not least what he was going to do about his sister, but he felt as if he had regained a little of his old self back. It was liberating, making the decision to refuse to bend to his father's will. For so long he had felt like there was nothing worth fighting for, that he might as well give in to his father's wishes, because he could not see that he would ever want to risk his heart again. It was only with Sarah's appearance in his life he'd realised he could not let the old man dictate his future.

'Not one,' he said, leaning over and kissing her on the top of her head. 'How about you?'

'I do,' she said, biting her lip. 'Just one, a tiny one.'

'Oh?'

'I regret not bringing some food into the bedroom.'

'You are hungry, my lady?'

'I am ravenous.'

'Then I have been doing my job right. You should be hungry after you have spent the afternoon making love.'

He sat up, reaching for his shirt and trousers, pulling them on. He was aware of Sarah's eyes on him the whole time and grinned as he saw a flicker of desire in them.

'Let me see what I can find.'

He padded barefoot into the sitting room, looking for his shoes, before heading to the stairs. There was a kitchen in the basement, and the maid he shared with his downstairs neighbour prepared a few light meals each week, as well as ensuring the essentials were kept well stocked.

He was halfway down the stairs when there was a frenzied knocking at the front door. It was a strange time for visitors, and at first he wondered if his downstairs neighbour might have forgotten his key. He hadn't heard him moving around all afternoon and it would not be the first time he had locked himself out.

Henry crossed to the door and opened it, cursing silently when he saw who stood outside.

'Good evening, Father,' he said, surprised when the older man pushed past him into the house.

'What do you think you're playing at, boy?' his father barked.

Henry felt a familiar mix of irritation and despair, as he always did when dealing with his father.

'What do you mean?'

His father did not answer, but to Henry's horror headed for the stairs and began climbing.

'We will discuss this in your rooms.'

'This is not a good time...'

'Nonsense. You're hardly dressed for going out. Anyway, I think you will want to hear what I have to say.'

With his heart in his throat, Henry followed his father up the stairs, hoping Sarah had heard the exchange and at the very least closed the door to the bedroom.

His father sat down on the sofa upon which Henry had started to undress Sarah only a few hours earlier. With a flash of panic Henry looked round the room for signs of anything untoward, but thankfully all their discarded clothing had made it to the bedroom.

'I received a note from Sir William earlier today. He told me he'd encountered you with a young woman he did not think I would approve of.'

'Of course he did,' Henry muttered, cursing Sarah's estranged father.

'Am I to understand it was the same young woman you were seen with in Hyde Park, and later that I met at the opera house? This poor relative of the Shrewsburys?'

'Yes. Miss Shepherd.' A long time ago he had realised it was best to keep his answers short when it came to his father. It gave the old man less to argue with.

Lord Burwell grunted in disapproval. 'As I've already told you, she is hardly the sort of young woman you should be focussing on.' His father narrowed his eyes. 'There is nothing romantic between you?' He didn't wait for his son to answer before pushing on. 'In fact, I do not care what there is between you. I came here to tell you I have found you a wife.'

'What?' Henry reeled back, stunned.

'A wife. A suitable young lady. A gem amongst next year's debutantes. This young lady can trace her ancestry all the way back to the Norman kings.'

'A wife?' Henry repeated, not able to take in everything his father was saying.

'She will be popular of course. Her fortune is incomparable, and she is passable to look at, but her breeding is the main attraction. You can be sure any children you have with her will be of good stock.'

'You make her sound like a brood mare.'

'Nonsense. She is much more valuable. You will need to strike quickly, before any of her other potential suitors can get in. Once she's been presented to the Queen she will be inundated with proposals.'

'I don't even know the name of this girl.'

'Lady Isabelle Stanwell.'

'Ah,' he said, understanding why his father was so keen. 'Daughter of the Duke of Hampton.'

'That's the one.'

'She's a child.'

'Not anymore.' His father was almost cackling with glee at the prospect of the match. 'She is seventeen, and ripe for the plucking.'

He shuddered at the thought. It had been a year or two since he had last seen lady Isabelle Stanwell, but she still very much seemed like a child on their last meeting. He could never even contemplate marriage to a girl so young.

'I expect she'll accept your proposal without much fuss. For all your faults you can be charming, when you want to be.'

'Father, I am not going to propose to her,' Henry said resolutely.

His father stilled—an air of contempt came over him. 'Oh, but you will, boy.'

'No.'

Lord Burwell gave a humourless smile and shook his head. 'You forget yourself, and the deal we made.'

'I wish to renegotiate.'

'So do I.' The words sliced through Henry. Suddenly he felt a cold chill, as if he had just caught a glimpse of the devil in his father's eyes. 'Did you know your sister is in London?'

Henry shook his head, on edge.

'I had her governess bring her down, when I saw a little leverage might be required to get you to step up and fulfil your side of our deal.'

'Sophia is in London?'

'Tucked away safely at One Grosvenor Square.'

'Can I see her?'

'Once you are engaged.'

'I am not going to marry Lady Isabelle.'

'Oh, but you are.'

'You cannot make me, Father.'

Lord Burwell smiled wickedly, his expression like that of a snake slithering towards its prey.

'There will be a wedding in three months. It can be yours, to Lady Isabelle, or it can be Sophia's.'

'Don't be ridiculous. Sophia is far too young to marry.'

'Yet I have arranged the most marvellous match for her. Old Lord Tutley is looking for his fourth wife.'

For a moment Henry could not believe what he was hearing.

'Lord Tutley is seventy.'

'A man still has needs at seventy.'

'Sophia is fourteen.'

'It is perfectly legal for her to marry, as long as she has my permission.'

'You cannot think to submit her to that. It would be too cruel, even for you.'

'It is not my decision,' Lord Burwell said with a shrug. 'As I said, there will be a marriage in three months. Either you marry Lady Isabelle, or Sophia marries Lord Tutley.'

Henry sank into a chair, leaning back and holding onto the arms.

'Why are you doing this? What have I ever done to make you hate me so?'

'I don't hate you,' Lord Burwell said, his voice without emotion. 'I am just not sentimental enough to pander to your whims instead of putting the good of the family first.'

'How is any of this good for the family?'

'You jeopardised our reputation and our bloodline once. I will not allow you to do it again. It was hard enough cleaning up your last mess.'

Henry felt his heart twist in his chest and glanced surreptitiously at the bedroom door. He did not want to marry Lady Isabelle. He did not want to marry anyone except Sarah, even though he had not officially proposed. But if he was selfish, putting his own happiness over the welfare of his little sister, how would he be able to live with himself?

'So what do you say? Do I contact Lord Tutley, or will you do your duty?'

'Leave Sophia alone.'

'I look forward to the announcement of your impending nuptials. Make it soon.'

Lord Burwell stood and walked away, not looking back at his son once. Henry hurried downstairs after him, more to make sure he had actually left than to be polite in seeing his father out.

Once the old man had gone he took a moment to himself, resting his head on the wood of the door. He felt panicked, forced into a corner, as if his thoughts were racing around in his head, crashing into one another and just confusing him more.

After a minute he climbed back up the stairs, his feet dragging as if he were wearing heavy metal boots.

Sarah was getting dressed, fighting against the laces and ties as her fingers fumbled.

'I expect you heard all of that,' he said quietly.

'I did.'

'He is threatening to marry Sophia off to a man five times her age.'

'Would he do it?'

'Yes,' Henry said without hesitation. 'He would probably derive some sort of pleasure from it as well.'

'What do you want to do?' Sarah asked him, her eyes wide and her face pale and drawn.

'I want to marry you. I want to rescue Sophia from that beast of a man and take her far away from him.'

'But you cannot do both.'

'No. I cannot do both.'

They both fell silent. Henry was desperately trying to find a way he could save his sister from the terrible fate their father had proposed, but also marry the woman he loved.

'I don't think there is a way,' Sarah said eventually, walking towards him slowly. She reached up and stroked his cheek, then raised herself up on tiptoes to kiss him on the lips. 'Your father has won.'

'I cannot give you up.'

She smiled, but it was full of sadness. 'Then let me do this for you. I love you, Henry Routledge. Do your duty and take care of your sister. Try to forget about me.'

'I can't forget about you.'

'You must.'

He shook his head, gripping hold of her hand, even though he knew she was right. Marrying Lady Isabelle was the lesser of two evils. He would be tied to a woman he did not care for, but it would be a relationship he would be in control of. Never would he be unkind to his wife, however little he enjoyed her company. If Sophia was forced to marry Lord Tutley she would have to endure unspeakable things.

Sarah pulled her hand from his and, before he could say anything more, she slipped past him and ran from his rooms, down the stairs and out into the street. He stood, unmoving for a minute, before cursing under his breath and following her out. He could not lose her, not like this, not when he had finally allowed himself to feel something real again.

The street was empty in both directions. He could try to follow her, but what would it change? Right now he needed time to think and time to plan. Perhaps he could find a way to get out of the wedding, and if not...

He let the thought linger. It was a cruel world sometimes.

Chapter Eighteen

Sarah dashed through the streets, not really paying attention to what direction she was going in. She felt numb, as if her whole mind and body had been chilled by a dip in a frozen lake.

She could not believe what had just happened. Despite all her reservations, all her vows that she would not end up like her mother, she had given herself to a man who was not truly free to be with her. It was not entirely Henry's fault—his father had put him in an impossible position, but a small part of her wished he had chosen her. Never would she want his sister to suffer, but surely there must be some way that she and Henry could be together, and Sophia could be rescued from her horrific proposed marriage. She wanted him to fight for her, but she had seen in his eyes that he thought he was defeated.

Taking a deep breath, she forced herself to calm down. This was an impossible situation and she was asking too much of Henry. He had come so far these last few days, realising he deserved a second chance at love and that he could trust his instincts and decisions. They had almost succeeded, almost had their fairytale ending, but Lord Burwell had slipped in right when Sarah had allowed her worries to float away.

A chilling thought hit her as she realised she and Henry had spent the afternoon making love. It was only one afternoon, but babies had been conceived after less.

'He is not like your father,' she reminded herself. Henry was a good man stuck in an impossible situation. If she did find herself pregnant, she did not think he would abandon her to deal with it on her own.

A little rebellious voice inside of her asked, *If he had to choose between supporting her and helping his sister, what would he do?*

Sarah let out a half-strangled sob of distress, startling a couple walking past. She gave then a weak smile of apology and hurried on.

She could not believe how foolish she had been.

She needed to go. To pack her bags and leave London. It was the kindest thing she could do for Henry, even though her heart was breaking at the thought of never seeing him again. But she just complicated matters—if she was not there, he could make a decision about his future, and his sister's future, without having to take a third person into consideration.

Tonight she would pack up her few possessions, and tomorrow she would enquire about a coach to Tunbridge Wells. From there it was not far to the house of the Huntley family. It would be difficult leaving, but eventually she would see it was for the best. In the quiet Kent countryside she could mourn the loss of her first love and slowly recuperate from the unbearable pain she was feeling.

Henry paced back and forth across the expensive rug in Lord Shrewsbury's study. They had been cloistered in there for an hour, discussing recent events, but right now Henry felt no further forward.

After an agonising hour at home—where he had tried to come up with a way to salvage his burgeoning relationship with Sarah, and stop his father using his sister as a pawn against him—he had admitted defeat. Once he would have kept his despair to himself, but right now he would do anything to find a solution, so he had made his way to Shrewsbury House.

'I can't do it to her. She's fourteen years old and he wants her to marry Lord Tutley.'

'There is a chance he could push through the marriage, whether you propose to Lady Isabelle or not,' Shrewsbury said.

'Surely he wouldn't.' Henry closed he eyes, knowing that, despite his protest, his father could.

'I do not mean to add to your distress, I merely wish to point out that, whatever you decide, it might not be the end of it. I would hate for you to sacrifice your own happiness for Sophia's, only to find your father has tricked you.'

'Why does he have to be such a rogue?'

'He is beyond a rogue,' Shrewsbury said. 'Lord Tutley is not a pleasant marriage prospect for a fourteen-year-old, but the main objection is his age. I know he has been married four times, but I have not heard he is a cruel man, or unkind to his wives.'

'There is something wrong with a seventy-year-old who wishes to marry a child,' Henry said harshly.

'You are right, of course. I thought only to say that we do not know how your sister has been living. It cannot be a pleasant existence, having her every move controlled by your father. Perhaps it would be wise to ask her what she wants. She might welcome a chance to get away from Lord Burwell's influence, even if it is to marry Lord Tutley.'

Henry inclined his head. He could not see his sweet little sister ever voluntarily choosing to marry the old man, but Shrewsbury was right, he should seek her opinion, if he could find a way to gain access to her. The last time he had seen Sophia she had been nine years old. She was much older now, and would have opinions of her own.

'What does Miss Shepherd think?'

'She told me she loved me, and then said I had to do right by Sophia.'

'A generous young woman then.'

Henry groaned. 'Up until yesterday I had resigned myself to marrying whatever debutante would please my father. I would not have chosen one as young and naïve as Lady Isabelle, but I expect there is nothing really wrong with her. It just feels so

cruel. I finally decide to open my heart again, and he manoeu-
vres the chess pieces on the board so I have no choice.'

'You have a choice.'

'Not one that I care to make.' Henry let his head sink into
his hands. Shrewsbury did not have any miraculous solutions
to his problems, but it felt good to share the burden, even just
a little. 'I think you are right. I need to go and talk to Sophia.'

'Your father will not let you in, not without an agreement
from Lady Isabelle that she will marry you.'

Henry thought for a second, then grinned. 'I have an idea.
Will you come and distract my father and the servants?'

'What are you going to do?'

'I know a good spot in the back garden where I can climb
up to a first-floor window. No doubt there will be one open on
a warm night such as this.'

'You're going to break into your father's house?'

'I am. I will break in, find Sophia and see my little sister
again after all this time.'

Chapter Nineteen

The garden was in darkness as he slipped around the side of the house. He went to stand in the shadows of one of the tall trees a little bit away from the house. A candle flickered in an upstairs window, and another in his father's study, but the rest of the house was dark and quiet.

Henry waited, assessing the best way up to the first floor. There was no handy wisteria here, as there had been at Shrewsbury House for Sarah to climb. Instead, he would have to rely on the grooves in the stone work and the window ledges.

After a few minutes he heard a loud knock on the door followed by the faint sound of Lord Shrewsbury's voice. At first there was just a murmur, but as the seconds ticked by Shrewsbury raised his voice as they had planned, demanding to speak to Lord Burwell.

Henry waited a few more seconds, then walked quickly towards the house. Without missing a step he launched himself at the wall, feeling a thrill of satisfaction as he gripped the first handhold and pulled himself up. It was only a short climb to the first-floor window, but the hardest part was pulling himself up on the window ledge without toppling over and crashing into the room, alerting the servants below that there was an intruder.

Once inside he took a moment to get his breath back, then

began to creep through the house. Things had changed a little since he had last been inside 1 Grosvenor Square, but not so much that he didn't know where all the creaky floorboards were and potential places he could trip.

The last time he had been in residence with his sister she had only been young and confined to the nursery. Now she was older—with Lord Burwell suggesting she would soon be ready to marry, no doubt she had moved into one of the other bedrooms.

There was nothing for it but to check each room in turn. Avoiding the master bedroom, Henry opened each door down the first-floor corridor. All the rooms were silent and empty. Hoping he did not meet anyone on the stairs, he climbed up to the second floor, considering two further bedrooms and then dismissing them. Instead he turned left and went to the end of the hall, to where the three rooms of the nursery were set up. It would seem Lord Burwell thought Sophia was old enough to marry, but not old enough to leave the nursery.

He did not wish to startle his sister. Having a strange man silently creep into your bedroom would be terrifying for anyone, but most especially for a fourteen-year-old girl. He was also conscious that there was likely a governess sleeping nearby who he did not want to wake.

His worries were unfounded, for Sophia was sitting up at a little desk, studying a book by candlelight. It was a huge atlas, the maps inside beautifully drawn, and with a pang of nostalgia Henry realised it was the same book he had lovingly flicked through when he was a child himself, dreaming of a different life far away.

Sophia looked up as he paused in the doorway, fear immediately replaced by joy. She stood and ran to him, throwing her arms around his body and embracing him with such unbridled joy that Henry momentarily forgot they needed to be quiet. Only when she squealed his name did he put a warning finger to his lips.

'Hush,' he said softly, 'Father does not know I'm here.'

'How did you get inside?'

'There was an open window. I climbed in. I heard you were in London and I could not wait any longer to see you.'

'Why have you left it so long, Henry? I waited for years for you to visit, but nothing.'

'Father did not tell you?'

She pulled a face, screwing up her little nose, looking like an angry mouse. 'He said you no longer wanted to see me, that you had grown bored of me, but I didn't believe him.'

'Never believe anything like that. I missed you each and every day we were apart, Sophia,' he said, enjoying the expression of pure happiness at his words. 'Our father withheld contact with you as a punishment for me choosing a wife he did not approve of.'

She nodded sagely. 'I thought as much.'

He suddenly realised how much she had grown in the last few years.

'Then, in the last couple of years, he has kept us apart as a way to coerce me into doing what he wants.'

'I'm so pleased you are here now. Will you take me away with you?'

'I cannot, Sophia. Father will raise the hue and cry and have me labelled as a kidnapper.'

She chewed on her lip and nodded. 'You are right, but I cannot stay here with him.'

'Has it been terrible?'

With a shrug she looked away. 'Most of the time I am in Yorkshire with Miss French, my governess. It is a dull but comfortable life. Father spends much of his time in London, and only comes back to Yorkshire for a few weeks at a time.' She paused, looking over at him with concern. 'He sent a letter to Mrs French a few days ago ordering us to come immediately to London. Mrs French said he probably just misses my company, but I worry he has summoned me here for some other reason.'

Henry looked at the worried, innocent face in front of him and knew he had to do whatever it took to protect her. In his chest his heart tore apart. He realised there might not be a way to be with the woman he loved, if she would even have him now.

'I am afraid that once again you are stuck in the middle of a feud between me and Father. He wishes for me to marry some well-born society lady. I have been resisting. Earlier today he told me either I get on and marry the young woman of his choosing, or he will arrange a marriage between you and an old friend of his.'

Sophia looked shocked, shaking her head in disbelief. 'But I am only fourteen.'

'I know.'

'Surely that cannot be allowed. Not until I have had my debut.'

'Girls can marry from the age of twelve, as long as they have parental permission.'

'No,' she said, her eyes wide in terror. 'I don't want to marry anyone.'

There was his answer. Whatever happened, he could not leave Sophia here with their father who would dispose of her however he wished.

He thought of all the times in the last few years that he had accepted his fate without a fight, and a surge of anger bloomed inside him. No more. Today he would fight for himself and fight for his sister.

'Pack a bag,' he said, his mind finally made up. 'Just the very essential items.'

'You're taking me with you?'

'Yes.' It was foolhardy and could end up with him facing the hangman's noose, but this time his father had pushed him too far. Sarah had made him see that he could still make his own decisions, that even though he had made one mistake in his life that didn't mean he shouldn't keep striving for autonomy. His father was not going to set the terms he lived by for the rest of his life.

Sophia gave a little shake of excitement, then quickly disappeared into the bedroom at the back of the nursery. Within three minutes she was back, carrying a small bag. She'd changed from her nightgown into a dress, swapping her slippers for sensible boots.

'Are you ready?'

She nodded.

Henry was aware this was not the sort of behaviour expected of a Viscount, but his father had forced his hand by trying to manipulate him for so long. He only hoped they managed to escape unseen.

'Henry?' His father's voice cut through the air as they reached the bottom step of the staircase. They were only twenty paces from the door—Henry considered grabbing hold of Sophia's hand and running, but he realised it was important he turn and face his father. Carefully he positioned Sophia so she was a little behind him, hopefully protected from the worst of their father's malice.

'I'm taking Sophia away from here,' he said. There was no point trying to make an excuse for what he was doing here so late in the evening. It was clear Sophia was leaving with him and, for all his other flaws, Lord Burwell was a clever man.

'Don't be ridiculous. Sophia, get back to the nursery.'

He was pleased to see his sister did not move.

'Mrs French,' Lord Burwell bellowed. 'Mrs French, get your incompetent, lazy self down here immediately.'

'We're leaving, Father. I am not going to marry Lady Isabelle and Sophia is not going to marry Lord Tutley.'

'No,' Lord Burwell said, a nasty little smirk on his face. 'Perhaps Lord Tutley is the wrong choice for her. Remember, I have absolute control over her and her future. I can marry her to a disgusting, perverted cowherd or a village idiot. I can marry her to anyone I choose. She will be begging for Lord Tutley when she walks down the aisle and sees her future husband, and it will be all your fault.'

'You won't do that,' Henry said. 'All you care about is carrying on the family name, of heirs to the earldom with a pedigree the Prince Regent himself would be jealous of. Sophia's future children might be your only grandchildren, you will not risk them having a cowherd or village idiot as a father.'

Henry felt better than he had done for years. Since he had gained his independence at university, and broken away from his father's control, he had not put up with his manipulative behaviour for some time. But in the depths of his grief this last year, he'd allowed his father to worm his way back in, planting seeds of doubt about his own abilities. Henry had ended up a wreck, unsure if he could trust his own judgement, and that state of affairs had meant he had allowed the old man far too much influence over his life and his decisions. He could see it now ever so clearly, but it had taken Miss Shepherd to open his eyes to it.

At that moment the governess came hurrying down the stairs, panic in her eyes as she saw her young charge dressed, with a packed bag, close to the door.

'Take her upstairs,' Lord Burwell commanded.

'No,' Henry said, his voice calm and collected. 'Sophia stays with me.'

'I am her father. You have no right.'

'You are no father. A true father loves and cherishes his children.'

Lord Burwell scoffed. 'You're soft, Henry. I should have seen it years ago. Losing that dumb wife of yours has just made you softer.'

'Don't speak to him like that,' Sophia said, surprising them all with her outburst.

Lord Burwell stepped forward, reaching out to grab her arm but Henry blocked his path.

'You can't hope to win this, boy. I have the law on my side.'

'Not in everything,' Sophia spoke again, this time much quieter.

Henry turned to her, wondering what she meant. His sister was brave to stand up to their father, but he did not want his wrath focussed on her.

'Be quiet, girl.'

'I am quiet. Ever so quiet,' Sophia said, holding her father's eye. 'Every night I creep out of bed whilst Mrs French is sleeping, even if we are in the same room, and sometimes when I cannot sleep I creep around the rest of the house. It started as a game, to see if I got caught. I never did.'

'No one wants to hear this,' Lord Burwell said, waving a dismissive hand. 'Take her to bed, Mrs French, and in the morning pack your bags and get out of my house. Do not expect a good reference.'

'I overheard a lot of stuff too,' Sophia said.

'What did you overhear?' Lord Burwell demanded.

'The last time I was in London, two years ago, there were a lot of comings and goings,' Sophia said, her gaze fixed on her father. To Henry's surprise, the old man shifted uncomfortably. He had never seen his father looking as he did now. 'I remember it was late, and a strange man came into the house. He was covered in soot and smelled like smoke. You took him straight into your study. The man was shaking and crying and you told him to pull himself together.'

Lord Burwell shook his head and glanced at Henry.

'Two years ago…' Henry began, but Sophia continued speaking.

'The man said there had been a terrible tragedy, that he had not known that the woman was going to still be in the house, and that there was no way she could have survived a blaze like that.'

Henry felt his blood run cold as the awful realisation hit him.

'You killed her.'

'No.' Lord Burwell shook his head.

'You told the man what was done was done, and perhaps it was for the best, and then you paid him handsomely.'

'You sent someone to set the house on fire.'

Lord Burwell looked at him long and hard, then barked an order to Mrs French. 'Get out of here. I wish to talk to my children alone.'

The governess looked from one face to another and then scuttled away, deciding it was not worth defying Lord Burwell when she was likely out of a job anyway.

'You paid a man to burn down my house,' Henry said, feeling sick to his core. 'And in doing so you sanctioned the murder of my wife.'

Lord Burwell looked from Sophia to Henry and back again, trying to work out how he could twist his daughter's words. And failing.

Henry felt an icy calm descend on him. 'You're a murderer.'

'No one will believe the word of a child. She has an overactive imagination.'

'People will believe her.'

Lord Burwell cleared his throat.

'Here is what is going to happen,' Henry said, not allowing his father time to speak. 'I will take Sophia away with me. There will be no more talk of her marrying some unsuitable gentleman. She will be allowed to enjoy the rest of her childhood without your interference. You will stay away from both of us. I do not want to see or hear from you again, and I certainly do not want your thoughts on who I choose to marry.'

'And in return?'

'In return we will not tell the world what you did.' Henry shrugged. 'Even without any proof whatsoever, some people will believe us. I expect with a little hard work I could track down the man you paid to set the fire.'

'Don't be ridiculous.'

'Your animosity towards me and Anne was well known.' Henry paused, shaking his head. All this time he had believed that his late wife had been so miserable she had taken her own life. He'd thought the little improvement he had seen in her before the fire hadn't been real, and he'd doubted everything that he had believed. He sent a silent apology to his wife. One day, once Sophia was safely well away from Lord Burwell's influence and reach, settled happily somewhere, he would break his word and expose what his father had done. It would be a difficult task, but he owed it to Anne to show the world who had been responsible for her death. 'Why did you do it?'

Even as the question left his lips he worked out the answer for himself. In the months before the fire, he had just started to make a decent profit from the rooms he rented out. He had been considering expanding his business, purchasing another property to renovate and rent out, as he had the first two. It would mean his independence from his father could be guaranteed, as little by little his income grew.

'You hated that I had made my way in the world despite you refusing to support me. You wanted me penniless, forced to return to you and back within your web of influence,' he answered for his father, shaking his head.

After the fire he had sold the second of his properties, the undamaged one, to allow him to cover his immediate expenses and to compensate the people who had lost everything alongside him. If the Shrewsburys had not come and swept him up, showing him such kindness, he would have had to go begging back to his father straight away.

Lord Burwell set his lips hard and jabbed a finger in Henry's direction.

'Cross me at your peril, boy. I can make your life very difficult.'

Henry shook his head and took Sophia by the arm. 'Leave us alone. Do not try to contact us, do not even think about contacting the authorities. I will fight you every step of the way, and you have far much more to lose.'

Without waiting for his father's answer, he turned and stalked out the door, ushering Sophia along in front of him.

Outside he felt a surge of elation followed by a deep feeling of dread. He was under no illusion that his father would leave them alone. The old man was stunned at the realisation that his past exploits were known, but when he had time to consider his options, Henry knew his father would lash out in retaliation. The key was to not be around when he did.

'Come quickly,' he said as they walked down the street. He was thankful when they rounded the corner to see the Shrewsbury carriage waiting for them, his friend's anxious face peering out. Quickly he helped Sophia up inside, ignoring Shrewsbury's puzzled look.

'I'll explain it to you later, right now we need to move.'

He loved his friend a little bit more as Shrewsbury rallied and thumped on the roof, calling out the window for the driver to take them home.

Chapter Twenty

Sarah smiled at the eldest of her charges, a fourteen-year-old girl who had impeccable manners, but underneath it all a wicked sense of humour. It had been difficult leaving London, and she wondered if her heart would ever recover, but being out here in the middle of the beautiful Kent countryside with the Huntley family was as soothing a place to rest and recuperate as she could hope for.

Her duties were not arduous. There were three Huntley children: Elizabeth, the oldest at fourteen, Georgina who was ten and little Annabelle who was only six. All three girls were keen musicians, and it was a pleasure to teach them. What was more, she did not have to wrangle all three at a time. The mornings were spent with the girls alternating through their other lessons and spending time with Sarah at the piano. In the afternoons they would come together to sing as Sarah took them through their scales, teaching them techniques to make their voices stronger and more harmonious.

She had been warned about the perils of living and working in someone else's home, but her experience so far with the Huntley family was relatively painless. Her room was spacious and decently furnished at the top of the house, close to the nursery.

It had lovely views out over the parkland, and every morning Sarah rose early and watched the deer frolic on the lawn in the early morning light.

She took her meals with Miss Wilson, the governess, and Mrs Renley, the housekeeper, and both were kind and friendly people. All in all, she could not ask for a better position. Every day she reminded herself to be thankful for what she had.

'That is beautiful, Elizabeth,' she said as her young charge finished the piece. 'Just be a little careful of the timing in the middle section. Don't rush it—this piece is made to be savoured, so linger over every note.' She pointed out the part she was talking about and played it to the young girl. 'Now you try.'

It was perfect the second time, and Sarah heaped praise on her pupil. Elizabeth in particular was talented as well as studious, never shying away from time at the piano.

'Shall we play it again, or would you like to move on to something else?'

'Can I play it again?'

'Of course. I could listen to you play this all day.'

Sarah sat back, allowing Elizabeth to get herself set up and position her fingers on the piano keys. She had only just started when the door burst open and little Annabelle ran into the room.

'There's a carriage coming up the drive and Mama says it belongs to one of the wealthiest men in England,' she squealed in excitement.

Elizabeth stopped playing and stood, immediately crossing to the window with her little sister. It was an idyllic life here in the Kent countryside, but Sarah got the impression the girls were a little starved of company their own age. She did not chastise Elizabeth for getting distracted from her music lesson, as she too wished to see who was visiting.

Sarah frowned as she recognised the gold crest on the side of the smartly painted black carriage. She blushed as she remembered the intimate moment she had shared with Henry inside that very carriage, when they had been unable to keep their hands off one another, despite knowing nothing could happen.

'It's Lord Shrewsbury's carriage,' Sarah murmured.

'You know Lord Shrewsbury?' Mrs Huntley said as she

walked into the room, joining her daughters at the window as the carriage rolled to a stop.

Sarah cleared her throat before speaking, worried her voice might betray her emotion.

'I had the pleasure of making his acquaintance whilst I was in London. He was very kind.'

Mrs Huntley raised an eyebrow but said no more.

'Come away from the window, girls,' she ordered, not wanting to be caught gawping by whoever stepped out. Elizabeth complied but Annabelle lingered, pressing her face against the glass.

Sarah watched, not daring to breathe as the carriage door opened and a young girl stepped out. Immediately she knew who it was—the family resemblance was uncanny, and she could have easily picked out Henry's little sister from a room full of girls of a similar age.

Her heart began beating faster in her chest as Henry hopped down from the carriage, looking up at the house. A beam of sunlight illuminated his face, and for a moment he looked like one of the Greek gods from ancient legend.

She must have made a little strangled noise, for suddenly everyone was looking at her.

'That is Lord Routledge,' Mrs Huntley said, her eyes narrowing ever so slightly. 'You know Lord Routledge, too, Miss Shepherd?'

'He is a recent acquaintance.'

'You are extraordinarily well connected for a music teacher.'

Sarah lowered her eyes and tried to stop her heart from thumping so hard that it exploded out of her chest. There was no good reason for Henry to be visiting the Huntleys. He did not know them, and they clearly were not expecting him.

This past week she had tried not to think of him. She was aware she needed to let her heart heal, but that would be impossible if she kept dwelling on every moment of their relationship.

'He didn't choose you,' she told herself quietly. She didn't harbour any ill will towards him, and in fact she probably respected him more for choosing to rescue his sister. Sarah had

never been in danger, she had a life to go to, a future waiting for her. Sophia was a child—she needed to be put first.

Yet, after all they had been through, Sarah had panicked, feeling as though he was pushing her aside. Never would she be the most important thing in his life. She'd wondered if that was how her mother had felt when her father had announced his intention to terminate their relationship. That sense of loss, but alongside it the feeling of helplessness. She had not liked being without any power. That was why she had left London. She had been desperate to grab control of her own destiny again, rather than waiting—pining—for the man she loved who might never be coming back.

They all remained silent, straining to hear as Lord Routledge was admitted to the drawing room with his sister. The minutes ticked by. No one even pretended to do anything constructive, instead straining to hear the conversation from the room on the other side of the hall.

'Lord Routledge is here,' Mr Huntley said, looking puzzled as he entered the room a few minutes later. 'He has begged my indulgence in giving him a few minutes to speak with Miss Shepherd.'

All eyes turned to Sarah, and she felt her hand begin to shake. Quickly she buried them in the folds of her dress.

'Do you wish to speak to him?' Mrs Huntley asked.

Sarah nodded, rising from her seat. As she entered the drawing room she had the urge to run to him, to throw her arms around his neck and lose herself in his kiss. Of course that was not possible, not after everything that had happened between them, and certainly not with her employer looking on curiously.

'Miss Shepherd,' Lord Routledge said, breaking out into a smile. 'It is very good to see you again.'

'And you, my lord.'

'I do not think you have met my sister while in London, this is Lady Sophia.'

'It is a pleasure to meet you, Lady Sophia.'

The young girl crossed the space between them and gripped Sarah's hand. 'My brother has told me ever so much about you. I know we are going to be firm friends.'

Sarah managed a smile but felt her world tilt and rock. She did not know why Henry was here. She wouldn't put it past him to come and check she was settled in her new position, to assure her everything in London was fine, and to quietly enquire if she'd had her monthly bleed yet. However they had left their relationship, he would not shirk his responsibilities.

'I know it is a little unusual, but Miss Shepherd and I have something of great importance we wish to discuss. Might you spare her for ten minutes? We could take a stroll in the gardens.'

'Of course,' Mr Huntley said amiably.

'Perhaps, Lady Sophia, you would like to join my daughters and I for some refreshment,' Mrs Huntley said, eyeing the pretty young woman. Sophia was the daughter of an Earl, and it was never too early to start cultivating connections in society.

'That sounds wonderful, thank you.'

A few minutes later Sarah and Henry were alone, although careful to keep within view of the house. Sarah walked with her head bowed, unable to believe Henry was here, but struggling to know what to expect from this meeting.

'I hoped to catch you before you left London,' Henry said as they strolled through the rose garden. There were a dozen different varieties laid out in neat beds, all in bloom. Bees buzzed around, darting from flower to flower, and the air was sweet with the scent of flowers.

'I did not linger,' she shrugged, 'there was no reason for me to.'

'A lot happened that night. I am still reeling from it.'

She inclined her head, unable to look at him. Inside she was a horrible mix of anxious and hopeful, although she would never admit the latter to herself.

He told her of the late evening trip to his father's house and how he had taken inspiration from her, climbing in through an open upstairs window. He explained how he had spoken to Sophia and realised he could not leave her there, under the control of their father.

She gasped when he told her of the moment Sophia had revealed what she'd overheard about the fire, gripping his arm.

'Your father arranged to have your wife killed? Henry I am so sorry.'

'I believe he did not know Anne was going to be in the house when it was set alight. His primary aim was to take my home from me, and my source of income. I told you before, he hated that I was not reliant on him for money, and although my income was modest, I was making enough to provide Anne and I with a basic but decent quality of life.' He grimaced and shook his head. 'I have to believe he did not order the man who set the fire to kill Anne on purpose. I do not know if I could bear to be related to such a monster.'

'It is such a tragedy.'

'At the time he was shocked that Sophia knew so much, and it allowed us to escape without too much fuss.'

'Surely he would do anything to keep this quiet.'

'My father does not like to lose. I am sure he is getting his affairs in order to mount an attack, but I have been busy too. I have found the man who my father paid to set the fire. He was wracked with guilt. It did not take much to get him to sign a sworn statement in the presence of a solicitor about what he did, and my father's role in it.'

'If he is arrested, he will hang.'

'I can be very persuasive, and I promised to keep everything anonymised, although I do of course know the man's name.' He pulled a face. 'And as grateful as I am for his sworn statement, the fact is that he did set the fire that killed Anne. As such, I am not overly invested in his fate.'

'I am sorry you have had to deal with all of this.'

'I am taking Sophia away for a while. The more physical distance there is between our father and us, the less he can do to us.'

'That sounds very sensible,' Sarah said, trying to stop the words from sticking in her throat. So that was why he was here. To say goodbye.

'I wanted to apologise, Sarah.'

'Thank you. Your apology is accepted.'

He raised an eyebrow. 'I have not made it yet.'

She waved a dismissive hand. 'I understand, Henry. What

else could you have done? Your sister was in danger, and I am glad you chose to help her. I would not have wanted you to choose differently.'

'That is one of the many reasons that I love you,' he said quietly.

Sarah's eyes snapped up.

'When I was standing in the hall of One Grosvenor Square, facing my father, I realised that over the last two years I have been stumbling, as if I was in a dream. Every decision I had to make I chose the easiest path, because I had no more fight left in me. When you came along, you showed me what I was missing, and what sort of life I could lose if I continued down the route of least resistance. I saw that my father had worn me down and wheedled his way into my life, when I should never have even considered allowing him close. When I was eighteen, I saw how malicious he was, and yet, at the age of thirty-two, I still needed you to remind me that I did not need to bow to his decisions.'

He took her hand in his and Sarah felt her pulse quicken. 'You also showed me that I deserved love. I didn't believe it, but you can be quite persuasive.'

'You do deserve love. You deserve every happiness.'

He shook his head, his eyes searching hers.

'I am sorry I did not handle things better. When my father gave me that impossible choice, after we spent the afternoon together, my head was spinning. I panicked, and I did not consider how it would feel to be abandoned after you had given me everything. Especially with the history of your mother and father. I know it meant it was an even bigger risk for you, that you worried about history repeating itself, and I did not reassure you as I should.'

'Thank you,' Sarah said. 'I admit I was upset, although I could not put into words exactly why. I wanted you to go to your sister, to rescue her...'

'But you also wanted me to choose you.'

'Which was impossible. You couldn't do both.'

'Sometimes we want impossible things.'

'I hold no grudge, Henry. I am just glad you see now that you know you are worthy of love, and that just because you were hurt once it does not mean you will be hurt again.'

He shook his head in wonder. 'How was I so lucky to fall for you? I wronged you, hurt you, and yet here you are, wishing me nothing but good things.'

She gave a little half-smile. 'That is what happens when you love someone. Even when you cannot be together you still want them to be happy.'

Henry felt his heart flip. She loved him. She still loved him. He could see the hurt in her eyes as he talked about the evening a week earlier, when he had been unable to assure her that, no matter what, they would be together.

He had known how important her virtue was to her, how she was afraid of ending up alone and abandoned as her mother had. Yet still he had not held her in his arms and promised her that he would find a way to be together. In that time of need he had disregarded her feelings and once again allowed himself to be sucked into his father's trap.

No more.

Sarah looked well, although there was a definite hint of sadness about her. The Huntleys seemed good people, and he wondered if she would accept him or whether she would choose a simpler life here in Kent.

'I need to ask you something,' he said softly. 'Please consider it before you give your answer.'

She regarded him cautiously, then nodded.

'I know there are so many things I still need to work on. I know my feelings are influenced so much by past events, and sometimes I forget that the man I am now, the life I lead now, is very different to a few years ago.'

'Henry, I...'

He pushed on quickly, not wanting to hear her say no, however gently. He needed her to hear everything he had to say.

'I do not have a lot to offer you materially, but I have a little money. I plan to retire to the seaside for a while, somewhere outside of my father's realm of influence. I thought I might start investing in some property again, renovating a few old buildings so they can be used as lodgings. After a few months of hard work it will give me a modest income, enough to support three if we live frugally.' He glanced down at her belly. 'Or even four.

'I love you, Sarah. I love everything about you, and I know I have not been the easiest person to fall in love with, but I think you love me too.'

She searched his face, uncertainty clouding hers.

'Marry me, Sarah.'

'What about your reservations about marrying a woman of a different class?'

He shrugged. 'I realised you were right, I cannot base all my future decisions on what happened in the past. Just because it did not work with Anne does not mean it will not work with you. You are an entirely different person. Anyway, a penniless Viscount and a successful music teacher are not so different in status. Marry me. I have been a fool, but you have opened my eyes. I love you, Sarah.'

It felt like the wait for her answer was never-ending, but finally she threw her arms around his neck and kissed him.

'Does this mean you say yes?'

'Yes. Yes, a thousand times. I do not know how this has happened, but I think I fell in love with you on that first evening we met in Lord Shrewsbury's library. You were so patient and kind, and you were the first person who truly listened to what I had to say.' She shook her head. 'Although, back then, I never thought we would end up here.'

'You do not mind marrying a destitute Viscount with a sister to care for?'

'It will just make it all the more interesting,' Sarah said.

He picked her up and spun her round, unable to quite believe she had said yes. He'd always known Sarah was reasonable and didn't hold a grudge, but the hurt he had seen in her eyes—that evening after his father instructed him to marry the young Lady Isabelle—had been deep and all encompassing. He was grateful she could move past it, and see he cared for her with all his heart.

'I will show you how much you mean to me each and every day,' he murmured as he set her on the ground.

Then, amongst the sweet-smelling roses, he kissed the woman he was going to spend the rest of his life with.

Epilogue

February was always a grim month at the seaside. The weather was cold and grey and the hours of daylight limited. No visitors came to stroll along the promenade, or stay in the little hotels and lodging houses that peppered the seafront. Yet Sarah could not feel happier as she looked out of the top floor window. They had a view of the beach and the sea beyond. Today the waves were crashing against the edge of the promenade, threatening to spill over, and it gave everything a dramatic look.

She rested a hand on her growing belly. She was seven months pregnant and getting uncomfortable. Henry had suggested she stop the pupils coming for their piano lessons soon, but she enjoyed it too much and did not want to get bored as she neared the time of birth. Not that there was much chance of that. With Sophia to look after, and the renovations of the rooms downstairs continuing, often both she and Henry would collapse into bed at the end of the day, absolutely exhausted.

It was a good exhaustion though, the sort of exhaustion that comes from being busy doing the things that bring you pleasure.

The door to their set of rooms opened and Henry walked in, his face set into a frown.

'I have a letter,' he said, coming over to kiss her. His passion for her had not dimmed, even as she grew bigger with the pregnancy, and she had not lost her desire for her handsome husband. 'In fact, I have two. One looks to be from your sister.'

'And the other?'

'The update from Shrewsbury I have been waiting for.'

'Let us read that one first.'

Henry moved a chair so they were sitting side by side, and carefully he opened the seal. He was right, it was written in Lord Shrewsbury's neat handwriting and was two pages long. Carefully they read it, sitting back in amazement as they finished.

'You've done it,' Sarah said, reaching out and taking her husband's hand. 'You've actually done it.'

Ever since arriving in St Leonards just days after their wedding, Henry had been working tirelessly on two projects. The first was to turn this dilapidated old house he had bought into something much more profitable. He'd started with the upstairs rooms, working day and night until they had a small but comfortable living space. Sophia had her own bedroom and so did they, alongside a sitting room and a kitchen. It wasn't much, but it was theirs, and Sarah loved it more than anywhere else she had ever stayed. Now Henry was working on fixing the three levels below them, planning on turning them into lodgings they could rent out. The ground floor had been completed a few weeks earlier and they had their first tenants, bringing in some much-needed money.

His second project had been to work on safeguarding Sophia's future. He had enlisted the help of his loyal friend, Lord Shrewsbury, and between them they had gathered the evidence that showed Lord Burwell had hired a man to set fire to Henry's house, ultimately killing the first Lady Routledge. Lord Burwell's social status gave him a level of protection that was not afforded to normal men, and all along they had been aware it would be nigh on impossible to get him tried in a court of law. Instead, Henry and Shrewsbury had raised such a fuss that Parliament had discussed the issue once they reconvened in the autumn. There was support on both sides, and the argument had raged backwards and forwards, until now.

'I can't believe it,' Henry said, leaning over to kiss her.

'Nor can I. I did not think they would truly do anything. I thought the protection would be from the world knowing the story, preventing him from doing anything to you or Sophia again.'

'So did I.'

Lord Shrewsbury had written to say Parliament had tired of the ongoing conflict and had reprimanded Lord Burwell for bringing the House of Lords into ill repute. They suggested he return to his ancestral seat in Yorkshire and remain there indefinitely.

Of course it wasn't an order. He could do what he liked, but a suggestion from Parliament was difficult to ignore.

'You did it, my love,' Sarah said, leaning in to kiss him again. 'You have finally broken free from him completely.'

'It is such a relief. Although I do not think I will feel totally at ease until either the old man is dead or Sophia is married off to some kind young man.'

'Of course not, but this is a victory. I doubt he will dare to hurt us now.'

Sarah stood and stretched her back, picking up the second letter. It was from her sister, the second letter this month. Selina had been a faithful correspondent these last six months. Each letter detailed her life in London. She was still not treated as part of the family, and Sarah thought she never would be, but she seemed happy enough.

She opened the seal and went to sit back down, but Henry caught her round the waist and pulled her onto his lap. As she read he kissed and nuzzled her neck, and a few times she had to reread a sentence as her mind was elsewhere.

'Does she say anything of interest?' Henry asked as Sarah folded the letter back up neatly.

'Sir William, Lady Kingsley and their daughter Catherine are planning a trip to Scotland, and Selina has been invited.'

'Perhaps they are starting to accept her.'

'Perhaps,' Sarah said, not sure she believed it. Still, her sister seemed happy in her letters. She was enjoying life in London, experiencing something different from a quiet, seaside town, and at the moment she seemed willing to put up with their horrible father and his family to do so.

'Now I suggest we make the most of this empty house. Sophia will be home in half an hour from her lessons, and I want to make the most of my time with my wife.'

She giggled as he stood, grunting as he lifted her from a sitting position.

'That is not the noise you want your husband to make when he lifts you.'

He raised an eyebrow and then pretended to stagger all the way to the bedroom.

'You are doing nothing for my self-esteem,' she laughed.

'Nonsense,' he said. 'You are the most beautiful pregnant woman I have ever seen.'

'Only you think that.'

'Only I have to think that,' he said, lowering her gently onto the bed.

'That is very true.'

'Now let me show you how beautiful I think you are.'

He kissed her, tangling his hands in her hair, and Sarah felt a wonderful wave of desire and contentment wash over her. Never had she thought her life would look like this. Henry pulled her back to the present as his lips trailed across the angle of her jaw, settling on the little spot below her earlobe that made her shiver with pleasure.

'I love you, Lady Routledge.'

'And I love you.'

As the waves crashed outside the window, Sarah forgot about everything else and lost herself in her husband's touch.

* * * * *

When Cinderella Met The Duke

Sophia Williams

MILLS & BOON

Sophia Williams lives in London with her family. She has loved reading Regency romances for as long as she can remember and is delighted now to be writing them for Harlequin. When she isn't chasing her children around or writing (or pretending to write but actually googling for hero inspiration and pictures of gorgeous Regency dresses), she enjoys reading, tennis and wine.

Books by Sophia Williams

Harlequin Historical

How the Duke Met His Match
The Secret She Kept from the Earl

Look out for more books from Sophia Williams coming soon.

Visit the Author Profile page
at millsandboon.com.au.

Author Note

I hope you enjoy reading *When Cinderella Met the Duke* as much as I enjoyed writing it!

I wanted to write a Cinderella-themed story, but with a bit of a twist.

James, our hero, needs to get married to produce an heir, but—scarred by bereavement—does not want to fall in love. But then he meets Anna at a ball and finds himself smitten at first sight... Only for her to run away at midnight, and for him then to discover that she is not who he thought she was. I loved exploring his internal conflict as his love for Anna grew.

In Anna, I wanted to write a heroine for the ages, a strong woman with a determination to make her own way within the constraints of the era she lives in. Offered the opportunity by her godmother to become her (actually quite unnecessary) companion, she turns it down and takes up a post as a governess to earn her living. Anna's life history has taught her not to trust men, specifically their loyalty, and I very much enjoyed following her path to finding the courage to allow herself to fall in love with James and marry him.

I also of course enjoyed, as always, the gorgeous Regency London setting—and researching all the different ice cream flavors available then... I'm quite tempted by artichoke and Parmesan!

Thank you so much for reading!

To William

Chapter One

Miss Anna Blake

London,
November 1817

'I am really not certain that this is a good idea,' Miss Anna Blake said, surveying herself in the looking glass in front of her. She *wanted* it to be a good idea, because she didn't know whether she'd ever again have the opportunity to wear a dress as wonderful as this or be able to go to another Society ball, but...

'Nonsense. You deserve to have one last evening of enjoyment.' Anna's godmother, Lady Derwent, tweaked the gauze overdress of Anna's ball gown into place and gave the tiniest of ladylike sniffs before wiping very delicately under her eyes with her beringed fingers. 'I declare, you look like something out of a fairy tale, my dear: so beautiful. Your mother would have been so proud.'

'Thank you, but...' Anna began again. She was quite sure that her mother would *not* have recommended quite such an audacious deception. She had practised a deception of her own, when she'd eloped with Anna's father, and had then had to spend

Anna's entire childhood attempting—with little success—to repair the damage done by the elopement. She had therefore been particularly desirous of Anna's living as respectably as possible. The plan for this evening was *not* respectable.

'You're being far too cautious,' Anna's best friend, Lady Maria Swanley, told her. 'If anyone should ever find out—which they won't—it will be *I* whom they accuse of wrongdoing.'

'Hmm,' said Anna.

Nearly ten years of close friendship with Lady Maria, since they had entered Bath's strictest seminary together, had taught her that Maria's plots gave rise to much enjoyment but usually ended badly, for Anna, at least.

As the daughter of a rich earl, Lady Maria was usually protected from reprimand. Anna, by contrast, was the daughter of a groom. She was also the granddaughter of an earl, and sponsored by Lady Derwent, one of Society's most redoubtable matrons and a great friend of her late mother's, but in the eyes of Miss Courthope, the seminary headmistress, she was her father's daughter and someone who could be punished much more thoroughly than could Maria, so whenever Anna had engaged in any mischief—usually with Maria—she had afterwards felt the full force of Miss Courthope's ire.

That was one thing, and Anna had considered Miss Courthope's punishments a small price to pay for how much she'd enjoyed misbehaving, but hoodwinking most of the *ton* was another. Surely that could give rise to any number of consequences considerably greater than having to write out one's catechism three times or pen a letter of apology to the dance master.

'What if Lady Puntney finds out? What if I oversleep tomorrow?' Anna was starting work as a governess for the Puntney family in the morning. 'And what if your parents find out?' *How* had she allowed herself to be talked into this? Well, she knew how: both Lady Maria and Lady Derwent could be extremely persuasive and, if she was honest, Anna had been very happy to allow herself to be persuaded, and it was only now that the deception was almost under way that she was beginning to acknowledge her doubts.

'If my parents find out, it is likely that they will also have found out about my engagement to my darling Clarence, and they will be interested only in that,' Maria said.

Anna nodded; that much was true. Lady Maria's beloved Clarence was a curate of very uncertain means, and her parents had their sights set on the Duke of Amscott, no less, as their only daughter's future husband.

Anna was not convinced that her friend was making a sensible choice; Clarence might seem perfect now to Maria, but what if things became difficult in due course? He was of course a man of the cloth, so would—one would hope—hold himself to higher standards than did other men, but if he was anything like Anna's father and grandfather, his love would not endure in the face of life's obstacles.

When Anna's mother had fallen in love at the age of eighteen with one of her father's grooms, and then become with child and eloped with him, her father—Anna's grandfather—had disowned her and refused ever to see her again. He had died a few years later. And after the money raised from the sale of Anna's mother's jewels ran out, Anna's father had left to make a new life for himself in America, with no apparent further thought for his wife and daughter. When Anna had lost her mother, she had written to her father, and had received his—very short and not particularly heartfelt—reply over six months later. She knew that he had written it himself—her mother had taught him to read and write in the early days of their marriage and she recognised his handwriting—so had to assume that it did express his own sentiments. He had not suggested that she join him in Canada or that he attempt to support her in any way whatsoever.

Anna had been rescued from penury by the women in her life—her mother's maid and then Lady Derwent—and she did not believe that men were to be relied upon. Lady Derwent had confirmed this belief; she had told Anna on more than one occasion that she was *extremely* happy to be a widow.

'And in the meantime,' Maria interrupted her thoughts, 'I *cannot* go to the ball.'

The Dowager Duchess of Amscott was holding the first

grand ball of the Season this evening, and, according to Lady Derwent, everyone expected the duke to be there, searching for a wife. Lady Maria's birth, beauty and large dowry made her an obvious candidate for the position. When her parents had been called away and she had been entrusted to Lady Derwent to chaperone her this evening, Maria had suggested, most persuasively, as was her wont, that Anna attend in her place.

She had waxed lyrical about the dress that Anna would wear, the people she would see, the dancing, the food, the enjoyment of participating in such an excellent but entirely harmless deception. Lady Derwent had immediately echoed her suggestions, and Anna had found herself agreeing most thoroughly with everything they said. Now, though…

'Lady Puntney will not find out,' Lady Derwent stated, with great certainty. 'Dressed as you are now, you look like one of Shakespeare's fairy queens. Lord Byron himself would write quite lyrically about you, I'm sure. When attired in the *garments*—' she scrunched her face disapprovingly '—you will wear as governess, you will still look beautiful, of course, but you will look quite different. I do not believe that anyone will make the connection. And we will leave at midnight so that you will not be too tired on the morrow.'

'The timing is quite serendipitous,' Maria mused. 'Had this ball not been my first, had I not been incarcerated in the country in mourning for so many years so that I know no one in London—' Maria's family had suffered a series of bereavements '—and had my parents not been forced to leave town and entrust me to the care of dear Lady Derwent—' Lady Maria's grandmother was ill and her mother had left post-haste, accompanied by her husband, to visit her in her hour of need '—this would not have been possible. And by the time my parents return, Clarence and I shall be formally affianced, and no one will make me attend any more balls as a rich-husband-seeking young lady. So it will all be perfect.'

She smiled at Anna.

'You look beautiful. That dress becomes you wonderfully. Perhaps you will find a beau of your own this evening, and marry rather than take up your position.'

Anna rolled her eyes at her friend. 'I shall be very happy as a governess.' She wasn't *entirely* convinced that that was true, but it would be better than relying on a man to protect her, only to be abandoned when he lost interest in her; and she was certainly very lucky to have obtained her position with the Puntneys.

'Harumph.' Lady Derwent did not approve of Anna's desire to be independent; she had asked her more than once to live with her as a companion, despite her obvious lack of need for one. 'Let us go. You will not wish to miss any part of the ball, Anna.'

'What if you change your mind in future, Maria?' Anna worried. 'How will you take your place in Society after I have attended this ball as you?'

'No one would ever dare to question me,' Lady Derwent said. 'Should you in the future change your mind, Maria, and decide that you do not after all wish to marry an impecunious curate with few prospects, and that you wish to take your place at balls as yourself, I shall inform anyone who questions me that their eyesight is perhaps failing them and that the Lady Maria they met at the Amscott ball was of course you, and no one will contradict me.'

Certainly, very few people, including Anna, chose to disagree very often with Lady Derwent.

Anna turned to look again at her image in the glass. She *loved* this dress. It would be such a shame not to show it off at the ball. She *loved* parties—the small number that she had been to. She *loved* dancing. And everyone who was anyone amongst London's glittering *haut ton* would be there, and she would *love* to see them all, and witness and take part in such an event.

She straightened her shoulders and beamed at the reflection of her two companions before turning back round.

'You are both right,' she said. She was going to take this wonderful opportunity and enjoy it to the full before starting her new, possibly quite dull life on the morrow.

'It will be so diverting to know that you are practising such a masquerade,' Maria said. 'A huge secret that no one else knows. And you will enjoy the dancing very much, I am sure.'

'Thank you, Maria,' Anna said.

'No, no.' Maria hugged her. '*I* must thank *you*. Just make sure you enjoy yourself.'

'I just want to check one final time that you are absolutely certain?' Anna asked again.

'We are certain.' Lady Derwent was already standing and moving towards the door. 'Nothing can possibly go wrong.'

Chapter Two

James, Duke of Amscott

'And that is all for now,' concluded the Dowager Duchess of Amscott, as she folded into neat squares the piece of paper upon which she had scribed her list of possible candidates for the hand of her son, James, Duke of Amscott, before leaving her escritoire to join him on the sofa opposite.

James raised an eyebrow. 'Are you intending to share the contents of your list with me?'

'Maybe. Maybe not.' She waved the piece of paper under his nose before whisking it away and tucking it into her reticule.

James laughed. The idea of getting married was not at all funny, but his mother could nearly always raise a smile from him. Which was impressive, given all that she had gone through in recent years, with the death first of her husband and then of James's two older brothers.

'On a serious note,' his mother said, 'I will of course discuss the list with you, but I feel that it might be best for you first to meet the various young ladies without any preconceptions. You are fortunate in having no need to marry for money and being able therefore to choose any young lady—of good birth, of course—for love.'

James looked down at his knees for a moment, to hide his eyes from her as a chill ran over him.

He did not want to marry for love.

He did not wish to love someone so deeply that he would be broken if anything happened to her, as his mother had been at the loss of her husband and two oldest sons, and as he and his sisters had also been.

Also, and even more importantly, he did not wish someone to love *him* deeply, because he wouldn't wish anyone else to be devastated if he died, and he veered between terror and resignation at the thought that it seemed extremely likely that he would die young; the doctors were not sure what had caused the early deaths of his father and brothers but their symptoms had all been similar, and it did not seem unlikely that their illnesses had been due to a family trait. It would be bad enough thinking of the pain that would cause his mother and sisters, but for him to choose to marry someone who loved him deeply only for the pain of loss to be inflicted on her too would be awful.

'James?'

'Yes, Mama. What an…excellent plan.' He could not tell her how he felt; he could not add to her sadness, especially when she was doing so well herself at pretending to be happy. He must maintain his own stiff upper lip, as she did.

And his emotions were confused. Because he *needed* to produce an heir. His current heir was a distant cousin residing in Canada, and James had no way of knowing whether the man would—in the event of James's death—look after James's mother and younger sisters in the way that he would wish. It would be infinitely preferable for a son of James's—infant or adult—to become the new duke.

And the existence of an heir—his son—would of course lessen his family's grief on James's death, in addition to securing their future. His wife would have a child or children to love, and his mother had already proved herself to be a most doting grandmother to his oldest sister's two young daughters.

He raised his eyes to his mother's and smiled as sincerely as he could.

'That is settled then.' She rose from the sofa. 'You will meet as many ladies as possible this evening, and should you develop a preference, you may undertake to improve your acquaintance of the young lady in question. If you do not have a preference, we will revert to my list.'

James rose too. 'Excellent.' *God.*

'We must hasten. The first of our guests will arrive soon.' She held her arm out imperiously.

They were hosting the first big ball of this year's London Season, and James's mother believed that the whole of Society would be scrabbling to attend. She was almost certainly right: wealthy dukes were always popular, irrespective of their personal attributes. They were even more popular when they were nearing thirty and unmarried.

He laughed at his mother's haughty gesture, and took her arm, wondering as he did so what chance there was that he would meet someone this evening with whom he could fall in love, should he allow himself to do so—he would not—or whether he would be happy to marry someone from the list.

He did need to marry.

And while he did not desire a love match, he did wish to choose his own bride rather than have one foisted upon him by his mother. He would like someone whose conversation he enjoyed, for example, although he probably wouldn't choose to live permanently with anyone quite as opinionated as his mother and sisters were...

As they entered the ballroom, his mother's voice pierced his thoughts. 'Amscott. I was telling you about my decorations.' She hadn't allowed him to see the themed room until now, eager, she said, to spring a surprise on him—or perhaps just to avert the strong possibility of his cavilling at her evident extraordinarily high expenditure. He had in fact been happy to indulge her, delighted to see her take an interest in something again; she had struggled with listlessness in the aftermath of their bereavements.

'I beg your pardon, Mama. I was lost in admiration of your

design of the room.' It was certainly remarkable—and must indeed have cost a small fortune. The ballroom of Amscott House had been transformed into an exotic fruit orchard. There were so many orange and lemon trees—surely more than in the glasshouses of the rest of England combined—that the room had a definite citrusy scent. And were those...pineapple trees?

'I wished to make a splash, and I believe we shall do so. In addition, our ball will *smell* nicer than everyone else's.' His mother's air of complacence made him laugh again. 'So many hot bodies in the same room can often be quite unbearable.'

'Impressive forethought.'

'I must confess that I did not realise how very much scent the trees would give off,' his mother confided, 'but I am quite delighted now at how I shall be setting both a visual design *and* an olfactory trend.'

The first guests were announced before they had the opportunity to engage in further conversation, and James became fully occupied in greeting dandified men, bejewelled matrons, their eager-to-please debutante charges and the occasional actual friend of his.

'Lady Derwent and Lady Maria Swanley,' a footman announced, as a tall woman, her air almost as imperious as that of James's mother, swept into the room with a smaller and younger lady, who was dressed in a silvery, sparkly dress.

'Good evening.' Lady Derwent curtsied the tiniest amount in James's mother's direction, her demeanour as though she was conferring an enormous favour on the duchess, who responded with the smallest of smiles. James made a mental note to ask his mother on the morrow what argument she and Lady Derwent held; there was clearly some animosity between the two women, and his mother's stories were always amusing. 'Lady Maria is under my charge this evening; dear Lady Swanley has been called to Viscountess Massey's sickbed.'

'I am so sorry to hear that your grandmother is ill,' James's mother told Lady Maria.

'Thank you; we hope very much that she will make a full and speedy recovery.' Lady Maria's voice was musical, clear and warm in tone, so lovely to listen to that James instinctively looked more closely in her direction.

Her hair was a light brown, thick and glossy, her eyes green, her skin clear and her features regular, and her dress—cut low at the bosom and high at the waist—became her very well. She was certainly attractive, but, when his thoughts wandered vaguely to whether she would be on his mother's marriage candidate list, he decided that it was irrelevant; she was probably a very pleasant lady, but there were any number of pleasant, attractive young ladies here, and he could think of no reason that he would choose this lady over any other.

Indeed, how *would* he choose a bride given that his choice would not be directed by his falling in love? Perhaps he should ask his oldest two sisters which young ladies they got on with best.

'My son, the Duke of Amscott,' James's mother said, and Lady Maria turned in his direction with a smile.

And, good Lord, the smile was extraordinary. It displayed perfect, even teeth, it was wide, it was infectious, it showed one delightful dimple just to the left of her mouth, it was *beautiful*. James felt it through his entire body, almost uncomfortably so.

'Delighted to meet you.' His own mouth was broadening into a wide smile in response to Lady Maria's, almost of its own volition.

Lady Maria curtseyed and held out two fingers, smiling now as though she was almost on the brink of laughter, her eyes dancing. James had no idea what she was finding quite so funny, but he knew that he wanted to find out. He had the strangest feeling, in fact, that he wanted to find out everything about her, which was a ridiculous sensation to have, given that the entire sum of knowledge he had about her was that she was a small, pleasant-looking woman with a musical voice and the most beguiling smile and was accompanied by Lady Derwent.

He leaned forward a little and spoke into her ear, just for her, comfortable in the knowledge that the hubbub of voices around them would make it very difficult for anyone else to hear.

'Do you have a joke that you wish to share?' He accompanied his words with a smile, to ensure that Lady Maria would know that he was funning rather than reprimanding her in any way. He would not normally speak to a stranger, a debutante, in such a manner, but then debutantes did not usually look as though they held a big and amusing secret. And he couldn't remember the last time—if ever—that he'd had such a strong sense that he *would* get to know a particular person very well.

'No, Your Grace.' Her smile was no less mirthful than before as she continued, 'I am perhaps just overwhelmed by the occasion.' Her words did not ring true; she did not seem in the slightest bit overwhelmed.

She looked around the room before returning her regard to his. 'I adore these plants. They are quite remarkable. I have never seen a lemon or orange tree outside the covers of a book.'

'Remarkable indeed,' James agreed. 'I have it on the highest authority that the scent as well as the décor will make this one of the most successful balls of the Season.'

'I think your authority is right,' Lady Maria said very gravely. 'Every ball is judged by its scent. And it is particularly clever to use trees that will, I presume, no longer be bearing fruit as we enter the winter, so that no other host will be able to replicate this.'

'I had not thought of that. The design is my mother's; you and she are obviously both more astute than I.'

'Thank you; I am of course regularly complimented on my ballroom scent knowledge.'

She twinkled up at him as she spoke, and James laughed.

And then he found himself saying, 'May I have the pleasure of taking the first dance with you?'

As he finished the question, he realised the import of his words: asking a young lady whom he had never previously met, and who was presumably at her first ball, for the first dance could be taken as a mark of quite particular regard. Certainly, if he did not then wish to further their acquaintance, he would have to navigate things very carefully: on the one hand, he would have to ensure on his own account that he did not appear to single her out for any other special attention; but he would also, for her sake, have to make sure that he did not appear to slight her.

Somehow, though, he didn't mind; he again had the strangest sensation that he *had* to get to know Lady Maria better.

'I'm sure Lady Maria would be delighted.' Lady Derwent had clearly overheard his words and, as any good chaperone ought to do when a wealthy unmarried duke asked her charge to dance, was doing her best to ensure that his request was granted. In fact, if he wasn't mistaken, she had just given Lady Maria a small but quite forceful nudge.

To James's admiration, Lady Maria didn't acknowledge the nudge at all, not even glancing in Lady Derwent's direction before saying, 'I would indeed be delighted.'

'Amscott.' His mother's tone was sharp; she had clearly overheard his question and was less happy about it than Lady Derwent had been. 'You will remember my dear friend Countess Montague and her daughter Lady Helena Montague.'

As the introductions continued, James found his gaze following Lady Maria until she was swallowed up by the hordes of people swirling around her. Once he'd lost sight of her, he couldn't find her again, however hard he tried. And, he realised a few minutes later, when his mother remarked acerbically on yet another lapse in his attention, he was trying very hard to see her.

It would have been easier had she been less diminutive in stature, of course.

James had hitherto always thought he was more attracted to taller ladies, but he now realised that he'd been quite wrong.

Good God. At the age of twenty-nine years old, he was behaving like an infatuated moonling in his first Season. One beautiful smile had turned his mind.

He couldn't even remember what he'd been thinking about women and marriage only an hour ago. He was certain that he hadn't wanted to find any woman this attractive, but he wasn't quite sure why. Attraction and love were not the same thing, after all.

'Amscott.' His mother's sharpness had reached the pitch where it could cut a steak; he should concentrate harder on these introductions. She was a devoted mother and a generous-spirited woman, but she did not appreciate inattention.

* * *

Eventually, the introductions were completed and it was time for the first dance.

As he made his way across the room to where Lady Maria was standing with Lady Derwent, James was conscious of a genuine increase in his heart rate, which had him almost physically shaking his head at himself. After all, he didn't even know now whether he'd been imagining how attractive he'd found Lady Maria; perhaps when he saw her again he'd realise that he'd been quite mistaken.

And then, over other people's heads, he did catch sight of her. She was standing with some other debutantes, laughing at something another young lady had just said. Lady Maria then said something in her turn, and the whole little group joined in with the laughter—full, shoulder-shaking laughter, not just polite Society titters. He couldn't help smiling just watching them and realised that he would very much like to know what the joke was. And when he saw Lady Maria beam at the other ladies, he knew that he had not been mistaken in the slightest; she was remarkably attractive.

Perhaps half a minute later, he was standing in front of Lady Maria and Lady Derwent, with his heels snapped together, bowing his head to both ladies.

Lady Derwent was, unsurprisingly, wreathed in smiles. James didn't flatter himself that he personally was a hugely attractive catch on the marriage mart; that would presumably depend on a lady's particular taste. He did, though, believe that an unmarried duke in possession of a good fortune must always be attractive to the vast majority of young ladies and their chaperones, and it appeared that Lady Derwent was no exception.

Lady Maria was also smiling, but not quite so widely as when they'd met or when she'd been laughing with the other young ladies. He hoped she wasn't regretting agreeing to this dance. Perhaps she was one of those rare debutantes who had no wish to marry a duke.

Good God. In the past few minutes he must have thought about marriage at least five times. It was as though he had, like many men before him, lost his head to one pretty face. And good

God again, he felt as though he didn't care and indeed would be more than happy to follow his instincts and court the young lady most assiduously.

As Lady Maria placed her fingertips lightly on his arm, he knew that he had to be imagining it, but it was as though this moment of their first touch was extremely significant, as though the contact was branding him in some way; he had the strangest sense that it would be the first of many such touches. Extraordinary; he was never this fanciful.

'You are recently arrived in London, I understand?' he asked her as they wove through the crowds of guests towards the dance floor.

'Yes,' she confirmed. 'I was previously in the country. I very much like London and over the past week or two have enjoyed prevailing upon my godmother to show me any number of places that I believe interested me a good deal more than they interested her.'

James laughed and then queried, 'You have been spending time with your godmother?'

'Yes. I… Yes, Lady Derwent, I mean. My mother was called away some time ago to be with my grandmother.'

'Oh, I see. I had understood your mother to have left town very recently.'

'I… No. Not particularly recently. Less recently than you might think. Do you reside in London all year round, Your Grace?'

Bizarrely, given that they really did not know each other, *Your Grace* sounded far too formal on Lady Maria's lips.

Suppressing a desire to ask her to call him James, and wishing that he could call her a simple Maria, he said, 'I have only recently inherited the dukedom. I imagine that I will spend the Season in London and the remainder of the year in the country.' He had the most insane urge to tell her that he was really quite flexible and, if his soon-to-be—he hoped—wife wished to spend all her time in London or all her time in the country, he would be quite amenable to either, as long as he could be at her side. He really did seem to have run quite mad. He didn't know Lady Maria. He didn't even know…well, anything at all about her.

And he did *not* wish to marry for love. Did he? No, he did not. *This* was clearly not love. He just had a very strong sense that she would be an excellent life companion, that was all.

He opened his mouth to ask any one of the many thousands of questions to which he'd like to have the answers—such as *Where would you like to live? How old are you?* and, quite possibly, *Would you like to marry me?*—just as she said, 'I'm so sorry to hear that. There can never be a good reason to inherit something.'

'No,' James agreed. 'My brother's death came as a devastating shock to all of us, but especially of course to my mother.' Good God. He never spoke about this, and here he was confiding in a complete stranger. Before he knew anything about her. Truly, something very odd had happened to him.

'I'm so deeply sorry. I can empathise. We have also suffered bereavement in my family. Like most families, I suppose.' Lady Maria paused and then, as though consciously changing the subject, looked around and said, 'I am enjoying this ball enormously.'

James smiled, grateful that she'd lightened the moment. 'So am I. I presume that this is your first?' He was clearly extraordinarily lucky to have met her immediately on her coming out. He was surprised though, now he thought about it: she looked a little older than he would have expected a debutante to be. In the most delightful way. On reflection, he would prefer his wife to be a little older than the youngest of debutantes. That way, their companionship, friendship—certainly not love—would be more balanced.

'Yes. I…' There was that hesitation again. Why did she seem to be choosing her words carefully? Did she have something to hide or was she just nervous at her first ball? He had so many questions about her; he *needed* to get to know her better. 'We were in mourning for a long period, which is why I haven't made my come-out until now.' Oh; perhaps the subject matter would explain her hesitation.

'Of course. I'm sorry.' He wanted to ask whom it was they had been mourning but didn't wish to upset her.

Neither of them had the opportunity to say any more for the time being. The band had struck up and all involved in the first dance—a quadrille—were taking their places.

'I must apologise,' Lady Maria told him as they came together at the beginning of the dance. 'It is some time since I danced, and I might have forgotten some of the steps.'

'You look remarkably proficient to me,' James told her, wishing very much that this was a waltz so that he might stand close to Lady Maria and talk to her for the duration of the dance. 'It is I who must apologise in advance; there is every possibility that I will tread on your toes.'

Lady Maria shook her head. 'I am not exaggerating when I say that I will be forced to count my steps or I risk causing the entire ensemble to fail. Look.' And she began to mouth numbers, all the while looking straight ahead and smiling serenely, her eyes dancing.

James choked back laughter as they came together and then drew apart, before Lady Maria moved round gracefully, throwing a final 'one and two' at him over her shoulder as he went. James didn't know what Lady Derwent would say if she could hear her charge now, but he was sure that his mother would disapprove; she was a stickler for only the most proper of behaviour in public. James, by contrast, he now realised, had been waiting all his life for a lady who laughed irreverently through her first formal dance.

The nice thing about their dancing a quadrille was that he was able to give full attention to the other ladies he crossed briefly while having ample opportunity to observe Lady Maria's very much in-time and particularly graceful dancing.

She was, he could see, perfectly polite to the other gentlemen she encountered as they all moved around, but perhaps, he fancied—hoped—not quite so sparkling as she had been when talking to him.

Every so often, when he was glancing in her direction, she would look over at him too, and their eyes would catch. James couldn't remember a time when he had felt a greater sense of anticipation and enjoyment of the moments in a set when he would come together with his original partner.

When the dance finished, James said with great reluctance, 'I must escort you back to Lady Derwent.'

'Oh, thank you, but I am taken for the second dance.'

'Oh, yes, I should have assumed that you would be.' He should *not* be feeling mildly—strongly—irritated at the thought of someone else wishing to dance with her. He himself, after all, was about to dance with a different lady. And he barely knew Lady Maria.

'You should indeed have done; once it becomes known that the Duke of Amscott wishes to dance the opening dance with one, one becomes extremely popular with other young men.'

'I am certain that it is you with whom they wish to dance, and not just my partner.' James was quite sure that it wasn't just the social cachet of dancing with him that had attracted others; all she had to do was smile and surely she would have the world at her feet.

Lady Maria smiled at him. He *loved* her smile. 'It is very kind of you to say so.'

He returned the smile and then said, because he couldn't help it, 'May I have the pleasure of dancing the waltz with you later?'

'I do have one dance left on my card,' she said, 'and I believe that it is a waltz,' and there was that dimple again.

Dancing twice with a lady at a ball was tantamount to stating a very serious intention towards her, especially when that ball was your own. James wondered very briefly what his mother and indeed the whole of the rest of the *ton* would think about the fact that he was making a statement of this magnitude at this very first ball of the Season. And then he realised that he did not care in the slightest. All he cared about, it seemed, was getting to know Lady Maria better.

'And perhaps I might take you into supper?' he suggested.

'That would be delightful,' she said, bestowing yet another stunning smile on him before being whisked away by a far-too-eager—in James's eyes—young viscount.

* * *

If his dance with Lady Maria had fairly flown by, the remainder of the dances until supper passed very slowly, other than when he was briefly partnered with Lady Maria during the movements within sets.

Each time that that happened, he felt the most ridiculous lifting of his heart. Truly, he didn't think he'd ever experienced such infatuation in his entire life. Every snatched touch of the hand, smile and couple of words exchanged felt like a gift from heaven. And every time they had to move on from each other, it felt as though he'd been deprived very suddenly.

Finally, supper was called.

James, wondering at himself, had been, as though under some kind of spell, waiting with increasing impatience for the end of the last set, knowing that supper would be coming. He'd also been unable to prevent himself through the entirety of the dance from keeping a close eye on Lady Maria's whereabouts. Truly, he was behaving like a love-struck youth.

He handed the young lady whom he had just partnered back to her mother and thanked her profusely for the dance, escaped before her mother could hint too forcefully that he might escort her into supper, and made his way over to where he'd last spied Lady Maria.

By the time he got to her, she was surrounded by several young sprigs together with several more mature gentlemen, two of whom were good friends of James's.

'Lady Maria.' James inserted himself between two of the men as he spoke.

'Your Grace.' She smiled at him and he realised that it had to have been at least half an hour since he'd last received a smile from her. He was already basking in the warmth of this latest one; each one felt as though it was a special gift just for him.

He held his arm out to her, internally raising his eyebrows at himself at the way in which his thoughts had suddenly become so poetic.

'Thank you.' She accepted the arm—and good God, he almost shivered at her touch—and smiled around the group of men, and then they began to process with all the other guests towards the supper room.

'I am looking forward to seeing how my mother will have had the supper room decorated,' he told Lady Maria as they walked. 'I have not yet seen it; I don't know whether she will have continued her theme in there.' Well. It was fortunate that he was a duke; if this was all the conversation he could provide, he would have to hope that his title would attract Lady Maria.

'I'm sure it will be as striking and beautiful as the ballroom. I look forward to finding out whether it smells as wonderful.'

James was spared from having to search for any more words—truly this was the first time in his life that he'd ever been struck so near dumb—by their entry into the supper room.

And... Good Lord. His mother had certainly not held back. James and Lady Maria both stood for a moment, staring.

It was Lady Maria who regained her powers of speech first. 'It's...most striking,' she said. 'And elegant.'

James nodded, still speechless. He wasn't sure that *elegant* was the right word for it.

'I like the green,' Lady Maria persisted. 'It's very...botanical. Like the ballroom.'

'It certainly is...apple-coloured,' James said.

'And the pink is quite like a fuchsia. Which is also botanical.'

'Indeed.'

The supper room was hung with lengths of bright pink-and-green-striped silk, and the colour theme continued to the tables, the plates, the *floor*. It was truly the stuff of intense migraines.

In addition, the stripes were so wide but so ubiquitous that certain people's clothing was almost camouflaged.

'I like it.' Lady Maria had clearly entirely recovered from the shock now, and spoke quite definitively. 'I foresee that this will set a fashion for stripes.'

'I sincerely hope that you are wrong. May I seat you at a stripy table and place a selection of food on a stripy plate for you?' James said.

'That would be wonderful. I shall of course view you as a failure if you do not manage to choose striped food for me. And I would expect you to match it to the plate.'

James laughed. 'Your word shall be my bidding.'

Once he'd seated her and was next to the buffet table, he realised that he had a dilemma: like the lovelorn juvenile he appeared to have become, he just wanted to rush straight back to Lady Maria, but he also wanted to impress her. Impress her with his food choices, though? Really? What was he becoming?

It was the first time in his life that he'd worked as fast as he could to match food to a plate but he did his best and soon he was back with Lady Maria. As he sat down, he was conscious of a lightening of his shoulders, a smile spreading across his face, really just a strong sense of *happiness*. Utterly ridiculous, really, because he didn't know her at all. By the end of this supper, he might have discovered that the two of them were extremely incompatible.

'I'm extremely impressed,' Lady Maria said. 'I had not thought you able to meet the challenge. I particularly like the way you have covered the food of the wrong colour with hams and asparagus to maintain the pink and green stripes without causing me to have too monotonous a meal.' The contrast between the seriousness of her tone and the laugh in her eyes was *adorable*.

As he grinned at her, and laughed, James was quite certain that he was not in fact going to find that they were incompatible.

As friends and companions, obviously. There would be no love involved.

Chapter Three

Anna

'I think you will find—' the duke leaned in as though he was about to impart extreme wisdom '—that the presentation of food in stripes to match a plate is one of the greatest challenges imaginable. Much greater, for example, than those undertaken by the dragon-slaying knights of yore.'

Anna laughed before inclining her head and saying with her best air of great seriousness, 'I think you're right. There is no ancient king who would not immediately reward such a knight with his daughter's hand.' She was enjoying herself immensely; she had never before in her life had this kind of conversation with an attractive man—other than the music master at her seminary in her last year of school, for which, when they were overheard by the Latin master, she had been roundly punished and the music master had not, which had not seemed very fair to her, but of course men and women were held to very different standards.

She was *very* glad that Maria and her godmother had persuaded her into attending this evening; she could be doing no harm to anyone and was having the most delightful time.

'If I were such a knight, I would be truly honoured to receive the hand of a maiden discerning enough to wish her food to be in stripes.' The duke looked directly into her eyes as he spoke, a half-smile playing about his lips. Anna felt her heart do a gigantic thump, and swallowed hard.

She and the duke were sitting close enough to each other that she could see the faint shadow where his beard growth was already restarting, the deep blue of his eyes, the thickness of his wavy dark hair. His shoulders were broad and she had the oddest feeling that if one allowed oneself to lay one's problems on those shoulders, one would be protected from the world. For a moment she felt a surge of real wistfulness when she thought of the fortunate young woman whom he would marry in due course.

Although, of course, he was probably just like all other men— kind and caring and dependable...until he wasn't.

At this moment, though, it was easy to imagine that he might be a rare, truly dependable man. She had had that impression of him from the very first moment she saw him; she'd been on the brink of laughter at the audacity of the deception she and her godmother were practising, and she'd felt so immediately comfortable with him that for one silly moment she'd almost confided in him.

They were still staring into each other's eyes, not speaking.

This would not do; she needed to look away, find some light words to cut across this...tension that she felt between them.

The duke was still gazing intently at her, and his smile was growing.

'I have so many questions for you,' he said.

'You do?' Anna's voice had emerged as a squeak.

'So many. I hope...' He paused for a moment, and his smile turned wry, almost as though he were laughing at himself. 'I hope that I may have the opportunity to get to know you well enough to ask them all.'

Anna swallowed again. She had no experience of meeting men in polite Society but she couldn't help feeling that—even though he knew nothing of her—the duke's flirting was in earnest. As though he was genuinely interested in getting to know her well.

Oh, of course: he was interested in getting to know *Lady Maria Swanley* well; as the daughter of an earl who was possessed of what Maria had confided was a truly enormous dowry, she would attract any number of suitors, including dukes, and that was exactly why Anna had not wished to attend this ball. She had *foreseen* this.

What Anna should probably do now was change the subject, converse on lighter matters, and certainly not flirt back. Except...

'*I* believe that I have a question for *you*,' she said, unable to resist the temptation. Although...what was her question? There were many things she would love to know about him, but all her questions would sound remarkably forward if she asked them now.

'I am all yours.' His smile was becoming ever more, well... intimate. As though it was just for her. 'Perhaps we could... *exchange*...questions.' The way he said it made Anna feel really quite warm, inside as well as out. It was almost as though he'd been about to say they could exchange...something else. 'A questions game, perhaps. She, or he, who can't think of another—sensible—question to ask on their turn, is the loser.'

'And what is the winner's reward?' she found herself asking.

'Perhaps that should be for the winner to decide?'

'I'm sure I will win.' Anna held his gaze and faux pursed her lips. She was quite sure that she shouldn't be conversing with the duke like this, but it was as though she was under some kind of compunction. Also, she never liked to turn down a challenge—which was, of course, partly why she was here in the first place; Maria had begun the whole charade by challenging Anna to take her place.

'I'm ready whenever you are. Ladies first.'

'Let me think.' Rational thought was quite difficult when she was sitting quite so close to the most intriguing and handsome man she'd ever met. 'If you were decorating a ballroom, how would you decorate it? Yourself. Not delegating to anyone else.'

Anna wasn't *very* pleased with her question, because it was a little dull, but it was better than nothing.

'Good question. In that it is one I have never before asked myself. I fear that my answer might disappoint you. I would aim for simplicity.'

Anna shook her head, mock sorrowfully. 'I am indeed disappointed. That is no answer.'

'You're right. I beg your pardon. I shall now apply myself to thinking of a better response. I do like the colour blue.'

'Better,' Anna approved. 'What kind of blue, though?'

'A mid blue. Similar to the sky on a summer's day, but a little darker.'

'That's a very nice colour. Stripes?'

'No stripes.' The duke looked into her eyes again and shook his own head. 'I must change my answer. I have just realised that my favourite colour is green. The green of your eyes.'

Anna chose to laugh. 'Now you are becoming ridiculous, Your Grace.'

'My name is James, and yes, I do fear that I am ridiculous. But at the same time...not.' His face was suddenly completely serious, and Anna was suddenly extremely breathless. 'Another colour that I now very much like,' he continued, 'is silver. The silver of your dress.' His gaze flickered lower, for the merest of seconds, to her chest, before returning to her face.

Anna came very close to repeating a very overcome *Oh!* before pulling herself together and saying, 'Would you have green and silver stripes?'

'I confess that I would not have stripes. I would instead decorate the entire ballroom in the green of your eyes and the entire supper room in silver spangles.'

'Would the green not feel a little monotonous?' Anna was *not* going to give in to the flutter in her stomach.

'Never. I feel it would be easy to look at the colour of your eyes every day for the rest of one's life.'

'If I had a fan, I would now rap you over the knuckles,' Anna told him, mock sternly. 'As you know, I was referring to the ballroom decorations. I feel, however, that we have exhausted this topic, and should move on.'

'Before I make further outrageous references to your beautiful eyes?'

'Exactly.'

'In that case, I believe that it's my turn for a question,' he said.

'I'm really not sure that I should grant it, considering how poor your response to my question was. I am, however, feeling generous.'

The duke's grin transformed his face from somewhat austere handsomeness into boyish cheekiness, and Anna was suddenly certain that she would remember this evening, this supper—and his grin—for the rest of her life.

'Thank you,' he said. 'So kind.'

She laughed.

'I have many, many questions,' he continued. 'It's difficult to choose. I will start with a small one. Of a different nature. What is your favourite food? Did I select well for you?'

'You did select well.' Anna had barely eaten a mouthful, she realised; she'd been too busy with their conversation. 'I like a lot of food; it's hard to choose a favourite.'

'No, no.' The duke shook his head. 'You are in danger of answering this question as badly as I answered yours.'

'Please accept my deepest apologies.'

'I will accept them *if* you answer the question properly.'

'That's very gracious of you, Your Grace.'

'James.'

Anna applied herself to deciding on her favourite food—asparagus and chicken—and then the duke (she really couldn't call him James) told her what his was—a most unimaginative steak, but he allowed that asparagus was delicious.

Eventually they decided that their question game had been a draw, and then their conversation—punctuated by mouthfuls of the most delectable food—continued in the same silly but utterly delightful vein until supper was ended.

Anna couldn't remember a time when she'd been more disappointed for a meal to finish. There was still, however, their waltz to look forward to. Although…she was beginning to be worried that for some strange reason the duke might like her for herself, rather than for Lady Maria's birth and connections, in which case would she be doing him a disservice to waltz with him? Maybe… But on the other hand, if he did enjoy her company, he would—perhaps she was flattering herself but he *might*—be sad not to see her again, and it probably wouldn't make much difference whether or not they shared another dance. Conversation, and getting to know each other a little, drew people together more than dancing, surely.

As he bowed deep over her hand when he released her to her partner for the next dance, a Mr Marsh, the duke said, 'I look forward to our waltz,' before raising his head and giving her that same intimate smile.

Anna was going to look forward with great anticipation to their dance.

As she walked towards the dance floor with Mr Marsh, she caught her godmother's eye. Lady Derwent was swivelling her eyes and jiggling her eyebrows in the most dramatic way.

'Would you mind if I spoke to my godmother for one moment before the dance?' she asked Mr Marsh.

'Certainly.'

'The duke is being most marked in his attentions,' Lady Derwent whispered as soon as Anna reached her side. 'There is every indication that he might wish to marry you.'

'Surely not.'

'Oh, I think so.'

'Well, I clearly can't marry him. I am about to become a governess.'

'Piffle. Your grandfather was the Earl of Broome, and Lady Puntney would certainly understand.'

'But I've lied to the duke. And I *am* ineligible. I mean, I'm sure it's moonshine anyway. But if it weren't, I wouldn't be able to.' And Anna had no interest in the institution of marriage; since men were not to be trusted to treat women well, she would probably be better off as a governess. At least she would have some independence and would not be relying on anyone other than her employer.

Lady Derwent wrinkled her brow and stared into the distance for a moment, and then said, 'I think on reflection that for the time being you are right. Now go and dance with Mr Marsh. He's delightful.'

'Thank you. Remember that we need to leave at midnight.' Anna could *not* be late tomorrow.

'Certainly. In the meantime, enjoy the rest of the evening.'

Mr Marsh was a very nice man, and Anna was determined to make the most of *every* dance this evening, not just the ones with the duke, because it was entirely possible that this was the only ball she would have the good fortune to attend in her entire life. But if she was honest, it was difficult not to be very aware of where the duke was at every moment—it was easy to see him because of his height—and also difficult not to fizz with anticipation ahead of her waltz with him.

She did enjoy dancing and some very nice conversation with Mr Marsh, and she was almost sorry to leave him at the end of the dance.

Except she wasn't really, because it was time for her second dance with the duke.

She had learnt the waltz during her seminary days, and earlier that day Lady Derwent had mangled one on the pianoforte while Lady Maria took the role of gentleman and led Anna round Lady Derwent's drawing room in a practice waltz. The practice had not gone well, due to Lady Maria's constantly forgetting that she was supposed to lead, but Anna was confident that she could remember the rudiments of the dance sufficiently accurately to acquit herself adequately this evening. Earlier, she and Lady Derwent had agreed out loud, so that others might hear, that she might waltz. She was quite sure that she was ready for the dance.

She had not, though, taken into account the way her heart would thud so very hard in her chest and that her anticipation of the duke's touch would cause her mind to falter.

'I've been looking forward to this dance,' the duke murmured as he took her in his arms.

Anna didn't trust her voice to come out sounding normal or indeed her mind to produce any sensible-sounding words, so she smiled and said nothing. How had she been naïve enough to think that a waltz would draw two people together less than conversation might?

Her senses were quite flooded by the duke, and in every way; he even *smelled* good. The only way she could describe his scent was just, well, *masculine*. A delightful kind of masculine. He *felt* good; his height and the width of his shoulders and the latent strength evident in his arms as he held her gave the impression of security and, again, extreme masculinity. Just *hardness*. And, of course, when she turned her face up to his, he *looked* good. His strong features and jawline, the way he looked harshly handsome in repose but delightfully cheekily handsome when he smiled… And the way his body looked in his perfectly fitting evening clothes.

The whole was just…magnificent. And, in this moment, she felt like the luckiest woman in the world. And, also, one of the least lucky, because nothing could ever come of her meeting the duke; this was for one evening only. She would remember it, however—perhaps be almost spoilt by it—for evermore.

Since it *was* for only one evening, she should *not* allow herself to feel maudlin; she should instead enjoy every last minute of this dance, and indeed the rest of the evening.

So she directed a huge smile in the duke's direction and sank into his hold. Her hand fitted perfectly inside his much larger one, and the way he was holding it made her almost shudder with delight. Although not as much as did the way his other hand rested lightly on her waist, and the way when they turned she sensed the hardness in his thighs and his chest. The way their bodies touched and moved together through the dance felt almost scandalous in its intimacy.

And then, as the duke led her through a turn, she looked up at his face, and if she'd already thought that this experience was intoxicating, well, she'd been wrong. What was truly intoxicating was the way he was looking at her now, as though they were the only two people in the world, as though with the half-smile on his lips he was making her some kind of promise, as though he saw deep inside her and very much admired what he saw.

Anna knew that she was being fanciful; from one smile one could hardly tell what a man was thinking. Perhaps he was just

thinking that he liked the—really quite lovely—flowers that
Lady Derwent had procured for her to wear in her hair, or perhaps he adored the waltz and smiled like that at everyone with
whom he danced.

And then she stopped bothering to think, because it was far
too much effort and definitely served no good purpose, and just
gave herself up to enjoying the dance.

Some time later—she had no idea how long—she, or the
duke, it was hard to tell, became aware of being jostled by others. She looked round and saw that the dance had come to an
end. She was still held in the duke's strong arms, and he showed
no sign of letting go of her yet, for which she could only be
deeply grateful.

It defied belief, but somehow, over the course of this short
evening, it felt almost as though he had become very important
to her, even though she barely knew him.

'That was...wonderful,' he said, still not releasing her.

'It was. I must thank you, very much.' She had a sudden mad
wish to tell him the truth about herself, but, no, she couldn't; the
secret was only half hers to impart, and, in addition, if he did
choose to tell anyone else, or anyone overheard them, it could
give rise to the most dreadful consequences.

'Would you like to take a turn outside on the balcony?' he
asked, *still* not relaxing his hold on her. She in her turn, she realised, was still clinging onto him.

'I believe that I am taken for the next dance.'

'It is not for a few moments and, if you were to feel faint,
I am sure the gentleman in question would release you from
your commitment?'

'I *do* feel somewhat faint,' Anna agreed. It wasn't even entirely a lie; surely any lady would be feeling somewhat wobbly
after being held quite so intimately for quite so long by a man
like the duke.

'Then you must immediately get some fresh air.'

They were interrupted by an elderly man, who was powdered
and painted in the way of the previous century. 'I believe that
the next dance with Lady Maria is mine.'

The duke and Anna both moved a little way away from each other and dropped their arms. It was as though they had been in their own little universe and someone else had entered.

'Sir Richard. I'm afraid that you will have to excuse Lady Maria,' the duke told him, his demeanour suddenly quite haughty and even a little intimidating. 'She feels ill and is in need of fresh air.'

'I would be very happy to escort the lady myself to seek fresher air.'

'That is very kind, but I will perhaps return myself to my godmother,' Anna said. However much her mother had come from this world and however much at all levels of society men had rights that women did not, she still could not stand and listen to two men discussing what she was going to do next without attempting to interject.

'Certainly,' the duke said very promptly. 'I will escort you over to her.' He nodded to Sir Richard, whose face appeared to be purpling beneath his paint, and then somehow manoeuvred himself and Anna so that they were walking away from him.

'Would you like to return to Lady Derwent now or do you perhaps feel that you might be better served by breathing some fresher air first?'

Anna was quite sure that she ought just to return to her godmother, because would it not be quite scandalous for her to walk outside with the duke? But no one knew who she was, and she wouldn't see any of these people again at an occasion like this. No one would connect her with Lady Maria after this because they looked so different, and, anyway, Lady Maria would be getting married. And Anna's future employer—should they see her—which she did not think likely—would never recognise her in governess garb after seeing her dressed like this. And she so *very* much wanted to steal just a few more moments with the duke.

'Upon reflection,' she told him, 'I do believe that fresh air would serve me very well at this moment.'

As the duke made a way for them through the crowd, Anna allowed herself for this one moment to feel special, to relish these few minutes where he was effectively hers. The lady for whose hand he offered would be very lucky.

She thought for a moment of Maria. How could she possibly wish to marry Clarence, her curate, when she could presumably have had the duke at her feet? It would be remarkably easy to fall in love with the duke.

But of course Maria had already fallen in love, and Anna had to admire her bravery; very few young ladies would have the courage to choose to marry someone in Clarence's straitened circumstances. Although Anna's own mother had of course been much braver than that: she had married her father's second groom. Anna hoped Maria was making the right decision; in the case of her parents, their difference in stations and the change in her mother's circumstances upon her elopement had put a strain upon her parents' relationship until eventually her father had left.

'You look as though you're thinking about something very serious,' the duke said as they stepped out of the long glass doors leading to a terrace along the back of the house. 'Please don't feel that you have to walk out here with me if you do not wish to; I would be more than happy to return you immediately to Lady Derwent.'

'Oh, no, I am very happy. That is...if you would still like to walk?'

'Very happy indeed,' he murmured, which made Anna smile.

As they moved along the terrace, he said, 'We are fortunate in having a particularly nice rose garden. Down those steps.' He pointed ahead. 'Would you like to take a walk around it? The moonlight and clear skies allow us to see quite well tonight.'

'I should very much like to, thank you.'

They continued towards the steps, Anna holding the duke's arm, and he said, 'I realise now that I was dreadfully short-sighted in not asking you what your favourite flowers were when we were asking questions of each other.'

'Fortunately, roses are some of my favourites.'

'Mine too,' he said. 'What a happy coincidence.'

Anna laughed; it was as though her senses were so heightened at this moment that the tiniest joke must seem hilarious.

'Take care on the steps,' the duke instructed. 'They are quite uneven and guests have been known to fall on them even in broad daylight. Allow me to hold your arm a little more tightly.'

Anna was more than happy to have her arm held more tightly. In fact, she couldn't think of anything she'd like more right now than to be held tightly by the duke.

'Thank you,' she said, a little breathlessly.

It was most enjoyable descending the steps clamped hard against his side. Anna couldn't believe that it was necessary for him to hold her steady with quite so much determination, but she certainly wasn't going to quibble. She had determined to enjoy this evening, and proximity to him could only enhance her enjoyment.

The steps safely negotiated, the duke drew her left. In the hazy light, Anna made out an archway into a walled garden, and then a profusion of rose bushes, laid out in a very regular fashion.

'These are indeed beautiful,' she said. 'I very much like seeing a gardener's work: the love and care put into the planting and nurturing of the plants.'

'I agree, although in truth our head gardener, Alliss, whilst very talented, is a very grumpy individual who would be most put out if anyone suspected him of putting love into his work.'

Anna laughed. 'I refuse to believe that no love has gone into this planting. Look at them. They're wonderful. Quite beautiful.'

'Mmm.' The duke was not looking at the roses; he was looking at her. 'You are also very beautiful,' he told her, his voice completely serious. 'Your smile is…perfection.'

Anna felt his words to the very core of her body, and swallowed, suddenly suffused with emotion. While she had been educated as though she would one day take her place in Society and she was now two-and-twenty years old, quite old enough to know the ways of the world, she had no idea to what extent men spoke to women like this just for fun. Lady Maria was a young lady of quality, though, and chaperoned by Lady Derwent, and the duke was under his own roof. It seemed quite unlikely that he would attempt to take advantage of her; it seemed possible therefore that he really might mean his words. For the moment, at least.

Perhaps she should tell him now who she really was; being here under false pretences was beginning to feel terrible. But no, she'd already been over this in her mind, and she couldn't. It was not Anna's secret to share; she would be betraying Maria.

'Would you care to sit down?' the duke asked. 'There's a bench over there in the corner, with a lovely view of some of the better rose bushes.'

'That sounds delightful,' Anna said primly. She would tell him *something* to ensure that he was not led into believing she could be courted. And she would enjoy his conversation. And then she would leave.

She gasped as she sat down; the stone was very cold against her skin through her thin dress.

'I'm so sorry,' the duke said immediately. 'I should have been more considerate. Allow me to warm you with my jacket.'

'Oh, no, I… *Oh!*'

The duke had immediately divested himself of his jacket and placed it around her shoulders, and it was the most wonderful sensation being enveloped in his clothing, his scent again and the warmth from where his body had just been touching it.

'May I…?' He lifted his arm as though to place it around Anna's shoulders. She was fairly sure that she should say no, but she couldn't quite remember why. It wasn't as though a gentleman placing his arm around one's shoulders was *kissing*, after all.

So she smiled at him, and he smiled back at her, and hugged her into him.

And this felt even more intimate than their waltz had, because now they really *were* alone, rather than just feeling as though they were.

She had no idea what might happen next, but she was aware that, even though she barely knew him, she did trust the duke. Which was ridiculous, of course, because all she really knew of men from first-hand experience was that they were not to be trusted.

'Where is your childhood home?' he asked. 'Is it similar to London or very different?'

'It is in Somerset, and very different from London.' Anna had grown up in Gloucestershire, but Lady Maria's family home was quite close to Bath. Anna knew it reasonably well, having been invited to stay with her best friend on three occasions.

'Oh, yes, you mentioned that you had been enjoying visiting the sights of London. What do you have planned for tomorrow?'

'Tomorrow, I... I think...' Anna suddenly had a large lump in her throat at the mention of the next day. Tomorrow she would be leaving behind any pretence that this life could possibly be for her, and moving into the Puntneys' home before beginning her employment in earnest the following day.

'I ask...' The duke shifted a little on the bench so that, while still keeping his arm around Anna's shoulders, he was now also facing her. 'I ask because I should very much like to call on you tomorrow.'

'Oh!' *Oh.* Oh, no. This wasn't the way Anna had foreseen the deception going wrong, but it definitely *was* wrong.

The duke was looking—gazing—at her in the most *exciting* way and all she could do was swallow.

'I would like to take you for a drive in Hyde Park.' He lifted the hand that was not around Anna's shoulders, and very gently traced the curve of her cheek with one finger, which caused Anna's breath to hitch. 'I would also like to take you for a drive in Richmond Park.' He moved a little closer. Anna could hardly remember how to breathe. 'And I would like to show you around my estates.' He moved even closer. 'Further, I would like to assist your godmother in showing you as many of the sights of London that you would like to see.'

He drew her a little closer to him with his arm, and moved his free hand so that it was in Anna's curls, cupping the back of her neck.

'I would like—' the duke's voice was low and husky now, and every word he spoke sent a shiver through Anna '—to do so many things with you. I know that we've only just met but I feel...' He paused and then continued, 'I'm sorry. That's far too much. To begin with.' He tugged her hair very slightly, very gently, so that her head was angled exactly beneath his. And then, very, very slowly, he leaned towards her and brushed her lips with his. 'I would very much like to call on you tomorrow.'

'I would like that too, but...' Anna barely knew what she was saying. She was very aware that she had to tell him something *now* so that he wouldn't be holding any misconceptions, but she was even more aware of how he was holding her and where his lips had just touched hers.

'That.' The duke brushed her lips again with his, for a little longer this time. Anna's heart was beating *so* hard. 'Is.' He dropped another kiss on her lips and Anna wondered through the mists of feeling whether she might explode with...something. 'Wonderful.'

And then he kissed her for longer. And then he parted her lips with his tongue, and Anna felt it throughout her entire body. And then she found herself kissing him back, and it was truly, truly the most delicious thing she'd ever done in her entire life.

Anna had no idea how long they kissed for. She was dimly aware of being held tightly by the duke, one of his arms now sliding around her waist, of winding her own arms around his neck and then plunging her hands into his hair.

When they eventually stopped the kiss, the duke took a deep breath and then just held her very tightly, his cheek against her hair. Being in his arms felt like the most natural place in the world to be, as though she *should* be there. Which was odd, because in reality she hardly knew him, and she was here with him under extreme false pretences.

As she thought that, she snuggled even more closely against him, wanting this moment to go on for ever.

And then, to her great disappointment, the duke planted a kiss on her forehead and drew back, easing his hold on her.

'We should be careful,' he said, his voice ragged. 'I could... I could... We could... We must not do things that a young lady should not do outside marriage. And to that end...' He moved a little further away and took his arm away from her.

'I would like to call on you tomorrow,' he said firmly. 'Much as I would like to stay out here, I think we should go back inside now. I do not trust myself to avoid temptation.'

Anna was going to have to tell him. As soon as possible. She needed to find the words.

'I should give your jacket back to you,' she said first.

'When we are closer to the house. Otherwise, you will catch cold.'

'Thank you.'

They stood up and began to retrace their steps towards the building.

'I have enjoyed this evening very greatly,' the duke said as they walked.

'So have I. Thank you. It has been one of the most enjoyable of my life.' Anna knew that she would treasure the memory; she also knew that she would find it hard not to wish that he really could have called on her tomorrow.

When he pressed her hand on his arm and she smiled up at him in the moonlight, she suddenly felt quite tearful at the tender look on his face.

They were nearly at the terrace now.

'I must return your jacket to you,' she told him.

As he helped her out of it, his hands lingered for just a little longer than necessary on her bare arms, and she shivered through the entire length of her body in response.

'Thank you.' Honestly, her voice sounded quite tremulous.

She now felt very cold. Not just physically, but emotionally. As though the most wonderful interlude in her life had finished and it would take her a long time to feel warm again.

They trod up the steps and along the path together, Anna keeping her eyes fixed straight ahead because she couldn't bear to look at the duke.

And then, just before they stepped back inside the ballroom, she moved away from him and said, 'I'm so sorry, but I think I return to the country soon and will not be able to see you again.'

She looked up at him for a second and saw him just staring, and slightly frowning.

He reached a hand out to her and, ridiculously, because in

reality she'd only known him for a few short hours, she felt as though her heart might break.

'Goodbye,' she said. 'Thank you so very much for a truly wonderful evening. Quite the best evening of my life. I have enjoyed it so very much.'

And then she walked away as fast as she could.

Chapter Four

James

James awoke slowly the next morning, from a dream where he'd been chasing something—maybe a butterfly—that he couldn't quite catch. He lay blinking for a few moments, conscious of a strong sense of dissatisfaction, waiting for clarity of thought to return, and then suddenly he remembered. Last night. Lady Maria. The strong sense of connection they'd shared, or he'd thought they'd shared. And then...her disappearance.

He pushed back his covers and swung his legs out of bed; he felt as though he had a lot to do.

Although, he realised, as he shook his head to clear it fully, it was far too early to pay a call on anyone. And he wasn't entirely sure that Lady Maria would *like* him to call on her. He couldn't decide which was the greater indicator: her sudden flight or the fact that she'd told him that yesterday evening had been wonderful, the best of her life.

He called for water and soap, still shaking his head a little, wondering what exactly had happened to him yesterday evening.

Before the ball, if he'd been asked, he'd have said that he

expected that at some point he would come to a sensible, measured decision regarding the choice of young lady to whom he would offer his hand in marriage. He had not had any real idea about how he might make that decision but he did know that he hadn't expected to know for certain after one evening—perhaps one minute—which lady he would choose.

He had also not expected that if he *did* meet someone with whom he could imagine spending his life, someone with whom he could enjoy companionship and friendship, he would be unlucky enough for the young lady to tell him that she would be leaving for the country and unable to see him again.

Had she meant it? He just didn't know.

He washed and dressed hurriedly—although he did take the time to ensure that his cravat fell well, in the hope that he would be able to speak to Lady Maria later—still with the strong sense that he was in a rush to take some kind of action, and then descended to the breakfast parlour.

As he sat to eat steak—which reminded him of eating supper with Lady Maria—he tried to marshal his thoughts.

The contrast between her telling him she was leaving for the country and that she wouldn't be able to see him again and the way she'd melted into the crowd of guests so quickly that he hadn't been able to follow her, and the fact that she'd told him with seeming great sincerity how very much she'd enjoyed the evening, was very confusing.

Perhaps she hadn't really meant that she wouldn't be able to see him again; perhaps she had just meant that when she left for the country she would be residing far from London and didn't expect to see him again *easily*. Or soon.

Perhaps she'd been as overwhelmed as he by the connection and tension there had been between them and had panicked a little. Perhaps she had thought he was merely trifling with her. She was certainly not experienced with men; he had had the strongest sense when he kissed her that it was the first time she had kissed anyone or been kissed like that.

He took a large swig of ale and frowned a little as he considered how he would plan his day.

It wasn't difficult, actually.

He *knew* that he wanted to marry Lady Maria. He needed to get married. He hadn't wanted to get married. He didn't wish to fall in love and he didn't wish anyone to fall in love with him. But they weren't in love. How could they be when they barely knew each other? They had merely experienced an intense connection of the sort that he could easily imagine would lead to an excellent understanding and partnership between them. And the intimate side of marriage would certainly be no hardship with Lady Maria. She would make the ideal bride for him.

And therefore he would like to propose to her today.

She would surely not be leaving for the country as soon as this morning, unless she had had word that her grandmother had taken a turn for the worse.

So he would pay a call on her as early as he reasonably could and hope very much that the reason that she had effectively run away from him last night was merely that she had felt overwhelmed by what had happened and had not understood that his intentions were serious and entirely honourable, and that she would accept his proposal.

And between now and then he should really do his best to do something better with his day than just kick his heels in impatience.

He achieved very little other than a ludicrous amount of pacing before the hour at which he might call on Lady Maria finally arrived.

He had sent a footman to enquire about where she was residing, given that her mother had left town, and had been told that she was staying in her own home, accompanied by two very elderly great-aunts. Their age would presumably explain why she had been accompanied last night by Lady Derwent.

Standing on the doorstep of the Grosvenor Square house, he found his hands going to his cravat to check it more than once, and realised that he was squaring his shoulders and taking deeper breaths than he might usually do.

The door was opened by a particularly stately butler, who showed him into a conservatively decorated parlour to the left of the hall.

James sat and then stood and then sat and then stood again as he waited.

And then, finally, the door opened and the butler announced Lady Maria and her aunt, Lady Sephranella.

The first lady to enter the room was aged and walked slowly with a stick. James greeted her politely, looking eagerly beyond her to where Lady Maria would appear.

The young lady who followed her into the room was not, however, Lady Maria.

He turned to Lady Sephranella, not wishing to be rude to whomever this young lady might be. Perhaps a cousin of Lady Maria's.

'I wondered whether I might be able to see Lady Maria,' he said.

'I am Lady Maria,' the younger lady said.

James frowned. 'I'm afraid I don't understand,' he said. This young lady was tall and blond-haired and blue-eyed, whereas the Lady Maria that he had met was smaller, brown-haired and green-eyed. This lady was beautiful, but his Lady Maria was *really* beautiful. Especially when she smiled. 'I wondered whether I might be able to see Lady Maria Swanley.'

'I am Lady Maria Swanley.' She spoke very slowly, as if to someone who did not have strong comprehension.

James shook his head.

'I met Lady Maria last night,' he said. 'Lady Maria Swanley.'

'Really?' The lady in front of him shook her own head. 'I'm so sorry but I don't entirely remember. It was of course a great crush—so wonderful that the whole world wished to attend your mama's ball—so one met a great many people. It is difficult to remember to whom one spoke.'

James frowned at her. She looked absolutely nothing like the actual Lady Maria. The only thing this lady and *his* Lady Maria had in common, he realised, was that this one's eyes seemed to be dancing with merriment, as his Lady Maria's had last night when he met her.

He… What? Could they… What?

Could they have played some kind of trick on him, on the *ton*? Surely not? *Why*? There had to be some other explanation.

This Lady Maria really did look, however, as though she was on the brink of laughter.

'I am the Duke of Amscott,' he said.

'Yes,' agreed the lady.

'Last night, my mother held a ball.'

'Yes.'

'At the ball, I met and danced twice with Lady Maria Swanley.'

'I am Lady Maria Swanley.'

'I do not, however—' James was starting to find it difficult to get his words out without shouting '—recall having met you before.'

The lady cast her eyes down. 'I must confess that I would be a little hurt by your words, Your Grace, were it not for the fact that I do not easily recall you either.'

'Are you indeed Lady Maria Swanley?' James asked baldly, ignoring her last sentence.

'Yes, of course I am.' The lady's smile was so bland as to be suspicious.

'Are you confused, Your Grace?' Lady Sephranella quavered from the corner of the room. 'This is my great-niece, the granddaughter of my sister. This is Lady Maria Swanley. Have you come to the wrong house, sir?'

Could it be possible that the elderly lady and the butler were both colluding in a plot to pretend that this lady was Lady Maria? Why on earth would they do that? They *couldn't* be.

He took another long look at the lady who called herself Lady Maria. She was still smiling blandly at him and her eyes were still dancing. She looked ridiculously mischievous.

'I have not come to the wrong house but I will bid you good afternoon.' Clearly, he needed to go and see Lady Derwent.

Twenty minutes later, he was waiting in a grand drawing room in Lady Derwent's Berkeley Square mansion, which, co-incidentally, was directly opposite his own, on the other side of the gardens in the middle of the square.

'Your Grace.' Lady Derwent swept into the room in a rustle of stiff silk.

'My Lady.'

Greetings dispensed with, James came straight to the point. 'I would very much like to pay a call on Lady Maria Swanley today.'

'I believe that Lady Maria resides in Grosvenor Square.'

'She is not here?'

Lady Derwent raised her eyebrows. 'No?'

James had rarely in his life spent so much time in one afternoon wishing to grind his teeth. 'Yesterday evening, at my mother's ball, you introduced your goddaughter, Lady Maria Swanley, to me.'

'That is correct.' Lady Derwent moved to a chair near the fireplace and said, 'Please sit down.'

'Thank you. I enjoyed meeting Lady Maria.'

'We enjoyed attending the ball; thank you so much. I particularly liked the decorations. I believe that your mama will have created a fashion.'

'Thank you. Indeed.' James did not wish to discuss ballroom furnishings. 'I am a little confused. I have just been to call on Lady Maria at her house.'

'How very pleasant.'

'The Lady Maria that I met at her house was not the Lady Maria that I met last night.'

'Did you visit the correct Lady Maria? Maria is quite a common name.'

James had to work hard not to grind his teeth. 'Yes. I understand from you that the lady I met last night was Lady Maria Swanley. And the lady I visited today was Lady Maria Swanley. They were not, however, the same person.'

Lady Derwent inclined her head to one side and frowned slightly. 'I myself am also now confused. How could that be? I was not aware that there were two Lady Maria Swanleys.'

'I am sure there are not.'

'Then I do not understand what you mean.'

'Last night—' James was surprised that he was not now yelling '—I met a Lady Maria Swanley, whom you introduced as your goddaughter. I danced twice with her, I ate supper with her, I conversed with her.' He had *kissed* her.

Lady Derwent nodded. 'Yes.'

'And this afternoon I went to call on Lady Maria Swanley, at her house. A young lady came into the room where I was waiting. The butler and a Lady Sephranella, described to me as Lady Maria's great-aunt, referred to the young lady as Lady Maria Swanley. She referred to herself as Lady Maria Swanley. She said that she had been at the ball and thought that she had probably met me but did not remember me. I did not remember her at all because I have never met her before because she was not *my* Lady Maria Swanley.'

'*Your* Lady Maria Swanley?'

'I had—' James was aware that he had lost all dignity and he did not care '—that is to say, I formed quite an attachment to Lady Maria over the course of yesterday evening. I wished to call on her today to further our acquaintance.'

'I see.' Lady Derwent looked thoughtful.

'Forgive me if I appear rude.' James did not care at all if he appeared rude right now. 'I wonder if you could explain what has happened. Where is the Lady Maria I met last night and what relation does she have to the Lady Maria I met this afternoon?'

Lady Derwent placed her hands together, palm to palm, and touched them to her chin for a moment, before relaxing her fingers so that they clasped each other and laying her hands in her lap.

Speaking slowly, as though choosing her words carefully, she said, 'I believe that you met Lady Maria Swanley this afternoon.'

'Who was the lady I met yesterday evening then?'

Lady Derwent paused for a moment and then said, 'Lady Maria Swanley.' She turned and rang the bell next to her. 'Would you like to take tea?'

James looked at her for a long moment and then said, 'Thank you; I am afraid that I have urgent business to attend to and must leave.'

Lady Derwent nodded. 'Do visit again.'

'I should be delighted.' James just wanted to swear.

* * *

Marching away from Lady Derwent's house, James had the strangest sensation that his head was going to explode. Someone—everyone—had to be lying to him, because clearly at least one of the two purported Lady Marias was not the real one. But *why* were they lying?

Something was nagging at the edge of his mind. As his thoughts began to crystallise, he stopped dead in the middle of the pavement, and a little boy out with his nurse for a walk ran right into him.

'I do apologise,' James said, his mind working hard.

Both so-called Lady Marias had seemed mirthful on his first meeting with them. It was easy to imagine that the mirth might have related to a secret. And that that secret might be the impersonation by one of the ladies of the other.

The first Lady Maria had *known* that she was going to be meeting people that evening, in the guise of Lady Maria. The second Lady Maria had not known until he arrived that James would call on her today. Had the first Lady Maria been the real one, she would not have been mirthful about the masquerade that neither she nor the second Lady Maria could know might arise, as neither would have known at that point that he would make today's call.

Of course, the mirth might have been for a different reason.

But logic suggested that if one of the two ladies was impersonating Lady Maria, and they both knew about it, which they must do, and that was what had caused both ladies' mirth, it was the second lady who was the real one, and last night's Lady Maria who was the fake.

He turned round. He was going back to see Lady Derwent again.

'What a delightful surprise,' said Lady Derwent five minutes later, indicating that James should take a chair near to hers. 'I had not thought to see you again so soon, Your Grace.'

'No, indeed; this is very soon,' agreed James, sitting as directed. 'I will not take up too much of your time. I have merely come to say that I believe that the lady I met yesterday evening under the guise of Lady Maria Swanley was not in fact Lady Maria. I must apologise for any implied rudeness—' he bowed '—but it seems to me that you were aware of the deception.'

Lady Derwent studied him for a long moment, and then said, in much milder tones than she usually used, 'That would of course be an astonishing deception. Quite unbelievable, in fact; ladies such as I do not practise such deceptions.'

She was clearly lying.

James leaned forward. 'Who was the lady I met last night?'

Lady Derwent shook her head, a little sorrowfully, and said, 'Lady Maria Swanley.'

James tried not to roll his eyes and failed. 'I should be very grateful if you would pass on a message to the lady I met last night.'

'What kind of message would you like to pass on to… Lady Maria?'

'I…' James could not just blurt out a marriage proposal by proxy. 'I… I would very much like the opportunity to see again the lady that I met last night.'

'That is not a particularly interesting sentiment.' Lady Derwent sounded a little disappointed. 'Perhaps a stronger message would have a greater effect.'

James narrowed his eyes. Was she *encouraging* him to make serious advances? How very peculiar. Had she somehow orchestrated his meeting with last night's Lady Maria so that he would propose to her? No. That was preposterous. She could not possibly have known that he would be captivated by one smile, and she was hardly making it easy for him to see her now.

'If I am able to see her again, I am sure that I will have a stronger message for her,' he said.

Lady Derwent inclined her head graciously. 'I will bear that in mind.'

Three days later, James was taking tea with his mother and sisters, his mood still fairly bleak.

He realised now that it was a good thing that the young lady he had met had disappeared; he had to admit that some would describe the level of infatuation he had experienced as close to having fallen head over heels in love on first sight, and he did not wish to fall in love. He was beginning to come to terms with the loss of his father and brothers, and he did not wish to experience further loss. Women died in childbirth all the time, for example. And if the lady reciprocated his feelings and he did die young like his brothers, that would be terrible for her.

So, yes, with hindsight, he was inclined—when reflecting rationally—to think he'd had a lucky escape. He could have been in danger of falling in love, and love was a dangerous emotion. Really, it was a good thing that he was unable to get to know the lady any better or propose marriage to her. He was quite convinced of it.

It was more difficult, however, to convince himself that he was feeling particularly happy or that life was particularly enjoyable. Stupidly, given that he did not know the lady at all—hell, he didn't even know her real *name*—he felt that he missed her. In addition, there was clearly an unsolved mystery surrounding her identity that he would have liked to have solved. And he didn't *think* she could be in any kind of trouble, given that she had been under Lady Derwent's protection, but he wasn't *certain* that all was well with her.

He had considered paying a detective to look for her, but rationally felt that he should not. He could not *force* her to tell him who she was.

'Ouch.'

His mother had just rapped him across the knuckles.

'James,' she tutted. 'You have been paying very little heed to us this afternoon. You appear to be wrapped up in thoughts of your own.'

'My apologies, Mama. I am a little tired.'

'You should get more sleep. We were discussing which young ladies you are considering getting to know better with marriage in mind.'

James suddenly felt very tired. 'I am not sure that I wish to marry soon.'

His mother frowned. 'I thought we had already discussed this.'

James sighed. In truth, they *had* discussed it, and he did have to produce an heir while he was still in good health. He'd been over this in his mind countless times now. He absolutely did not wish to marry someone with whom he was in love or who loved him. It was for the best that Lady Maria—or whoever she had been—had disappeared. As long as she was in good health, happy and safe. *No.* He was not going to start worrying about this again.

He took a deep breath and turned to his mother. 'Whom do you suggest I meet?'

Two days later, James and his mother called on a very pleasant young lady, a Lady Catherine Rainsford, a marchioness's daughter with a large dowry, a pretty face and easy but not overwhelming conversation.

On their return home, his mother pulled her gloves off and handed them to their butler.

'Lady Catherine is a delightful young lady.' She walked into the smaller of the two saloons leading right off the hall, her demeanour very much indicating that she expected James to follow. 'Do you think that you might like to marry her?'

'I...' James really had no idea whom he might like to marry. Well, he had an idea whom he would *like* to marry, but not whom he *would* marry. 'She does seem very pleasant.' He could certainly imagine being friends with her. 'And quite attractive.' He *supposed* he could imagine making love to her.

It was probably *good* that he didn't feel terribly excited by that. As he had told himself many times before, he did not want to be in love with his wife, and he didn't think he would fall in love with Lady Catherine. And she really would be very suitable. She was well-formed. Not too tall, not too small. She had a nice face and nice hair. She seemed reasonably intelligent but not a bluestocking. He presumed that she would be a good mother for his children.

Really, he couldn't imagine a better wife.

Except, well, he *could*...

This was ridiculous.

What had his mother asked? Whether he might like to marry her.

'Perhaps I might,' he said.

'James.' His mother's hand went to her mouth, and then she reached up and hugged him before releasing him and patting her hair in the mirror. 'Darling, I'm quite excited.'

'So am I,' he told her untruthfully.

'When will you propose to her?'

'Soon. I think. Although, I am not certain.'

'Oh.' His mother plumped herself down on a chair as though all the stuffing had suddenly gone out of her. 'I do think you should marry soon, my dear.'

James nodded. 'I know. I will.' He looked at his mother. He loved her and his sisters very much. He did need to ensure that their future was secure, and for that he did need at least one son. 'Soon. I just need a little time to get used to the idea.'

'Darling, if you don't feel comfortable marrying, please don't let me push you into it.'

James raised his eyebrows wryly. 'Really?'

'Yes. I'm aware that I have indeed been trying to persuade you into it, but I believe that you would be happy, should you find a young woman with whom you were compatible. I would be delighted for you if you came to love her as deeply as I loved your father.' She and James's father had had an arranged marriage that had turned out to be a very happy one. 'I thought... I wondered whether you were singling out Lady Maria Swanley at our ball, but you haven't mentioned her since then.' She had mentioned Lady Maria obliquely once or twice since the ball but this was the first time she had mentioned her explicitly.

'Yes. No. I haven't, no. She...left London.'

'Oh, I know why.' James's sister Charlotte had come into the room and caught the latest part of their conversation. 'Have you not heard the latest *on-dit*? Lady Maria has become engaged to a penniless curate, although he is of very good birth, I believe. Her mama is very unhappy about it, but I have it from dearest Eliza Featherley that because Lady Maria is now twenty-one she is old enough to make her own decision and intends to marry and retire to the country with him. He has a living in Hampshire.'

'Really!' their mother said.

Really, James thought. If this had been going on for some time, perhaps that was why Lady Maria had practised her deception. Perhaps she had sent a friend to the ball in her place because she did not wish to participate in the Season's marriage mart when she was already promised to her fiancé. But why would Lady Derwent have colluded in that?

'What is it about Lady Derwent that you don't like?' he asked his mother.

'We know each other well but we've never really been good friends. We came out in the same year and she nearly ran away with your dear father, before he saw sense and married me. She's always been quite wild. Even now. She acts the grand Society matron on one hand but on the other does not have a great regard for convention.'

'Very interesting.' Very interesting indeed.

They attended a musical soirée together that evening, because James's mother had ascertained that Lady Catherine would be there.

Shortly after they arrived, James looked round to discover Lady Derwent at his elbow. It seemed very much as though she was there by design. Perhaps she had more to say about Lady Maria.

'I wondered if you might be able to procure some lemonade for me,' she said.

When he had the drink, he found her sitting in a corner, waiting for him.

'Thank you.' She took the glass from him and patted the empty chair next to her. 'Do sit and keep me company for a moment.'

'Of course.'

James was barely seated before she said, 'I believe that you would find it of interest to walk near the cows' pasture in the north-west part of Hyde Park in the morning. At perhaps eleven o'clock.'

James raised his eyebrows. Presumably this had something to do with the fake Lady Maria.

'Indeed?' he asked.

'I am thinking about our last conversation,' she pursued. 'I would recommend that you take a walk there before coming to any important decisions.'

'For a particular purpose?' he asked.

'Eleven o'clock,' she repeated, as though he had not spoken.

'I will bear that in mind,' he said, blinking.

'Are you a musical devotee?' she asked.

'Erm, no.'

'Never mind.' She smiled at him and then launched into a description of the renowned soprano who was going to be singing to them shortly.

James nodded and said very little—he had no opinions to offer on the soprano in question—until eventually Lady Derwent said, 'You must go and find your mother. Don't forget. Eleven o'clock. Tomorrow.'

As James bent his head over her hand, he had no idea whether he would take himself to Hyde Park on the morrow or not.

He still wasn't entirely sure whether he would go to Hyde Park the next day, he told himself, as he endured a lengthy monologue from Lady Catherine on the subject of music, wondering the whole time whether he really would like to be married to her, and unable to stop thinking about Lady Maria—*his* Lady Maria—and wondering whether her presence would have made this evening more enjoyable (he was quite sure that it would).

He would not yet propose marriage to Lady Catherine. He needed to think a little more about it.

He was always going to have come to Hyde Park, he reflected fourteen hours later, as he walked his horse, Star, down the path that led to the spot that Lady Derwent had described to him the previous evening. Of course he was. As he'd listened to a succession of warbling sopranos and growling tenors, he'd reflected on the conversations that he'd had with her and had concluded that of course her suggestion—command—had something to do with his Lady Maria.

And if Lady Derwent was trying to arrange a meeting between him and the fake Lady Maria he couldn't resist attending.

When he came upon the clearing that Lady Derwent had

mentioned, he found that there was no one there. His pocket watch told him that it was still five minutes before eleven.

The next few minutes passed unutterably slowly as he walked Star round, just waiting to see what would happen.

When he did eventually hear people approaching, he turned quickly, only to see that it was not Lady Maria.

Rather, the little group that was approaching comprised three children, a nursemaid and a grey-clad lady who was presumably a governess.

James's gaze rested on the group very briefly, before he resumed looking around to see if other people—in particular a small lady with a beautiful smile—might be approaching. And then, he could not say why, he found his eyes being drawn back to the little group, and in particular to the lady in grey. There was something about her...

He looked hard at her and, as he stared, her head turned in his direction, and she gave a noticeable start.

He hadn't been able to make out her features fully, due to the bonnet she was wearing and the fact that on glimpsing him she had then turned away, and yet he had the strongest feeling...

Was she...?

He dismounted, looped Star's reins around a tree and strode over to the group.

'Good morning,' he said, directing his words at the grey-clad woman. His accosting the group was of course somewhat irregular, but he felt a strong compulsion to confirm his suspicions.

'Good morning.' She kept her head lowered so that it was difficult to see her face, but her voice was recognisable, and so was her posture. Good God.

'Lady Maria!' he exclaimed.

She froze and then, after a long moment, looked up at him.

If he wasn't mistaken, her eyes were filling. Surprisingly, given that surely *she* had wronged *him*, he found himself feeling guilty.

'I'm afraid that you are mistaken,' she told him, shaking her head. There was no trace of her smile. 'Good morning. We must be on our way.'

'No,' he blurted out. He felt as though he *needed* to find out more about her. And Lady Derwent had clearly meant him to find this lady, whoever she really was. As though in some way they were *intended* to meet again.

The lady tilted her head very slightly to one side and said, 'No?' Her tone was significantly frostier than he had assumed her capable of.

Which was arguably quite ridiculous given that *she* had lied to *him*.

'I should be very grateful if you would afford me a few moments of your time,' he said.

'I...' She took a deep breath and then glanced over her shoulder at the nurse and children behind her. 'I am unfortunately busy.'

'Please?' Apparently he was begging. Which, again, felt quite ridiculous. 'Just a minute or two?'

She looked into his face for quite a long time before pressing her lips together and saying, 'One moment.' She turned to the maid and said, 'Elsie, I should be grateful if you would take the children for a short walk along the path over there. Children, please could you look at the different leaves on the trees and try to ascertain what type of tree they are?'

James waited a few moments so that the remainder of her party would be out of earshot, and then said in a low voice, so that they would not hear, 'I would appreciate an explanation. I take it that you masqueraded as Lady Maria at the ball.'

'Yes, I did. I am sorry if I offended you in any way.' She gave a small nod, as though to end the conversation, and took a step or two away from him.

'I don't think this is the end of the conversation,' James stated. How could she possibly think that it was acceptable to practise such an outrageous deception—in his house—and admit to it but behave as though that would be the end of it? At the very least, surely, she should tell him why. And apologise. And...

Well, he didn't know what else. He couldn't really work out how he felt about her any more.

Good God, he'd been on the brink of *proposing* to her. And she was... Well, he had no idea who she was. She was a governess. Who'd been pretending to be Lady Maria Swanley. The whole thing was preposterous.

Perhaps the personality she had presented to him had also been fake. He wasn't sure whether that thought made him feel angry or sad or... Maybe confused. And, yes, definitely angry.

'I would suggest that you owe me an explanation,' he told her.

'I...' She stopped and turned back to face him fully, before saying, 'Yes. The explanation is not entirely mine to give, however. Lady Maria and I are very close friends. Lady Derwent is my godmother. Lady Maria did not wish to attend the ball for reasons of her own, which I cannot disclose, and she asked me to go in her place. Lady Derwent persuaded me that it would be a good idea to enjoy one ball before I began my employment here. I beg of you not to tell my employer that I undertook the masquerade.'

'Your employer?'

'I am a governess.'

Of course. That explained the grey dress. And the children. It did not explain how Lady Derwent was her godmother and Lady Maria her good friend.

'I will not tell your employer.' He was still very angry but he had no taste for vindictiveness. 'I would ask, however: did none of you think of the consequences of your action? I cannot understand how any of you would think that it was an acceptable thing to do. It was rude, it was ridiculous, it was preposterous, it was *stupid*.'

'I'm sorry, I...' she began. And then she stopped and pressed her lips together and tilted her head slightly. 'I do understand that Society might not look kindly on such a masquerade. However, I am sure that it is rare for two people to meet and make a strong connection on such an occasion. Had I just danced and talked to a succession of different people that evening, and then disappeared, no one would have been any the wiser. Whilst I would have had one very enjoyable evening. I believe that your disapprobation is perhaps due to the fact that you and I spent a long time talking and that you feel that I misled you.'

James shook his head, not wishing to acknowledge that he

had a personal reason for his anger. 'I cannot think it acceptable that you practised such a deception.'

'I would suggest—' her voice had turned to ice and somehow he liked her all the more for it '—that, as Duke of Amscott, it is perhaps difficult for you to understand the realities of life for women or less privileged men. Lady Maria had a very good reason for not wishing to attend the ball, and, had she not gone at all, people would have asked questions. Because she is a woman. I did not wish to become a governess, but I have no alternative. I do enjoy parties; that was the only ball I will ever have had the opportunity to attend as a guest. Because I am poor. When you have experienced being either a woman or poverty-stricken or both, I shall accept your criticism.'

James frowned. 'I do of course have the advantages of birth, wealth and sex, and I am sorry that you have had no alternative but to accept a role that you do not want.' They should not have practised their deception, however. Although...her words about being poor and having no further opportunity to attend a ball were very sad. She had seemed to enjoy the dancing very much.

He still didn't know who she was, other than Lady Derwent's goddaughter, or how she came to be in this position.

'You are a lady,' he stated.

She inclined her head.

'May I ask your name and why you came to be a governess?'

'I am sorry but I can see no reason to prolong our acquaintance. I wish you very well, and I apologise for any distress I caused you with the deception.' She gave him a quick smile— a small one, not one of her wide, joyful, wonderful ones—and then turned and hurried in the direction of the maid and her charges, calling to them as she went, so that if James attempted to speak to her again he would cause a scene.

He couldn't do that to her, of course, so he just stood, impotent, hands on hips, watching her walk away from him, wondering what he would do next.

He had the strangest sense that if his life were a play, everything up to the evening he'd met her had been the first act.

And now he'd entered a different stage of life, one in which this lady—whose name he still did not know—might, perhaps, feature heavily.

She couldn't, though. She had deceived him and she was a governess.

He should probably stop being so fanciful and put her out of his mind.

The nameless lady—*she*—was now surrounded by her charges, whose smiles and laughs, their faces upturned to hers, suggested that they were very fond of her.

The little group disappeared around a corner, and James felt, well, bereft.

Maybe he should go after her after all. Find out her name and direction, request further conversation with her.

He took a couple of steps in the direction of the path they had taken, before checking himself. He should not cause the lady any difficulties with her employer unless he was going to propose marriage to her.

This morning, he had been certain that he would propose to her.

Now, however, he really wasn't sure. Well, of course he wasn't. All he knew about her was that she was a governess who had pretended to be Lady Maria Swanley and had spent an evening dancing and conversing with him.

He was definitely not going to propose to her.

He had had a lucky escape.

Chapter Five

Anna

Anna felt as though her legs would barely hold her up as she shepherded the children and Elsie around the corner.

What a horrible coincidence that the duke had come upon them like that. She came here every morning with the girls and rarely saw persons of quality out exercising. It was the wrong time of day for them—too late for gentlemen's morning gallops, and several hours earlier than the fashionable hour for the *ton* to be seen driving in the park—and it was also not the fashionable part of the park.

It had been extremely unlucky.

And extremely...upsetting.

She had spent a lot of time since the ball thinking about the duke and their evening together. When she'd told him that it had been the best evening of her life, she had not been exaggerating. It had been truly wonderful. Their dancing and their kiss had been truly perfect. But the thing that had been the best of all had been their conversation. She had felt as though they had had a genuine connection. And then, afterwards, she had wondered whether she had imagined it; she had thought that the duke probably met and forged connections with women all the time.

And then she had discovered from Lady Maria and her god-mother that he had been to call on her the day after the ball. Her godmother had told her that he had at the very least wished to pursue his acquaintance with her, given his tenacity in asking about her.

It was hard not to wonder whether he might even have proposed to her.

And whether she would have liked to have accepted such a proposal.

She wasn't sure.

He had occupied much of her thoughts and dreams since she'd met him. She had replayed various parts of the evening they'd spent together over and over in her mind.

But men were not to be trusted.

Her mother had brought her up as a lady. When Anna's father had left, they had moved to a well-appointed, medium-sized house in a Cotswold village, living as a respectable widow and her daughter. They had socialised with the local gentry and had attended assemblies in Cheltenham. Anna had had every expectation of continuing to live in such a way. And then her mother had become ill and Anna had spent a lot of money—all their money—on doctors. And then, after her mother had died, she had discovered that she was entirely penniless. Lady Derwent had taken her in and had asked her, many times, to live with her as a companion, as the daughter she had never had. But Anna could not bear to take charity, and had decided that she must earn her living.

And here she was.

Of course the duke would never propose to her now.

And that was probably—certainly—for the best. Because she would never wish to be trapped in an unhappy marriage, and she knew that men's affection and love for their wives—and daughters—could fade.

Although she would have liked to have had children. But she must not dwell on these things.

She should be grateful for her employment and her friends

and not think about the duke or about her life before her mother had become ill.

The way to avoid thinking about things was to keep her mind occupied in other ways. It was reasonably easy during the day, because looking after children made one very busy; it was the evenings that were more difficult.

Her employers, Sir Laurence and Lady Puntney, were very kind people.

Lady Puntney had told Anna that she did not wish her to be worked to the bone and that she must have early afternoons, evenings and regular days off, and enjoy excursions with any friends she might have.

Which was very kind, but it did mean that Anna had a good deal of spare time.

Sir Laurence had generously told her that she might read any of the books in his extensive library, and she had been doing her best to distract herself with literature. Unfortunately, his tastes, or those of his forebears who had stocked the library, tended towards the stuffier sort of fiction, and what Anna needed right now was something like a modern romance to keep her fully engrossed. She was currently reading Virgil in the original Latin, and it was a struggle to maintain her concentration; she regularly found herself staring at the same page for what felt like hours on end.

She had also tried to occupy herself in writing letters to friends, in particular Lady Maria and Lady Derwent, but had found it difficult to write much. Her words had tended towards the melancholy, and she did not wish to be or sound melancholic.

And she had never been particularly gifted at needlework.

'Anna.' Isabella, the youngest of her charges, was pulling at her arm. 'You weren't listening.'

'I'm so sorry, Isabella; I was momentarily distracted. You should nonetheless strive for greater politeness yourself. One should not pull on another's arm like that.'

That evening, when she had finished her work for the day and was about to go to the library to try to find herself a more enthralling work of fiction than Virgil, perhaps something writ-

ten in English, at least, the Puntneys' butler, Morcambe, handed
her a note that had been delivered to her during the afternoon.

It was in a thick envelope and addressed in a decisive-look-
ing script.

Something made her heart beat a little faster as she pulled
it out, and as she read the signature, she began to feel almost
faint with shock.

The note read:

Dear Miss Blake,
Would you be so kind as to accompany me for a short
drive or walk when you are next able?
Yours,
James, Duke of Amscott

How had he found out who she was?

Well, that was a silly question. She realised that she had
been naïve to think that she could effectively remain hidden
from him.

It would have been easy for him to establish her identity in
any manner of ways. Dukes had all the means in the world to
undertake detective work, or of course her godmother might
have decided to tell him; she had certainly been vocal about her
disappointment in Anna's choice to become a governess rather
than accept her charity and had begged her to remember that
she could always choose to live with her, and Anna was sure
that she had been trying to make a match between her and the
duke. No, her godmother had promised her that she would not
betray her to him, and Anna did trust her. He must have found
out some other way.

Her mind was wandering; she didn't need to speculate how
he'd discovered her name and where she was staying. She
needed to decide what she was going to do now.

She couldn't see him. It would be too difficult and there was
no point. And people might see them and talk.

However...

He seemed very determined and very tenacious.

Perhaps it would be better in fact to meet him once in person and explain definitively that she would not be meeting him again.

Maybe she would not reply immediately but instead reflect on the matter for a while.

Half an hour later, she was still in the library, having completely failed to choose a new book because all she could do was think about whether or not she should meet the duke.

She *was* going to meet him, she suddenly decided, as she picked up and discarded a book containing the poems of John Dryden. Otherwise, she would constantly wonder whether she might see him again anyway. Every time she left the house she would be distracted, looking over her shoulder, wondering whether he might be around the next corner. That would not be an enjoyable way to live; it would be better to meet him once and be done with it.

She sent off a note suggesting that they meet in three days' time—sooner than that seemed *very* soon—she felt as though she needed to prepare herself in some way—but longer than that would just be a *lot* of probably disagreeable anticipation—and within the hour received an affirmative response in his decisive script.

And so now she just had to wait and wonder. For three whole days. She should in fact have suggested tomorrow.

The day of their meeting dawned fine and fair. They had agreed to meet at two o'clock in the afternoon, a time at which the children were regularly looked after by their nursemaids while they played for half an hour after their luncheon.

Anna had already taken a small number of solitary walks in the early afternoon to visit shops to purchase necessaries and on one occasion to take a walk with Lady Maria, who had told her all about the duke's visit to her. Anna had not enjoyed hearing about his evident bewilderment, anger and perhaps misery when he'd realised that he'd been deceived, but had been powerless to stop herself asking for every detail of Lady Maria's conversation with him.

Despite her busyness with the children, the morning and luncheon passed very slowly until eventually it was time for Anna to ready herself for her walk with the duke.

Regarding herself in the looking glass, she reflected that she looked very different from how she had at the ball. Her hair was dressed in a plain manner now, pulled close against her head and fastened into a knot at the nape of her neck, and her dress was equally plain: a brown serge morning dress, which paid no particular note to the fashions of the moment.

Anna sighed, and then chastised herself mentally. She had known that this was her lot and she was extremely lucky to have found herself employment with such a pleasant family; and she had had the good fortune to enjoy that one week in London with Lady Derwent and the experience of attending the ball. There were many people in significantly worse situations than she, and she must not complain.

Five minutes later, she let herself out of the front door of the house and trod down the four wide steps leading to the pavement, before turning left towards the corner where she'd agreed that she would meet the duke.

He was already waiting for her.

He had taken her breath away when he was dressed in pristine evening dress, and he took her breath away again now clothed in plain but exquisitely tailored morning dress.

'Miss... Blake,' he said as she drew near to him.

'Your Grace.' She could hardly hear her own voice over the immense thudding in her ears from her racing heart, and all of a sudden her legs felt quite weak.

This was silly. She was just...

She was just going to go for a walk with the only man whom she had ever kissed, a man who was devastatingly attractive and to whom she had lied. Of *course* her heart was beating fast.

'Shall we walk?' He held his arm out to her and, after a little hesitation—it seemed odd for a governess to walk holding a duke's arm—she took it. 'This way?'

They turned left from Bruton Street, where the Puntneys lived, into Berkeley Square, and began to stroll along the side of the square.

A silence, which Anna did not like, began to stretch between them.

'It is a beautiful day for the time of year,' she ventured.

'Yes, we are lucky.'

They relapsed into silence for another minute or so, until the duke said, 'Could I ask… That is to say: I am aware that this is of course none of my business, but are you happy; is your employment palatable to you?'

'Certainly I am happy, thank you,' Anna said robustly. It *was* none of his business, but she had already treated him shabbily in deceiving him at the ball; she could not be rude to him now as well.

And she was *not* going to give in to the thoughts that intruded too often that the life of a governess could become very sad; she would of course have the opportunity to become involved in and shape the lives of her charges but she would be entirely at the mercy of her employers as to how long she remained with them and whether she was able to continue her acquaintance with the children when she no longer worked for the family. And as a governess she was now in a strange position, neither servant nor member of the family.

No. She should not allow herself even to think these things. She was very fortunate in her employers; they were very generous and paid her a salary of eighty pounds per year, where many governesses in their first role with a good London family might expect no more than forty pounds, and if she was careful she should be able to save most of it. And she had very good friends in Lady Derwent and Lady Maria. Indeed, Lady Maria had recently informed her that she would be appointing her godmother to her first child.

So Anna would certainly not end up in the poorhouse and she would have friends to correspond with and she was much more fortunate than many.

And she would of course become used to her new situation very soon.

'I am glad that you are happy,' he said.

'Why, thank you,' Anna said, allowing herself to sound a little acerbic. She did not require his pity.

'I apologise. Perhaps that sounded a little patronising.'

Anna *really* didn't want to be rude, whatever the provocation, and she also still, obviously, felt guilty about her masquerade at the ball, so she didn't exactly agree with him; she just murmured something that he might interpret how he liked.

He laughed. 'You're right. It did sound patronising and you are too polite to say so. What I meant was...well, yes, I would like to think that you're happy and, yes, I think I should perhaps say nothing else on the subject.' He paused, while Anna tried to hide a smile because it was really quite endearing how much he was tying himself into knots, and then he continued, 'This is another thing that is difficult to say without sounding patronising or odd but I would like to let you know that I have not asked any further questions about you other than your name and direction. I did not wish to intrude.'

'May I ask which of my friends furnished you with those details?' She could not help feeling that, if one were prone to melodrama, one might describe it as a betrayal.

'I did not ask your friends and I do not think they would have told me. I mentioned it to my man of business. He has his ways. I apologise; I should have told you that immediately so that you would not feel let down by Lady Derwent or Lady Maria.'

'Thank you!' She smiled at him; whatever else, he was very thoughtful.

There was a brief pause again, and then the duke said, 'This way perhaps?' when they came to the corner of the square, and they continued straight ahead, in the direction of Hyde Park.

'The trees are turning very autumnal,' Anna said.

'Indeed they are. The leaves are most attractive at this time of year.'

'Yes indeed.'

Anna suddenly realised that she did not wish to feel any regrets after this walk. There could be no friendship between a governess and a duke, and, even if there *could* be, it was quite possible that if the duke ever found out that her father had been a groom he would cease any acquaintance with her, so there was no point in their seeing each other again. If there was anything she would like to say to him she should say it now.

'I would like to apologise for having deceived you,' she said. She had partially apologised when they'd met in the park, but not entirely, because at the time she'd been quite angry with him. She *should* apologise, though. 'I would like to explain in more detail how it came about, if I may.'

'I should be very interested to hear in full.'

'Lady Maria and I went to the same seminary in Bath. She is my dearest friend. She is a few months younger than me. I am now two-and-twenty years old. She did not come out when she was younger because very sadly her family suffered a series of bereavements. Her parents wished her to make her come-out this year. But she, for reasons that are not mine to divulge, did not wish to do so. When her parents left town to visit Maria's grandmother, Maria's mother asked my godmother, Lady Derwent, to chaperone Maria to the various balls she was to attend. She came to take tea with Lady Derwent and me, and told us how she felt.

'It was my godmother who suggested the deception, thinking that it would be nice for me to go to a ball and that there could be no harm in it. Lady Maria thought it an excellent idea and I, despite seeing the obvious problems that might arise, such as did in fact arise, allowed myself to be carried along with the plan because I had never been to a ball in London and desired to go to one. My godmother provided me with my dress and escorted me there. I do realise that we should not have entered into the deception and I apologise for having got a little angry with you in the park.'

'No; I must apologise for my initial lack of understanding. And my own anger. And you are right that had you and I not met and…and spent time together…it might have been possible for the deception to go unnoticed, had Lady Maria not been home to callers the next day and then retired to the country.'

'That is exactly what my godmother said when she was persuading me into joining in her plan.'

'Clearly it is a case of great minds thinking alike.'

Anna laughed. 'Perhaps.'

She was very pleased to have had the opportunity to say all that she'd just said, she realised.

Clearly, frankness was a good thing.

'Why did you wish to meet me for this walk?' she asked.

'I...' The duke paused for a while, and then said, 'That is a good question. I don't really know. I think I just wanted to confirm to myself that you were happy. And find out—perhaps entirely out of curiosity, which is of course quite reprehensible—why you indulged in your masquerade. And perhaps I had some residual anger about it, which is now dissipated, because I accept that you could not have predicted how the evening would progress.'

'I see.' She did not entirely see, but of course a duke had a different life from that of most people. He probably wasn't used to not finding out the answer whenever he felt curious about something. It would be like a normal person having an itch that they couldn't reach.

'May I ask why you consented to come for the walk?'

'You may.' There could be no harm in her being honest. 'I think that had I not met you today I would have wondered if I *should* have met you, and what you wished to say to me, and I do not find it particularly comfortable constantly wondering about something.' And *that* would have been an itch that continued to irritate.

'I see. You know, I think I have just worked out why I asked if we could meet.' He paused for a moment as they entered the gates of the park. 'I feel that it is possible that even by the end of my sentence I will regret saying this to you, but I think that I wished to see you again because I...missed you.'

'Oh!' Anna felt her heart give the most enormous lurch.

'Yes, *oh*. I think I was right in predicting that I would regret my words. May I change the subject and draw your attention to that particularly assiduous woodpecker there?'

'Certainly you may. I have always liked the green of a woodpecker's beak.'

'Green is a delightful colour.' A laugh entered the duke's voice as he continued, 'I believe that I have already mentioned that I very much like the green of your eyes.'

'It is very kind in you to say so, and also something that a duke should not be saying to a governess,' said Anna repressively. She really did not wish him to flirt with her now. When she had been playing the role of Lady Maria, that had been one thing, but now, well, now she needed to maintain her reputation and she did not wish to be beguiled into thinking in *that* kind of way about the duke.

'I must apologise,' said the duke instantly. 'You are quite right.'

Anna did not wish any further awkward silences to arise between them. It was clear that this should be their last meeting, and from his immediate agreement with her words it was obvious that he agreed. She knew how much she could enjoy his company, and she might as well make the most of it now, for these last few minutes.

'We could perhaps take a turn around this small pond,' she said, 'and then I will need to return. I will be instructing my charges on geography this afternoon.'

'Indeed? Which geography will you be teaching them today?'

'I found an atlas with a particular emphasis on the British Isles in my employer's library, and whilst, being girls, they might not have the opportunity to travel further afield than England, I hope that they might be able when older to travel to other parts of this country, so I plan to instruct them most carefully in the geography of England.'

'I agree that a knowledge of geography is a very important part of a good education. Have you travelled yourself?' asked the duke.

'I know Gloucestershire well, as I grew up there, as well as Bath and Somerset, where my seminary was and where Lady Maria's family home is. I have never, however, travelled to the north of England. I believe the Lake District amongst other areas to include wonderful scenery that I should like to have the opportunity to visit one day, but of course I don't know whether that will happen. It is something to aspire to for the future. Have you travelled, Your Grace?'

'Yes, I was fortunate enough to do a Grand Tour when I was younger, and have also had the good fortune to travel within England.' He stopped, and then said, 'I am aware that I have been very lucky to have the opportunity to travel; I'm not sure that I recognised that sufficiently at the time.'

'I hope you don't feel that you must almost apologise to me for your fortune in that regard,' Anna told him. 'It is not your fault that you were born to the life you lead, any more than it is a chimney sweep's fault that he was not.'

'That is true, but it is difficult at times not to feel the weight of good fortune.'

'That is of course to your credit, but, rather than apologise to me, tell me some of your most interesting stories. I love to hear first-person accounts of such travels rather than reading about them in fusty books.'

'Well now, that is quite a challenge. I feel beholden to tell you some stories that are either genuinely amusing or genuinely interesting or genuinely not common knowledge.'

'Yes, indeed.' Anna found herself twinkling up at him as they walked slowly along beside the pond. 'I shall certainly be judging you most severely on the quality of your anecdotes.'

'How many anecdotes would you like?'

'Hmm.' Anna pretended to consider. 'Since you have raised the categories yourself, I should like one amusing, one interesting and one not common knowledge.'

The duke nodded very seriously. 'I accept your challenge. Let me prepare for it first.' He squared his shoulders and then rolled them, which made Anna giggle.

And then he told her some truly *excellent* stories, which took them most of the way back to the Puntneys' house and made Anna wish greatly that she could walk with him again.

When she had finished laughing at the conclusion to a story about how he had mistakenly stumbled into a literary salon, when under the impression—due to his imperfect grasp of the Italian language—that he would be attending a masquerade and was therefore dressed as a monk, they were at the end of the Puntneys' road.

'You have succeeded very well in the challenge,' she told the duke, trying very hard not to feel low at the thought that she might well never see him again. 'I am most impressed.'

'I feel a little guilty that I have monopolised the conversation since we were at the pond.'

'Not at all; I very much encouraged you to tell me your stories and I very much enjoyed them. For example, I have never had another first-hand account of someone meeting an elephant and do not think I shall do so again.'

'In that case I shall say that I am pleased to be of service.' The duke stopped walking, and Anna did too, because she was still holding his arm, very much as though their arms belonged perfectly together, which was clearly a silly thing to be thinking. 'I am not pleased, however, that you have not had the opportunity to tell me any of *your* stories; I should very much enjoy hearing anything you might say, getting to know you better.'

His words made Anna feel both very warm inside and very sad that there would be no opportunity for them to talk further. She took her arm away from his because there was no need to hold it when they weren't actually walking, and she was a little worried that she might start to cling on to him if she didn't move away a little.

'It is very kind of you to say so,' she said in as hearty a voice as she could muster, to avoid any of the emotion she felt surfacing, 'but I am sure that I have nothing of interest to say.'

'Firstly—' the duke turned a little so that they were facing each other under the tree beneath which they were standing '—everything you say must be of interest to me, and secondly I cannot believe that you do not have interesting stories. Looking after young children must give rise to many anecdotes. Who is the naughtiest of them?'

'Lydia, the youngest, is particularly naughty,' Anna owned, 'but in the most adorable way. It is in no way a character defect—' she was already extremely fond of all the girls '—but merely liveliness. But it does give rise to some quite extraordinary situations at times.' And then, as they continued to stand there under the tree, she found herself telling him about the slugs that Lydia had smuggled into her mother's bedchamber and the ensuing screams when they had been discovered by Lady Puntney and her maid.

'Oh, my goodness,' she suddenly said across the duke's

laughter, which was truly the most attractive laugh—deep and rumbly—that she'd ever heard; she was sure that one could listen to it every day and not get bored. Clouds had crossed the sun and caused the sky to grow much darker. 'Do you know what time it is? I must hasten back.'

'Of course,' the duke said immediately. 'I must apologise for keeping you.'

He held out his arm to her and she took it wordlessly and they began to walk along the road towards the house at a very fast pace.

'I very much enjoyed the walk; thank you,' the duke said when they reached the house. 'May I have the pleasure of walking with you again?'

'Oh, no, I'm not sure…' Anna was suddenly a little breathless. 'I thought… I'm not sure that we should make a habit of this. I don't think that it is usual for a duke and a governess to walk together.'

'Perhaps just one more walk, so that we might finish our conversation?'

'Is it indeed unfinished, though?'

'I believe that it is.' Anna knew that she had to be firm, even though it felt so—stupidly—deeply sad to say goodbye now. It could not benefit either of them to spend more time together. And, even if she were someone whom a duke might marry, would she want to place all her dependence on one man with whom she had already, she had to admit, felt such passion? Knowing the way her grandfather and father were capable of treating women, could she trust any man? If ever she were to have the occasion to marry, would it not be better—safer—for her husband to be someone whom she liked but did not feel great passion for?

'Perhaps one more walk? In due course? If you like?'

'I don't know.' She was very tempted but really she shouldn't. She looked up at the house; she didn't want anyone to see her with the duke. 'I must go inside now; goodbye.'

'Of course.' He immediately let go of her arm, which instantly made her feel a little bereft. Truly, she was ridiculous. 'Goodbye. I hope to see you again.'

'Goodbye.' Anna decided not to reply to his last few words; she didn't trust herself not to be weak and say perhaps they might meet again.

She purposely didn't look back at him as she went through the door, and then, as she closed it behind herself, regretted not having allowed herself one more look at him.

It would definitely be for the best not to see him again.

Chapter Six

James

James was disappointed that Miss Blake didn't turn for one last goodbye as she entered the house, and then he was disappointed in himself for being such a fool.

Bruton Street, where she now lived, gave directly onto Berkeley Square; it was astonishing to think that the entire time he had been wondering about her whereabouts she had been living so close by. As he walked the short distance in the direction of his home, he found himself scuffing at leaves with his foot, dissatisfied with…well, life. And himself.

Was Miss Blake right, that dukes and governesses should not go for walks? Would he be compromising her? He wouldn't be compromising her in terms of her eligibility for marriage in that he didn't know of a single bachelor of his acquaintance who would look amongst the ranks of governesses for a wife. Would he, though, be compromising her in the eyes of her employers? Would she be in danger of losing her job if she were seen with him regularly?

Maybe. If so, he should of course not see her again.

Perhaps, though, it would not matter.

He did not, he realised as he kicked a particularly large pile of leaves, have any idea what Society's rules were for governesses, beyond being aware that they occupied quite a unique space in the social hierarchy. They were ladies, and certainly not servants. But they were working for a living and could not therefore be regarded as part of Society.

Why did he care? Why was he interested? Did he really wish to see her again? Was he still tempted to propose marriage to her?

Did dukes marry governesses? Could *he* marry a governess?

What was her birth? It must be respectable, presumably. Lady Derwent was her godmother and she had been educated at the same Bath seminary as Lady Maria.

Why was she a governess?

And had he not decided last week that he had had a lucky escape because he didn't *want* to fall in love with the lady who would become his bride, and hadn't it occurred to him that he could be in danger of falling in love with her?

So would it perhaps be better if he did not pursue their acquaintance any further?

He rounded the corner of the square. More leaves. He gave those a kick too.

Maybe he would ask her if she would like to take just one more walk.

Not immediately, though. It would be poor behaviour to make her feel under any kind of obligation or pressure to meet him again.

When he walked into the main drawing room in his house, very ready to bury himself in the newspapers for some time, to give himself some respite from thinking too much about Miss Blake, he found his mother and two of his sisters in the room.

'James.' His mother beckoned him over to her. 'We should decide on the date of your wedding.'

'We should? But I have not yet decided on a bride. And I have not yet ascertained whether any young lady would consent to marry me.' He didn't sit down because he clearly wasn't going to want this conversation to continue for any length of time; he would much rather go to his study to look through some papers there.

His mother frowned and indicated very forcefully with her eyes and raised brow that he should sit beside her.

'I thought we had agreed that you were on the point of proposing,' she said.

'It is a very big decision. I need time to feel certain that I am making the right one.'

'I do understand that.' His mother's tone had softened. 'But equally I do feel that time is perhaps of the essence.'

From his side, James could understand his mother's impatience. She had lost her husband and two oldest sons in the space of only two years and was obviously still grieving, and much more anxious generally than she might have been before, and she had her five youngest daughters to think about. The oldest of his sisters was four-and-twenty and had been married for four years and had two daughters of her own now. His next oldest sister was only seventeen and not coming out until next year—his mother, while eager to know that her children were provided for, did not approve of marriage for young ladies before the age of eighteen. And his four youngest sisters were two sets of twins of fourteen and twelve.

That was a lot of people to ensure security for.

'Yes,' he said. She was right. Time was of the essence. He did need a son as soon as possible. What if the same illness that had struck his father and brothers struck him?

He wished he'd never met Miss Blake. She was confusing him too much. He needed to be able to think clearly.

Three days later, James had boxed hard at Gentleman Jackson's Boxing Saloon, he had ridden hard, he had boxed again—Gentleman Jackson had asked him if it was anger that was causing him to spar so well and James had just boxed even harder—he had played cards with friends and drunk far too much the evening before last, and he had attended two balls and the opera once, and he was still struggling not to think about Miss Blake. But he was now, with his mother, standing outside a house on Clarges Street, about to pay a call on Lady

Catherine Rainsford, who remained his mother's preferred candidate for his hand.

'Perhaps after today you will feel inspired to make an offer,' his mother said to him just as the door was opened by the Rainsford family's butler.

'Perhaps,' said James unenthusiastically.

Within fifteen minutes, as he and Lady Catherine sat and smiled at each other and occasionally produced a few insipid words before smiling some more, he knew that he couldn't do it. So many little snippets of sentences or references reminded him of Miss Blake, or made him wonder what her views on them might be, or caused him to imagine her laughing when he responded with sarcasm or wonder what joke she might make. It was as though he was under a spell, and he could not in good conscience propose to one woman while temporarily in thrall to another.

He intended to be an unfashionably faithful husband, as his own father had been, and, while he did not want to fall in love, he did not want to be thinking about another woman throughout his marriage.

What he should probably do was see Miss Blake again, if she were willing, and have a long conversation with her, get to know her better, and see if that put paid to this inconvenient hankering after her company that he was currently feeling. It felt like an infatuation; he needed to cure himself of it before committing to marriage with someone else. And everyone knew that familiarity bred contempt; if he spent more time with Miss Blake, he would no doubt cease to be so curious about her.

Three hours later he was waiting with bated breath for a response to the note he had dashed off asking Miss Blake if she would care to accompany him to Gunter's Tea Shop to sample their ices. Four hours later he was still waiting. And by the time he left the house for a dinner with close friends at White's, he still felt on tenterhooks even though it was clear that he was not going to receive a reply this evening—or, perhaps, at all.

There was still no reply by the time he took luncheon the next day.

And then, late in the afternoon, he received a note addressed in Miss Blake's hand. Even her handwriting appealed to him, he realised, as he tore open the envelope. It was well-formed, easily legible, very attractive to look at... Reminiscent of the lady herself in many ways.

If her handwriting appealed to him, the content of her note did not.

Your Grace,
I regret exceedingly that I am unable to meet you again.
Yours sincerely,
Anna Blake

And that was obviously that. Clearly, he could not beg her, or make her feel uncomfortable, by asking again. He could, of course, hover regularly in Bruton Street or go to Hyde Park when she would presumably be walking with her charges, but that would be shocking behaviour when she had told him so definitively that she did not wish to see him again. That really was very much that.

And everything suddenly felt very flat.

He didn't particularly want to do anything now, but he was not going to allow himself to sink into any kind of misery just because a young lady—a governess—had told him that she did not wish to accompany him to a tea shop.

He had managed to keep his own spirits and those of his mother and sisters reasonably steady through the terrible loss of his father and brothers, so he was certainly not going to succumb to despondency over Miss Blake.

She was just a lady with whom he had enjoyed a very pleasurable evening and a nice walk.

And now he was going to go into the library and look through the post that he had received earlier in the day and had not opened because he had been waiting for Miss Blake's note.

The usual invitations and various other missives he had received caused him to sigh with boredom, but he continued. Soon, this feeling would pass and he would carry on with his life perfectly happily, and by the end of the Season he would, he trusted, have come to an agreement with a pleasant and suitable young lady.

He was almost yawning as he pulled out yet another note, written in an ornate script. He'd begun to make little bets to himself as to what each invitation would be. This one he would wager would be a dowager's musical soirée.

It was in fact an invitation to call with Lady Derwent in two days' time.

He re-read it. Yes, it was indeed addressed to him rather than to his mother.

Well.

It seemed very likely that the invitation was related to his acquaintance with Miss Blake. And therefore of course he was going to go.

When he arrived very punctually—at the somewhat surprising time of half past two—to see Lady Derwent, her butler showed him immediately towards the same saloon in which he had been on his previous visit.

As he approached the room, he heard more than one female voice from within. And…if he wasn't mistaken, one of them was Miss Blake's. Or was that just wishful thinking? He had thought he'd caught a glimpse of her more than once in the park and in the street and had whipped his head round each time only to discover that he'd been wrong; this was probably just the same.

The butler opened the door for him and announced his name.

And if James wasn't mistaken, there was an audible gasp from within.

And, yes, as the door opened wider, he saw Miss Blake, sitting directly opposite, her beautiful mouth formed into an O shape and her eyes wide.

She remained like that for a long moment, before recovering her composure and casting her eyes down, whilst murmuring, 'Good afternoon, Your Grace.'

'You are early,' Lady Derwent admonished him. 'I had not expected you for another hour.'

James looked at the clock on the mantelpiece and frowned.

He could not directly contradict her but he *knew* that he was exactly on time.

And then he looked at her more closely. He couldn't say exactly in what way, but he could swear that she looked almost sly at this moment. As though she were plotting something.

Had she planned this on purpose? Invited him at the same time as Miss Blake so that they would meet each other again?

He looked back to Miss Blake. She was now sitting with her hands folded in her lap, her eyes downcast but otherwise looking entirely composed.

'I do apologise,' he said to Lady Derwent. 'I must have misread your writing.'

'Or perhaps misremembered,' she said. 'Well, no matter. Now that you are here, you must take tea with us. I shall ring for Buxton.'

'I must take my leave,' Miss Blake said.

'Nonsense,' Lady Derwent told her. 'You have only just arrived, and I still need to hear your news and tell you mine. The duke will not mind. None of us need to pretend that you have not already met.'

'No, indeed,' agreed James. 'I think we are all aware that we met at the ball.'

A tiny gasp came from Miss Blake's direction.

James was tempted to ask her if she was quite all right but decided that it would be better to ignore the sound.

'Your news, Anna,' Lady Derwent said. 'You were telling me about your excursion to the British Museum. I am sure His Grace would be interested to hear about it.'

'I am afraid that I have little of interest to tell,' Miss Blake—Anna—said. 'As we were on the point of looking at the Rosetta Stone, Lydia declared herself quite ill, and we had to leave very quickly.'

'Was she genuinely ill or just not very interested in historical artefacts?' James asked.

'The latter, I fear. I considered reprimanding her and then decided that a far better punishment would be to take her very seriously and insist that she keep to her room for the remainder of the day and take just some chicken broth. She was extremely bored and recovered remarkably quickly.'

'You are clearly an excellent governess,' Lady Derwent said approvingly, while James smiled. 'I should not like to think of your allowing the girls to be naughty.'

James raised one eyebrow very slightly at Lady Derwent. Surely this was the pot calling a kettle black; pretending to be ill to avoid being bored at a museum could not compare with instigating an impersonation of a ball guest.

'I know what you are thinking.' Lady Derwent leaned forward and rapped him over the knuckles, which James saw out of the corner of his eye caused Miss Blake's eyes to dance. 'Irrespective of what they might do in later life, it is important for children to be taught to behave properly.'

'Indeed it is,' Miss Blake agreed. 'And I am doing my best to instil discipline into them. It is hard sometimes, because one is tempted to laugh.'

'Did you have a governess, my lady?' James asked Lady Derwent very blandly.

'I did, and she failed utterly to indoctrinate me with discipline, but that is not to say that other children should not be taught better than I.'

Miss Blake laughed. James adored her laugh. It was light but full, and, if you caused that laugh you felt very proud of yourself, and if you did not know the reason for her mirth you immediately wished to find out the reason for it.

And now he was laughing at himself for thinking far too much about *her* laugh.

'Were you educated at home or at school, Your Grace?' Miss Blake's question was the first of a personal nature that she had asked him; he had had the impression that she did not wish to discuss either his life history or her own. Perhaps she felt on safer ground with Lady Derwent present.

'I began with nurses at home in the country, and then had a succession of tutors—some did not stay long because my two older brothers and I were close in age and not well disciplined, and then I went to Eton, followed by Oxford.' He looked at Miss Blake. He would very much like to know more about her background. 'I understand that you were educated in Bath, at the same establishment as Lady Maria?'

'Yes, I was, and we both enjoyed it there most of the time.'

'Were you both angelic students?' he asked.

'Not always,' Miss Blake admitted. 'But I flatter myself that my experience of breaking the rules a little will make me a wiser governess.'

'I think you're right,' James agreed. 'In fact, one might say that you were particularly prescient in undertaking any naughtiness. You were merely exploring all options for the future.'

'Exactly.'

'Did you ever swap identities with someone?' he asked.

'I must reprimand you, Your Grace, for such a particularly indelicate question.' Miss Blake tsked. 'We do not refer to specific past misdemeanours.'

James laughed out loud. 'Apparently I must apologise.' He realised that at some point he had clearly entirely forgiven Miss Blake for her deception at the ball.

'Indeed you must,' Miss Blake told him.

'Were you instructed at home before you entered the seminary?' he asked, still very interested to hear all about her early life.

'Her mother, my dear friend, instructed her,' Lady Derwent said. 'Your Grace, are you a devotee of poetry? Before you came, we were discussing Lord Byron's *The Bride of Abydos*.' It was very much as though she was changing the subject. Did she not wish him to discuss Miss Blake's childhood with her?

'I must own that I do not regularly read verse,' he said, and the conversation continued from there, through literature—with minimal contribution from James—and a discussion of the library of Miss Blake's employer and James's own library.

'Sir Laurence's library is remarkably well-stocked,' Miss Blake concluded.

'Does he have copies of the romances you like so much?' asked Lady Derwent.

'Sir Laurence does not share my taste in that regard, for which one can only admire him.'

'I, however, *do* share your taste.' James could not believe his luck. This would give him a very good excuse to see Miss Blake again. 'That is to say, my mother does, and she would very much like to lend her books to you, I know.'

He would have to remember to purchase the necessary books. He could enquire of his married sister perhaps which would be the best ones to buy. Or perhaps he would just buy all such books stocked in London so that there could be no possibility of his disappointing Miss Blake.

'Oh, no, I couldn't possibly.' Miss Blake shook her head firmly.

'Nonsense.' Lady Derwent sounded even firmer. 'I think it a marvellous idea. You are working very hard, my dear, and you will be a better governess to your charges if you enjoy your reading when you are resting. His Grace will, I am sure, bring the books to you when you next have a spare moment. Perhaps tomorrow? Or the day after tomorrow?'

'Thank you.' Miss Blake spoke a little faintly—Lady Derwent was indeed very forceful—and James would almost have felt sorry for her if he had not been so pleased that he would have such a good opportunity to see her again. 'That is extremely kind. Perhaps if you…you could perhaps send a footman with them?'

'I am sure His Grace will be very happy to deliver them to you himself. In fact…' Lady Derwent looked thoughtful.

James had the strongest sense that he and Miss Blake were pawns in some game that Lady Derwent was playing. Did he mind? He wasn't sure. It would of course depend on whether the aim of her game aligned with his own. At this point he wasn't entirely sure of his own aims. He did want to see Miss Blake alone again, for the purposes of curing himself of this ridiculous infatuation. And then he would like to marry someone with whom he would not be desperately in love. It did not seem particularly likely that that was what Lady Derwent was planning.

'I'm afraid I must leave now.' Miss Blake gathered her gloves and reticule and rose to her feet before her godmother could continue down whatever line of thought she had begun. 'Thank you so much; I have very much enjoyed our tea.'

Lady Derwent rose too. 'I would usually suggest that His

Grace escort you home, but as he is so recently arrived I should like to talk to him for a few moments. One of my footmen will walk with you.'

James also rose, in order to bid Miss Blake goodbye. As he took her hand in his and looked down into her beautiful green eyes, he found it an effort not to press her fingers far more tightly than a mere goodbye warranted.

'I will look out for those books for you on my return home,' he told her.

'Thank you; that is very kind.'

And then she was gone and the door was closed behind her, and Lady Derwent was gesturing him to be seated.

'Now.' She leaned forward and tapped him on the knee. 'I believe that my goddaughter's reluctance to prolong her acquaintance with you comes from a belief that a governess cannot have a friendship with a duke. Of course, one would imagine that it might be quite irregular. But it would not be irregular for a duke to propose to a governess who was a gentlewoman of good family. It *would* of course be irregular for a duke to pursue a friendship with a lady whom he did not wish to marry.'

'Yes.' He would have liked to have asked what Miss Blake's birth was, but did not, he realised, have quite the same knack for outrageous frankness that Lady Derwent had.

'I expect my goddaughter to be treated well, as you would treat any other gently born lady,' Lady Derwent said.

'I would never wish to do her any harm,' James told her.

'Then I imagine that you will make up your mind one way or the other as to what you want as soon as possible. In the meantime, I shall be holding a literary salon on Friday. Given your interest in modern literature, you will be pleased to attend.'

'Thank you.' Good God. James very much hoped that Miss Blake would also be made to attend, otherwise it would almost certainly be a torturous experience. *Could* governesses venture out in the evenings? Did they? He really did not know. He would just have to hope.

'And now, I find myself a little fatigued,' Lady Derwent told him. 'I look forward to seeing you on Friday.'

James laughed. It didn't surprise him that his mother and

Lady Derwent did not like each other. They were so similar that they could be nothing but bosom friends or sworn enemies.

The next afternoon, at two o'clock, after a very busy morning visiting first his astonished sister—she had not seen him before luncheon for several years—to ask about the latest popular novels, and then Hatchard's bookshop on Piccadilly, James was outside the Puntneys' mansion, looking forward to seeing Miss Blake.

As he lifted the knocker, though, he suddenly realised that he couldn't do this. She had been cajoled, effectively, into seeing him, by her godmother and by him.

If she did not wish to see him then he should certainly not force her to do so.

It was pure selfishness in him to wish to see her, spend time with her, in order to cure himself of the infatuation he currently felt. He had felt that there was a mutual attraction between them. What if she had felt it too, and what if she were disappointed if he asked her to accompany him for a walk and then did not wish to see her again?

He should not do that.

So when the Puntneys' butler opened the door to him, he asked him if he would be able to present the books to Miss Blake with his compliments on behalf of Lady Derwent, before handing the pile to him and leaving.

He would just have to hope that time would help him forget his ridiculous infatuation.

Chapter Seven

Anna

Anna had been—pathetically, she knew—unable to help herself peeking out of the window at the street below to see whether the duke would indeed come to see her with the books.

She had known that she would be very grateful to have them, if he did come.

She hadn't been sure whether or not she would be grateful to see the duke himself, though.

If she was honest, she *loved* his company, but it could be of no benefit to her to see him again, and so she would prefer to put an immediate end to their acquaintance.

And yet…when she'd seen him round the corner into the street and walk along with what looked like four books under his arm, her heart had given the most tremendous lurch.

When he disappeared out of sight after going up the steps from the pavement to the front door, she couldn't help going over to the looking glass above the mantelpiece to pat her hair into place, and then allowing herself to give her cheeks just the tiniest of pinches to bring a little colour to them. She smiled at her reflection and almost danced to the door to begin to descend the stairs from her attic floor in anticipation of being told that she had a caller.

She was in the hall before a footman had reached her and... Oh.

There was a pile of books on the marble-topped chiffonier to her left, with a card on top of the pile, and no sign of the duke.

She felt her smile drop and her hand go to her throat.

She'd been so silly. *So* silly.

The duke had obviously *not* been intending to see her or as interested in her company as she was in his. He had obviously just been *made* by her godmother to provide the books and had been too polite to demur. So he had clearly dutifully collected some together and had brought them and...gone away again.

And that was *perfect*, she thought, as she looked at his card. *Perfect*. Exactly what she would have chosen, in fact. Definitely.

Three days later, at eight o'clock in the evening, she alit from Lady Puntney's carriage outside her godmother's house. Truly, Lady Puntney was the most wonderful employer; she had told Anna that she positively *insisted* that she attend Lady Derwent's literary salon because it could only benefit the girls if their governess discussed literature with people who knew the great Lord Byron well. She had also whispered to Anna, in a joking fashion, poking fun at herself—because, as she had already owned, she was hoping to climb as high in Society as possible, in as nice a way as possible—that if Anna wished to introduce her to such an illustrious personage as Lady Derwent, that would be wonderful.

Truly, there was no need to hanker after the friendship of the duke. Anna was most lucky in both her employer and her godmother, not to mention her wonderful best friend, Lady Maria, who would be here this evening.

Lady Derwent had told Anna that the evening would comprise a select group of ladies meeting to discuss the most recent work of Jane Austen, *Emma*.

Most fortuitously, *Emma* was one of the books that the duke had delivered to Anna on Tuesday, and from the first page she had loved it. She had read late into the night, until her candle burnt out, for the three nights since she had received it, unable to put it down. She had finished it that afternoon, while her charges rested with their nurses, in lieu of taking her usual afternoon walk around the garden square. Forgoing her daily exercise was in direct contradiction of her own strict tenets on how a lady should live, but it had been worth it because she had very much enjoyed the ending of the story and would now be in a position to discuss it with the other ladies.

Lady Maria greeted her at the door to the salon with her arms held out, and Anna embraced her gladly. Her godmother then hurried over.

'Anna, dearest.' She pulled her properly into the room, and said, 'Allow me to introduce you to our fellow devotees of literature.'

As Anna was introduced to a series of ladies, she was extremely grateful for the dresses with which her godmother had presented her before she took up her governess role; the one she was wearing now was a delightful primrose yellow muslin, which she knew was of the latest mode and hoped became her quite well. Everyone here was smartly attired and she would not have enjoyed wearing one of her brown or dark blue day dresses.

'I'm delighted to...' She suddenly gave the most tremendous start in the middle of greeting a very well-dressed lady of perhaps forty years old whom Lady Derwent had introduced as a Mrs Travers; she had perceived out of the corner of her eye, at the far end of the room, a group of three men.

Two of them were dressed rather unusually, the way one might imagine poets to dress, with loose jackets and spotted cravats. And the other...

The other was a tall and broad gentleman with thick dark hair and very neatly fitting and not at all poetic-looking clothing, and an expression of slight horror on his face, which made Anna's lips twitch, even as she felt her stomach churn.

She forced her attention back to the ladies to whom she was being introduced, and flattered herself that she managed to produce quite acceptable smiles and greetings, despite the whirring of thoughts inside her head.

And then her godmother took her over to the men.

She introduced Anna to both the spotted cravat wearers, while Anna tried very hard to focus on the introductions and produce a few polite words, while her mind whirred and her eyes seemed to want to swivel in the direction of the third gentleman.

And then Lady Derwent said, 'And, of course, you are acquainted with His Grace,' and Anna was able to look directly at him without appearing rude.

Anna and the duke said, 'Indeed,' at the same time. He inclined his head slightly, his expression unmoving, and she gave him a small smile.

'Thank you so much for the books.' Anna had of course written a note thanking the duke—a note that had taken her far more time than it should have done to compose—but obviously must thank him properly now.

'It was my great pleasure. I hope that you will enjoy them.'

'I have already finished reading *Emma* and enjoyed it exceedingly; I am sure that I will enjoy the others too, and am very grateful for the opportunity to read them. I must confess that I was so engrossed in the story that I read late into the night three evenings running and was only stopped by my candle burning right down; I am very eager to start the next one but will wait a little, both to enjoy the anticipation of it and to recover from the lack of sleep that I experienced this week.'

The duke laughed, and said, 'I'm very pleased to hear how much you enjoyed it and will be equally pleased to lend you more books from my mother's collection when you have finished those. Which do you intend to read next?'

Anna's reply—Fanny Burney's *Evelina*—was interrupted by Lady Derwent clapping and addressing the assembled company.

'We are now going to discuss Jane Austen's *Emma*. For those who have not read it but intend to do so, those of us who *have* read it will take great care to avoid telling you what happens at the end. Let us arrange ourselves so that we can converse more easily as a group.'

Within a small number of minutes, with a firm and slightly terrifying authority that Anna imagined many army generals could only dream of attaining, Lady Derwent had directed the assembled company to sit in a semicircle.

Somehow—Anna was sure that it was by design but had not been able to pinpoint how she had actually managed it—Lady Derwent contrived to seat the duke on the left-hand end of the half-circle, with Anna immediately to his right, so that if he wished to enjoy any quiet conversation it could only be with her.

Truly, her godmother was incorrigible in her apparent quest to throw Anna together with him.

And truly, Anna's heart should not be lifting in the way that it was at the prospect of more time talking to him. Allowing herself to enjoy his company could only lead to despondency in the future. Clearly nothing could come of an acquaintance between them; dukes did not marry the daughters of scandal, and indeed that was a good thing: Anna should keep on reminding herself that she had seen the misery caused by her parents' incompatibility—both in rank and in temperament—and did not wish to participate in such a union herself. Husbands in general were rarely to be relied upon.

Having finished her directions, Lady Derwent seated herself in a large chair that had been placed facing the middle of the semicircle, and some distance back so that she was able to see everyone without having to turn her head too much.

'With whom should we commence?' She looked in the duke's direction, very much as though she had always intended to ask him first. 'Amscott, as one of the few gentlemen here, should you like to give us your thoughts on the main themes of the book?'

'I...am...still reading it and so would not like to say too much now in case my views change when I reach the end of the book. Which I am very much enjoying.'

'What did you think of Emma herself at the beginning? And of Mr Knightley of course?' asked Anna, unable to help herself poking a little fun at him. It was extremely obvious that he had not read any of the book at all.

'I thought Miss Austen's execution of the entire book was masterful. I like her use of literary devices and the setting in which she places the story and her characters. I should be very interested to hear your views on her writing, not to mention her characterisation. Of Emma and Mr Knightley in particular,' the duke replied. Quite masterfully, in fact. He really did give the impression of almost knowing what he was talking about.

'One last question,' Anna said, really unable to resist. 'What did you think of the relationship between Jane Fairfax and Frank Churchill?'

The duke narrowed his eyes at her for a moment, which made her lips twitch further, before smiling blandly and saying, 'I very much enjoyed reading about their relationship. I thought that it was written very well. I should very much like to hear your thoughts now, though. I fear that I have been monopolising the conversation for too long.'

'I would be very happy to—perhaps—bore you with my many thoughts, as I quite devoured the book, but have one final question for you,' she said.

The duke nodded and murmured, 'Of course you do.'

'Who was your favourite character, and why?'

The duke shook his head. 'No,' he stated. 'I enjoyed the book so much that I cannot choose. I do not mean to imply that I found each character equally worthy of my liking or equally flawed, but they were so well drawn by the author that I cannot choose one above the other.' His head was turned in the direction of Lady Derwent, but he shot a triumphant glance in Anna's direction as he finished speaking, which caused her to have to swallow a giggle.

'Most illuminating,' Lady Derwent said. 'Anna, do you agree with the duke's thoughts?'

Looking straight back at her godmother, trying hard not to be very conscious of the duke's eyes on her, Anna said, 'They were certainly very comprehensive. More specifically...'

She had a lot to say, having read the book so very recently and having enjoyed it so very much, and soon was so engrossed in conversation with others who had genuinely read it that she almost at times forgot how close to the duke she was sitting and how if she moved a little to her left their shoulders and thighs might almost brush against each other.

It was wonderful. She hadn't previously experienced discussing literature with others in this way; her parents had not been readers, and Lady Maria and her other friends at the seminary had been reluctant scholars at best—although it did seem this evening as though Lady Maria had read at least some of *Emma*. Perhaps the problem had been the dry nature of their reading material at the seminary.

The discussion—with nods and murmured agreement from the duke—continued for a gratifyingly long time, with, amongst other things, different opinions offered as to Miss Austen's motivation behind her writing, the reasons that the writing was so particularly effective, and discussion as to whether any of her characters might be based on people whom Miss Austen knew, and whether any of the present company might have met any of those people.

As the conversation eventually descended into general gossip, Anna found herself turning to the duke—it would have been rude of her not to have done so as he would have had no one else with whom to converse—and being unable to resist the temptation to say, 'You must be pleased not to be dressed as a monk this evening.'

He cracked a laugh. 'I am delighted not to be dressed as a monk and even more delighted that my telling you that story clearly made an impression.'

'I must confess I would have enjoyed seeing you in religious garb this evening.' She smiled at him and added sarcastically, 'You look as though you are *very* pleased to be here.'

'As you will have noticed, I am extremely devoted to all forms of literature and very much in my element here,' he said, rolling his eyes just a little, which made Anna laugh.

'I do hope that hearing our thoughts will not have ruined the end of the book for you, Your Grace,' she said with faux sincerity. 'I understood you to say that you had read most of it already, and certainly your expressed thoughts indicated a wide knowledge of the book.'

'What I was most proud of in the expression of my thoughts,' he replied, 'was that they were so very applicable to almost any well-written work of fiction. And of course one's views on any book one has read are subjective, and so I could not be called wrong.'

Anna laughed. 'Very cunning; I am not surprised that you feel proud. Are there any books that you have read recently that you would like to discuss in more specific detail?'

The duke narrowed his eyes at her. 'Without wishing to be impolite in any way, I cannot answer that question until I understand the possible consequences. Would I be required to discuss the book more widely, and is there a risk that I would have to do so today?'

'My godmother wrote to me yesterday to ask if there was a particular book that I should like to discuss at this salon, and I understood from her that our conversation would be confined to the works of Jane Austen, but I'm sure that if you wished to hold forth about another author we should all be most eager to hear what you had to say. I would be very happy to suggest that to my godmother.'

'I cannot believe you would treat me so shabbily after I sent you the book that you have just enjoyed so much.'

'You are quite right.' Anna gave him a fake contrite smile. 'I am very grateful and must no longer torment you.'

'Indeed you must not.' His smile, coupled with the way he was gazing into her eyes as though the rest of the company did not exist, was suddenly making her feel quite breathless.

'If I give you my assurance that I will not mention your answer to anyone else,' Anna said, trying hard not to be too overcome at his proximity, the intimacy of his lowered and beautifully deep and raspy voice and the squareness of his jaw, 'would you tell me your favourite author?'

The duke leaned another inch or so closer to her. 'If it is to remain our secret—' the increased raspiness of his voice caused Anna's skin to raise in goose bumps '—I am prepared to confide in you.'

'I shall be honoured,' she said, still breathless, 'to be the holder of your confidence.'

The duke's eyes dropped from her eyes to her mouth for a moment, and Anna swallowed.

'That is…good to hear,' he said.

Anna found herself moistening her lips with her tongue.

'So…my secret.' He was looking at her lips again, and Anna felt as though they were the only two people in the world.

'Mmm?' she breathed.

'You must remember that you have promised not to tell another soul.'

'I shall remain faithful to that promise.' She could not have told why this conversation felt so extremely daring.

'So your question was…? I just want to make sure I answer it quite correctly.' The duke turned a little further in her direction, his eyes not moving from her face, and the sides of their knees brushed.

'Oh,' Anna squeaked.

A small smile played about the duke's lips and Anna smiled back.

They were just *looking* now, gazing at each other, as though they were quite alone.

Which they were not, she suddenly remembered.

'The question,' she said, as firmly as she could.

'Ah yes, your question. *Any* question, Miss Blake, and I will answer it as long as my response remains secret.'

Anna took a deep breath. Her stomach seemed to have turned completely liquid. A very warm liquid.

What had they been talking about? What *was* her question? Oh, yes.

'Who,' she breathed, 'is your favourite author?'

'My favourite author,' the duke said very slowly, and Anna could not help watching his beautifully firm mouth as he formed the words, 'is—' he leaned even closer to her and their knees brushed even more '—Jethro Tull.'

'Jethro Tull?' Her voice had gone squeaky again.

'The only author I have read recently.'

'I am not—' she was almost forgetting what they were talking about, because the way he was gazing at her was so—well—*exciting* '—familiar with Mr Tull's works.'

'He wrote about agricultural machinery and farming methods in the last century. I have just been dipping into his work *Horse-hoeing Husbandry*.'

'Oh. How...fascinating.'

'Extremely fascinating.' The duke's lips quirked up and Anna couldn't find any more words, because it didn't feel as though it was just Mr Tull whom the duke found fascinating.

And then they just sat and smiled at each other, and Anna felt as though her heart might beat right out of her chest.

She loved the tiny lines at the corners of the duke's eyes when they creased as his smile grew, as it was doing now, and she loved the sheer breadth of his shoulders and the way she could see his muscles move under his tight-fitting jacket. And she loved just *being* with him.

He was looking at her lips again and she wondered whether she might explode. She really did need to re-start some sensible conversation.

'How often do you read Jethro Tull? And how many books did he write?' she asked, trying not to sigh at the sheer deliciousness of this conversation.

'I am not sure exactly how many books he wrote and I am not an avid reader but I do on occasion enjoy reading—' the duke's voice dropped a little '—when I am in bed, before I go to sleep.' His throat worked as she stared at him, unable to stop herself imagining him in, well, *bed*. The way he was swallowing indicated that perhaps he was having similar thoughts. Perhaps in relation to her.

'In bed,' she repeated, and then gasped. What was she *saying*? Respectable governesses did not talk about *beds* with unmarried men. Especially not in a literary salon in the company of others.

She took a very deep breath and said, 'I must try Mr Tull's works myself,' with as much briskness as she could muster.

'I would be very happy to lend them to you any time you should like to read them.' The duke's tone was very serious, but his eyes were very playful, and the combination was irresistible.

'I should not like to deprive you of your own reading matter,' Anna replied, only just capable of forming a rational sentence.

'My feeling...'

To Anna's huge disappointment, the duke was interrupted

by Lady Derwent clapping her hands. 'I think it's time that we all took some refreshment.'

She had groups of small tables surrounded by chairs at the other end of the salon, and they all dutifully followed her over to them.

'I would like to sit with my goddaughter and of course the duke,' she announced. 'I make no pretence that I don't enjoy the company of a handsome young man.'

And before Anna had time to think about whether she was pleased or not to be seated at the same table as the duke and her godmother, she'd been marched by Lady Derwent over to her table.

'I must say, Amscott—' Lady Derwent took a dainty bite of a small crab tart '—your blathering about the book was admirable. One might almost have imagined that you had read it.'

The duke leaned back in his chair, his broad shoulders far too wide for its back, and grinned. 'I was not aware until four days ago that you were summoning me to this salon. Had I had longer, I would of course have been delighted to have read the entire book.'

'In that case—' Lady Derwent smiled triumphantly '—I shall tell you now what book we intend to discuss next time.'

Anna felt herself smiling inside at the thought that there would be a *next time*, even as she realised that it would be very dangerous to allow herself to become too attached to such occasions.

Perhaps, though, perhaps she might have an interesting and full life if she could continue to attend select events like this with her godmother. And perhaps one day she might meet a man whom she could hope to marry who might make her feel the way the duke made her feel. Actually, why had she just thought that? Hadn't she decided that if she could avoid it she would not like to be married? Or if she did marry should her husband not be someone who did *not* make her feel the way the duke did?

'Next time?' queried the duke, and Anna immediately felt her spirits sink a little. Which was very silly; this salon would have been hugely enjoyable even without the Duke's presence, she was sure.

'Next time,' her godmother said firmly.

The duke laughed. 'I will of course be more than happy to attend—' he glanced for the merest of seconds in Anna's direction, which made her smile '—any number of book discussions.'

'Do you undertake to produce an equally profound analysis of any book, Your Grace?' Anna asked with her most demure air.

'Certainly,' he said.

And then he nudged her foot very gently under the table with his own foot, while continuing to hold a particularly bland expression on his face, which made her gasp considerably less gently.

'Are you quite well, Anna?' her godmother asked.

'Very well, thank you.' Which was true as long as her heart didn't jump right out of her body with all the thudding it was doing as she wondered what the duke might do next.

The three of them then conversed amicably on a number of unexceptionable topics, and the duke behaved equally unexceptionably throughout. Which was really quite disappointing.

When in due course some of the guests began to take their leave, Anna stood up too, with some reluctance.

'Thank you so much for the evening,' she said to her godmother. 'I have enjoyed it exceedingly.'

'You will go home in one of my carriages,' Lady Derwent instructed. 'The duke will escort you outside.'

'Of course.' The duke stood up very promptly and held his arm out to Anna, and to her shame she felt herself almost wriggling with internal delight to have another opportunity to touch him, even in a completely innocent way.

As they descended the steps outside the front door, he leaned down so that no one around might hear, and said, 'We were interrupted in the middle of a conversation earlier. Perhaps we should resume it. Would you care after all to visit Gunter's with me? I believe the ices there are the best in London.'

Anna knew that she'd thought about this and decided that it was not a good idea to see the duke alone—or at all—again, but right now she couldn't remember why she'd thought so, and it also seemed that there could be little point in not accompanying him there if she was, for example, going to see him again at another literary evening.

So she said, 'Oh, well if they are the best in *London*, perhaps I cannot refuse.'

'Excellent.' His smile melted Anna's insides. 'I shall look forward to it. I will write to you tomorrow to arrange the time.'

As he handed her into the carriage, the duke pressed her hand just a little more than was necessary, in the most delicious way, almost as though he were promising something, and held her gaze for far longer than necessary as he smiled at her.

Anna smiled back at him, wordlessly, and knew that she would look forward to their visit to Gunter's far more than she ought.

Chapter Eight

James

James had made hay while the sun shone and had written to Anna immediately on waking the next day to arrange to visit the ice cream parlour.

The response had taken far too long for his liking; it had not arrived until the afternoon. It was an excellent response, though: Anna had agreed to go to Gunter's with him the next day.

He drew up on Bruton Street in his curricle at the time they had agreed, feeling far more excited than any grown man should at the prospect of going to a tea shop and eating ices.

He needed to remind himself that the reason for spending a little more time with her was to confirm that they would not in fact be compatible as life partners. He just needed to cure himself of his ridiculous infatuation.

As he lifted the knocker on the Puntneys' front door, he reflected that he could no longer think of Anna as Miss Blake after hearing Lady Derwent address her by her Christian name. The name Anna was perfect for her: classic, poised, elegant, lovely-sounding and with a little cheekiness to it. Good God.

It seemed as though the literary evening might have had an effect on him; he had become quite poetic.

The Puntneys' butler asked him to wait in the hall for a moment and rang a bell. Shortly afterwards, he heard steps and Anna came into sight around the bend in the staircase.

She smiled when she saw him and James smiled too and all of a sudden it was as though his day had brightened. And there was that damned poeticism again.

'Good afternoon,' he said, more interesting speech having deserted him for the time being while he got used to the very pleasant fact that he was with Anna again. 'You look very nice today. As always.'

She laughed. 'Thank you.'

She was wearing a dark green velvet pelisse over a dress of the same colour, with a cream beading. She looked delightful, and also expensively dressed. She couldn't possibly have the means to buy herself such clothes on a governess's salary, and indeed when he had seen her in the park she had been wearing a much less fashionable and intricately tailored gown. She had obviously fallen on hard times to have chosen to become a governess. How, he wondered, did she afford her clothes? Perhaps they were from her previous life. Or a gift from someone, perhaps Lady Derwent.

He would like very much to know how it had happened that she had become a governess. He did not like to think of her being in need.

'It is a beautiful day,' he observed, as they descended the steps outside the house.

'It is indeed,' Anna agreed. 'I had feared that it would continue to rain but the clouds seem to have entirely disappeared now.'

'Were you able to take your charges out this morning for their walk between rain showers?'

'We did manage a short one and I think that their nurse will take them into the garden for an hour now.'

'Let me help you up into the curricle. I have a blanket for you to wrap around your legs to keep you warm.' It was very pleasant taking her weight on his arm for a moment as he handed her up, and really quite disappointing that she had already arranged the blanket entirely successfully by herself before he was seated next to her and could offer to help with it.

'Thank you,' she said. 'I have not been in a curricle before; this is the most wonderful treat.'

'I am pleased that it is.' He took the reins and nudged his horses to start walking. 'Do you...' James very much wanted to ask her more about her background. Was he being curious for the sake of curiosity? No, he realised; he had begun to care about her and wanted to know whether she was genuinely happy. 'How did you come to be a governess?' Asking leading questions could only seem patronising; it was surely better to ask directly. Although...she might not wish to tell him. 'I'm sorry; please don't feel that you have to answer that question.'

'I am happy to answer it,' she said after a short pause. 'I think mine is not an unusual situation. My parents were sadly somewhat impecunious, and while my mother was alive we had enough money, but with her loss I also lost all financial means. I realised that I would have to earn some money, and was extremely fortunate to find this position with the help of Lady Derwent. She would have very happily paid me to be her companion, but she is not yet at the stage of life where she genuinely requires one, and I would prefer to maintain our relationship as it is, without receiving too much charity.'

'I'm so sorry about the loss of your parents. Was it recent?'

'Thank you. My father, he, that is to say, I... We...' She paused and then continued, 'We lost him some years ago. My mother more recently. I am very lucky in having such a wonderful godmother, however. I know that you have also experienced loss; it is deeply tragic but I believe those of us who have the good fortune still to be here must do our best to enjoy the life that we have, when we are ready, of course, after the first deep grief.'

'I agree.' He took the reins in one hand and covered her hand for a moment with his own. What he wanted to do, he realised with a shock, was hug her tightly against him to comfort her if he possibly could.

'Thank you. And that is why,' she said, a slight tremor in her voice indicating perhaps that she felt more emotion than she was owning to, 'we must enjoy every last morsel of our ices today.'

James laughed. 'I agree with that too.'

As they drove at a leisurely pace down the road and into Berkeley Square, where Gunter's was located, part of him just enjoyed being physically in her presence, part of him produced vague small talk to match hers, and part of him reflected on what she'd just said. He realised that she had answered his question about her background without answering it in the slightest. What was the story behind any lady of quality becoming a governess? Any such lady would have been brought up in the way Anna clearly had, and would then have fallen on hard times and decided that she needed to seek employment.

And while she had confided in him the information about the loss of her parents, of *course* she had lost them; she would presumably not otherwise have to work as a governess.

Her answer had in fact been very similar to his about Miss Austen's book: quite generic.

Of course, she had answered in that way because she didn't want to give him any further details, whereas the reason that he'd answered in that way had been that he hadn't read the book. He should respect her wish not to disclose more. And since he was only here to cure himself of the ridiculous infatuation he felt for her, there was no need for him to find out anything else about her background.

'On a different note,' he said, 'but continuing with the theme of making the most of life, I was so taken by your passion for *Emma* that I have started reading it myself. I don't think many amongst my friends have read it and presume that Miss Austen might have had a female audience in mind when she wrote it, but I must own that I am enjoying it and that I do, like you, very much like the way she writes, and her wit.'

'Well! I am very pleased to have been of service to you. And I have to admit that I am a little surprised. On Friday you did not have the air of a man who wished to engage closely with literature.' Anna glanced sideways up at him as she spoke, with a smile that held a cheeky edge, and James smiled back at her.

And then they had one of the moments that they'd been having where they just smiled—foolishly—at each other without speaking.

James had slowed the horses to a standstill outside the tea shop. Anna's face was tilted up towards his, and he had a feeling that if they were not in quite such a public space, he would not be able to help himself doing what he'd done at the ball, and leaning down and kissing her. *Damn*, he wished he could. Her lips were slightly parted, her cheeks were a little flushed, her sea-green eyes were framed by long eyelashes, her gaze was direct, and the whole made for, well, for extreme temptation.

They were, however, surrounded by other stationary carriages; it was common practice for people to drive up and be served as they waited.

'A waiter will come soon to take our order,' he told Anna, to distract himself from the lushness of her lips.

'I am very much looking forward to tasting the ices.' She frowned. 'How are you reading *Emma* having given your copy of it to me?' she asked.

Damn. He was an idiot. If he wasn't careful, he'd end up admitting that he'd bought all the books he'd 'lent' to her. He had in fact bought a second copy of *Emma*.

'My sister and mother both had copies of it. You can never have too many copies of a good book.' He was an excellent liar, it seemed. He wasn't sure whether he should be proud of that or not.

'Oh, I see. Thank you again for lending the books to me. I am of course able to give them back to you any time you desire.'

'I would be very happy for you to keep them for as long as you like. From what you have said, I believe you to be a much keener reader than any in my family other than perhaps one or two of my sisters, and I'm sure that every author would like his or her books to be read as widely as possible.'

'Thank you.' The smile she gave him would have been more than enough reward for something considerably greater than the procurement of a few books.

'My very great pleasure, I assure you,' he told her.

'Tell me about your sisters? It sounds as though you have several?'

'Well.' James was more than happy to talk about his family, whose company he liked very much. 'You must interrupt me immediately if I talk for too long. There is a lot to say: I have six sisters.'

'My goodness.'

'Indeed.'

He had her laughing with several anecdotes about his sisters, which he found immensely gratifying. He liked the sound of her laugh, and he liked to think that he had made her happy in some way, and everyone enjoyed laughing.

As he watched a waiter approach them, he finished another story about his two youngest sisters, and said, 'I have been speaking for far too long. Do you have any siblings?'

'No, I don't. I would have liked to, I believe. It must be wonderful to be surrounded by so much family. Oh, look at the different ices that people are eating.' She nodded at the occupants of some of the other carriages. 'I have no idea what flavour I'm going to choose.'

She clearly did not wish to talk about her family for long. Perhaps it was understandable given her recent losses. And of course he certainly should not lead the conversation in directions she did not wish to follow.

'There are certainly some quite remarkable flavours,' he said. And then he added, 'I have been here a few times before, always with my sisters,' because for some reason he did not wish her to think that he'd escorted any other young lady here in the way that he'd escorted her.

A few minutes later, as Anna perused the menu, he took the opportunity to watch her. Her face was beautifully expressive and the colour of her hair quite delightful. He could happily just look at her for a long time. Which, frankly, seemed a little odd, as though he'd lost his wits.

'My goodness,' Anna interrupted his thoughts, looking up from the menu. 'I know that you've been here before but I can't resist reading some of these flavours out loud; some of them seem quite remarkable. We may choose between maple, bergamot, pineapple, pistachio, jasmine, white coffee, chocolate, vanilla, elderflower, Parmesan, lavender, artichoke, and coriander.'

James could not recall a time when he had more enjoyed someone reading a list. He very much liked Anna's voice, and he very much liked the way she wrinkled her nose at him when she found something amusing.

'By what are you most tempted?' he asked.

'I can't quite decide. I should like to taste the ones that I think will be *nice*, obviously, but I should also like to taste the ones that I think will be *odd*. Just to see what they're like. So I fear that I am going to be most indecisive.'

'May I make a suggestion?'

'Of course.'

'Why don't you choose several ices—some odd and some nice—and taste them all?'

'I don't like to waste anything,' she said. 'One sees and hears of such poverty. It does not seem right to order food that one knows one cannot finish.'

James wondered what poverty she had experienced herself to have decided that she needed to work.

Her point was valid and he did not wish to waste food either, but he did want her to have a good time and to taste whatever she wanted.

'I have an idea,' he said, pleased with his own genius. 'Choose a small selection now and we will return soon and taste more of the flavours. I am very happy to return as many times as you like.'

'You are very kind,' she told him, smiling.

That *smile*. James was almost sighing just at the sight of it.

'I am not kind, I am quite selfish,' he told her. 'I very much enjoy your company and therefore I am heartily enjoying our visit. I would enjoy a second and indeed third or as many as you like.'

'I cannot trespass upon your kindness to that extent, but I am certainly looking forward to tasting the ices now.'

James was *definitely* going to want to persuade her to return, he thought, but he could pursue that later. Perhaps when she had tasted some of the ices and was feeling wistful about the ones she had not sampled.

'For the time being,' he said, 'I feel that you have a big decision to make. We can certainly manage four flavours between us; I am a very competent eater. Which will you choose?'

After much deliberation, during which James could not take his eyes off her as she read the menu, tilting her head to one side to think, she announced, 'I think I am quite decided. Parmesan. Obviously.'

'Obviously. You have to have a cheese one.'

'Yes indeed. Also artichoke, because I have to have a vegetable. Violet, because I have to have a flower. And pineapple and maple because I have to have one that I think I will actually like.'

'The perfect combination. Parmesan, artichoke, violet, pineapple and maple. I can't imagine a more delectable mouthful.'

'Your Grace.' She fixed him with a stern look. 'Are you trying to put me off? Because I must tell you that you are succeeding quite well and I might have to reconsider my choices.'

'Miss Blake.' He wished so much that he could call her Anna. This formality seemed ridiculous. 'Firstly, I should like it very much if you called me James.'

'Do you not think that is perhaps too familiar?'

He lowered his voice so that there could be no possibility of anyone else hearing and said, 'I do not wish to be indelicate, but I feel that when one has kissed someone, it cannot be thought improper to call them by their Christian name.'

'Oh!' Her squeak was one of the most adorable things he'd ever heard. 'Your Grace. *James.*'

'Yes?'

'You are quite outrageous.'

'I cannot apologise, unfortunately, because I enjoyed it very much.'

'I really do need one of my godmother's fans to give you a well-deserved rap.'

'My knuckles are very grateful that you do not have one. Although… I think you would look delightful peeking over the top of a fan.' He could not resist teasing her; the combination of her laugh and her pout was one of the most alluring things he'd ever seen.

'I feel that our conversation is going sadly awry. I believe that you had something else you wished to say to me?'

'Yes, I think I did.' James smiled at her. 'I think I've forgotten, though. You make me forget myself.'

Anna leaned towards him and very deliberately did a large and most unladylike roll of her eyes.

'Miss Blake. I am shocked.'

'So am I,' she said sunnily, which made James laugh, a lot.

Soon Anna joined in with the laughing, and it turned out that there was little he would rather do than laugh about absolutely nothing with this wonderful woman.

They eventually calmed down, and as they wiped their eyes, Anna still hiccupping slightly with giggles, it occurred to him that he really hadn't done very well at pushing this infatuation out of his mind.

He hadn't actually spent that much time with her yet, though. Maybe the way she ate her ices would give him pause for thought. Or maybe the way *he* ate ices would cause *her* to wish herself anywhere but here. Maybe by the end of this afternoon, they would both be heartily relieved never to see the other at close quarters again.

A waiter interrupted his thoughts to place their ices in front of them, so he was going to find out sooner rather than later whether ice-eating made any difference to his silly infatuation.

'I intend to be scientific about this,' said Anna, clearly not as distracted as he was. 'I think I'm going to start with the one I think I will like least and finish with the one I expect to like the most.'

James shook his head. 'Is that not very risky? What if the one you think you will like the least is in fact the one you like the most? It would be disappointing to begin well and finish badly.'

'That is very true.' Anna paused, her spoon mid-air. 'I need to think about this carefully.'

'But not too carefully in case the ices melt.'

'Very true. Perhaps I should take one mouthful of each in the order I expect to like them going from worst to best, and then re-evaluate the situation.'

'Very sensible,' James approved.

'However—' her spoon was still in the air '—I now realise that I am being very rude to you. Very self-centred. Which ones would *you* like to try first?'

'No, no, this is your treat and we agreed that I am just here to finish up whatever you do not wish to eat.'

'Are you sure, though? I feel that I am imposing on you.'

'You could never impose on me,' James said, very seriously, meaning it.

Anna looked at him for a long moment, her own face very serious all of a sudden, and then said, 'You are a very kind man.'

'Really, no,' he said. God. He was in fact only here because he wished to clear his mind of the infatuation he felt for her. That was not kind at all.

'We must agree to differ and we must begin to eat or as you say they will melt.' She looked between them. 'I am of course going to try the artichoke one first, because I do not expect to like it as much as the others.'

'Of course.'

She placed her spoon in the artichoke ice and scooped a little out.

And so far, watching her take ice cream was not helping James's infatuation level at all. The way she held her spoon, the way she concentrated and then looked up at him with a little smile, were all quite delightful. Delicate but not *too* delicate.

And then she opened her beautiful mouth and put the spoon in and, oh, good God, the way she held the spoon in her mouth for a second; James was imagining her holding *other* things in her mouth. And the way she was tasting it, savouring it.

How had he managed to sit opposite her and eat an entire meal with her during the supper at the ball without exploding with desire?

As she finished the mouthful, Anna gave a little wriggle, which caused her chest to move far too alluringly for James's sanity, and said, 'I was mistaken.'

'You were?' James managed to ask.

'Yes. Artichoke ice cream is divine. You must try some immediately.'

'Certainly.' His voice sounded somewhat like a croak.

He put his own spoon into the ice and then put it into his mouth, incredibly conscious the entire time of Anna's eyes on his hands and mouth.

'That is wonderful.' He wasn't certain whether he was referring to the ice or to the way it felt having Anna's eyes following his every movement.

She swallowed and raised her eyes to his. 'Yes.'

Their eyes held for a long time, before Anna pulled hers away with what looked like an effort and said, 'We should try the next one.'

'We should.'

'Violet,' she said decisively.

And then she took a spoonful of it, and, even though he'd already seen her place a spoon in her mouth and suck gently, the sight of her doing it still caused his body to respond most uncomfortably. At this rate, he was going to be a gibbering wreck by the end of the afternoon.

Anna closed her eyes for a second and put her head to one side, looking as though she was focusing very much on the taste she was experiencing, and then opened her eyes and swallowed.

James took a deep breath and shook his head slightly to clear it.

'How was that one?' he asked, very impressed at how normal his voice sounded.

'Very nice but not as truly wonderful as artichoke. Which is the opposite of what you would expect.'

'That *is* interesting.' James plunged his own spoon into the ice, trying hard not to think crude thoughts about plunging other things into places, and tasted. 'You're right,' he said. And then for some reason he couldn't resist adding, 'It seems that we have *very* compatible taste in ices.'

'I think,' said Anna, placing her spoon very deliberately into the next ice, 'that that remains to be seen. For all we know, we might disagree enormously on the next ones.'

'That is a very fair point,' James acknowledged, as he watched her again before taking his own mouthful.

As they continued to taste the ices together, James's enjoyment of watching Anna only grew, if that were possible.

'The artichoke is still my favourite,' concluded Anna after their final tasting. 'Although the pineapple and maple is a close second.'

'I agree.' James would agree with absolutely anything she might say right now. 'And that proves that we are compatible when it comes to ices.'

'No, it proves we are compatible when it comes to *these four* ices.'

'In that case,' he said triumphantly—although he wasn't even sure that this what he wanted; he knew that at the beginning of the afternoon it hadn't been entirely—'we will have to come again and sample another four.'

'You might be right. Not definitely right, but probably. Now, I am afraid, with great regret, that I ought to return to the house.'

'Of course.' James was conscious of huge disappointment, which was at odds with what he'd intended from this afternoon. He thought. It was actually quite difficult to remember.

Maybe because his infatuation was, if he was honest with himself, growing. And maybe that was because, once Anna had told him the bald facts about her family, they'd just reverted to engaging in frivolous small talk. And so, really, he still knew hardly anything about her.

As he collected up his reins and encouraged his horses to move forward, he found himself asking, 'Do you drive?'

'No; I have never had the opportunity. I do love horses, though, and much admire this pair.'

'And of course the skill with which they are being driven.'

She laughed. 'Of *course* I admire your skill.'

James laughed too, and then found himself saying, 'I think we are fated to visit Gunter's again. We need to sample a lot more ices, as you rightly said, because we need to determine whether our ice cream tastes are indeed compatible, and I feel that you should have at least one opportunity to drive a carriage. We could combine the ice-eating with a driving lesson.'

And, good God, what had come over him? He *hated* being driven and under no circumstances—normally—would he acquiesce to a request to drive his horses, let alone *offer* such torture. He would worry about his horses and he would worry about his sanity. But now, when he thought about it, he didn't even think it would *be* torture.

Apparently he would do almost anything to spend time with Anna.

Chapter Nine

Anna

Anna did a gigantic swallow as she looked at the duke—James—holding his horse's reins and smiling at her. He was…he was…*sublime*.

His humour.

His kindness.

His strong, handsome features.

The evident strength in his arms, across his shoulders, ensured that she felt safe at all times in his presence. Well, not *entirely* safe; she was beginning to think that her *heart* might not be safe. But physically she knew he would protect her. She was *sure* he was a good driver.

She was also sure that she would be much better served to thank him for the ices and say goodbye and that she would perhaps see him another time, perhaps at another literary salon at her godmother's.

But…

'I should like that very much,' she heard herself saying.

'Why don't you take the reins now?' he suggested.

'Now?'

'Well.' He looked around at the relatively narrow road they were in. 'Not exactly now. But perhaps we could go somewhere less busy and you could begin your first lesson. I think the village of Kensington might be a good place to start.'

The sensible thing to say would of course be that she should go back now...except Lady Puntney had suggested that she take the entire afternoon to herself as she had admitted to having a headache yesterday—probably due to such a lack of sleep from reading late and then thinking about the duke—and Lady Puntney did not wish her to be ill. And so she *could* stay for just a little bit longer.

'I'd love to just for a few minutes,' she said. 'Thank you.'

'There is really no need to thank me,' he said as he manoeuvred them through what felt like an impossibly small gap and which at the hands of a less confidence-inducing driver would have caused Anna to close her eyes and cling tightly to the side of the carriage. 'Really, I'm being quite selfish; I'm sure I will enjoy teaching you.'

'In that case, I must ask you to thank me for agreeing to your suggestion.'

He smiled at her as though her very weak humour had amused him deeply, which made her smile in her turn.

They lapsed into silence, but it was a nice, comfortable one, unlike the one they'd had at the beginning of the walk they'd taken. It felt as though—even though Anna had been careful to keep their conversations quite frivolous—they had become friends.

Well, it wasn't *entirely* comfortable. Anna felt as though her heart was bursting with...something, and she was most *un*comfortably aware that she very much wanted him to kiss her again.

When they went over a bump in the road and they were jiggled in their seats and their legs almost touched, it felt incredibly exciting and then very disappointing that they settled back into the same positions they'd been in before.

And as she watched his hands—so strong and yet light on the reins—she found herself wondering how it would feel to have them on her.

And when she looked at his profile as he concentrated on

the road, and then caught his eye when he glanced briefly at her with a smile, well then her mind was filled with memories of their kiss.

'I think this is as good a place as any,' the duke said after a few moments.

'For what?' asked Anna, unable to collect her thoughts.

'For teaching you to drive?'

'Oh! Yes, of course.' She hoped he hadn't realised that her mind had been quite so far away from driving, focused at that moment on his thigh next to hers. She looked around. They were in a wide, quiet, tree-lined road, bordered by pretty houses. 'Is this Kensington?'

'Yes, it is.'

'It's very peaceful after the hustle and bustle of London. And yet really quite close.' Perhaps one day in ten or twenty years' time, when she had saved enough money from her salary, Anna might be able to purchase a small house in a place like this.

'Yes, it's very nice.' The duke smiled at her in such a way that Anna felt as though all he could see at this moment was her. It was quite intoxicating being regarded in such a way. And she feared that she might be returning his gaze with an identical one.

After a few beautifully long moments, he lifted one hand towards her, and then replaced it at his side and swallowed.

'Perhaps you should move a little more towards the middle of the seat,' he said.

Anna just stared at him, in mute question. Was he suggesting that they...

'So that we might begin the lesson,' he clarified.

Oh! Of course. Of *course* he hadn't been suggesting that they move closer so that they might kiss.

Anna nodded and slid sideways, as he did the same, until they were seated very close to each other.

Their upper arms were touching now, which was making Anna very warm inside. Apparently it wasn't making the duke's insides turn to mulch at all, though, because he was able to speak in a perfectly normal voice, saying, 'I'm going to give you the reins now and show you how to hold them. Perhaps...'

She looked up at him as he regarded her and then the horses as though he was trying to solve a particularly knotty problem.

'I must confess that I haven't ever tried to teach anyone to drive before,' he said. 'I feel that it would be prudent to make sure that I am able to stop the horses bolting if they get alarmed in any way or if you pull on their mouths, which I am *certain* you won't, but we should consider all eventualities.'

'Mmm.' Anna's heart was beginning to bang very loudly in her chest; at this rate it would be so loud that it might cause the horses to take fright. She had no space in her brain to think about holding the reins correctly because her entire being seemed to be taken up with drinking in the duke's proximity and wondering what would happen next.

'I wonder,' he said, 'whether the wisest thing might not be for us both to hold the reins, like this. If you agree.'

And he put his left arm around her so that she was encircled by his arms and held the reins in front of her. He was warm and hard and big and smelled wonderful, and Anna couldn't imagine that there could be a nicer place in the world to sit than right here, right now, within his hold.

'Is that all right?' he asked, his voice low, his breath whispering across her cheek.

'Mmm.' She really didn't have any words. She glanced over her shoulder at him and saw that he was smiling at her in such a fond manner that she almost had to close her eyes to recover from the...well, the sheer delight of it.

'So you should take the reins,' he said.

'The reins,' she repeated. All she could think about was the way her back was against his chest and just how big and hard it felt.

'Maybe we should hold them together.' His voice was low and husky and he could have said any words at all and they would have sounded delightful, exciting, fascinating...

'Mmm.'

He put both the reins in his right hand and then took her left in his—it fitted *beautifully* inside his larger hand—and transferred both reins to their left hands, and then took her right in his and transferred the right rein back.

'Look,' he said. 'You're driving.'

'Mmm.'

'You seem—' his mouth was even closer to her ear now, his breath almost tickling her '—to be unusually lacking in speech at the moment. Perhaps you are overcome by...the idea of your first driving lesson?'

Anna took a very deep breath, which caused her to be pressed more tightly against his chest, and found some words.

'That is exactly it,' she achieved. 'I am extremely overcome by...that.'

'I find you to be an excellent driver.' His voice had sunk extremely low.

'I'm not sure that I am actually driving. The horses are stationary.'

'That is a mere detail.'

'An important one, though?'

'You are demanding, Miss Blake.'

'In *every* way.' She had *no* idea where her words had come from but she had *loved* saying them. She didn't even really know what she meant by them but...

'In that case—' he tightened his arms around her a little '—perhaps you would like to move the horses on a little.'

'I think I would.'

'Go like this with the reins.' He took his hands away from hers for a moment—which she really did not like, and not just because it was a little terrifying thinking that she was the one in charge of the horses for that moment, but because she *liked* his hands on hers—and showed her what to do.

She moved the reins herself and the horses began to walk forward, in perfect harmony with each other.

'Oh, my goodness,' she said, entranced. 'They're beautiful. And I'm driving them.'

'Indeed.'

They continued to move forward in a straight line, Anna watching the proud backs and haunches of the horses and feeling the duke's embrace.

She was so deliciously happy with where she was that she almost didn't register that there was a bend coming up.

'We will need to turn,' the duke said, his mouth against her temple. 'The horses are extremely intelligent but it would nonetheless be wise to encourage them a little to follow the line of the road.'

'By pulling gently with the left rein?'

'Exactly,' the duke approved. 'You are indeed a natural driver.'

As they rounded the corner, Anna said, 'I see that it is in fact the horses who are natural drivers.'

'I did choose this pair for today knowing that they are reasonably placid, as they were going to be standing for some time while we ate,' he acknowledged, 'but I am quite certain that you would drive any horses very well with very little practice.'

They continued for a few minutes until they were beyond the village and then he said, 'Perhaps we should take this turning here.'

After a few more moments, they came to a clearing.

'I wonder whether we should stop for a moment to enjoy the scenery?' he suggested.

'I think that would be very nice.' Anna suspected that he was tempted to enjoy the scenery in the same way that they had enjoyed the rose garden at the ball. The sensible part of her mind was suggesting that it would not be a good idea to engage in any more flirting, or kissing... But the rest of her was, frankly, quite desperate to be kissed just one more time.

'We stop the horses like this,' the duke told her, helping her to apply just a little pressure with the reins.

They came to a halt under a large oak tree, still not entirely divested of its leaves despite the progression of autumn. The duke removed his arms from around Anna, leaped down and looped the reins around the tree's trunk, before returning to the seat in one lithe move.

And then he settled himself back where he had been sitting before.

'I wonder whether, without the horses and reins to distract us, we might find an even better position for you for driving,' he said, his voice very throaty. 'Like this, for example.'

He placed his hands on her waist and lifted her a little so that she was in a slightly different position against his chest.

'I think that might work particularly well.'

'Mmm.' Anna could hardly breathe. She *loved* his hands on her waist, large against her body.

'Did you enjoy that?' His mouth was almost touching her temple as he spoke.

'Enjoy…?' Enjoy his hands on her waist? Very much so, yes.

'Your first driving lesson.'

'Driving.' Of course that was what he had meant. 'Yes, thank you.'

'I enjoyed it too.' His voice was *so* deliciously throaty.

She turned a little to look up at him over her shoulder, wriggling a little against him as she did so, and smiled at him.

'Damn,' he said.

She raised her eyebrows, suddenly—even though she wasn't sure how—feeling in some way as though she was in control of this conversation. A conversation without words.

He gazed at her eyes, her mouth, her tongue as she moistened her lips.

And then she wriggled more against him and pouted a little at him.

'Damn,' he repeated.

And then, very slowly, but with very clear meaning, as though nothing could have altered his course, he leaned down and kissed her on the lips.

This kiss was different from the first one they had shared at the ball. It was not tentative, or a mere brushing of lips. It was immediately hard, and demanding, the duke's tongue entering her mouth immediately, *wanting*, wanting things from her, and causing her to want too.

She turned further towards him and reached her arms up around his neck, loving the way that the movement meant that their chests pressed against each other.

The duke groaned and then slid his right arm further around her waist.

His left hand was on her waist, his fingers on her ribs, and then it began to move up her body.

Anna took a sharp intake of breath as his hand moved to cup the underside of her breast, as all the while they continued to kiss. This felt so very, very daring, and so very, very perfect, and she just wanted him to touch her more, further...

She pushed her hands into his thick hair, almost as though she wanted to anchor him to her, as they continued to deepen their kiss. His hand was moving further now, on her breast, and *oh*. Even through the fabric of her dress, his touch felt wonderful.

And then he lifted her so that she was on his lap. He put his right hand into her hair, and tugged very gently, so that she leaned her head back a little, and then he began to kiss her very slowly along her jawline, as she sat encircled in his arms, her hands still in his hair, her body truly on fire.

With one hand he continued to caress the underside of her breasts and with the other he somehow undid the buttons of her pelisse until he had it open and was kissing her along her collarbone and then down and down, with what felt like great intent, towards the neckline of her dress.

And then, somehow—he had very clever hands—he had the neckline lower and had her breasts released from their constraints and he was kissing, caressing, nipping, and Anna was just *shuddering* with the sheer delight of it.

As he continued, she pushed her hands inside his shirt, wanting to feel his hard chest. She could feel corded muscle, and strength, and she could feel what he was doing to her, and it was utterly, utterly blissful.

As they continued to explore each other with their hands, she found herself kissing, almost biting his neck as he sucked and nipped on her, and it was one of the most wonderful things she had ever experienced.

And then...one of his hands moved to her leg, and he began to run his fingers along the length of her thigh, and even through the fabric of her dress his touch made her shiver even more, as his hand rose higher. She reached down to his thigh, marvelling at the solidity of it and the bunching of his muscles, and enjoying how as she moved her fingers higher up his thigh, his breathing became faster.

And then he moved his hand under her skirts, and now his

hand was on her bare skin, tracing further and further up her leg to where she now felt liquid and...almost *desperate*.

He continued to kiss her neck, her breasts, her shoulders, tormenting and delighting, as his fingers circled closer and closer, ever higher on her thighs. She was clinging to him, one arm round his neck again now, holding his shoulders, the other on his hard thigh.

And then, finally, his fingers reached her most intimate parts, the shock of his first touch there causing her whole body to shudder.

'Your Grace,' she panted, as he began to move his fingers with what felt like real purpose. She could barely think but she knew that she wanted to feel him too.

He halted the movement of his fingers. 'I'm sorry; would you like to stop?'

'No, no, please, please carry on.'

He laughed and resumed his touch.

Anna couldn't think now, all she could do was feel, and judder and cling to him.

She reached for his breeches, feeling the hardness of him there, and worked to open them. When she had her hand on him, she felt—with great satisfaction—him judder too.

'Oh, my God, *Anna*. Call me James.'

'James,' she said on a long pant—maybe a little scream if she was honest—as his fingers began to move more and more and the pressure built.

As she spoke his name, she suddenly wondered *what* she was doing, and whether it could be dangerous for her.

'James. Stop,' she managed to say. 'Could I become with child like this?' She didn't *think* she could, but she *had* to be sure.

'Not if I do not enter you.'

His fingers and mouth had immediately stilled when she'd asked him to stop, and she didn't like it, and if it couldn't result in a baby, then she couldn't bear the thought of stopping *now*...

She didn't have the words to ask him to continue, though, so instead she just increased her hold on him and began to move her hand.

'Anna? Do you…?'

'Mmm, yes.'

'You are certain? Because maybe…' He ended on a groan as she moved her hand more.

'Extremely. Certain,' she said, moving very deliberately.

And then he moved his hand back and kissed her hard and deep on the mouth before beginning to kiss her breasts again, and then she was lost to the pressure and sensation that began to build, just on the perfect side of unbearable.

Release came for Anna, and, she realised, for James, at almost the same time.

And then they just half lay, half sat under the blanket on the carriage seat, their limbs entwined, both of them still shuddering.

Anna was the first to stir. The day had become quite gusty, it seemed from the leaves beginning to blow around them, and the breeze on her bare shoulders had made her very aware of her nakedness under the blanket. She wriggled away from him so that she could adjust her dress. *Big* adjustments were required; she was quite scandalously undressed. Well. The undress was clearly not as scandalous as what they'd just *done*. All the kissing and touching and… Her stomach was dipping just at the *thought* of it all.

'Would you like any help?' James's voice was still quite ragged, which Anna had to admit she *loved*.

'I think—' she smiled at him as she adjusted her dress across her chest '—that I might have had quite enough *help* from you today.'

He returned her smile and lifted both his hands to cup her face, and then he placed a lovely little kiss on her lips.

'I don't think I could ever have enough such *help* from you,' he said.

'James! I can't believe you just said that.'

'Really? I have a *lot* to say in response to that.' He kissed her on the lips again and then smoothed her hair back and helped her to pull her pelisse around her shoulders. 'Firstly, I love hearing my name on your lips like that.'

'Secondly,' he continued, 'you can't believe that I just made a slightly warm comment about what we just did? Because I *assure* you—' he kissed her again before tracing one finger down her chest between her breasts, which made her shiver quite delightfully '—that what we *did* was a lot more shocking than what we might say.'

His face became very serious, and then he continued, 'I must apologise if you feel uncomfortable in any way about what happened, but I assure that you cannot possibly become with child without...'

Anna shook her head. 'We had already kissed and that was quite scandalous enough already to ruin a young lady of quality such as Lady Maria. And no one knows we are here...' She knew that she should regret what they'd done, because of course it was truly shocking behaviour, and it couldn't happen again, because even an employer as kind-hearted and caring as Lady Puntney would really probably have no choice but to ask her to leave if she knew of such an indiscretion, but if she was never to be married, which seemed probable, she would at least have this memory. 'And so...' She smiled at him, to signal to him that she had no regrets, and then bit her lip, because his expression was *so* serious.

'I would never, ever want to hurt you in any way, Anna,' he said.

'I know that.' She realised that—insofar as a woman could trust a man, she did trust him very fully. Well, she trusted him fully to treat her well within the context that he had of her, which was that she was a lady who had fallen on hard times. Arguably they should not have kissed, but many people kissed, and more, before they were married, even Lady Maria and her *curate*, it seemed. She wasn't sure how he would treat her if he knew that she was the daughter of a groom. She was sure that he would still be kind to her, because she was certain that he was a very kind, honourable man, but she wasn't sure that he would wish to spend any more time with her. In her experience, even the nicest of men were bound by Society's code. 'Thank you.'

'I think I should take you back now.' He tucked the blanket around Anna and gathered the reins. 'Perhaps I will drive now, if you don't mind, for speed. We have been out for quite a long time and I should not wish Lady Puntney to comment.'

'No indeed, and yes, I will allow that your driving is a tiny bit faster than mine. For the time being. Until I have spent a few more minutes practising and have become an expert.' It felt important to try to turn the conversation entirely away from what they had just *done*.

James smiled obligingly and said, 'Of *course* you will be an expert with the reins with only a few more minutes' practice.'

They both laughed and then lapsed into silence as they began to drive back towards London.

Anna did not wish to be silent; she would not be able to avoid being alone with her remarkably confusing thoughts later on and did not wish to be free now to reflect too much on what had happened.

'It really is very autumnal now,' she observed.

'Indeed it is. I particularly like red leaves at this time of year.'

'Have you travelled to Scotland? I believe that the forests there are particularly fine?'

They passed the next few minutes in most enjoyable discussion about the different botanical and zoological features of Scotland and its islands. That is to say, at times Anna almost managed to stop incessantly replaying in her mind what she and James had *done*. Most of the time, though, if she was honest, she had only half her mind on the conversation.

Eventually, as the conversation slid somehow to the discussion of some rather scandalous *on-dits* that James had heard from his mother about some of the ladies who had been present at the literary salon evening, Anna managed to participate more fully in the conversation, and soon couldn't stop herself giggling hard at some of James's more outrageous stories.

They arrived too soon at Bruton Street, and Anna was conscious of a sense almost of loss that she would be leaving James's company so soon.

As he drew up, he said, 'I very much hope that you would like to return to Gunter's to taste more ices. We have a lot of them to experience. And also, of course, you might wish to un-

dertake more…*practice*.' He accompanied his last word by a
meaningful eyebrow raise and a *wink*, which made Anna gasp.

'James!'

'Anna! What did you think I meant? I was referring to driving. Obviously.'

'Obviously indeed,' she said, and he laughed. 'Thank you
very much for a wonderful afternoon.'

'I was extremely pleased to be of service,' he said, with another eyebrow raise, causing Anna to gasp again.

'I am afraid,' she said, adopting her primmest manner, 'that
I can no longer thank you *for the delicious ices* because you appear determined to make inappropriate references at every turn.'

'You are correct,' he said. 'I would like to apologise but I
fear that I do not feel particularly sorry.'

Anna held her arm out as haughtily as she could. 'I feel that
it is now time for me to go inside.'

'Your word is my command.'

It took a very long time for them to say goodbye to each
other—without touching each other at all, because of course
there might be many witnesses—until eventually Anna went
inside the house.

She found it remarkably hard to concentrate on—well, *anything*—because her head was full of this afternoon with James,
and, like a young miss with nothing else to think about than
pretty dresses and ribbons, rather than the mature governess
she was, wonder how long it might be until next she saw him.

Gratifyingly, she discovered within the space of less than
two hours that James perhaps felt similarly, when she received
a card in the handwriting she now recognised. The more she
knew him, the more she liked his script.

She was all fingers as she fumbled to get the card out of its
envelope, so keen was she to read its contents.

She found when she opened it that he had written in entirely
formal language, with no reference to anything inappropriate.
She was heartily relieved, because one never knew when something might fall into other hands, but also she was a little disappointed, she realised.

The import of what he had written did not disappoint, however; he wished to make an arrangement now to take her back to Gunter's to continue their ice-tasting experience. As soon as possible, he had suggested.

Anna knew that it would be very silly to repeat what they had done. She also knew that she couldn't think of anything she'd rather do.

Lady Puntney had been quite outspoken about how pleased she was for Anna to continue to see Ladies Derwent and Maria, and any other friend she might wish to meet. And it was quite unexceptionable for a lady to visit Gunter's alone with a male friend. And she would probably meet James again at her godmother's next literary soirée. It could do no harm to meet him on occasion. She was sure they wouldn't be silly enough to kiss again.

Before she could change her mind, because it really was quite tedious going back and forth with pros and cons in her mind, she dashed off an acceptance of his invitation. She would look forward to seeing him again, but just for the ices. Nothing else.

The next morning dawned grey, the clouds in the sky heavy with water. By the time breakfast was finished, the heavens had opened and Anna had to acknowledge that she would not be able to take the girls for their usual morning walk; they would get drenched if they left the house.

It was the first day since she'd begun her role as governess that they weren't able to go out at all in the morning, and it was—as she could have predicted—not particularly enjoyable; the girls steadily became less well-behaved than usual, and Anna began to feel as though the four walls of the house were closing around them.

Finally, at around half past three in the afternoon, the rain had cleared up and the sky was cloudless.

Anna, with Elsie's assistance, hurried the girls into their outer garments and boots and set off as quickly as possible, just in case the clouds were going to change their minds and return.

As she did every time she walked out of the house now, since the duke—James—had told her that he lived in Berkeley

Square, which was adjacent to Bruton Street, she couldn't help wondering whether she might bump into him while she was out.

It was *impossible*, she was finding, not to think about him quite regularly when she was inside the house too.

And, as they walked into the park at this very different time of day from usual, it was impossible not to look into each of the carriages of the fashionable people that they passed, just in case she saw him...

He wasn't in any of them.

Until...there he was.

Anna almost gasped out loud at the sight of his now achingly familiar profile and broad shoulders.

Her lips began to form into a smile and then she suddenly realised that he was not alone in the carriage. He was accompanying two ladies.

One of them was his mother; Anna recognised her from the ball.

The other...was a very young and very beautiful lady, who Anna did not recognise.

Perhaps she was the duke's sister, Anna told herself.

Except...she did not resemble James or his mother at all.

And the expression of extreme politeness on James's face indicated that she was not a sibling. Anna had met enough people with siblings to be aware that they rarely behaved together as though they were only acquaintances.

James was driving with another young lady. And his mother.

Which surely could only mean one thing.

He was planning to marry the young lady.

'This way,' she told the girls and Elsie a little more sharply than she'd intended, shepherding them as quickly as she could down the first path she saw, desperate for James not to see her.

She was *so* humiliated, she thought as she sniffed back tears. And the lady should feel humiliated too, of course, because he had been doing *that* with Anna while about to become, or perhaps already, affianced to her.

Actually, she thought, staring hard at a tree trunk as though that might give her inspiration, he couldn't already be betrothed. If he were, he could hardly risk being seen at Gunter's with Anna.

Gunter's. Should she still go there again with him? She didn't know. Should she write him a vicious note saying she had seen him with someone else and both she and the other lady deserved better than that and she never wished to see him again? Although maybe she would like to say that in person. Or perhaps she should just ignore him when he arrived in Bruton Street. That would be petty, though, and she didn't want to be petty, however badly he might have behaved.

Maybe she would go with him to Gunter's, enjoy his conversation in a very dignified manner and then tell him at the end that she would not be seeing him again and that she wished him well. And perhaps she would mention that she had seen him with the other young lady. Perhaps that would be the most dignified approach, with the added benefit of telling him that she *knew*.

Yes, that was what she was going to do.

She still felt *very* low, though. Which was of course very, very silly, because she had known all along that dukes did not marry governesses. And she didn't even *want* to get married.

And, since it was silly, she was going to pull herself together and concentrate on the children.

She gave a huge sniff—rather a honking one, which caused the girls to stare at her and Elsie to ask if she was quite all right—and gave them all a big smile. The Duke of Amscott was *nothing* to her. A mere acquaintance. She was not going to let him affect her at *all*.

The next afternoon, she went shopping for paints with Lady Derwent, who had decided that she would like to produce some watercolours.

Anna decided on the way there that she would not mention *anything* about the duke.

And she stuck to her decision very well until, as they were standing deliberating in Ackermann's Emporium, she saw on the other side of the shop the young lady with whom the duke had been driving yesterday.

'Who is that?' she asked her godmother in a whisper.

'Lady Catherine Rainsford,' Lady Derwent told her, still concentrating on the picture frames between which she was choosing. And then she suddenly looked up at Anna, her eyes slightly narrowed. 'Why do you ask?'

'No reason,' Anna said airily.

'I have seen the Duke of Amscott with her a few times. I believe that his mother is perhaps promoting a match between them. I have not seen great enthusiasm from his side, however.'

'Oh, I see,' Anna murmured.

It did make more sense that spending time with Lady Catherine had not been entirely the duke's choice, but it underscored the fact that he and Anna really could not continue as friends or acquaintances or whatever they were any longer.

She would meet him one final time tomorrow. And she might as well enjoy that meeting as much as she could before she finally told him that they must no longer see each other.

Chapter Ten

James

Three days after he'd last been with Anna, five minutes before the time he'd agreed with her, James drove up Bruton Street, already smiling at the thought of seeing her again.

He'd missed her, more than it should be possible to miss someone whom you last saw less than half a week ago. He wanted to hear what she'd been doing and thinking, and he wanted to tell her countless small anecdotes about what he'd been doing, from the most mundane, like what he'd eaten, to the social events he had been to and the gossip, through to important things like decisions he was making about his estates. He would also like to ask her opinion on when his seventeen-year-old sister, Jane, should make her come-out.

She was fast becoming—had already become—someone with whom he felt that he wanted to share everything: of *course* the lovemaking, although that really ought not to happen again, but also, really, *everything* else.

He couldn't help feeling that that might not be a good thing, but he also couldn't help just wanting very much to see her.

She was ready when he arrived, dressed this time in a mid-blue, delightfully form-fitting pelisse and a jaunty-looking hat.

'Good afternoon. You are looking very well.' He took her hand and kissed her fingers.

'Thank you.' Her smile had the same effect on him that it had done each time since he had first seen it, at the ball, and he beamed at her in response.

Then he frowned. Her smile—while always beautiful—was in fact not quite so wide as usual, as though she felt some constraint.

'Are you quite all right?' he asked her.

'Yes, thank you. I...' She paused, and then looked him directly in the eye. 'Yes, I am, thank you.'

And then she walked with him to his curricle, and as he handed her up into it, she seemed completely herself again.

He realised, once he had her settled on the curricle seat with a blanket around her legs and had jumped up on his own side, that he had so many things to speak about with her that he didn't know where to begin.

He should be polite, of course, and ask in greater detail how she was.

'Very well, thank you,' she replied, 'although I am at grave risk of becoming very tired again thanks to *Evelina*, which I started two days ago and am enjoying almost as much as I enjoyed *Emma*.'

'I am very pleased that you are enjoying it, and shall read it myself when I have finished *Emma*. And I am also very pleased that you have immediately led the conversation in this direction, as I—genuinely—very much wished to enquire about your thoughts on the relationship between Emma and Mr Knightley.'

'Your Grace...'

'James?'

'James.' She twinkled at him as she spoke his name and he nearly dropped his reins. She was so very alluring. 'Am I to understand that the man who told me recently that he did not read fiction is not only reading it but *enjoying* it?'

'That is correct.' He couldn't remember the last time he had read a work of fiction, and he didn't think he'd *ever* read something quite so...*romantic*...but he was not ashamed to say that he was enjoying it greatly.

'I would like to take sole credit for your epiphany but must allow that there were many others present at the salon, so I must share it.'

'No, no, it is all you.' He smiled at her. 'I assure you that there was no other lady there who could inspire me to stay up far too late at night.'

She gasped and he said, 'Reading, I mean.'

Anna visibly swallowed and then laughed, and said, 'I am flattered, Your Grace.'

'So you should be. Every tutor I ever had, as well as my schoolmasters and dons, would be deeply impressed. And now tell me your thoughts on Emma and Mr Knightley before your head is turned by my compliments.'

'Well. How far along in the story are you? I do not wish to spoil the end for you.'

They did not stop talking about *Emma* until after they arrived at Gunter's, when they had to break to place their order.

'I must tell you,' James said, 'that I take full credit for introducing you to these ices, in the same way that you have introduced me to Miss Austen's works, and as such I allowed myself to order a special ice for you, with a flavour combination that I hope you will like.'

'Oh, how exciting.'

'I feel that you should also choose another four to sample. In case you do not like the one that I chose. And you are certainly under no obligation to say that you like it.'

Anna laughed. 'I am sure I shall. Thank you!'

'I think that you should withhold your thanks until you have tasted it. Now, which others would you like?'

'I feel that it should be a joint decision.'

'No, no; you chose very well last time and I think we should maintain tradition.'

'In that case...'

She chose lemon, carrot, cinnamon and Gruyere cheese. When she had finished ordering, James said, 'And we would like a little artichoke ice cream as well, if possible.'

'You're very clever,' Anna said approvingly. 'We will need to compare the best of these against the artichoke so that we may find the best of all.'

'Exactly. And I am really not sure what I wish to happen: will we be sad if artichoke is removed from its position of superiority or will we be delighted to have found something even more delicious?'

Anna frowned and nodded with an air of great seriousness. 'You pose a very important philosophical question.'

James laughed and reflected yet again that he couldn't imagine a better way of spending an afternoon.

When the ices came, Anna said, 'I am quite agog to see what flavour you asked especially for.'

'Chicken and asparagus,' James said, as the waiter got them ready for them.

'Oh, those are my two favourite foods.'

'I remember from the ball. I think I remember everything you have said to me.'

'Oh!' The little squeak she gave made James smile a lot. 'Thank you!'

After a pause, she said, 'We must taste it first, at exactly the same time.'

They took their spoons, and...the taste was...odd.

'I like it excessively,' said Anna, in a most determined manner.

'I must own,' James said, 'that it is not my favourite.'

'I like it very much.' Anna took another spoonful.

'You really don't have to,' said James as she failed to hide a quite alarming wince.

'I really do like it very much—' she looked a little as though she was going to be sick '—and I am extremely grateful for the lovely gesture, but I think it would be remiss in me not to try the other flavours.'

In the end, they determined lemon to be as good a flavour as artichoke but no better, and Anna had admitted that while she was extremely grateful that he had remembered her favourite food, she would not choose to eat chicken ice cream again.

'I foresee that we will have to return here many times to determine the absolute best,' he said, as they prepared to leave. He looked over at her, smiling at him with laughter in her eyes, and wondered if it was possible that his heart had just actually turned over.

He had fully intended to drive her straight home after they had finished their ice creams, with no detour during which any lovemaking of any kind might occur. And of course, he should certainly not kiss her again, as he had no thought—well, he didn't know whether he did or not, but he probably didn't—of proposing to her. As he'd determined before, he did not wish to experience any further loss, and marrying someone he loved would of course endanger him in that way. So they ought to go straight home. But on the other side of the coin, it would be a shame for her to have no further driving practice.

'Would you like to take the reins for a short while?' he asked. 'When I have driven us somewhere a little less crowded again.'

'Oh, yes, thank you, I would.' She hesitated, and then said, 'There should be no need for us to stop along the way, though, I think.'

Which was of course ideal. It really was. Really.

Her driving was genuinely impressive and he allowed her to take the reins by herself for a while—she was a very fast learner—and James genuinely did not intend that they stop along the way...

But somehow, when she handed the reins back to him, and their hands brushed, and she smiled up at him in *that* way, he was unable to resist the temptation just to give her the tiniest of kisses, and she responded in a way that he had not entirely expected but did very much appreciate. And then it would have been, well, really quite impolite, had he not secured the reins so that he could kiss her for just a little longer, and then it seemed that neither of them wished to stop kissing. And more.

And this time it was even better than before, because this time, while they were still exploring each other, they also already knew a little about what the other liked. James realised that a man could happily spend a lifetime making Anna shudder and moan in just that way.

When they finally finished, and he was trying to help her tame her markedly dishevelled locks and adjust her clothing to an acceptable state, all he could do was smile.

'You are very, very beautiful,' he murmured in her ear as he smoothed her pelisse into place over her extremely well-formed breasts and she shivered again under his touch.

He was beginning to think that he might have fallen in love. Did he *want* to be in love?

On the way back into London, he managed to lead quite naturally, he hoped, into a question he very much wanted to ask. 'Tell me more about your parents?' It felt odd that, though they now had a very strong connection and he knew so much about her tastes in ices, literature, travel ambitions and stripy food, he knew absolutely nothing about her background.

'They were... I'm not sure how to describe them. That is not a question that I've been asked very often. Or ever, perhaps. Since I...lost them, no one has asked.'

And she had not answered the question in the slightest. Would it be rude of him to ask again?

'I'd very much like to hear if you would like to tell me.' He would not repeat the question if she brushed him off this time.

'My father was...hard to describe. I remember him laughing with his friends. My mother was very kind and enjoyed helping others.' And that was that. She sounded very final; she clearly did not wish to say any more.

James realised that he didn't wish to know just about their personalities. He also wanted to know *who* they were, how they had spent their lives. He wasn't sure whether he *ought* to want to know those things: did they really matter or was it enough that they were *kind*? If he hoped to make Anna his duchess, though—which, thinking rationally about what he *wanted* in a wife, he still wasn't sure he did, but supposing he did—the world, Society, would want to know those things about her parents.

Did he want to make her his duchess? He just did not know. The desire that he felt for her was one thing. He could manage that. The love for her that he felt building inside him, though:

he was not sure whether he could cope with that. Because what if something happened to her, as it had to his father and brothers in such quick succession? He couldn't bear to lose her. And what if he did indeed die young, like his brothers, as his mother feared he would, and Anna loved him the way he loved her, and she was left bereft? It did not bear thinking about; he was almost shuddering at the horror of it.

'Tell me about your father and brothers?' Anna asked at that exact moment.

Was she a mind reader, or was that a natural question following his to her?

'My father was unfashionably and unashamedly most attached to his family and very much enjoyed spending time with us. He enjoyed hunting and shooting and fencing, and took my brothers and me out with him as soon as we were out of leading strings. And my brothers were both, I suppose, very similar to me in personality and tastes.'

He had also, he realised, described *them* as opposed to their status in life, but Anna *knew* who they were. And he had mentioned his father's activities, whereas after what Anna had said he was none the wiser about her parents' tastes.

'They sound wonderful,' she said. 'I'm so sorry for your loss.'

'And I for yours.' He reached out to squeeze her hand and she squeezed his back.

He was probably reading too much into her choice of words. It was after all difficult talking about relatives one mourned. Perhaps she had said all she could bear to say at this point.

When they reached Bruton Street, he felt a strong urge to ask Anna now when they could meet again. It was beginning to feel to him as though the days on which he did not see her were empty.

He did not ask, however.

'Thank you again; I very much enjoyed the afternoon,' he told her. And then he watched her inside before driving off.

He needed to restrain himself until he had made sure of his own intentions. He did not want to hurt her and so if he did not have serious intentions he should probably stop seeing her. She would be utterly ruined if anyone saw what they had done.

And, good God, he had run quite mad. After what they had done, he owed it to her—irrespective of his thoughts on love within marriage—to marry her. Of course he did. He should propose to her very soon. He...

Now was not the time, though.

He needed a little more time to think.

He should perhaps pay a call to Lady Derwent.

The next afternoon he was seated in Lady Derwent's drawing room wishing that he had called at almost *any* other time, or agreed in advance a particular time to see her; she had been taking tea with three dowagers when he arrived and they were all *extremely* interested to see him.

'Amscott, how are your dear mothers and sisters?' Lady Forcet asked him.

Time dragged as the ladies drew from him very small details about his family's health and whereabouts and marital intentions.

'None,' he said shortly in reference to his five youngest sisters.

Eventually, after he had wasted a good half hour of his life in her drawing room, Lady Derwent took pity on him and said, 'Perhaps we might drive in the park together, Amscott. You may call for me at half past four tomorrow.'

Twenty-five hours later, James was finally able to speak to Lady Derwent alone.

'I had expected you to bring your curricle,' she said as he handed her up into the chaise he had brought, assuming that she would not want to ride in a curricle. 'I am not in my dotage yet, thank you.'

He laughed. 'I must apologise. I will bear that in mind for any future drives we take together.'

As they moved forward, he opened his mouth to ask her immediately about Anna, but was thwarted when she began to talk to him about the weather. She continued onto the latest gossip from Court, and then the weather again, and then some exclamations about how bare the trees seemed now. And then the weather again.

Finally, she began to describe—in stunning detail—the exhibition at the Royal Academy that she had been to earlier in the week. She began with descriptions of what every lady she had seen there had been wearing, while James began to wonder if he would be able to speak at *all* during the drive, or whether this would be a wasted afternoon from the perspective of finding out a little more about Anna.

And then Lady Derwent moved on to talking about some of the paintings, before saying, 'My goddaughter would certainly appreciate the exhibition. Perhaps you should take her.'

Finally!

'Perhaps I should,' James said. 'I do not, however, know whether Miss Blake is particularly interested in art.'

'I am sure she would enjoy it.'

'Has Miss Blake visited many art exhibitions before now?'

'One or two only, I imagine.' Lady Derwent smiled at him. 'I commend you for hiding your frustration so admirably during the first part of our drive.'

'I assure you that I have enjoyed your company during the entirety of this afternoon,' James said cautiously.

'Fiddlesticks. The only reason that you wanted to see me was to ask me about Miss Blake, was it not?'

'A little,' said James, trying not to wince, 'but I am also enjoying the drive and hearing your views on other topics.'

'Gammon.' Lady Derwent rolled her eyes so thoroughly that James was worried she might give herself a headache. 'Enquire of me whatever you like about my goddaughter, and I will answer you where I am able and deem it acceptable.'

Good God. James was suddenly almost nervous. He had been trying to ask such questions for some time, and now he had carte blanche to ask what he liked. What if he did not like the answers? Also, was this really acceptable? To ask questions about Miss Blake to which she might not like him to know the answers?

It was not acceptable, he realised. He would *like* to find out everything about her, but he could not in all conscience go behind her back like this. He could not ask Lady Derwent a question about Anna that he would not ask her directly.

He was quite sure, however, that Lady Derwent had only Anna's best interests at heart.

Perhaps his best course of action was honesty.

In moderation. He was not going to disclose what had happened between him and Anna on their ice-tasting afternoons.

'In truth,' he said, hoping that he was indeed about to speak the truth, because he wouldn't like to lie to Lady Derwent, 'I did intend to ask you some questions about Miss Blake, but on reflection I find that I should not ask you anything about her that I would not ask her to her face. And therefore I do not have anything to ask about her.'

'I see.' Lady Derwent observed him for an unnervingly long time through her lorgnette, for so long in fact that James found himself struggling to keep his focus on his horses and the road.

Eventually, she cleared her throat and said, 'May I ask your intentions towards my goddaughter?'

James gave an involuntary twitch and caused one of his horses to stop for a moment, and the carriage to lurch a little.

'I must apologise,' he said, when he had them back under control a few moments later. 'I cannot remember the last time I drove so badly.'

'Perhaps you also cannot remember the last time someone asked you if you intended to marry their goddaughter or not.'

This time James laughed rather than jobbing his horses' mouths, which was an improvement.

'That is true,' he said.

'And what is your answer?'

'I...' This was not good. He should really have thought of this when he decided to call on Lady Derwent.

'Yes?'

'I admire Miss Blake very much,' he said. 'She is a most... admirable young woman.'

'Do you intend to propose to her, though? Do you love her?'

'I...' Good God. What if Lady Derwent relayed the import of this conversation to Anna? And what would Anna's thoughts be at this moment in time? 'I am not certain and—without wishing to sound arrogant and assuming that anyone to whom I might propose marriage would accept—I would not wish to raise anyone's hopes of a proposal—which of course they might or might not choose to accept or be happy about—before I knew myself what I intended.'

He did intend to propose, he was certain of that now, but he did not wish his proposal to be via Lady Derwent as proxy.

'So you called on me with the intention of asking about Anna? And then thought better of it because you did not feel it fair to ask about something that you would not ask her directly.'

James nodded ruefully. 'That is correct,' he said. 'I cannot ask you anything that Miss Blake would not choose to tell me herself.'

'That is laudable. If a little dull.'

'Thank you?'

Lady Derwent ignored him and continued, 'I am going to give you one important piece of information. I am also going to give you a warning.'

'Indeed?'

'I will begin with the warning. Do not trifle with my goddaughter's heart. She is a wonderful young lady and I should not like to see her upset.'

'I would not like to upset her,' James said.

'That is good. I understand that you have been seen with other young ladies, including Lady Catherine Rainsford. For everyone's sake, you would be wise to make your choice sooner rather than later.'

'Yes.'

Lady Derwent was, he had to admit, correct; and it was right and proper that she should attempt to protect her goddaughter.

'I would not like to upset Miss Blake,' he repeated.

Lady Derwent ignored him again. 'The information that I think you might like to have concerns Anna's birth.'

James did of course wish to learn such information, but, the more he thought about it, the more uneasy he felt about betraying Anna's trust—such as she might have—and speaking about her in her absence.

'I'm not sure...' he began.

'Nonsense.' Lady Derwent spoke over him before he could finish his objection. 'She is the granddaughter of an earl.'

And there he had it, or part of it. Her background.

He couldn't tell whether he had been expecting that or not. Part of him, he realised, had worried that she might be of low birth, which would make marriage between them more difficult. His mother was a stickler for tradition and good breeding, although he hoped that her wish for him to be happy would transcend any feeling that the woman he married might not be of exactly the family his mother would have chosen. He had also, however, been quite sure all along that Anna was a lady.

'A particularly august earl,' Lady Derwent continued. 'Of a very old family. Anna's grandfather was the late Earl of Broome. The ninth earl.'

James frowned. He knew, distantly, of the Earl of Broome. The new—tenth—earl was young, younger than him. Perhaps something had happened within the family of the sort that he and his mother worried might happen if he, James, died without issue. Perhaps the earldom had passed to a distant cousin who had not provided for Anna on the death of her mother. The cur. If the man were in front of him now, James would want to throttle him. How could he live with the knowledge that his cousin was now forced to work as a governess? Surely the man could make her an allowance of enough to live modestly without working?

Perhaps he would ask his mother about the earl. Perhaps not, on second thought, or not until he had made up his mind exactly when—and how—he would propose to Anna.

Because, yes, of *course* he was going to propose to her. He had to. He had compromised a young lady of quality and it was irrelevant whether or not anyone else knew. *He* knew. He had to do the right thing by her.

Good God. He was going to propose to Anna. As soon as he could.

And if she accepted, they would marry. They would be husband and wife.

And that would be…well, it would be a lot of things.

It would be terrifying, because, obviously, due to the fact

that she was wonderful in every way, he would end up—if he wasn't already—deeply in love with her. His wife. And so, if anything happened to her, he would be heartbroken, bereft.

But it would also be exhilarating, life-affirming, perfect... Because being married to Anna would enable him to see her every day: talk to her, laugh with her, make love to her, just *be* with her.

He would be the luckiest man alive.

He realised suddenly that he had been staring ahead while he thought, completely ignoring Lady Derwent.

'I must apologise,' he said. 'My thoughts were elsewhere. Thank you for letting me know.'

'There is no need to apologise. I presume you were thinking of my goddaughter.'

James inclined his head.

'I must remind you.' Her tone had hardened significantly. 'I would expect to hear either a happy announcement in relation to you and Anna, or nothing at all. That is to say: you must not trifle with her affections. If you do not intend to marry her, I would expect you no longer to spend any time with her. Her work as a governess does not preclude her from marrying and I do not wish her reputation to be sullied by you.'

'Of course.' James had nothing further to add, because he was certainly not going to tell Lady Derwent before he asked Anna that he hoped very much that Anna would like to marry him.

He would have liked Anna to have told him herself about her background, but he understood that it must be very hurtful and humiliating effectively being rejected by one's own family, and perhaps it was something that she did not feel she could discuss with anyone. Hopefully, in time, she would feel that she was able to confide in him—hopefully her husband.

Now he just needed to plan his proposal.

The next morning, after much thought, he sent a note inviting Anna to the opera that evening. She had mentioned in passing that she had never been, and he had been sure that, while she was not a woman to evince any self-pity, he had caught a wistful note in her voice.

He had been careful in his planning not to organise an evening that might compromise her; he had also invited Lady Derwent—and had received her acceptance before he penned his invitation to Anna—as well as his mother, his married sister and her husband, and two or three other friends, and had told Anna that he was doing so.

He had thought long and hard about the timing of the opera trip. Should it be before or after he proposed—assuming she accepted the proposal? He had decided that it would be more comfortable for Anna to enter into a betrothal with him if she already knew his mother and sister a little better. And from their side, if they got to know her, they could not fail to like her, and he would wish his family and his wife to get on well together.

He was sure that Lady Derwent would then happily allow him to escort Anna home himself while she travelled in her own carriage.

He waited on tenterhooks for Anna's reply and was heartily relieved when he received an acceptance of his invitation within three hours of issuing it. Now he just needed to wait for the evening to come.

Chapter Eleven

Anna

Anna had just arrived back from her morning walk with the girls when she received James's card. As she had looked at the envelope and recognised his handwriting, her heart had—annoyingly—quickened, and she had decided to put it to one side and open it later. She had resolved yesterday evening not to continue her outings with him, however much she might like ice creams. And his company. And what they'd done together in the carriage each time.

She had been very lucky that no one had seen them on the three occasions that they had kissed—and more—and she couldn't risk being caught in such a compromising situation.

In addition, she had, she realised, developed feelings for James that were much stronger than mere liking, and she did not wish to have her heart broken. He would clearly not contemplate marrying her, as evidenced by his dallying with her in this way; she was sure that dukes did not do such things with young ladies of quality. Clearly, therefore, he knew her to be inferior to him socially, and that was why he had behaved the way he had. Equally clear was that he would need to marry and produce at least one heir relatively soon.

She did not wish to be heartbroken when he married someone else—Lady Catherine Rainsford for example—and she did not wish there to be any possibility that he might attempt to set her up as his mistress. Everyone knew that even the nicest of men behaved quite awfully in this regard.

So she hoped very much that he would be happy with whomever he married and she was glad—honestly, she was—that it wouldn't be her. Being deeply in love with one's own husband was a recipe for deep unhappiness. Dukes frequently had affairs outside marriage. Everyone knew that. Even if they did not abandon their wives in the way that her father had left her mother.

It was for the best, then, no longer to see each other. She did not wish to be any more heartbroken than she had to be.

Before she had opened the note, she had spoken quite sternly to herself. She would not accept whatever invitation it might contain.

Except...oh!

He had invited her to the opera with her godmother—who had apparently already indicated to him that she would be attending—together with his own mother and sister, and several other people.

Perhaps he held her in higher esteem than she had thought. It could not be possible—surely—that he would introduce her to his mother and sister in such a small group if he had dishonourable intentions towards her. Even though she was a governess and he had driven in the park with Lady Catherine between his two outings with Anna?

Or did he just regard her as a friend whom he would like to introduce to other friends? *Could* a duke openly have a governess as a friend?

Did he perhaps have intimate relations with all sorts of women? Anna had pushed that thought out of her mind as fast as it had entered; it did not make her feel good.

Whatever James's intentions, it must be quite unexceptionable to visit the opera with her own godmother as guests of a duke and his wider family and friends, and she would very much like to have the opportunity to go. There could be no risk on such an occasion of them succumbing to any temptation to kiss, so it could surely do no harm.

Once she had decided that, she had asked Lady Puntney if she would be happy for her to go. Her employer had, as usual, been quite delighted at her governess's moving in such august circles, and had told her 'dearest Miss Blake' that she must of course attend, and must enjoy herself as much as she could during her evenings off, so there had been nothing preventing Anna from accepting the invitation.

'Good evening, my dear,' Lady Derwent greeted her when— as agreed by an exchange of notes during the afternoon—Anna entered her godmother's carriage later that day. 'That mantle is most becoming; I am so glad that we bought it.'

The mantle in question was powder blue and lined and trimmed with fur and sewn with gold thread, and worn over a pale green silk evening dress. Both garments had been among Lady Derwent's more extravagant gifts to Anna, and she adored them both.

'Thank you. I am very grateful to you; I like it exceedingly.' She returned her godmother's embrace and said, 'You are also looking particularly fine this evening.'

Lady Derwent adjusted her own mantle into place and then spread her heavily beringed hands in front of her and regarded them with a complacent air.

'Yes, I think I am,' she said, which made them both laugh.

Laughing with her reminded Anna of laughing with James.

And this was silly. Really, *anything* nice reminded her of him. She wondered… She didn't want to wonder. She should *not* wonder; even if he did for some strange reason perhaps wish to…well, she couldn't even think it, but if he did wish something honourable, she was sure he would change his mind if he knew about the scandal of her parents' elopement and the fact that her father had been a groom.

If it began to look as though his intentions really might be honourable, she would have to tell him about her parents, as soon as possible.

The fact that he was introducing her to his mother did indicate that...

No, she mustn't think it.

She must, however, decide whether, should such a thing occur, she would disclose the truth about her parents or just say no with no explanation.

When they arrived at the Theatre Royal, where they were to watch the opera, James was waiting in the road to meet them.

As he handed Anna down from the carriage, he applied just a little more pressure to her hand than might be usual, and fixed her with a particular look which made her feel quite warm inside; the look seemed to signal that he was extremely pleased to see her. A small smile was playing about his lips as he looked at her, and his eyes were focused on hers, as though she was the only other person that existed in his world.

The way he was looking at her was actually making her feel quite breathless.

'I am particularly pleased to see you here this evening,' he told her.

Anna had no words other than, 'Thank you,' accompanied by a shiver of pleasure.

As they made their way to his box, the hordes in the opera house's foyer parted easily for them due to James's broad shoulders and natural air of command. Anna could not remember a time when she had felt more protected within a crowd. It was a sensation that anyone would surely revel in.

The box was entirely velvet and gilt and felt beautifully luxurious. Glancing up, Anna saw that the ceiling was also very intricately decorated, with blue panels, relieved by white and enriched by gold.

James's entire *life* was luxury. She wondered briefly how he would feel about her if he knew that after her mother's death before Lady Derwent had effectively rescued her she had been living in a very small and somewhat damp cottage with a friend of her mother's, a Miss Shepson, another gentlewoman who had fallen on hard times, and had been forced to take in sewing to try to earn a few pennies so that she had money enough to eat. Heating had been a luxury she could not often afford, so both ladies had enjoyed the summer months considerably more than the winter ones.

'Miss Blake, you have already met my mother, the dowager duchess. I am not sure you are acquainted with my sister Lady Mallow and her husband, Lord Mallow.'

'I am very pleased to meet you.' Lady Mallow patted the empty chair next to her. 'Come and sit next to me so that we may talk more easily. You must call me Sybilla.'

'Thank you. And you must call me Anna.'

She and Sybilla exchanged mutual smiles, and immediately began a very comfortable cose; it quickly felt as though they had known each other for quite some time.

Just before the opera—Mozart's *The Magic Flute*—began, James made his way to the seat next to Anna's, on the other side from Sybilla, and Anna could not help feeling that there could be no more enjoyable way to be seated. Other than alone with James in his carriage but that was quite inappropriate and should not—could not—happen again, and she should not even think about it.

'Are you too warm?' James asked her in an undertone. 'Your cheeks are a little red.'

'Oh, no! I just...' She wondered what he would say—or indeed *do*—if she told him that she had been blushing at her own scandalous thoughts, involving him... 'I am very well, thank you, and it is the perfect temperature in here. I am very much looking forward to the performance.'

'I am pleased to hear it. And I too am looking forward to it; I shall very much enjoy watching it with you.'

Sitting next to James in the near darkness, knowing that he was so close to her, almost able to touch him without moving far, knowing what he felt like and how it felt when he touched her but prevented from doing anything of that nature by the presence of his sister on her other side and the others in their group around them was quite overwhelming.

The performance was wonderful. Anna was transported to ancient Egypt and fully engrossed in the story. Knowing that she was sharing it with James made it an even more intense experience.

When the interval came, she realised that she was almost tearful from the beauty of the story and the singing. It was blissful to be able to discuss and exclaim over the performance with James and his sister, and to witness their funning with each other and the sibling bond they shared.

A few minutes into the interval, there was some movement around the box. Sybilla rose to go and speak to a cousin, and another lady seated herself in her place.

James had just started saying something, but was interrupted by the lady in Sybilla's seat leaning very rudely across Anna as though she were a piece of furniture rather than an actual person, and saying, 'I should love to hear your views on this particular production of *The Magic Flute*, Your Grace.'

Anna couldn't work out whether she was more annoyed by the rudeness or sad about the very strong reminder that James—the lofty Duke of Amscott—could not possibly contemplate, even if he wanted to, marrying a woman like Anna. If someone were this rude when they believed her to be of acceptable birth, then how much ruder or dismissive would they be if they knew about her parents?

She glanced up at James and saw that his eyes were suddenly like flints and his expression rigid.

'I believe that introductions have not been performed,' he said in chilly tones. 'Miss Blake, this is Mrs Chilcott, an acquaintance of my mother's. Mrs Chilcott, this is Miss Blake, a particular friend of my family's and goddaughter of Lady Derwent.'

Anna smiled at him and tried not to feel horrified about the fact that her presence had caused James to be in this position.

'Oh. Miss Blake. Yes. Forgive me… I'm not quite sure…' The lady raised one eyebrow in a very haughty fashion. Anna stared back at her, quite taken aback at her rudeness.

'Not sure about…?' James's voice was now so cold it could have frozen water. 'As I said, Miss Blake is Lady Derwent's goddaughter and is also known by my mother. I am surprised that you do not know her, but she is recently arrived in town, and perhaps you were not at my mother's ball, where you would have met her.'

'Of course I was at your mother's ball,' the lady trilled. 'You and I conversed for quite ten minutes.'

'Forgive me.' The Duke's voice was still as hard as stone. 'It was a busy evening for me and I spoke to a great many people.'

Anna did her best to smile as the lady began to brush over her rudeness in the face of the Duke's evident distaste for it, but it was difficult. Quite aside from the fact that men were not to be trusted, *this* was why she would never be able to marry someone of his standing in Society. When it became known that she was the product of her mother's scandalous elopement with one of Anna's grandfather's grooms, she would regularly be the subject of this kind of rudeness, and it would be very difficult for her husband. How long would it be until he tired of the difficulty?

'Indeed,' said James for about the fifth time in response to yet another opening sally from Mrs Chilcott.

Eventually, Mrs Chilcott rose and said, 'It has been most pleasant to converse.'

Anna smiled blandly and James inclined his head the merest fraction, and Mrs Chilcott turned and left in what could only be described as a flouncing manner.

'I'm so sorry,' James said. 'I abhor such rudeness.'

'No, no; it was my presence that caused it.'

'Well, it *was* your presence, but it was not *you*. Many people envy a young lady who is singled out by an unmarried duke of marriageable age.'

Anna screwed her face up a little. 'I am not sure it is that; I think it is rather that she did not deem me a suitable person with whom to converse.'

'Nonsense. That could never be the case.' James's smile was so warm that Anna felt her eyes to be suddenly moist. 'Let us not waste any more time talking about someone neither of us knows; instead let me introduce you further to my mother.'

He drew Anna over to the duchess, who was conversing

with Lady Derwent, and soon had all three of the ladies laughing with his observations on the evening, before asking Anna, 'What aspect of the opera have you enjoyed the most so far?'

'That is a very hard question to answer,' she said. 'It's all wonderful. The theatre itself, the way the set on the stage is designed, the costumes, the music, and of course the singing and acting. I would find it very difficult to choose a favourite. The whole combine to make it a truly intoxicating experience.'

The duchess nodded. 'I agree. Too many people come to the opera merely to see and be seen. We must not forget that we are very lucky to witness such wonderful art on the stage.'

'That is very true, Leonora,' said Lady Derwent, and the two matrons smiled at each other. From what Anna had heard, this was a remarkable achievement on the part of James.

The three ladies found themselves in strong agreement on a variety of topics, and Anna enjoyed their conversation so much that she was almost sorry when the second half of the opera began.

As they re-seated themselves in preparation to begin watching again, James said sotto voce to Anna, 'I'm so pleased that you and my mother have established such a rapport, and that you seem to have struck up an immediate friendship with Sybilla.'

A shiver ran all the way down Anna from the back of her neck almost to her toes. It was nice—she thought—to know that it was unlikely he would do her the dishonour of wishing to set her up as his mistress; no one sane would introduce their paramour to their own mother. However, his clearly wishing that she and his mother become better acquainted did indicate that he might indeed be considering proposing to her.

If she were an entirely different woman, who could ever dare to entrust her heart and independence to a man, and if she were from an entirely different, scandal-free family, that might be—would be—wonderful.

But as it was it was quite awful. Rejecting him *would* be for the best because it would protect her from being tossed aside by him at some point in the future.

She would have to tell him about her parents. She *couldn't* just turn him down with no explanation. If she didn't have the opportunity to do so this evening, she would ask him for a short meeting as soon as possible.

She didn't want the opera to end. In itself, it was a wonderful spectacle, but the reason she wanted it to continue for ever was that she was quite sure that it would be the last time that she would have the opportunity to spend time with James like this. And that was deeply, deeply sad.

She didn't want to be sad. She should make the most of these last few moments, enjoy the way that when anything particularly dramatic happened he turned to her, enjoy the way their glances caught, enjoy being able to look at his handsomeness, enjoy the sensation that for now, this evening, he was *hers*.

And when he smiled at her—in that particular, just-for-her way that she *adored*—she should just drink it in, for one last time, rather than stupidly feeling her eyes fill with tears.

Eventually, too soon, the performance was over, and Anna didn't want to think about the imminent end to the evening, so instead she busied herself with chatter to the people around them.

And then everyone began to take their leave.

As she was about to thank James for a wonderful evening and say good-night—knowing that this was the last time she would see him before their friendship ended—he turned towards her godmother and spoke in a low voice to her.

Then he turned back to Anna and spoke quietly to her. 'Lady Derwent is happy for me to escort you home in my carriage; I have something most particular to ask you.'

Ohhhh, goodness.

Oh, dear.

Well. She couldn't say no to the suggestion without making a scene and drawing attention to them in a way that could do neither of them any good. And it would be the ideal opportunity for her to tell him about her parents.

So after a pause, she just said, 'Thank you.'

She would tell him everything as soon as they got into the

carriage and thank him personally for the lovely times they had spent together, and then he would take her back to Bruton Street and that would be the end of things. She should not be devastated at the thought that she would not see him again; she should be grateful that she had experienced Gunter's and the opera and…all that *pleasure*…with him.

When they reached James's carriage, he held his hand out for her to take as she ascended the steps, and held on to hers for a little longer than necessary, looking into her eyes as he did so. He had his lips half pressed together, half smiling, as though he was full of happiness.

Which made Anna feel the exact opposite.

She purposely avoided his eye while she was seating herself on the forward-facing velvet-upholstered seat of the carriage, both because now that the end was so near, even just looking at him was painful, and because she didn't wish to lead him to think that she was hoping for or would accept a proposal.

She was tempted to sit right in the middle of the seat to imply that he should sit opposite her rather than next to her, and then moved towards the right-hand corner at the last minute, worried that he would still sit next to her and they would then be far too close to each other.

He closed the carriage door behind him and did indeed sit down on the same seat as her, angling his body towards hers.

She lifted her regard from the floor to him and nearly gasped at the expression on his face. It was so…well, adoring. He was just *looking*, as though his entire being was focused on her and only her, and it was so much she could barely breathe. If only she hadn't been born of scandal; if only she could trust that he wouldn't cast her aside, as her father had done to her mother. She had to tell him. And she would do so, as soon as they set off and she was certain that no one could hear their words.

And then, before the carriage had even shown any signs of moving, James reached forward and took her hands in his, and said, 'Anna.'

'Oh,' said Anna. 'James.' No, that wasn't the right thing to say. He'd sounded as though he was speaking in a very romantic kind of way, and so did she. And she mustn't. 'James, I...'

'Anna, I have a very particular question to ask you and I'm not sure I can wait any longer.' He moved a little closer to her so that their knees were touching.

Even though she *knew* she was about to put an end to all of this, Anna's insides were turning to liquid just at his touch, which was just so silly.

She felt the carriage begin to move forward and wondered how long it would take to get back to Bruton Street. Not very long.

He leaned forward and kissed her lightly on the lips and she wanted *so much* to reach for him, pull him close to her, kiss him properly. But no. She must not and she needed to stop him before he said anything that he would clearly regret later.

She wriggled backwards a little, and said, 'James, no, I...' She had to tell him *now*.

'I'm sorry; you are of course right. We should not...yet.'

Before she could react further, he lowered himself to one knee, re-gathered her hands in his, turned them over and pressed his lips hard to each of her palms in turn, before saying, 'Anna, dearest Anna, will you marry me?'

Oh!

No.

No.

She was—for this one moment—the luckiest woman in the world.

But really, she felt like the *un*luckiest.

She had so much she needed to say, immediately, but all she could manage was, 'Oh, oh, *James.*'

He kissed her hands again, before turning them back over and drawing them close to his chest and saying, his voice hoarse all of a sudden, 'Is that... Might I hope that that is a yes?'

Oh, no. This was truly, truly awful.

Anna closed her eyes. For one long moment she wished that she could just accept. But at some point she would *have* to tell him about her parents. And men being what they were, he would no doubt pull out of the engagement at that point. Better for both of them for her to tell him now.

She took a deep, juddering breath before trying to pull her hands away.

'I'm so sorry.' Her words were little more than a whisper; it was as though her voice did not work properly any more. 'I cannot marry you.'

He froze for a moment, and then let go of her hands and bowed his head briefly before slowly rising and sitting down on the seat behind him, opposite Anna.

The space between them suddenly seemed huge.

'I'm so sorry,' he said in a horribly croaky voice, after an awful silence. 'I had perhaps misunderstood; I believed... That is to say... Of course. Might I... There is of course no obligation to reply but might I ask your reason?' His voice, his demeanour seemed horrifyingly diminished somehow.

Anna had never seen him like this before and it was dreadful. Previously he'd always seemed so big and strong—he *was* big and strong—but big and strong in spirit as well as body. He'd always seemed in command of every situation, confident, powerful.

It was terrible to think that her words could have reduced him somehow, and she very much needed to explain to him that her reason did not relate to *him*, it related to *her*.

She couldn't believe that at any point she had imagined that she might refuse a proposal without giving him a reason. She could never in reality bear him to think that she might not love him. No one—pauper or duke—should be led to believe that they were unlovable.

'Of course I will tell you the reason,' she said, despising herself for the fact that her voice was wobbling.

She drew a deep breath.

'I am not someone you can marry,' she told him when she was certain that she had command of her voice. 'I am not an appropriate wife for a duke.' She felt a tear dribble down her cheek and wiped it away with her fingers. 'I want you to know that any woman—lady—would be very lucky to marry you. It is not that you are not an acceptable husband; it is entirely that I am not an acceptable wife.'

'Anna. No.' James rose from his bench and moved back to sit next to her. 'That is not true.' He put his arm round her and pulled her against him with one arm before with his other hand very gently wiping the tears that were now coursing freely down her face.

Anna gave a gigantic sniff and said, 'It is.'

'No.' He pulled her even closer and kissed her forehead. 'Never. You are funny, kind, interesting, clever, wonderful, and of course very beautiful. You have all the attributes that any man could ever desire in a wife.'

Anna sniffed even harder, but nothing could prevent her tears now. She couldn't imagine a more wonderful set of compliments. All given under false pretences, of course, because she was not who he thought she was.

James wiped her tears again with his fingers, and then, taking her chin in his hand, gently turned her face towards his and then lowered his mouth to hers.

Anna allowed herself to return his kiss for one long—blissful—moment, before drawing back a little and saying, 'No, you don't understand, I can't.'

'I'm sorry. Of course.' James kept his arm round her but didn't attempt to kiss her again.

'I need to tell you something.' She took another breath, wiped under her eyes again, and squared her shoulders within the circle of his arm. 'You are wonderful. I have enjoyed spending time with you so very much.'

'Thank you. And I you.'

'I do very much wish you to know that.' She had to tell him *now* but it was hard to get the words out.

'I have also enjoyed myself with you very greatly.' He smiled at her and it felt as though her heart might crack.

When he reached for her again, she allowed herself for one moment to be drawn into his arms, to feel one last time the strength of his arms around her, his body against hers. If only she could stay here for ever.

As she clung to him, her face buried against his chest, she

heard him say, his voice sounding impossibly deep, 'Anna, I love you, so very, very much.'

'I love you too,' she whispered, and then she lifted her face to his, even though she shouldn't, because she couldn't prevent herself.

It was inevitable that they would kiss. There was passion, fire, and on Anna's side huge regret and sadness at what she knew was coming.

They kissed urgently and hard, before their hands found each other's bodies and they began to fumble with clothing, fast, telling each other to be quick because the journey was not that long.

Soon they were both hot and panting and, *oh*, the incredible pleasure of the cleverness of James's fingers and tongue. Anna was almost tempted to *beg* him to do *everything* with her this time—one final time—but sanity—a tiny modicum at least—prevailed.

As they helped each other return their clothing to a semblance of modesty, laughing and kissing as they did so, James said again, 'I love you so much.' The happiness and laughter in his voice was heart-rending, because he was about to be told something he clearly wasn't going to want to hear.

And that thought brought Anna to her senses.

'James, we shouldn't have, *I* shouldn't have... I'm so sorry. I have to tell you.' As she spoke, she felt the carriage come to a halt. 'But I think we've arrived. I need to tell you now.'

'My coachman will not open the door; we have as long as we need.' He was still smiling at her, clearly unaware that she was about to burst the bubble of happiness he seemed to be wearing, clearly assuming that her earlier refusal had perhaps been maidenly confusion.

'I am just going to say it,' she told him. 'I have been trying to preface it with softer explanations, and that led to what just happened, which really should not have happened again.'

James's eyes had narrowed and his smile had dropped as she spoke.

'Yes?' he asked.

Anna looked away from him for a moment, and then back into his eyes.

'My father was my grandfather's second groom. My mother and he fell in love and they ran away together. It caused a great scandal, and my grandfather disowned my mother and they never saw each other again. We lived quietly in the country, in some penury.'

James shook his head, his brow furrowing, as though he couldn't immediately understand her words. 'I... I'm afraid...'

'I should have mentioned: it's even worse than that, if that were possible. I was born six months after my parents ran away together. The scandal was great. My grandfather disowned my mother. Some of her friends remained loyal to her, in particular my wonderful godmother, Lady Derwent, but most did not. Things became even worse when I was about nine, when my father left us. He now lives in Canada. I wrote to him when my mother died, but he showed no interest. When I referred to our having lost him, I meant that he had abandoned us.' Anna looked hard at James. The duke. His face had become like a mask, with no emotion showing. 'As you can see,' she pursued, 'I am not someone the Duke of Amscott can marry.'

James was entirely silent. He had released her from his arms and was sitting, with his hands on his knees, just staring at the floor of the carriage.

Anna felt very, very cold, and quite mortified at the way her dress was still in some disarray. How could she have touched him, allowed him to touch her in that way only a few minutes ago? Now it just felt sordid, embarrassing.

This was exactly like she imagined her mother's experience had been, when she'd been rejected by her own father when she got pregnant, and then rejected by her own husband when times were hard.

She realised now that a tiny part of her had hoped that the duke might say that he did not care about her birth. But of course he cared, and was rejecting her. That was what men did.

When, after what felt a very long time, the duke raised his head, she saw that his eyes had gone unpleasantly hard.

'You lied to me,' he stated.

Anna felt herself stiffen. It mattered to her, she realised, what James thought of her probity. And it mattered, more broadly, how men treated women, and how more privileged people treated less privileged ones.

She was not going to be accused of something she had not done. Yes, her birth was undesirable, but no, she had not lied. 'No, I did not. Obviously I did go to your ball in the guise of Lady Maria, but when I did that I was not lying to *you*; it was, as you know, just a silly deception. And since then I have not lied to you at all. I have not at any point pretended to be anything other than an impecunious governess who has had the great good fortune to be sponsored by Lady Derwent but who otherwise cannot take any place in Society.'

James's lips had formed into a hard line. 'You must have known what I intended. And yet you said nothing.'

'I believe that that is unfair,' Anna said. 'I saw you driving in the park with Lady Catherine Rainsford earlier in the week. Why would I presume that you were intending to marry me?'

'I was driving with her because my mother arranged it. It was not my choice. And you and I had already been intimate by then.'

'I could not have known that it was your mother who had arranged your outing. And—' her voice was suddenly shaking with anger now, at the injustice of *his* anger '—if I should have assumed that our being *intimate* would cause you to propose to me, should not that proposal have come immediately?'

'You should have told me sooner,' he repeated.

She glared at him. It was suddenly like looking at a stranger.

A stranger with whom she had had really the best times of her life and who had just proposed marriage to her.

No, he had not in fact proposed marriage to *her*; he had proposed marriage to someone else, a woman he had thought suitable to be his bride. A woman of excellent birth who had sadly fallen on hard times but who had no scandal in her background.

There could be no point in continuing this dreadful conversation.

And, frankly, if he could be this unreasonable, she didn't even care any longer what he thought of her. Because this proved that her fears had been right, that men's affections were always conditional and easily lost.

'Goodbye,' she said. 'Thank you for——' she could not call it a nice evening; it had begun gloriously but ended terribly '——thank you.' It had, after all, been kind of him to invite her to the opera.

'Allow me to help you down,' James said stiffly. 'Excuse me.'

His arm brushed Anna's for a moment as he reached for the door handle, and she had to swallow a sob at how it was now extremely awkward for them to touch at all.

Once out of the carriage, he held his arm out for Anna to support her as she descended the steps. She placed two fingers very gingerly on his arm and released it as soon as she was sure that she wouldn't trip; touching him in any way felt very wrong now.

'Thank you again,' she said in her most formal tone.

'It was a pleasure,' he said, with great insincerity. 'Good night.'

Anna nodded and then began to walk up the steps towards the house, before suddenly freezing.

James—she must begin to think of him as *the duke* again, rather than in such familiar terms—had looked incredibly angry, and perhaps hurt, and seemed still to believe that she had purposely deceived him. What if he told someone else her secret and the Puntneys found out and she lost her job?

She turned back in his direction. 'Your Grace.'

He turned round instantly. 'Miss Blake?'

She very much did not wish to have to do this. But she *needed* her employment and must swallow her pride.

'I am a devoted governess and irrespective of my birth I do have the education and knowledge to instruct my charges,' she said. 'If I lose this position I will be destitute. I would be very grateful if you would undertake not to discuss this—or anything we *did*—with anyone.'

'Of course.' He was extremely tight-lipped. 'I should not dream of it.'

'Thank you.' She must get inside and up to her bedchamber before she allowed herself to *sob* as she felt she was about to do. 'Good night, then.'

'Good night.'

And that was that.

Chapter Twelve

James

James had cried at the deaths of his father and his two brothers but other than that he couldn't remember the last time he had even had a tear in his eye.

Now, watching Anna—Miss Blake—walk up the steps, her slim back held very straight, he didn't just have a lump in his throat; he felt as though he could easily spend a considerable amount of time bawling his eyes out.

He had expected this evening to be one of the happiest of his life. Instead, this. A real grief.

Suddenly, he took two steps forward. He couldn't let her go inside without apologising. He had accused her of lying. She was right: she had not lied to him. He had *felt* in that moment that she had, but she hadn't. He had lashed out from the depths of his misery, and that was a terrible thing to have done.

'Anna.' His voice sounded low, urgent to his own ears.

She froze for a moment, and then turned round, very slowly. 'Yes?'

'I am so sorry,' he said, in a rush to get his words out, feeling as though she might turn and slip inside at any moment. 'I apologise for having accused you of lying to me. I know that you did not. I am aware that much of our...relationship...has been instigated by me, and that you would not have been aware of my intentions initially. And you did of course tell me the truth as soon as I made my intentions clear. I must apologise from my side for not having made them clear immediately, the first time we...did things that we should not have done. I am sorry for everything and I would like you to know that I have very much enjoyed all our time together.' He was babbling, he realised, trying to make the situation better.

'I love you,' he concluded.

'I love you too,' she said. 'I wish you very well. Goodbye.'

And then, while he stood there staring, aghast but his mind strangely frozen so that he could not work out what he should do or say next, she turned back round and continued her way up the steps.

When she closed the front door behind her, it felt as though a door was closing on an unlived chapter of the rest of his life that he hadn't known he wanted until he met her.

He stared at the door for a long time, before turning and telling his coachman in a flat voice that he would walk.

And then he set off down the road. Walking felt like an extraordinary effort, as though his limbs had become entirely leaden.

God. Only perhaps twenty minutes ago, he and Anna had kissed, touched each other intimately, the precursor, he had assumed, to what would be blissful full lovemaking when they were married. And now...now they were entirely separate, and there could be no reason for them to see each other again.

His mind felt as leaden as his limbs.

He couldn't go home yet. He turned left instead of right and began an aimless walk through the streets of Mayfair as he tried to make sense of how he felt.

He hadn't wanted to marry at all but he needed to do so in order to produce an heir to secure his mother and sisters' futures.

If he had to get married, he had been adamant that he hadn't wished to fall in love with his wife, because he hadn't wanted to put himself in a position where he might experience further loss.

The entire reason that he'd planned to marry now was to take care of his mother and sisters. His wife being known to be some-one of such scandalous background could cause his own family to be embroiled in the scandal. What if that harmed his sisters' marriage prospects? What if *they* then ended up as governesses, or in undesirable marriages? What if one of them, for example, fell in love with an impecunious curate as Lady Maria had done? In that instance, if she was no longer under the protection of a powerful man, could it cause her problems if her sister-in-law were someone from a scandalous background? What if he mar-ried Anna and they had a son and then he, James, died young as his brothers had, when their son was still a minor? Would Society accept Anna as effectively a regent for a child duke?

Life was damned difficult for women and it was a huge re-sponsibility having so many sisters to set on a happy path in life, not to mention his mother, who had borne so much grief with so much dignity.

He could not bear any of his sisters to have to become a governess.

He did not like the thought of Anna being a governess.

He also didn't like the thought of her being sad. She'd cried so much. She'd looked stricken.

He'd been awful to her. He'd accused her of lying. She hadn't lied. She hadn't even knowingly misled him. She couldn't have suspected until recently that he planned to ask her to marry him. If doing things together that would clearly compromise her had caused him to propose, why had he not done so immediately? How could she have known that he would suddenly realise that he should, and that in that moment he was happy to do so be-cause he loved her?

At least he had apologised to her. But the fact remained that he had done things with her that one should not do with a lady of quality who was not one's wife. She *was* a lady of quality; her grandfather was an earl. She hadn't told him that. She had only told him that her father was a groom. She had not tried to protect herself in any way.

He'd been right about never wanting to fall in love: this hurt damnably.

So maybe this was for the best. As long as Anna wasn't too miserable.

Chapter Thirteen

Anna

Anna awoke the next morning lying on top of her bed still in her opera-visiting finery, her head feeling as though a metal clamp was squeezing it and her mouth as though she'd munched through the feathers in her eiderdown during her sleep.

As she blinked painfully dry eyes, she remembered that she'd walked blindly through the house and dissolved into tears the second she'd closed her bedchamber door behind her. Eventually, after much revisiting of painful conversations and misery in her head, she had gone to sleep there without changing out of her gown.

She had been very naïve, she realised. During the early hours of the night she had admitted to herself that she *had* actually hoped that James would propose to her *and* that he would somehow convince her that the scandal surrounding her parents did not matter. But of course it mattered, and of course James—the duke—could not ignore it. Her grandfather had abandoned her mother. Her father had not been the best of husbands to her mother. She knew that men expected women to adhere to higher standards than those to which they themselves adhered, and if they fell short—often through no fault of their own—they did not support them.

Really, she was lucky that things had come to a head now and that the farce of their friendship had ended.

It did hurt very much, though. As did her head.

She *really* did not want to look after young children this morning. She didn't really want to do anything. But if she *had* to do something, it would be much more akin to crawling behind a large rock and hiding there than plastering a smile on her face and attempting to instil discipline and knowledge into someone else's children, however generous a salary she was being paid to do it.

She was ready for breakfast—which Lady Puntney had kindly decreed from the beginning she should take with the family—only a little later than usual. Her looking glass had told her that her face was unusually pale and that the smile that she practised was sadly lacking in authenticity, but she hoped that no one would notice.

She managed to force down some toast and some tea, and discovered that the old adage that food and drink always made you feel better was absolute nonsense. She just felt now as though she was going to be sick. She wasn't sure whether her nausea was due to tiredness or misery or both, but it wasn't helping.

Two hours of instruction on arithmetic followed by some handwriting practice just increased the headache that accompanied her nausea, but it was very helpful to be occupied so that she did not have to be alone with her thoughts.

She and the children took their usual Hyde Park walk later in the morning, and as they reached the pond they liked to walk around, Anna realised that the fresh air was doing her some good; it was clearing her head a little, and looking at the trees and birds was an excellent reminder that life was bigger than just one man. She *would* be happy again, and she *would* make a good life for herself. She was lucky to have this employment, after all, and she was lucky to have Ladies Derwent and Maria as good friends.

By the time they arrived back at Bruton Street, Anna was

still feeling deeply miserable, but she had pulled herself together sufficiently to enjoy the company of the children and
to be sure that she really could recover from this; it would be
a temporary misery.

As she was removing her brown wool pelisse, the one she
wore when she was performing her governess role, Morcambe,
the butler, said, 'Lady Puntney would like to speak to you in
the library.'

Anna had been looking down as she unfastened buttons, but
glanced up at his face in surprise, because the tone of his voice
was odd, quite cold. She almost gasped out loud at the look on
his face. He had always behaved very paternally towards her,
and had always had a smile for her and often a word of advice,
but now he was entirely unsmiling, and staring at her almost
insolently.

A cold dread began to creep over her as she stared back at
him. What had happened?

'Thank you,' she said, mortified to hear her own voice shake
a little. She gave herself a little shake and then said, in a much
stronger voice, thank goodness, 'I shall go to her directly.'

'See that you do,' Morcambe said, and Anna nearly gasped
again at the rudeness.

A minute later, purposely having taken her time, to persuade
herself that she could not be intimidated by Morcambe—but in
reality really quite terrified by the change in his demeanour—
she entered the library.

'Please close the door.' Lady Puntney was standing behind
a writing table. When Anna had closed the door, she indicated
a chair in front of the table, and said, 'Please sit down.'

Anna seated herself, feeling quite wild with fear now, as
though her head might explode from inside.

Lady Puntney sat down too, and clasped her hands in front
of her.

'I am sorry about this,' she began. And then she paused, for
a very long time, while Anna swallowed hard.

Perhaps they no longer needed a governess. Although why
then would Morcambe have been so insolent in his manner
towards her? Surely he should have been more sympathetic?

'I have, as you know, been very pleased with your service.' Lady Puntney's voice faltered. 'The children have very much liked you and indeed I have too. However...' She paused again as Anna blinked to dispel sudden moistness in her eyes. Clearly, she was being asked to leave for some reason. She *needed* a job, though, and this one was better than any other she might hope to get.

'The problem is...' Lady Puntney cleared her throat. 'That is to say...' She unclasped her hands and pressed her fingertips together and then re-clasped them. 'I do not wish to be unfair.'

Then please keep me on, Anna screamed inside. Externally, she kept her face immobile and concentrated on not crying.

'Mrs Clarke told me this morning that she had overheard something last night of which she felt it her duty to inform me.'

Anna went very cold all over.

Lady Puntney pressed her lips together before continuing, 'She told me that you had had a conversation on the doorstep late last night with the Duke of Amscott that clearly indicated that you have had some form of intimacy with him.'

Oh, no, no, no. Mrs Clarke was the Puntneys' housekeeper. What exactly had she heard? What had they said after they left the privacy of the carriage? Oh, no. This had happened because she had implored the duke not to tell anyone about what had happened between them. How *stupid* of her. Or perhaps it was his apology that Mrs Clarke had heard. Whichever, Anna had been stupidly, *stupidly* rash spending any time with him whatsoever.

She shook her head, speechless.

'Are you able to tell me that this was a mistake?' Lady Puntney continued.

'I...' Anna wanted so much to lie. Would it hurt a living soul if she *did* lie? She didn't think it would. She *was* a good governess; she cared about the children and she felt that she was educating them well. She was *not* a debauched person. She would not influence them badly in any way. She didn't like lying, especially to someone who had treated her as well as Lady Puntney had. But could it hurt anyone if she denied it? She wouldn't want to get Mrs Clarke into trouble for having invented something that she had not in fact invented. What should she say? 'I...'

'Miss Blake! Your hesitation tells me everything I need to know. I had hoped to be told that Mrs Clarke was mistaken. I am distraught.' Lady Puntney was indeed twisting her hands most agitatedly and her eyes looked moist, but it was hard to imagine that she could be as distraught as was Anna.

Anna took a deep, juddering breath. She could not allow herself to dissolve in tears or indeed to say nothing; she had to find some words to explain her situation reasonably, if Lady Puntney would allow her. And then, obviously, she would almost certainly still ask her to leave, but at least she would hopefully not then think ill of her for ever.

'I met the duke at his mother's ball at the beginning of the Season,' she said.

Lady Puntney nodded, as though she wanted to hear more, and Anna realised that of course she wasn't going to refuse to listen to her; she would be agog to hear any gossip about the duke. Well, Anna was not going to give her any gossip, including about her masquerade as Lady Maria, but she would do her best to clear her own name. Just in case. She was not going to volunteer the details about her parents, because that could do her no good and was nobody else's business, and if she was lucky Mrs Clarke would not have overheard that.

If Mrs Clarke *had* heard that, Anna would have to obtain a post far from London if she were to continue as a governess. Most families wished for governesses at least as well-born as they were—just a lot more impecunious.

She should continue her story.

'At the ball, we danced twice and spoke for a while. Subsequently he asked me to go to Gunter's, as you know, and to the opera. And yesterday evening after the opera he escorted me home and we had—' she was almost choking on the words '—a small disagreement and are no longer friends.'

'Mrs Clarke gained the impression that you and the duke had, in her recital of what passed between you, "done" some things together.'

'We, no, that is...'

'I must tell you that she then felt herself obliged to question the staff and a number of them were suspicious, and disclosed that there have been strong whisperings about you and the duke. They had assumed that if you were…exchanging intimacies with him…you were perhaps secretly betrothed.'

Anna closed her eyes for a moment.

'I am afraid,' Lady Puntney said, 'that, even though you might be innocent of anything untoward, there will now be questions about you in people's minds, and that could extend to me and to my daughters. And I have to be prudent.'

'So,' asked Anna slowly, 'even if you knew things that people had said were just rumours, you would still feel that you had to act on them as though they were truth?'

Lady Puntney stared at her for a long time and then nodded. 'Yes, I think perhaps I would have to. For my family's sake. Such is the world in which we live. My status is not sufficiently high to withstand any kind of scandal.'

Anna nodded. Of course Lady Puntney had to think of her daughters' future, and they could not have a governess to whom was attached any scandal.

And, of course, the scandal was *true*. And Lady Puntney didn't even know about Anna's parents, or the extent of the scandal that *might* attach to Anna now.

She paused and then continued, 'Miss Blake—Anna—I very much like you. I do not know what has happened between you and the duke. I must confess—speaking very frankly—that I had hoped on your behalf that perhaps the duke's interest in you might lead to marriage. I believe that it is very wrong that any indiscretion between you means that you must lose your employment while he loses nothing.' She sniffed. 'I do wish that I did not have to let you go. But I am afraid that I have to think of my family and our reputation. Servants do talk. And others might have heard.'

Anna bowed her head. 'I understand.'

'Anna, I will do what I can. I will not tell anyone about this, and I will provide you with a reference so that you may find another position. Perhaps, though, it would be best for you to move to another part of the country so that rumours do not follow you via my servants. I do not like to think that they gossip widely, but one must be realistic about human nature.'

'Thank you,' Anna managed to say before her voice threatened to give way to tears. She did feel very grateful; with a reference from Lady Puntney, and perhaps more help from Lady Derwent, she should indeed be able to find a position in another part of the country. She also, however, felt deeply, deeply sad.

Lady Puntney pushed her chair back, stood, walked round the table and held her hands out to Anna. 'Come.' As Anna stood, she pulled her into an embrace.

Anna did not mean to cry—in fact she was very keen *not* to do so—but somehow she found herself weeping onto Lady Puntney's shoulder as the other woman held her.

Eventually, she pulled away, and saw that Lady Puntney's cheeks were also tear-stained.

'I shall miss you greatly,' Lady Puntney said. 'I am angry with the duke and with this situation. I can no longer employ you but please remember that you have a friend in me.'

'Thank you.' Anna was still sniffing a little. She did fully understand Lady Puntney's position. If one were fortunate enough to have a good reputation, one had to guard it fiercely, and Lady Puntney had her three young daughters to think about.

'I cannot bear to think of you cast out entirely,' Lady Puntney told her. 'I am sure I could find somewhere in the country for you to stay, a cottage for you to reside in perhaps. Perhaps you should stay in a hotel while I attempt to organise something for you.'

Anna shook her head. 'Truly, that is most kind, but I can't allow you to do that.'

'You will have to make me a promise. You must not allow yourself to become destitute.'

Anna swallowed as she nodded, all too aware that such a promise might be difficult to keep.

Chapter Fourteen

James

Two days later, James handed his horse's reins to his groom and strode into his house, almost knocking over his butler, Lumley, on his way in.

'Is everything all right, Your Grace?' Lumley asked.

'Yes, thank you,' James lied.

'You seemed to be in a hurry,' Lumley persisted.

It was excellent having household retainers whom one had known one's entire life. Usually. Sometimes, like now, it was not excellent; it was really quite annoying.

'No particular hurry,' James said, and hurried away. Truth be told, he'd been doing everything fast over the past couple of days. This morning, he'd been dressed before his valet had had a chance to get his hands on his wardrobe and he'd practically gobbled his breakfast. He'd galloped hell for leather down Rotten Row. And now he was going to read his correspondence fast before perhaps going and raining blows in Gentleman Jackson's Boxing Saloon.

It was as though he had a compulsion to do things fast and

furiously, to try to prevent the thoughts and the misery and the worry that kept intruding.

It wasn't working; as he sat down at his desk, he was, yet again, thinking about Anna. He was angry, although not with her; it was the situation. And himself, of course; he was definitely angry with himself. He was missing her. And he was worried about her; he hoped that she wouldn't be too upset.

He was *really* missing her. He just wanted to see her, talk to her, kiss her—obviously.

God.

Correspondence rushed through, followed by furious sparring with Gentleman Jackson himself, the freneticism of which earnt him some puzzled questioning, and then a gobbled luncheon and some more high-speed work, he found himself sitting with his mother in her boudoir.

He'd been avoiding her for the past two days, sure that she would ask him about Anna, and very eager to avoid talking to her about the situation.

'I am just returned from a call to the Countess of Maltby,' she told him. She looked down at the sewing in her lap for a moment. 'She had much to say on many topics.'

James felt himself tense a little. He did not wish to discuss Anna at all. Thank heavens he had not at any point told his mother that she was the ninth Earl of Broome's granddaughter.

'She asked about you and Miss Blake,' his mother continued, still looking at her embroidery, meaning that he was unable to see the expression in her eyes, 'and I told her, of course, that Miss Blake is an acquaintance of yours and the goddaughter of Lady Derwent, and that I have no further information about her.'

James said nothing.

'I presume that others will also be asking about her. Your attentions to her were most pronounced at the opera, and I hear that you were seen with her more than once at Gunter's.'

This was why he'd been avoiding his mother.

James drew a deep breath. He should say something that would ensure that Miss Blake's reputation would be damaged no further; if there was gossip surrounding her, she might lose her position.

His attentions to her *had* been very pronounced. He should acknowledge that to his mother, and ensure that she believed that Miss Blake had turned him down. Which she had. Except... Had it, in fact, been the case that he had walked away from her once she had told him about her parents? Without trying hard enough to persuade her to accept his proposal?

No, that was something to think about later.

'I was indeed courting Miss Blake,' he said. 'Unfortunately, she does not wish to marry me.'

'What?' His mother dropped her embroidery and her head came straight up. 'Am I to understand that you proposed to her?'

'Yes.'

'You did not tell me of this.'

'I am a grown man, Mama. There are some things that one does not wish to discuss with one's parent or indeed with anyone.'

'You proposed to her and she refused you?'

'That is correct.'

'Why would any young lady in her right mind turn down a proposal from you? You are handsome, you are a wonderful man, and you are a *duke*.'

Because she was a very courteous and considerate young lady. And honest. She could have withheld the information about her parentage until he was too far embroiled in their betrothal to be able to withdraw, had he been so minded.

Why *had* he been so minded when he heard the information?

Oh, yes. The impact that the scandal might have on his mother and sisters.

Miss Blake, though. What if he had compromised her? Well, he had. It was just that no one knew. *He* knew, though.

'James?'

'Sorry, Mama.' He'd been asked why Anna would refuse him. 'I believe that she just did not wish to marry me. She thanked me for my very kind offer and told me that she was very grateful but believed that we should not suit.'

'How could the life of a duchess not suit a *governess*?'

'Perhaps she—' James swallowed '—perhaps Miss Blake wishes to marry for love, as I know you did.'

'Well.' His mother's eyes were practically flashing with anger. 'How could she not love *you*? She could not find a better man.'

'I believe that you are biased, Mama.' James knew that she was wrong. A better man than he would not have allowed things to develop the way they had with Anna. And, having allowed that to happen, he would have worked out a way to do the right thing for her while avoiding scandal for his family.

'I am not wrong. The young lady is clearly addle-brained.'

'Mama!'

'I make no apology, James. If I cannot state my mind in front of my own son, before whom might I speak frankly?'

James nodded. Fair enough, he supposed.

'I will say that I hope that you are not too distraught. While I am not sure of what family Miss Blake is, she is clearly a lady, and if she would have made you happy, I would have been pleased to welcome her into our family. If she refused you, perhaps she has a reason and perhaps it is for the best. There are many other young ladies who would like to make your acquaintance.'

'Indeed.' James nodded unenthusiastically. Of course there were. He was a duke. Unfortunately for him, he couldn't imagine ever liking—loving—another young lady in the way that he did Anna. And while he had not wanted to marry for love, he also couldn't imagine spending time with another woman, making love to another woman.

'I see that your spirits are currently low.' His mother shook her head. 'I am sorry, James.'

'Thank you, Mama. For your concern. We do not need to speak of it, however.'

'I shall not mention it ever again,' his mother said, almost certainly inaccurately. 'Let me distract you by telling you about some of the other *on-dits* that the countess shared with me.'

'Mama, this is how unpleasant gossip spreads.'

'James. You are my son. Neither of us needs to repeat any of this further, but one needs to be able to talk to *some*one.'

James immediately felt guilty. He knew how much she missed his father, and his brothers, and of course she needed to be able to talk to him.

And she was right; he needed to be distracted.

'Tell me everything,' he said.

'And *that*,' concluded his mother at least fifteen minutes later, after she'd regaled him with a series of the most bewilderingly convoluted anecdotes he'd heard in some time, 'goes to show that Miss Blake is indeed an unusual young lady. And while she is of course not of a family of note—' she was entirely wrong there, with regard to both the Earl of Broome, and the scandal Anna's parents had caused '—she is very prettily behaved and quite beautiful. And if the Marquis of Blythe can marry an *actress*, you can marry a nonentity.'

'Firstly, Miss Blake does not wish to marry me. And secondly, will the marquis not be subject to approbation?' James asked.

'Some perhaps, but it will soon be forgotten if he ignores it. He is the Marquis of Blythe, James.'

James stared at his mother. Was she…right? If he were to marry Miss Blake—if she would have him, which he strongly doubted now—would Society effectively forgive him? And therefore might there be no negative effect on his mother and sisters?

'There are so many instances of august men marrying women of inferior status,' his mother was continuing. 'If the lady in question is very lady*like*, her supposed unsuitability is easily forgotten as soon as the next little scandal comes along.'

'I had not thought you so pragmatic,' he said. 'When you were compiling a list of prospective brides for me, you were particularly interested in birth.'

'I was. But…' His mother paused and then placed her embroidery on the little side table next to her. 'Come and sit next to me.'

James rose and took his place on the sofa next to her with a level of enthusiasm not much greater than he would have felt had she been a hungry lion.

To his alarm, his mother took his hands in hers.

'I want you to be happy,' she said. 'I know that you did not expect ever to inherit the dukedom and that you now bear a great weight of responsibility that you did not expect.' She hesitated and then squeezed his hands. 'I...saw you with Miss Blake. She is perhaps not of the highest birth, but she is of course vouched for by Sophonora, Lady Derwent. While Sophonora is, as you know, not one of my closest friends, no one can say she is not of the highest *ton*. Anyway, when you were with Miss Blake, you looked...happy, carefree, playful...in *love*.'

James was almost physically squirming by the time she had finished. *Who* had to endure such a conversation with anyone, let alone their own mother? This was even worse than being fussed over by one's housekeeper or butler.

'Sadly,' he said, wondering how soon he could pull his hands out of his mother's clasp, 'as I mentioned, the lady does not wish to marry me.'

'That is a great shame and I think she's very silly and I am quite angry with her.' His mother still wasn't letting go of his hands.

'No. There is no good reason to be angry with her.' He couldn't believe that he himself had felt anger with her for one second.

If Anna *would* have him, if he told her that he did not care about her birth, would he wish to marry her? He *should* do so, obviously, having compromised her, even if no one had seen them. But would he *wish* to? Given that loving someone deeply carried such a risk of terrible pain if you lost them?

He looked at his mother, who was still holding his hands, and felt a sudden almost overwhelming pang for her loss. And for his own.

'Since we have been speaking plainly,' he said, 'may I ask if you would do it again? Marry my father? Even though you have now lost him?'

His mother stared at him for a long moment, and then said, 'That is a silly question, because I have my children. But even without all of you, certainly I would. I am very lucky to have had the time with your father that I did, and I would have been lucky however long it might have been. I would not have changed anything. James… Are you concerned about loving someone and then losing them?'

'Well, I…' Suddenly he really wished that he could confide in her, talk to her, tell her everything about Anna. But he couldn't, because she had already borne great loss and she already had far too much to worry about. And she was clearly wondering whether the loss of his father and brothers had damaged him in some way. Perhaps it had, but she did not need to know that.

'No,' he said. 'No. The truth about my acquaintance with Miss Blake is that I liked her very tolerably and proposed marriage to her, but she felt that she did not wish to become a duchess with all that that entailed. And that she did not love me quite as she felt she would like to love a husband.' It was a little horrifying how easily the lies rolled off his tongue, but it was necessary, he felt, to protect his mother.

He suddenly felt as though he would like to go for a walk, to clear his head.

'Would you care to accompany me for a walk?' he asked her, out of politeness, because now he really wanted to be alone, to have the time to clarify his thoughts.

'I should have liked that very much, and would like to do so tomorrow, if you have the time, but today I have agreed to shop for a new muff with Sybilla, a most important task, you must recognise.' She twinkled at him and kissed his cheek.

He smiled back at her and stood up. 'I will take my leave of you now, then, and will perhaps see you for dinner later.'

He let himself out of the house shortly afterwards and began to walk aimlessly down the road, as though all his energy had been diverted to his thoughts.

It all suddenly seemed quite simple.

He was a duke. Anna's grandfather was an earl. Her parents had created a scandal. She was, however, indisputably a lady of quality, in her demeanour, her personality, everything. More importantly, she was kind and honourable. She was also very beautiful, and he loved being with her. He loved everything about her in fact. And one of the advantages of being a duke was, as his mother had said, that his status would transcend a

generation-old scandal. And his sisters would have large dow-
ries, which, combined with their birth, should of course allow
them to marry whomever they chose.

And, really, that had all been obvious, or should have been,
all along.

Had he been using it as an excuse?

Because he had been scared of getting hurt?

He'd behaved appallingly. *Appallingly.*

He had compromised her, whether or not anyone else knew
about it—he trusted they did not. He should have proposed to
her irrespective of whether or not he *wished* to marry her.

But he *did* wish to marry her, he realised as he rounded another corner and nearly walked into a tree. He wanted to spend
as much time with her as he could, make her happy, look after
her. If that time was limited, then he would still be lucky to
have had that time with her.

But, good God, what if *she* loved *him*—if that were possible
after the way he'd behaved—and he died young like his father
and brothers had?

According to his mother, being with James would still have
been worth it for Anna.

And from a practical perspective, Anna would still, presumably, be much better off as a dowager duchess than as an impecunious governess.

His pace had picked up, he realised, and his steps were leading him in the direction of Bruton Street.

By the time he arrived there, not long afterwards, he was almost running, in a particularly undignified fashion.

Banging on the door knocker, he realised that he must be
wearing a very foolish grin at the thought of seeing Anna again.

God, he hoped that he would be able to convince her that she
should marry him. If, of course, she did wish to. Perhaps she
didn't. Perhaps she didn't love him. Perhaps...

'Good afternoon. I am come to visit Miss Blake,' he said to
the butler who had just opened the door.

'Miss Blake no longer works here.' The man's sneer was extraordinary.

James's natural inclination would usually be to give him a

severe dressing-down, except now he was more concerned with what had happened to Anna and why the man was speaking in such a derogatory fashion.

'Is Lady Puntney at home?' he asked.

'I will enquire.' And, good God, there was that sneer again. James had rarely ever been spoken to like this and he did not appreciate it. And damn, if the man would speak to *him* like this, how had he spoken to Anna?

As he waited in a very luxuriously decorated drawing room, his level of anxiety about Anna climbed as he had time to wonder further what might have happened to her.

The butler's sneering indicated that she might well have left under some kind of cloud; James very much hoped that that had nothing to do with him but the more he thought about it…

'Good afternoon.' Lady Puntney's smile was pleasant; James was not surprised given what Anna had told him about what a generous employer she had been.

'Good afternoon.' James had no appetite for small talk. 'I came to call on Miss Blake but I understand that she has left your employment. I wondered if you would be able to reassure me that she has come to no ill, and to furnish me with her new direction.'

'I…' Lady Puntney looked over her shoulder, and then took the few steps necessary to reach the door and close it, before moving to a chair near the fireplace. 'Please sit down.'

James inclined his head and took the chair to the other side of the fireplace, and waited, with some impatience.

'I very much like Miss Blake,' Lady Puntney began. 'And I have worried about her since she left.'

'May I ask why she left?'

'She… Well. This is awkward, but I feel that for Miss Blake's sake I should speak plainly. My housekeeper overheard a conversation between the two of you, and one of our housemaids had seen some rather…warm…behaviour between you. I could not, for the sake of my daughters and our reputation as a family, keep Miss Blake on.'

Damn. *Damn*. James had caused Anna so much harm. He wished she had told him what had happened; she could obviously have contacted him. She would not have wished to put him to any trouble, though.

God. He *hated* to think of her enduring the misery of losing her position. And where was she now? What if she had been cast out by all her acquaintance for what was *their* indiscretion, his and hers, not just hers?

'Could I ask where she is now?'

'I'm afraid that I promised her that I would not tell you. I assure you, however, that I understand her to be well and safe for the time being. We have corresponded.'

Lady Puntney was unshakeable in her refusal to betray her promise to Miss Blake, and James left soon afterwards.

He went straight to Lady Derwent's mansion. If anyone knew where Anna was, it must surely be her.

Lady Derwent was not at home.

'Is Miss Blake residing here?' James asked.

'I have not seen her.' The butler *might* be lying. Or he might be telling the truth. He had the art of impassivity very well mastered.

'Do you know when Lady Derwent will return home?'

'I'm afraid not.'

'I will wait,' James said firmly, and sat himself down on an intricately carved oak chair in the hall, so that no one might enter the house without him seeing.

The chair was hard, the afternoon was long, and James did not enjoy his thoughts; he was very worried about Anna, he felt incredibly guilty, and he was essentially just desperate to see her. It didn't bear thinking about where she might be if she wasn't with her godmother. Except he did think about it.

When, eventually, Lady Derwent did return, James was extremely disappointed to see that she was alone; he had been hoping that Anna might perhaps be with her.

'Your Grace,' she said. 'Interesting.' She handed her gloves to her butler. 'Come into my saloon.'

'What a pleasure it is seeing you,' she said, unsmilingly, as she settled herself on a sofa. 'Please do sit down.'

'Thank you.' James eyed her. He suspected that he would

fare a lot better with her if he made the effort to engage in some social niceties, however much he wished—frankly—to yell *Where is my Anna?* 'I hope that you are well?'

'Very well, I thank you. A little frustrated, I must admit.'

'Frustrated?' James felt as though he was at the beginning of an intricate chess game, to which he did not fully know the rules.

'Frustrated,' she confirmed, before lapsing into what he knew was an uncharacteristic silence, and which he felt was perhaps designed to induce him to speak.

He had nothing to lose, he decided, in indulging her, as long as he was cautious.

'I am sorry to hear of your frustration. I myself am also a little frustrated.'

Lady Derwent raised an eyebrow.

James decided to plunge straight in.

'I love your goddaughter, Miss Blake,' he stated. 'I understand from Lady Puntney that she terminated her employment because of our friendship. Most immediately, I am concerned about her, and hope that she is well and in a place of safety. I would also like very much to speak to her, to explain that I was stupid and how much I love her.'

Lady Derwent nodded, thoughtfully. 'I see.' She looked as though she was thinking very hard.

'I would, therefore, be very grateful if you were able to tell me where she is.'

'I am able,' she said, speaking slowly, 'to tell you that she is safe and well and that I have seen her. And that I will do my utmost to ensure that she remains safe and well.'

'Thank God,' James said.

'Yes.'

James looked at her, looking at him, as though she was sizing him up, and waited. He had already asked if she knew where Anna was, and he didn't think she was a lady who would appreciate repetition.

'I understand that you and my goddaughter visited Gunter's together twice, in addition to our evening at the opera. My observation was that you had seemed to have become quite close.'

'Yes. I love her,' James repeated.

'And?'

'And I would like to marry her.' He supposed that this was the equivalent of asking a young lady's father if he might be permitted to propose to his daughter. It was not very enjoyable; Lady Derwent's eagle eye was making him squirm as though he were a child, and there was something quite peculiar about declaring his love for Anna to someone other than her. Had he, in fact, told her properly how very much he loved her? He wasn't sure that he had.

He cleared his throat. 'And therefore I would very much welcome the opportunity to see her again. I wondered if you knew where she was.'

'My goddaughter was very distressed, although doing her best to hide it, when I saw her. She asked me to promise that I would not tell you whither she fled.'

James nodded. Damn.

'I cannot break my promise to her,' Lady Derwent said. 'She needs to be able to trust *someone*.' A low blow, but fair enough. James should have been thinking more clearly and should not have let things happen the way they had.

'I would like to be able to prove to her that she can trust me,' he said. 'Because, as I mentioned, I would like to marry her, because I love her and would like to do my best to make her happy.'

'Prettily spoken,' Lady Derwent finally approved. 'I would like you to be able to propose to her again, *properly*, but I cannot break my promise. Perhaps... Let me think.'

And then she sat and thought, while James fought very hard not to tap his fingers or his foot or just say—shout—*Yes, what?*

Eventually, she said, 'I will send you a note later.'

That was it? She was going to send him a note? What if she didn't send it?

He looked at her. Yes, this was, unfortunately, clearly the most she was going to give him.

'Thank you,' he said, managing not to grit his teeth too much, and rose to leave.

* * *

Lady Derwent's note arrived in Berkeley Square shortly after he did.

Pulling it out of its envelope with fingers that were suddenly all thumbs, he discovered that Lady Derwent had merely written:

I will be at Hatchard's bookshop at eleven o'clock tomorrow morning and should like to meet you there.

The frustration was immense. Maybe he should try to ask Lady Maria Swanley if she knew where her friend was now. He half turned back towards the front door, before checking himself. He should not cause any more gossip than had already arisen. He would have to wait, and hope that Lady Derwent had something more interesting to tell him on the morrow than she had today.

He was at Hatchard's the next morning ten minutes before the hour, wishing to make very sure that he did not miss Lady Derwent.

The last time he had visited this shop had been to purchase books for Anna.

Really, everywhere and everything reminded him of her.

Dear *God*, he missed her.

Her humour.

Her quick understanding.

Her smile.

The way she made him feel when he was with her…complete, happy, as though there was nowhere he'd rather be.

He hoped so very desperately that she was all right.

As he stood there, thinking and worrying about Anna, he realised that he was beginning to *see* her everywhere, imagine that she was in front of him.

At this rate he would be accosting complete strangers thinking that they were her.

For example, at this moment he could see a smallish woman making her way along the road towards him, and for some reason—probably the way she moved—she reminded him so strongly of Anna that he could almost believe that she *was* Anna.

So much so, in fact, that it was difficult not to stare at her.

Especially since, as she drew closer, he could see that her hair was of the same colour and...

And... He blinked hard. It *was* her.

It was Anna.

Walking down Piccadilly towards him.

Chapter Fifteen

Anna

Anna had not particularly wished to visit Hatchard's—or anywhere else—this morning, but she was deeply beholden to her godmother, and it did do her good to leave the house and take some walks, rather than moping inside, wondering what was to become of her, so she had agreed to join her when she had suggested this excursion.

The proposed outing had been for them to visit the shops together, but at the last moment Lady Derwent had told Anna that she was a little fatigued and thought that she would do well to rest this morning as she had a busy day ahead of her, but that she most particularly wanted to purchase Jane Austen's *Northanger Abbey*, and she would be very grateful if Anna would go on her behalf to buy it.

Anna had vaguely wondered that her godmother wouldn't send a footman in her stead, but perhaps Lady Derwent was trying to ensure that Anna was kept occupied. She was clearly right to do so, because it had certainly not been making Anna happy sitting inside reflecting on the turn that her fortunes had taken and what might have been.

She would also, of course, be able to browse the bookshelves herself, which she would enjoy. Reading was always helpful in taking one away from one's own problems.

As long as one could concentrate and a large duke did not intrude too much into one's thoughts.

She looked along the road at the shop as she approached and...

Discovered that the duke was yet again intruding into her thoughts.

Because, being fanciful, she could easily imagine that the large man standing outside the building was him.

Oh...*was* she imagining it, or was it actually him?

It couldn't be.

But that height and those broad shoulders, topped by his handsome face and thick, dark hair.

It...*was* him.

It was definitely him.

He was his usual elegant self, attired in a plain but perfectly cut dark coat, *very* attractively fitting breeches—*why* was her stupid brain thinking about *that* at this moment?—and impressively shiny boots.

His expression and posture were not as usual, though. He was entirely still, almost frozen, his hands fixed to his stick, his eyes staring and his jaw a little dropped.

If she hadn't been so stunned, she might almost have laughed at the way in which he was the personification of astonishment; it seemed that he had expected to see her as little as she had expected to see him.

For a long moment, Anna felt very much as though she imagined a chicken might in the presence of an unexpected fox—panic-stricken and unable to think—before she gathered her wits and wondered whether she might be able to just keep on walking, into the shop, and pretend she had never seen him. Apart from the stomach churning and near-faintness she was feeling, of course, but if she could just sit down for a moment, she was sure she would recover quite quickly.

Or perhaps she would just turn about and go somewhere else for a while and return when she was sure he would have left.

But, 'Good morning,' he said, while she was still trying to work out what she should do.

Oh.

'Good morning.' Her voice sounded distinctly odd.

'Good morning,' he repeated, before shaking his head. 'Apparently my wits are addled; that is the second *good morning* I have offered you.' His rueful smile was *so* attractive.

Anna found her own lips curling into a little smile too, which was odd, because she was fairly sure that she was still angry with him. She would not show it, however; she would rather retain any scrap of dignity she might have.

'Well, thank you for those good mornings.' She pointed at the clouds above them. 'They are not particularly apt.' Conversing about the weather was always a good ploy when there were no other topics that one wished to discuss. A few more weather-related words and she would be able to go inside and try to forget that she had seen him.

'Oh, no, they are extremely apt. Seeing you makes this morning good.'

'Oh!' Really? He sounded as though he was flirting with her. Was that usual behaviour in this situation? Surely not.

She should go; she really did not want to talk to him. Well, if she was honest, she *did* wish to talk to him, but it could only lead to further misery.

'It was most enjoyable to see you but I'm afraid I am rather busy.' She began to move past him towards the shop entrance.

'I had expected to see Lady Derwent here,' he said, just as she drew level with him. 'She asked me to meet her here. Is she joining you?'

Anna slowed to a halt. 'I… Oh. No, she isn't. She is unfortunately a little tired this morning, so she asked me to come and purchase some books for her.' She frowned. 'When did she ask you to meet her here?'

'I received a note from her yesterday evening instructing me to meet her here at eleven o'clock this morning.' He looked at his watch. 'Exactly now, in fact.'

Anna frowned. 'She is not forgetful,' she said slowly.

'Indeed,' the duke agreed. 'She could not possibly have forgotten that she had arranged to meet me here...'

'...when she requested me to join her on an excursion here, and then at the very last moment said that she was too tired to come but urged me to leave immediately because it looked as though it was going to rain,' Anna finished.

She shook her head.

Her godmother had *promised* her that she would not tell anyone—especially the duke—that she was staying with her.

She had not told him, it seemed. She had planned this meeting instead. Why, though? What purpose could it serve?

None. No purpose. And, for goodness' sake, now her eyes were filling yet again.

'I think we both know,' she said with an effort, 'that there can be no benefit in our conversing. I will bid you goodbye.' She stepped towards the shop door.

'Lady Derwent had good reason to decide to orchestrate our meeting,' the duke said.

Anna stopped again and turned to look at him.

'I visited her yesterday afternoon,' he continued. 'Do I understand that you are staying with her? She did not tell me that.'

'Yes, I am; I asked her to tell no one.'

He nodded. 'It seems that she wished us to meet but did not wish to betray your confidence.'

'Yes.' Anna knew that she shouldn't ask, but she couldn't help it: 'May I ask why you visited her?'

'Because I wanted to tell you...' The duke looked around. 'This is really not the place for it. Would you care to walk with me?'

Anna was so very tempted. But she had been tempted by him before now, and it had cost her dearly. Now, on the off chance that she still had any reputation left, she must guard it carefully, and could not be seen with any men, especially the duke.

'No, thank you.' She took another step towards the door. 'I am going to do the errand I came to do for my godmother and then I am going to leave.'

'You know, I think I also have a fancy to purchase some books.'

'That was really not what I intended,' Anna told him. A little weakly, because, if she was honest, she didn't entirely want him to leave.

'I think it might have been what your godmother intended.'

'My godmother is wonderful but she is not always right. As we have already ascertained.'

She was very frequently right, though.

The duke pushed the door open and smiled at her.

Anna rolled her eyes at him and then stepped inside. He had a look in his eye that told her that he was about to say something quite outrageous. He would not be *able* to be truly outrageous inside the shop, though; they would run the risk of being overheard, and, while she didn't think he was easily embarrassed on his own account, she did think that he was likely not to wish to embarrass *her*. So there couldn't *really* be any danger in talking to him. Just a little.

When she got inside, she realised that this place was quite heavenly. She would have to return, if she was able, another time, when she wouldn't be distracted by the duke's presence.

'Is this the first time you have been here?' he asked as she looked around. Gazing at the shelves and shelves of books was infinitely easier than looking at him and reflecting on the miserable fact that their lives would diverge again after this ridiculous meeting.

'Yes.'

'It is quite special, is it not? Even I—not, as you know, a great book-lover—can sense magic here.'

'Yes.'

'What books are you here to purchase?' the duke pursued.

'I have a list from my godmother and she suggested that I also buy one or two of my choice, which is of course very kind in her.'

'What books are you thinking of purchasing for yourself?'

'I don't know. I'm afraid that I will need to take some time choosing them. Probably in silence.' She didn't want to sound as though she was encouraging him to talk to her.

She took a few steps further into the shop.

The duke followed her.

Several pairs of eyes rose from books and shelves to look at them.

'I wonder whether you should leave me now,' she whispered. 'We have been remarked. I do not wish to be the subject of any further gossip.'

'Of course,' he replied, also whispering. 'And of course I do not wish to force my presence on you, and indeed should probably not have followed you in here, so, if you would like me to leave immediately, I will do so. But before I go could I possibly explain that I have something of great importance to say to you?'

'I think we have already discussed everything there is to say.' Sad but true.

He leaned closer to her and, still whispering, said into her ear, 'I love you.'

Anna froze.

'What?' she said, quite loudly.

'Shhh,' several voices said.

'I love you,' he whisper-repeated.

Anna ignored him and marched down an aisle between two sets of shelves. She was suddenly almost *throbbing* with annoyance. Why had he said that? Why was he torturing her like this? Why was he still following her?

'Please leave,' she hissed over her shoulder.

'Please marry me,' he whispered back.

Anna stopped stock still, and he bumped into her back, nearly sending her flying.

He caught her with a hand on each of her upper arms as she stumbled.

When she was steady, she turned round to face him, filled all of a sudden with heat—*furious* heat—from head to toe.

'We—' she prodded him in the chest with her finger '—have already discussed this. The answer, if you remember, was no.'

'You told me that the reason was that your parents had caused a scandal.'

'Shhh,' someone said.

'My apologies,' the duke said.

'I don't care about scandal,' he whispered. 'The only reason I cared about it was that I was worried about my sisters. But that is ridiculous. I love you more than words could ever say and, if you love me too, I would like to spend the rest of our days together doing my best to make you as happy as possible.'

'No,' Anna stated.

'No what?'

'No, I will not marry you.'

'You should marry him,' a woman said from the other side of the shelves.

'Hmmmph,' Anna told her.

'Would you like to go outside to discuss this better?' the duke whispered. 'I had not planned to propose here in such a manner.'

'I am so sorry that your proposal is ruined—' Anna hoped that her words sounded as insincere as they were '—but I'm afraid that I do not wish to go outside with you.'

'Oh, please *do* go,' the woman from the other side of the shelves begged.

James mouthed, 'Please?' at her.

'Well…'

'Only if you don't mind,' he suddenly said. 'I do not wish to pressure you into doing anything you do not wish to do.'

'Indeed,' replied Anna, even as the treacherous part of her brain reflected that however annoying and infuriating James might be, he could not help himself also being remarkably kind and chivalrous; it did not occur to a great number of men to allow women the courtesy of making decisions, big or small, about their own lives.

'Good day to you,' she told him, conscious of a great weight of misery descending as she uttered the words.

Her misery was reflected in his face, she saw, as he opened his mouth to reply.

She didn't hear what he had to say, because they were interrupted by a woman sweeping into the end of their aisle.

'Amscott!' she said.

'Lady Fortescue.' He bowed his head slightly.

'I am the lady with whom you were communicating through the shelves,' she said. She turned her gimlet gaze on Anna and said, 'I do not know who you are, and do not think that now is the time for introductions. I am come to say that I think that you really ought to hear him out, in a better location than here. Now that I see who it is who loves you and wishes to marry you, I have to tell you that you are quite mad if you do not accept him, although that is of course entirely your own business.'

A *shhh* came from behind the shelves opposite where Lady Fortescue had been.

'Quite.' She made a shooing motion with her hands. 'Off you go.'

'I should very much like the opportunity to have private conversation with you.' James was not moving, the shooing apparently having no effect on him. 'But I do understand if you wish not to.'

As a matter of principle, Anna did not wish to speak further to him. But, also, she very much did.

It would be silly to allow her principles to cause her to wonder for ever what he might have said.

And she had already been very miserable because of him; it could hardly make matters worse.

'Perhaps a very short conversation,' she said.

'Very sensible,' Lady Fortescue approved. 'Please go now and leave the rest of us in peace. I shall of course say nothing about this to anyone should it come to nothing. If it *does* come to something, I shall expect to be a guest of honour at your wedding.'

Despite everything, Anna felt her lips twitch a little. She wondered if her godmother and Lady Fortescue knew each other well. They would certainly be a match for each other in the forcefulness stakes.

'I will bear that in mind.' James indicated behind him with his eyes and Anna nodded. 'Good day, my lady.'

And then they traipsed out of the shop, regarded the entire way—Anna could feel her eyes boring into her back—by Lady Fortescue.

When they got outside, they discovered that it was raining.

'Oh, dear.' James looked down at her with a rueful smile. 'I must hope that the weather is not indicative of the outcome of our conversation. Let us find a hackney. If you would like?'

'I would prefer to walk.' Anna tried not to be conscious of the damp already working its way inside the neckline of her pelisse. 'Your reputation is already going to be quite ruined by Lady Fortescue having overheard our conversation. If we enter a carriage together it will be even worse. And I myself must be very careful.'

'I do not care about my own reputation but fully understand your point about your own. I apologise. Let us walk instead, if you would like?'

'Thank you.'

As they began to stroll up Piccadilly, James said, 'Your comment about my reputation leads me directly to one of the things I was going to mention to you. If you are happy to hear what I have to say?'

'I am not sure that *happy* is the word,' Anna said cautiously. 'But?'

'But if you wish to say something to me, please do.' If she was honest, she was quite desperate to hear what he had to say.

It began to rain significantly harder.

'Should we perhaps stand over here?' James led her in the direction of some large trees. The rain was so hard that Anna could ascertain no more than that they had very broad trunks.

It was a little less wet under the trees, but by no means dry.

'A good thing about it being so rainy is that we are unlikely to be remarked by anyone at all.' Anna was damp all over now. This was the kind of weather that caused less robust persons to become quite ill; and she had a nasty feeling that it would take her several hours to feel completely dry again.

'That is very true. A good thing.' James cleared his throat. 'Thank you for agreeing to listen to what I have to say. I don't think now is the time for small talk. Both because of the rain and because, well, because of what has already passed between us.'

'I agree.' Anna slightly wanted to stamp her foot. 'So what is it that you wish to say?'

'You are right; I was in fact engaging in small talk.'

'As you still are...'

He laughed. 'Sorry. Yes. Right. Well.'

Anna finally lost the ability to be at all patient. 'Oh. My. Goodness,' she said.

'Yes. Of course. Well. I have one big message for you.'

'What is that message?' Anna asked.

'I love you and would be the happiest man alive if you would agree to marry me, and I have several smaller messages which combine to create that one. Are you happy for me to continue?'

'Yes I am and thank you for asking.' Really, she didn't feel at all thankful; she just wanted him to *get on with it.*

'I spend a lot of time with sycophants, who will listen to anything I say merely because I am a duke,' he surprised her by replying, 'and I have no desire to force my conversation on you. Although I *am* extremely pleased that you are happy to listen.'

Anna nodded, just about managing not to roll her eyes. Had anyone, ever, in the history of irritating conversations, been as slow to say whatever it was they had to say?

'So,' he said. 'I didn't know that I would see you this morning. I feel as though I should really have prepared a speech. As I did not, I must apologise if my train of thought is a little rambling.'

Anna could contain herself no longer. 'It is extremely rambling,' she told him.

James nodded and smiled ruefully. 'I'm sorry. I feel as though this is the most important conversation of my life and as though I must not get it wrong.'

Anna just raised her eyebrows.

He laughed, before looking serious again.

'Here I go, then,' he said. 'You referred to my reputation. As I mentioned just now, I am surrounded by sycophants. That is because of my rank and my wealth. And as mentioned by mother recently, if I marry someone whose parents acted in a scandalous fashion a generation ago, no one would dare to mention it to me, and it would not have any impact on my mother and sisters, about whose reputations I of course care deeply. It would also not have any impact on my wife because I would not permit that to happen.' He looked suddenly very haughty and very ducal.

'I'm not sure...' she began to reply.

'Not sure?'

'I don't know.' If it was genuinely the case that the scandal would not ruin him—or his family—should she, could she marry him?

She didn't know. He had walked away from her very fast after his proposal the night of the opera. Why hadn't he tried to convince her immediately that they should marry? Would he be just like her grandfather and her father and not remain steadfast in the face of difficulty, or when he perhaps grew bored with her?

He cut across her thoughts. 'I'm not sure that that was the first thing that I should have mentioned. In fact, on reflection, I know that of course it isn't. I wish I had prepared what I was going to say.' He drew a deep breath. 'What I should have told you just now—and what I should have told you when I asked you to marry me—is that I am scared.'

'Scared?' Anna frowned, confused.

As she looked up at him, she saw him swallow and press his lips together, and suddenly she just wanted to put her arms around him, pull him against her, and provide reassurance against whatever was worrying him. Of course, on the face of it she had a lot more to be scared about than she did—for all she knew she could easily end up in the workhouse after all—but huge privilege did not preclude someone from feeling fear, and he had of course lost several close relatives quite recently. Perhaps it was related to that.

'I have been scared about many things. My father died quite young and my brothers very young, as you know. I found the pain of losing them very hard, both on my own account and that of my mother and sisters. I do not wish to experience such pain again, and I also do not wish to be the cause of someone else experiencing such pain. It seems to me that loving someone is therefore dangerous.'

Anna nodded slowly.

'With regard to loving you, I now realise that living without you, missing you, worrying about you, will cause me huge pain. And so, selfishly, I would like to marry you. I am worried, though, that I will die young as my male relatives did, and leave you to experience pain. I believe, however, that what I have to offer you is—baldly speaking—more than just myself as a husband; if something *were* to happen to me, you would be the Dowager Duchess of Amscott and—if we were lucky—the mother of the next duke, and your future would be secure.'

'Is that your reason for proposing?' she asked. 'Pity? Charity? To secure my future now that you know that my employment was terminated?'

'No. *No*. Of course not.' He sounded almost impatient. 'I could settle a large sum of money on you. I could employ you myself. I could buy you a house. Anonymously so that no scandal would attach to the purchase. I could do any manner of things to secure your future. And if you do not wish to marry me I will of course accept that, and I will beg you to allow me to help you financially. But securing your future *would* be a happy side effect of your marrying me.'

'Oh.'

It was a lot to comprehend.

After a few moments of reflection, she said, 'I am scared too.'

James nodded, his eyes fixed on her face, but did not speak.

'I'm scared of losing someone, as you are, but I think perhaps we all are, and something I have learnt is that it is wise to take happiness wherever one finds it.'

'I agree that that is wise.' He had his hands clasped in front of him, so hard that the knuckles were whitening, and his gaze was very intent.

'However,' she continued, 'I am also scared of relinquishing my independence to any man. My grandfather disowned my mother. My father abandoned us both.'

James swallowed visibly and said, 'I can understand that. I can offer you every assurance that your heart and your security would be safe with me, but I don't know how to convince you of that. Maybe... I can't. I love you, though. I would never...' His voice sounded harsh, raw.

Anna just stared at him, mute.

'I...' He stopped, swallowed again, and then continued, 'I believe that my happiness is bound up in you. I would very much like to marry you. I love you. I love your smile. I love your laugh. I love the way you make *me* laugh so much. I love your kindness. I love the way you tilt your head to one side and press your lips together when you are particularly annoyed and clearly fighting with yourself not to give someone—me—a stern set-down.'

Anna laughed, and then sniffed.

'I love everything I know of you,' James continued, 'and I would count myself indescribably fortunate to have the opportunity to spend a lifetime learning as much about you as I may. I would never disown you or abandon you.'

Anna sniffed tears back, suddenly—she could not say why—sure that he was not like her grandfather or father.

Of *course* not all men were the same. Take the Puntneys. Sir Laurence was clearly a most devoted husband. And Lady Maria's parents were happily married. Perhaps Anna had just been unlucky with her grandfather and father.

Perhaps her luck had turned when she met the duke.

'Oh,' she said.

'I would like so very much to marry you. And love and protect you for ever. I have never been surer about anything in my life.'

Anna sniffed and smiled at the same time.

For the first time since they'd moved under the tree, James began to smile too.

He unclasped his hands and reached for hers, before pulling her gently so that they were standing quite close together.

Then he got down on one knee, on the very wet ground, in full view of anyone who might walk past, and said, 'Anna Blake. I love you more than I can describe. Would you do me the great honour of accepting my hand in marriage?'

His features—so harshly handsome in repose, so delightful when laughing, but always giving the impression of strength, were arranged now in what Anna could only think of as vulnerable hope. It was the most beautiful expression she'd ever seen anyone wear.

'I love your face,' she whispered.

James screwed his loveable face up a little and then raised his eyebrows.

'And I also love *you*,' she told him.

James was still kneeling, still holding her hands.

'I cannot imagine anything better than being able to spend every day at your side,' she said.

'And without wishing to sound too impatient...?'

'I would love to marry you.'

'Oh, my God. Thank you.' He kissed each of her hands in turn, before rising to his feet—a most delightful flexing of his thigh muscles visible through his breeches as he did so—and drawing her into his arms. 'I love you more than words can say.'

And then he kissed her extremely thoroughly and extremely scandalously right there on the pavement, under the trees, in the rain, and it was quite wonderful.

Epilogue

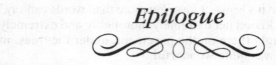

Anna

The Lake District,
Christmas 1827

Anna tilted her head to one side as she regarded herself in the floor-length looking glass in front of her.

James appeared behind her. 'You look beautiful, as always.' He slid his arms around her waist and kissed the top of her head.

Anna allowed herself a moment to enjoy the pleasurable shiver his touch always gave her, before putting her hands over his and saying, 'We must hurry.'

'Really?' He turned her in his arms so that she was facing him, put one finger under her chin so that her face was raised to his, and kissed her full on the lips.

And then he kissed her again, hungrily, as though he *needed* her, now, even though they had been together only last night and after their ball tonight would be able to fall into bed together again.

Anna *knew* that they should go down to greet their guests,

but she couldn't help herself reaching her arms round James's neck, anchoring him to her as their kiss deepened.

Still kissing her, teasing her tongue with his, he suddenly lifted her and carried her the few paces to the bed in the middle of the room and sat down on it with her on his knees.

As his mouth traced kisses into the sensitive skin at the base of her neck, he murmured, 'I very much like this costume.' And then he did something very clever with his fingers, so that suddenly the bodice of it was loosened. With one hand he cupped her breast and with the other he lifted her skirts, and Anna found herself wriggling so that she could move against his hardness.

'I like your costume too,' she panted, as he lifted his pharaoh tunic.

'You make,' James said between groans, as he moved inside her a few minutes later, 'the most alluring Cleopatra.'

'Thank you,' Anna managed to say. 'Oh, *James.*'

Afterwards, he held her close in his arms, until they were both calm.

And then Anna sat up and said, 'James! Our guests are probably already here.'

James moved so that he was lying on his back, looking at her, his hands behind his head.

'If you aren't careful,' he said, 'there will be no possibility of my going downstairs for a *long* time. You look extremely debauched, my beautiful duchess.'

Anna looked down at herself, entirely naked, save for her Cleopatra robe around her waist.

'Honestly,' she tutted. 'We have *guests* downstairs. Many dozens of them.'

It was the tenth anniversary of their wedding and James had arranged for them to visit the Lake District with their children—a long-held desire of Anna's but one that she had been unable to fulfil until now due to regular pregnancies—and spend the Christmas period there in a house on one of his estates. They had invited a large number of house guests, including, naturally, Lady Derwent, Lady Maria and her husband, Clarence—now a vicar with a sizeable parish—and their three children, and the Puntneys, with whom they had become firm friends, and this evening were holding a Christmas ball.

'Lady Derwent will be more than happy to greet them in our absence.'

'That is true but we really should go.' Anna hopped off the bed before James could tempt her to engage in any further love-making, and began to re-dress herself.

'I am the luckiest man in the world,' James said, sitting up. 'I have the most wonderful wife a man could ever wish for and five perfect children.' They had four boys and a baby girl, all of whom they doted on most unfashionably.

'And I the luckiest woman.' Anna never referred to the fact out loud, because she did not wish to remind James of past tragedies, but he had now lived several years longer than both his brothers, and appeared in excellent health. And he was the best husband a woman could ever wish for, having proved time and time again to her by his actions and words that he was entirely trustworthy, a very different kind of man from her grandfather and father. Not to mention, of course, very good company and extremely handsome.

They shared one more lingering kiss on the lips before Anna pushed James firmly away, patted her hair back into place and declared herself ready to descend to their party.

As they made their way down the house's grand staircase, they were greeted by a clamour of voices and an almost bewildering array of brightly coloured costumes. They had chosen a masquerade as a nod to Anna's impersonation of Lady Maria on their first meeting at James's mother's ball.

Anna put her mask on and said, 'We should have hidden our costumes from each other to see if we could find each other.'

'There would have been no point. From the very first moment I met you, it was as though I recognised you, even though I did not know your real identity. I would know you anywhere, whatever your disguise.'

'And I you.'

They smiled at each other, before Lady Derwent and James's mother came towards them. The two ladies had buried their differences and were now—usually—on the best of terms.

Except...oh, dear.

Anna glanced at James and saw that he was as wide-eyed as she felt she must be.

'You...both...look magnificent,' he told the two ladies, the merest tremor of laughter in his voice.

'Thank you,' they replied in tandem, neither of them smiling.

Anna decided to address the situation directly.

'I think that you both look truly spectacular and that, since Queen Elizabeth is widely regarded as having been the best of queens, and you are both the best of ladies, it is only right that you should both be her this evening. One can never have too many Queen Elizabeths.'

'Were that true,' Lady Derwent said, 'it would be a very fortunate thing.' She indicated behind her to the room.

And, oh, dear, again. There were a *lot* of Queen Elizabeths.

'I flatter myself that I am wearing better jewels,' Lady Derwent whispered, far too loudly, to Anna.

'I flatter *my*self that I have a smaller waist,' James's mother told James, not bothering to whisper.

James laughed out loud while Anna took an arm of each of the other ladies and said, 'Let us go and seek some refreshment and then perhaps sit down for a moment before the dancing begins.'

They were joined shortly afterwards by Lady Maria. Who was also dressed as Queen Elizabeth.

None of the Queen Elizabeths looked remotely amused.

Anna clapped her hands loudly in panic. 'I think it is time for the dancing to begin.'

Three hours later, she had danced until her feet were sore, including, extremely unfashionably, *three times* with her own husband (he had speculated that no one would know because they were in costume, and Anna had pointed out that everyone would know because there was no other man in the room with the same thick head of hair—greying most attractively now—and broad shoulders), and eaten supper with the openly warring Queen Elizabeths, and she was now taking a little rest, when the most handsome pharaoh in the room approached her.

He bowed low. 'Cleopatra. Would you do me the honour of taking a walk outside with me?'

'I should be delighted.' Truly, she was incredibly blessed that just the sound of her husband's voice could still send a shiver through her after ten years together.

She was shivering in a different way within seconds of going through the doors at the end of the ballroom, onto the terrace that ran along the back of the house above lawns that led down to a lake and beyond that a wood, the whole illuminated now by the full moon in the most fairy-tale-like way.

'It's *freezing*,' she squeaked.

'Indeed it is.' James put his arm round her and hugged her into him. 'This is the only way I can think of to warm you given that I have no coat or jacket to give to you.'

'Mmm, that is nice, but it's still *very* cold.'

'It is indeed too cold to be outside without very warm outer garments,' he agreed. 'I wonder... Perhaps we could sneak around the outside of the house and enter by a side door and make our way up to our chamber without anyone noticing...'

'That is a very good idea,' Anna approved.

And ten minutes later, they tiptoed into their bedchamber, both of them almost snorting with the laughter they were trying to hold back.

And then, almost before the door was closed behind them, James had Anna in his arms.

'You know that I thought about marriage from the very first moment I met you,' he told her between kisses. 'And that I loved you infinitely almost immediately, and yet I love you more with every day that passes. How is that possible?'

'It is the same for me,' Anna told him, as he began to make her gasp with pleasure. 'Thank you for being my wonderful husband. I love you.'

'I love you too.'
And then they spent the night celebrating their first decade of marriage in the most delightful way.

* * * * *

HISTORICAL

Your romantic escape to the past.

Available Next Month

Tempted By Her Enemy Marquis Louise Allen
The Duke's Guide To Fake Courtship Jade Lee

....

Miss Anna And The Earl Catherine Tinley
The Lady's Bargain With The Rogue Melissa Oliver